HEART QUEST

More to Love

HeartQuest brings you romantic fiction
ndation of biblical truth.
stery, intrigue, and suspense
se heartwarming stories of
en of faith striving to build
hat will last a lifetime.

tQuest books sweep you
s of God, who longs for you
and pursues you always.

Jewels for a Crown

LAWANA
BLACKWELL

HEART QUEST

Romance fiction from
Tyndale House Publishers, Inc., Wheaton, Illinois

www.heartquest.com

Visit Tyndale's exciting Web site at www.tyndale.com
Check out the latest about HeartQuest Books at www.heartquest.com

HeartQuest edition published in 2004 under ISBN 0-8423-7228-8.

Scripture quotations are taken from the *Holy Bible,* King James Version.

Library of Congress Cataloging-in-Publication Data

Blackwell, Lawana, date
Jewels for a crown / Lawana Blackwell.
p. cm — (Victorian serenade ; 3)
ISBN-8423-7960-6 (sc : alk. paper)
I. Title II. Series: Blackwell, Lawana, date. Victorian serenade ; 3.
PS3552.L3429J48 1996
813′54—dc20 96-18986

Printed in the United States of America

10 09 08 07 06 05 04
9 8 7 6 5 4 3 2 1

To Matthew

You fill our home with music

and our hearts with joy.

May God guide your steps forever.

With special appreciation to Gilbert Morris,

my writing mentor and friend.

Let us not grow weary in the work of love;
Send the light! Send the light!
Let us gather jewels for a crown above;
Send the light! Send the light!

—*Charles H. Gabriel*

Prologue

London, 1871

An archway of forsythia, gilded with yellow blossoms, beckoned guests to the formal garden of Orham Park. Inside, pensive Greek statues rose above beds of perennials, and a light May breeze caused the flowers to sway and nod, as if keeping time with the orchestrated strains of Verdi's *Rigoletto* overture.

The most lovely ornament in the garden, however, was Claudette Everly, now Lady Hastings. With a radiance in her expression that could only come from being deeply in love, she stood at the side of her new husband and accepted the good wishes of family members and friends.

"She's beautiful, isn't she?" nineteen-year-old Beryl Courtland murmured to her escort, Lieutenant William Landon, who sat beside her on a teak bench. Beryl had a hard time taking her eyes from the bride's face, so full of promise and joy.

"You would make a far more beautiful bride," he replied with a meaningful squeeze of her hand.

Beryl tore her eyes from the happy wedding party and smiled at William. She knew he spoke the truth. On an ordinary day, Beryl could outdazzle any of the women present. But Claudette's beauty today came from the happiness in her expression.

Beryl wondered if she, too, could be that happy if she agreed to marry William Landon. She could have a good life, being the center of William's universe. While she had never returned his declarations of love, she did feel a deep affection for the young officer—more than she had felt for any of the other beaus who had pursued her. Of Teutonic heritage, William was tall and fair-haired and carried himself regally in his scarlet-and-white uniform . . . and he never seemed to notice the admiring female glances that were sent his way from every quarter.

Most important, William was a consummate gentleman. He behaved as if his life's mission was to see that Beryl never lacked for anything she set her heart upon.

Beryl sought Claudette's face again. *I could be just as happy.*

"Beryl . . . darling!"

From out of nowhere her mother advanced upon them, her lorgnette held out in front of her like the figurehead of a ship. *"Ah, vous voilà!"* she panted. Before Beryl could answer that they had been there all along, Mother drew in a stout breath and turned to William. "Would you mind fetching us some punch, *s'il vous plaît?* And some of those marvelous shrimp pastries?"

Gentleman that he was, William left at once, not bothering to point out that one of the myriad of servants would likely be by with another tray shortly. He had been gone for only a second or two when Beryl's mother reached down and pulled her to her feet. "Come with me," she ordered. "I want you to meet someone."

"I've met enough people today," Beryl answered with a shrug of her shoulders.

"Graham Harrington," her mother went on, her opal earrings bobbing with every syllable. "He hardly ever goes out socially since his wife died. This may be your only chance to make his acquaintance."

"And why should I want to make his acquaintance?"

"Because he's richer than Croesus, that's why."

Beryl glanced toward the refreshment canopy. "But what if William comes back while we're gone?"

Her mother's face loomed closer, and the tone of her voice grew uncharacteristically hostile. "You would be better off if he never came back."

"What do you mean by that?"

"I mean that your young lieutenant is the fourth son in the family and will likely inherit nothing when his father dies. Do you want to live on the generosity of his older brother for the rest of your life?"

"But he loves—"

"Loves?" She spat out the word as if it were an oath. "What a comfort that will be when you end up scrubbing your own floors and tending to your own brats!"

As her mother's grip tightened on her arm, Beryl looked once more at the new Lady Hastings. This time it was not the joy in the bride's expression that drew Beryl's attention, but the lines of the sateen gown, obviously crafted in Paris. Sunlight danced off the huge diamond-encrusted brooch fastened upon her bodice. The lace veil, most likely woven in Brussels just for the occasion, spilled out from behind her curls.

Beryl brushed the wrinkles from the skirt of her gown. It was a copy of one of the latest French fashions, and had, until just this moment, been her favorite. Ignoring an almost overwhelming urge to look over toward the refreshment canopy once again, she straightened her shoulders and smiled at her mother. "Did you say that Mr. Harrington is a widower?"

1

London, 1875

JUST as the omnibus rolled to a stop at the corner of Park Lane and South Street, Jenny Price caught sight of an old Gypsy woman. The woman's wizened looks and filthy clothing contrasted sharply with the backdrop of Park Lane mansions. The Gypsy only stood there, hunched and statuelike behind an upturned apple crate, yet something about her posture gave the impression that she was waiting for someone.

Jenny moved to the front of the horse-drawn vehicle, handing the conductor fourpence before stepping down to the pavement. She had taken only two or three steps when an inexplicable impulse seized her and she looked to the right. As departing passengers and pedestrians passed by on both sides, Jenny found herself locking eyes with the old Gypsy woman.

A gold tooth gleamed as she smiled, but the woman's eyes were as dark and lifeless as bits of coal. "Read yer fortune, pretty miss?" Surprisingly, the soft voice carried through the frenzied street noises. A clawed hand scooped up several tarot cards from the apple crate. "Tell yer future?"

For a fraction of a second Jenny stood frozen to the spot, unable to tear her eyes from the woman. Then a loud clattering startled her, bringing her back to her senses. "Hey! Watch where yer goin', you clumsy lout!" an angry voice railed.

Jenny looked through the crowd to see a crimson-faced peddler on his hands and knees, chasing after the snuff tins that had been knocked from his tray.

She started down South Street at almost a run, not looking back at the Gypsy and not slowing down until she reached the stoop of a narrow four-story house. Leaning against the door-post, Jenny let out a long breath and waited for her heart to stop hammering against her chest.

Tell my future? A shiver ran down her neck at the memory of those dark eyes. *I hope I never get that desperate.*

Straightening, she forced the old Gypsy from her thoughts. Her future, at least for the next two years, had already been decided by God . . . and the woman who lived inside the house in front of her. That *had* to be the reason for the invitation Mrs. Wardroper had delivered that morning. The matron of the Nightingale School of Nursing had smiled broadly as she held out the invitation to afternoon tea, penned in a distinct and familiar script.

Florence Nightingale often sent notes of encouragement to "her" students, sometimes accompanied by flowers, fruit, or little gifts. Miss Nightingale had yet to visit the nursing school that she had founded fifteen years ago, yet she was heavily involved in every aspect of running the place.

"You should wear your nicest dress," Mrs. Wardroper had advised. Jenny reached behind her waist to make certain that the velvet bow was still tied securely over the bustle of her mauve silk gown. She hadn't needed to be told to dress nicely. Any summons from Florence Nightingale was a special occasion.

Except for church, it was practically the only time that Jenny wore anything other than her brown uniform gown, white apron, and cap. Nursing was a vocation, according to

Miss Nightingale—not just a career, but a calling from God. Dressing the part only seemed natural and proper, even when a student was not actually at her studies.

Confident that her bow was still in place, Jenny took a few more seconds to tuck some loose strands of hair under her bonnet. Her hair, so straight that a curling rod was of little use, had a tendency to slip out of her hairpins, no matter how tightly they were fastened. When she was younger, it had grieved her that she had no curls to frame her heart-shaped face. Now she had little time for vanity, and her hair was annoying only because of the stray tendrils that tickled the back of her neck or dangled in her eyes.

You'll be standing out here all day if you wait till your looks are perfect, she told herself, then took hold of the brass knocker on the door in front of her. A young housemaid answered almost immediately, as if she had been waiting on the other side of the door. "The missus is ready to see you," she told Jenny with a smile, then accompanied her up two flights of stairs.

Miss Nightingale's bedroom did not have the appearance of a sickroom. It was a bright, airy chamber with white walls, and the windows had no blinds or curtains to keep out the light. The furnishings were cheerful as well—a cozy bed, tables and chairs scattered about, pictures, a rose-shaded lamp, and a bowl of flowers on a chest of drawers. Miss Nightingale sat propped up on several pillows in her bed. Two cats lay curled at her feet, and another occupied a place on one of the Persian carpets.

"Cook should have our tea ready, Abigail," Miss Nightingale said to the maid. She smiled at Jenny and nodded toward the chair at the right side of her bed. "Come sit close so we can talk, Miss Price."

Jenny always felt a sense of awe in the presence of the great lady, whose revolutionary ideas had brought about improvements in hospital procedures as far away as the United States and Australia. Invalid that she was, Florence Nightingale was not feeble looking. A visitor did not notice the silver in her hair so much as the strength in her eyes. They were gray, like Jenny's, and didn't appear to miss anything.

Jenny's chair was placed only inches away from a square table covered with neat stacks of correspondence from all corners of the globe. Miss Nightingale faithfully kept up with her graduates. And now that Jenny's year-long internship at St. Thomas's Hospital was almost finished, she was about to join the ranks of those nurses. Exactly *where* she would serve was a decision that lay in the hands of this deceptively placid-looking woman before her.

"I hope you are feeling well, Miss Nightingale," Jenny offered. It struck her that it was a superfluous way to greet an invalid, but what else could she say? The opposite, that she hoped her hostess was *not* feeling well?

"Very well today, Miss Price. I've already lived a good ten years longer than I imagined I would, so it would be ungrateful of me to complain." She shifted on her pillows a bit, causing one of the cats at her feet to rouse and stretch. The animal gave Jenny a bored look of appraisal and curled back up into a ball.

With typical straightforwardness, Miss Nightingale got right to the point. "I asked you to come here so that we could discuss your assignment upon graduation. You've been a most exemplary student in all areas, according to Dr. Sutherland and Mrs. Wardroper."

"Thank you. It's hard to believe the term is almost finished."

To Jenny's surprise the woman in the bed laughed, bringing spots of color to her plump cheeks. "I like people who are mature enough to take a compliment without blushing and simpering little protests to prove their humility. My main reason for not accepting probationers under the age of twenty-five is because I don't want anyone who is likely to marry and leave the profession, wasting the effort put in to train her. But I must confess there has always been an ulterior motive in the back of my mind." She shook her head. "I simply don't have the patience to deal with anyone much younger than that these days."

"And yet you accepted me."

"The first exception I've made in the fifteen years since the school began. And only after Mr. Adam Burke assured us of your maturity and sobriety. Rare qualities in a lass of twenty two, if you ask me."

Jenny smiled at being referred to as a "lass"—after all, most women her age were already married and starting families. "Mr. Burke has been a good friend to my family," she responded.

"And a generous contributor to the school at St. Thomas." Miss Nightingale paused briefly. "And speaking of school, I've decided where you are to serve after you graduate."

Jenny sat straighter in her chair. "You have?"

The maid returned just then, carrying a silver tray of sandwiches and biscuits. She was followed by another maid with their tea. The two servants drew a round table up to the bedside between Jenny and their mistress, arranged dishes and poured cups with practiced ease, then slipped out of the room with the mewing cats at their heels.

All of this took less than three minutes, but to Jenny the time seemed to crawl by. *She was about to say Ontario,* she told herself. After all, Jenny had requested to fulfill her two-year commitment to the Nightingale Fund there, and the rumor in the halls of the nursing school was that the top graduates usually were given a choice of assignments.

Jenny hadn't gone into nursing because of its opportunities for travel. Nurturing others had been a basic part of her personality for as long as she could remember. But ever since Jenny was eleven years old, when her mother had married a former private detective named Joseph Price, she had loved to hear about the countless places her stepfather had been in the course of his career. His stories awakened a desire in her own heart to see something besides Leawick, Bristol, and London.

How exciting life would be if *both* of her interests, nursing and travel, could be combined! Of course she would miss her family. Her parents and younger brother and sister, as well as the numerous relatives on her adoptive father's side, were all very important to her. But two years wasn't a terribly long time. And think of the experiences she would be able to write about in letters back home!

Miss Nightingale reached for her cup, took a sip of her tea, and then continued as if the conversation had never been interrupted. "I was paid a visit last month by a Mr. Graham Harrington, an acquaintance of my sister and her husband, who lives here in London. Mr. Harrington is a widower, and his daughter has epilepsy. The child's nurse is to be married next month."

The older woman smiled, and the only sound Jenny was aware of was the pounding of her pulse in her ears. *What does this have to do with Ontario?* she wondered, then felt a twinge of guilt for not considering the plight of the poor child. She had been praised for her maturity only a few minutes ago, and here she was thinking only of herself. "How . . . how old is the little girl?" she asked.

"Twelve years old. Mr. Harrington has asked for someone with a great deal of compassion for children, along with more than competent nursing skills. Someone who is willing to attend the Church of England, too, for the child will need to have a nurse in attendance even on Sundays. You came to my mind right away, but of course I wanted to spend some time in prayer about it. Such decisions shouldn't be made lightly."

Miss Nightingale set her cup down on the table, dabbed at the corner of her mouth with a napkin, and turned her attention back to Jenny. "You look distressed, dear. Is something wrong?"

Her appetite suddenly gone, Jenny set her half-empty cup on the table as well. "I appreciate your confidence in me, Miss Nightingale," she said carefully. "But I was hoping . . ."

"You were hoping to be assigned to the hospital in Ontario."

Jenny's breath caught in her throat. "I don't wish to sound selfish, Miss Nightingale, but there are other students who are competent enough to take on this assignment. And I know several who are hoping to stay here in London."

Miss Nightingale was quiet for a long time, staring down at her folded hands. Finally she said, "Why do you wish to go to Canada?"

"I'm going to be a nurse. There are people there I can help."

"Even if God would rather you stay and help someone here in London?"

I've got to make her understand, Jenny thought. "I've lived in three places in my life, Miss Nightingale," she began with a respectful firmness. "I've been praying God would send me to Ontario so that I could help people and, at the same time, see something of another part of the world. You've traveled . . . I've read your journals. Didn't you feel the same way?"

"I went where God directed me," the older woman answered. "And only to the places where I felt his leading." Her eyes became somewhat sad as she studied Jenny's face. "You just said that you've prayed to be sent to Canada. Has God answered? Do you feel he has directed you to go there?"

"He has," Jenny replied immediately. Even as she spoke, she chose to ignore the voice of her conscience, reminding her that she had suffered doubts. Who didn't have doubts at some time or another?

Even her calling to be a nurse hadn't always been crystal clear. Jenny had always loved children, having practically raised three younger cousins when she was just a child herself. At one time in her life she thought that her nurturing spirit could be satisfied by marriage and a family. At the age of nineteen she became engaged to a fine young man, an architect. His death in a train derailment near Manchester had sent her into mourning for months.

Afterward Jenny had turned down invitations from other prospective suitors. She was determined never again to allow herself to attach all of her dreams for the future to one person. People had a way of dying—people like her natural father, and her fiancé. Depending on another person was likely to end in disappointment.

By the time Jenny had begun to cope with her grief, she started to feel that there was a higher calling to her life—something that hovered, especially in the wee hours of the night, just out of her mind's grasp. She prayed for direction while she kept herself occupied, helping her parents care for her two younger siblings and operate the bookstore they had founded in Bristol shortly after their marriage.

One day in the store she came across a pamphlet entitled *Una and the Lion,* written by Florence Nightingale herself, about Nightingale nurses working at a Liverpool workhouse infirmary. She could not read fast enough. Every word seemed to drive away more and more of the restlessness that had taken hold of her. By the time she knelt for her bedside prayers, she knew with all certainty that God was calling her into the nursing field.

And she was *still* certain of that. After all, hadn't God miraculously opened the door for her to come to school here in London, in spite of the age requirement? And surely he was calling her to go to Ontario. There weren't enough trained nurses to meet the demand over there. Wasn't it written in the Bible that one of the signs of true Christianity was visiting the sick? Well, there were sick people in Canada, too.

Jenny realized that Miss Nightingale was still staring at her. The woman had not replied to the affirmation she had spoken seconds ago, that God was indeed directing her to go to Ontario. Jenny cleared her throat. "I don't feel that our Lord would be displeased if I helped others in any location, do you?"

"Of course not." She smiled. "Ours is a noble calling. And I know you want to please God. Your character as a Christian has been obvious from the first time I interviewed you." After a thoughtful pause, Miss Nightingale went on. "It saddens me to postpone your dream, but I wonder why God would put *you alone* in my heart every time I tried to think of a nurse to send to Mr. Harrington and his daughter?"

"Why wouldn't he put the need in my heart as well?" Jenny pressed.

"For one thing, how would you understand the message he was sending? You haven't even known about the Harringtons until just now. But most important, Jenny, God is very wise. He is aware that this isn't *your* decision to make."

The sound of her given name coming from the famous Miss Nightingale disarmed Jenny. "I haven't had the peace of mind about Canada that I had about becoming a nurse," she admitted miserably. Her heart was beginning to feel like a stone in her chest. "My prayers have mainly been that God would send me there."

"Then keep praying about it," advised the older woman. "You're still young. You can always go when your two-year obligation is over . . . if you find that it is indeed the Lord's will. I will even help you find a position."

"You're still sending me to Mr. Harrington's then?"

Miss Nightingale's eyes radiated kindness, but her voice was firm. "It is solely my responsibility to assign the graduates, dear, and every decision I make is bathed in prayer. You are the person I'm to send to nurse that child."

There was nothing Jenny could do but agree to what was expected of her. Yet before totally surrendering her will, she had to make one more feeble effort. "You're certain of this, Miss Nightingale?"

"I'm certain," the woman said with a smile. "I've grown too old not to recognize the voice of God when it echoes against the walls of my heart."

~

Two weeks later Jenny, her parents, and her younger sister and brother occupied a trio of wingback chairs and a small settee in a corner of the sitting room of the Nightingale School of

Nursing. A handful of other families were assembled in similar groups, but most of the students were still upstairs dressing for the graduation ceremony that would be starting at ten o'clock that morning.

"Have you met this Mr. Harrington yet?" her mother asked.

"Not yet, Mother." Jenny shifted in her starched uniform and looked around at the dear, familiar faces of her family.

Even though she would be returning to Bristol with them for a fortnight, Jenny had gotten up earlier than usual so that she could spend more time with them. Once she was settled at the Harrington estate, she would see them only occasionally over the next two years, whenever her parents could leave their thriving business and come to London.

Her only consolation for not getting the assignment of her choice had been their relief when she told them that she wouldn't be going to Canada after all. Even though her adoptive father, Joseph Price, had understood her longing to see the world, he had worried along with her mother about the hazards of a young woman being so far from home and family.

"Is she as big as me?" Jenny's sister, Nicolette, asked. The lisp caused by two missing teeth was every bit as charming as the ivory sateen and lace dress the six-year-old wore.

"Who, Nicolette? Mr. Harrington's daughter?"

When the girl nodded, nine-year-old Joseph Jr. cut in. "Jenny already told us that she was twelve." He spoke with the slightly condescending air that Jenny supposed was typical of all older brothers. "That means she's twice as old as you are."

"Well, she's twice as old as you are, too."

"She can't be twice as old as me," he retorted with still more superiority. "That would make her eighteen years old."

Jenny reached over to tousle the boy's hair, sending a wink

to her little sister at the same time. "Mr. Harrington divides his time between London and Liverpool, tending to his shipping business," she said to her parents. "His steward, a Mr. Palmer, sent a letter last week asking what I'll need for personal and medical supplies. I'll be staying in the nursery wing with the governess, right next door to Celeste."

"Celeste is the little girl?" Joseph Price asked.

Jenny smiled at her adoptive father. His dark hair and beard were now flecked with gray, but she still found him as handsome as her mother was beautiful. "I forgot that I hadn't mentioned her name. She's a rather pitiful child, or so I hear. Her mother died right after she was born."

"The poor dear!" Jenny's mother exclaimed, her face suddenly clouded with emotion. "Why do children have to suffer so?"

Jenny and her father locked eyes for a brief instant. Clearly, they shared the same thought. Her mother was feeling more than just sympathy for the little girl. Remorse, like some monster from the ocean depths, sometimes reached out its tentacles to squeeze at Corrine Price's heart, attempting to choke out any confidence that her past sins had been forgiven by her daughter and by the Almighty.

"Celeste has not been as fortunate as I have been," Jenny said gently, slipping her hand into her mother's gloved one. "I have a mother I wouldn't trade for anyone else in the world."

Her mother smiled and squeezed Jenny's hand, but her eyes had grown moist. "I know, dear. And I've thanked God for every day that we've been back together."

The laughter of a group of people over by the fireplace caught their attention. Jenny recognized the family of Martha Westcott, one of the five graduates who would spend the next two years in Canada. Before envy could take root in her thoughts again, she considered her mother's words and imagined the loneliness little Celeste surely felt. The nights could be unbearably lonely when no maternal hand had fluffed up a pillow or tucked a blanket around little shoulders.

Too well Jenny could empathize with the child, having experienced countless such nights during her early childhood. Suddenly it dawned upon her that she had more to offer Celeste Harrington than just competent nursing skills. And for the first time, it began to make sense that God would keep her here in London.

2

THE Treaty of Waitangi," Celeste Harrington mused out loud, while absently tracing with her finger the letters engraved on the leather cover of her text, *The Illustrated History of Britain*. "Wasn't that the one between France and . . . Prussia?"

"No, Miss Celeste, that was the Treaty of Basel." Across the oak study table in the girl's schoolroom, governess Elaine Barton struggled to hide her boredom, even though her young pupil did not bother to do the same. "When the Treaty of Waitangi was signed, New Zealand became a British Crown Colony. Do you remember the date?"

The girl yawned, then guessed, "1792?"

"No, later than that. Why don't you look it up in your textbook and show me?"

"Can't you just tell me?"

"You'll remember it better if you find it yourself," Elaine said gently. "It's in the chapter we read yesterday, so it shouldn't take long."

The sad part was that history wasn't the only subject Celeste, who was brighter than any child Elaine had ever tutored, did not take seriously. Every subject was an exercise in tedium, and had been for the past year, since the day Elaine had come to the Harrington household.

Elaine had no family, save a grandmother in Essex who wanted nothing to do with her, so teaching was her life. Always in the past she had relished her task of opening doors to knowledge and ushering students through. At her previous position, she had tutored the Ogelsby sisters in Kennington so well that the youngest was now making excellent marks at Girton College.

With Celeste Harrington, it hadn't taken long for that enthusiasm to dry up. Sometimes while going over the same details again and again, Elaine felt she would like to go to a window and scream. Better yet, grab the child by the shoulders and give her a good shake!

She can't help being sick, Elaine reminded herself for the thousandth time. She pushed down her dislike for the girl and tried to dredge up what compassion she still had left. The seizures were a drain on the twelve-year-old's energy and often left headaches in their wake. *I would be irritable, too, if I were sick most of the time.*

And irritable the girl was. Given the features of Celeste's oval face, a more pleasant-tempered child would have been declared pretty. The girl's long lashes and dark chestnut curls were inherited from her mother, whose portrait hung over the fireplace in the morning room. With time even the pug nose and dimpled right cheek might develop into the face of a beautiful young woman. But as Celeste listlessly turned one page at a time in her textbook, the frown at her lips was such a permanent fixture that it seemed to be chiseled out of stone, frozen there for perpetuity.

As much as the girl loved her father, one would think that her disposition would improve during the times Mr.

Harrington was at home, but it only seemed to get worse. In fact, the only one who had any positive effect on the child was Mr. Harrington's fiancée, Miss Beryl Courtland. Elaine found herself wishing that Miss Courtland would visit, but that was highly unlikely as long as Mr. Harrington was still in Liverpool.

"I can't find that date," Celeste finally said. Her face brightened when she turned another page. "But see here—this man looks like you."

Elaine stiffened. *"Man?"*

"Well, he's certainly got your nose."

Leaning forward, Elaine realized that the girl was pointing to a portrait of King Charles II. The monarch's profile indeed showed a hawkish nose, more pronounced than her own, but sadly, only by a small degree. She could feel her cheeks start to burn. As mean-spirited as the girl could be at times, Celeste had never before mentioned her appearance.

Yet there was no evidence on the girl's face that she was making sport with her blunt words. In a way, that was worse. Had Celeste been deliberately spiteful, that would at least demonstrate an acknowledgment that Elaine had *feelings.* Instead, the child spoke as one would speak when describing the flaws of an inanimate object, such as a painting or piece of furniture.

Now that she had broached the subject, Celeste apparently was determined to go the full route, for the next thing out of her childish mouth was, "And why do you have those pits all over your face?"

"Smallpox."

The girl's eyes grew wide. "Why didn't you get the vaccine?"

"The vaccine wasn't available back then. I was only seven when I contracted smallpox," Elaine answered flatly while reaching forward to close the textbook. "Our lessons are finished for today."

"Is that why you never got married?"

Elaine pretended not to hear as she replaced the cap on the inkwell, then wiped the tips of the two pens with a linen cloth. She expected the girl would get tired of waiting for an answer and find something else to amuse herself. On the contrary, Celeste sat there waiting, appraising her with curious brown eyes. Too bad she was never so curious about history.

"Is that why you never got married?" she asked again.

"I expect so," Elaine murmured.

"You most likely never will," the girl declared. "You have to be pretty like Miss Beryl to get married. Or like my mother was."

"Yes."

"You have to be young, too. How old are you?"

"Thirty-six."

"The same age as my father—but it's different with a man. That's what Miss Beryl says, and she knows all about such things." Celeste pursed her lips for a moment. "It's a pity—your hair is such a pretty auburn. Your eyes are a nice shade of green, too. If your face were only pretty, someone would have probably asked you to marry him by now."

Elaine picked up a copybook and added it to the stack of textbooks on the shelf just under the table. "Your new nurse is coming tomorrow morning," she said in an attempt to change the subject.

The child wrinkled her nose. "I hope she's not as stupid as Miss Templeton."

First glancing at the open door behind her shoulder, Elaine put a finger to her lips. It was unlikely that the nurse could hear her from the room next door, but a child shouldn't be allowed to speak this way of an adult—or of anyone. "Miss Celeste, you shouldn't say that."

"She can't hear me. And you know I'm telling the truth. All she talks about is her fiancé and those silly magazine stories."

"Nurse Templeton is a very kind person."

Celeste shrugged. "I surely don't know how she got someone to ask her to marry him. Men like ladies who are smart, too. Miss Beryl told me that."

"I'll wager Miss Templeton knows about the Treaty of Waitangi," Elaine muttered under her breath as she pushed out her chair and got to her feet.

"What?"

She straightened and gave the girl a tepid smile. "Nothing."

"Well, it's almost time for my nap," yawned Celeste, pulling the kid slippers from her feet and tossing them aside. "I do get so tired of reading those books."

"I'll turn down the sheets for you," Elaine said. She picked up the discarded slippers and followed the girl into her bedroom, then helped her slip out of her dress so that she could nap in her shift. When Celeste was tucked into bed under a bedspread of white satin, Elaine unfolded an apple-green velvet counterpane and spread it over her. There was no chill in the room, but the child was cold by nature.

Elaine pulled the bell cord at the head of the bed. Seconds later one of the upstairs maids, a short, heavyset girl named Reanna, showed up in the bedroom carrying a basket of needlepoint. She sent a polite nod in Elaine's direction and plopped down in the Windsor side chair for the naptime vigil. Her duties thus relieved for an hour, Elaine went back through the schoolroom and into the room she shared with Lucille Templeton, the child's nurse.

"Ready for our walk?" she asked from the doorway.

From the bed where she sat propped up with pillows, Lucille held up a magazine with one hand and wiped her eyes with the other. "This story is so beastly sad," she sniffed. "Just three more pages—would you mind waiting?"

"I'll straighten the schoolroom," Elaine whispered back. She turned and began putting the rest of the school materials in order, slipping the geography book into its place on the shelf, then extinguishing the lamp that hung from a brass pole next to the study table. With a sigh she looked around in the dimness of the room. What a happy place this surely was intended to be! Stripes of green, yellow, and orange ran up from white wainscoting to meet the ceiling, interrupted only by framed pictures of happy children playing. Below the wainscot was painted a garden scene of grass, carrots, pumpkins, marigolds, and green beans.

A sofa covered with yellow-and-white patterned velveteen sat against one wall, next to a huge toy chest. The fireplace was polished oak, and green curtains hung at the four windows. An abundance of school supplies—a chalkboard, maps, books, drawing supplies, and puzzles—would have been coveted by any teacher in any school in England.

I wonder if this new nurse has any idea what she's getting into, Elaine thought. Most household employees of Mr. Harrington didn't stay long—at least the ones who had any contact with Celeste. She wondered if Lucille Templeton, still reading in the next room, was getting married because she was truly in love with the loud, boorish solicitor who had proposed to her, or because tending to the child had soured her on the nursing profession as a whole.

Elaine sometimes entertained the idea of looking for other

employment, but reality always interceded before she could actually take any steps to do so. The salary Mr. Harrington paid was extremely generous—more than enough to allow her to save for her winter years. A woman with no inheritance had to plan ahead for such things, unless she wanted to end up in a workhouse.

Turning, she nearly stepped on a doll that lay on the carpet—one of the toys Celeste had been playing with before her lessons. She bent down to pick it up. Vacant eyes of dark blue glass stared back from the tiny face as Elaine touched its cheek with a finger. So smooth was the flesh-colored porcelain, not cratered like her own cheeks.

Every one of Celeste's dolls had beautiful features, as if the doll makers had ladies like Miss Beryl Courtland in mind when the molds were cast. Elaine raised a hand to touch her own cheek. *I can't blame them for that,* she thought. *What little girl would want a doll that looked like me?*

Walking over to Celeste's huge dollhouse, she propped the doll in one of the rooms, then turned when she heard a footstep behind her. Lucille Templeton stood there tying the strings of her bonnet.

"Thank you for waiting," she sniffed, her hazel eyes rimmed with red. "I just had to see if Genevieve D'Arcy would be rescued from the Robespierrists."

Elaine managed a sympathetic look, for she was well aware of how deeply Lucille felt about the misfortunes of her favorite fictional heroine, serialized in *Goodwyn's Lady's Gazette.* "Was she rescued?" Elaine asked, though she already knew the answer.

"Practically snatched from the guillotine at the last minute," the nurse breathed, a hand up to her chest. "My heart is still racing from it!"

"Well, she's safe now," Elaine soothed. *Until next month, that is.*

"Yes, thank goodness." Lucille perked up and pulled the bill of her bonnet over her forehead. "I don't want to have sunburned cheeks at my wedding ceremony," she said with a nervous giggle. "I'll likely be blushing enough as it is."

Elaine smiled at her jitteriness. "You will be a beautiful bride."

"Oh, I do hope so," the nurse gushed as they started for the door to the hallway. "I wouldn't want to embarrass Shelton. He comes from such good stock, you know. His father was *almost* awarded knighthood once!"

Lucille's future husband may be a pompous braggart, Elaine thought, *but at least she's found someone who wants to marry her.* She wondered if she herself would choose to marry someone like that just to get away from an unhappy situation. *No,* she decided. Better to remain a lonely spinster than to marry a loutish man.

The two walked in silence down the servants' staircase and through the morning room, to the French doors leading to the terrace. When the sunlight hit their faces, Lucille threw out her arms and sighed. "Just think! In one week I'll be Mrs. Shelton Newly!"

In spite of her misgivings about Lucille's fiancé, Elaine couldn't help but envy the happiness on the nurse's face. *It would at least be nice to have been asked.*

3

PADDINGTON Station was a sea of people on the Monday afternoon of August second when Jenny Price arrived back in London. Under the majestic ironwork that arched overhead, she balanced on her toes in an effort to add another inch to her five feet two. She was supposed to locate Mr. Palmer, Graham Harrington's steward, in the crowd. The booking office seemed the logical place to go, so she pushed the perpetually loose strand of hair back under her hat and headed in that direction.

"Miss Price?" Through the tumult of depot sounds came a voice behind her. Jenny turned to find a slightly built, bespectacled man of an indeterminable age, along with a footman in powdered wig and full livery.

"Mr. Palmer?"

The man smiled. "Mrs. Wardroper described you perfectly."

After they shook hands, Mr. Palmer instructed the footman to see about Jenny's trunk, then he led her to the line of carriages outside the station. Mr. Harrington's waiting barouche was well appointed, black, trimmed in silver, with even the driver sporting a black silk top hat.

"Mrs. Ganaway, the housekeeper, will explain your duties

to you," the steward said a few minutes later as the carriage wheels started rolling.

Jenny nodded across at the man. "I'm looking forward to meeting Celeste."

"I don't have much contact with the child," Mr. Palmer said after a slight pause. The sunlight reflecting from his spectacles made the expression in his eyes unreadable. "Managing the expenses of the household, the stables, and the gardens occupies most of my waking hours. So . . . did you have a pleasant visit with your family?"

"Most pleasant," Jenny replied, smiling.

Mr. Palmer gave a polite nod and motioned toward the white-and-cream stucco houses lining Bayswater Road. "This area is growing rapidly since the underground was put in. Mr. Harrington's home is not far from here."

For two years it'll be my home, too. Jenny's hand went up to the gold locket and chain she wore at her collar, a graduation gift from her mother and father. The warmth of the heart-shaped metal, etched with her initials, was a reminder that there were people in another part of the country who thought about her every day. *Take care of them, Lord,* she prayed silently.

Ten minutes later the pace of the horses slowed as they began the ascent up Campden Hill. Rising more than one hundred feet above the gray London fog and overlooking the Thames in the distance, the neighborhood had the appearance of a rural district far removed from the center of London. The carriage passed several stately homes, some apparently built quite recently, and turned onto a street named Phillimore Gardens. Minutes later they pulled into the brick carriage drive of a gleaming white stucco mansion. A blue-and-green mosaic stretched from corner to corner and separated the windows of the two stories, below a roof of Mediterranean red tiles.

Though the status of a trained nurse was a degree above that of a household servant, Jenny still expected to come and go through the back entrance. She was surprised, however, when the horses came to a stop at a walkway leading down the center of the lawn to the front portico of the great house. "Mrs. Ganaway would like to give you a tour," Mr. Palmer explained, tipping his hat. "I'll have your trunk sent up from the back."

The footman, whom the steward had addressed as Reeves, was already at the side of the carriage, extending a gloved hand to help her to the ground. He led her up the steps and over another mosaic pattern, this time set into the portico floor. A pair of ebony doors opened into an entrance hall flooded with light from a glass and wrought-iron dome overhead.

"Would you mind waiting here?" Reeves asked as he showed her to a dimly lit front parlor to the left of the entrance hall. When Jenny had taken a seat on one of the damask-covered chairs, he went to the wide window behind her, pulled aside the drapes, and opened the window. "I'll send some tea and let Mrs. Ganaway know that you've arrived."

A young maid arrived with a tray at the same time as the housekeeper. "Please, have your tea," Mrs. Ganaway said when Jenny made a move to get up from the chair. She was a formidable figure, dressed all in black. An immaculate white frilled cap concealed most of her graying hair, and a huge bunch of keys dangled from a chatelaine at her ample waist. She sat down in a chair across the tea table from Jenny, waving away the maid's offer of tea. "We will go ahead and discuss your duties, and see the house afterwards."

Jenny nodded and wished she hadn't accepted the watercress sandwich and shortbread from the servant's tray. She had been too anxious about her pending employment to eat the lunch her mother had sent with her on the train, so she now felt hungry enough to consume twice the amount she'd been served. But she hadn't planned on being appraised as she ate.

"Mr. Harrington is most particular about his daughter's health," Mrs. Ganaway began. Her pale blue eyes seemed to be fastened upon a pattern in the wallpaper just above Jenny's right shoulder, and her lips had yet to curve into a smile. "Miss Celeste has to be watched constantly, even while she sleeps. One of the maids sits in her bedroom during her afternoon naps, and another servant watches her at night, so you will have a little time to yourself."

"I don't mind," Jenny said, and she meant it. Since her graduation, she had found herself eager to apply her training to real life.

"I'm afraid that Mr. Harrington is unable to offer you Sundays off like most of the other staff, but you'll find that your salary more than compensates for it." Mrs. Ganaway raised a thin eyebrow. "Will that be a problem?"

Jenny had just taken a bite of her sandwich, so she swallowed it quickly and shook her head. "My family lives in Bristol, and I haven't anyone in the city to visit."

"No friends from nursing school?"

"My two closest friends have been sent to hospitals outside of London." A question darted into her mind about how the nurse she was replacing managed, with such restricted hours, to meet a beau and get engaged. *Not that I'm interested in meeting anyone,* she reminded herself.

"There is a small sitting room in the nursery wing, outside the bedroom you'll be sharing with the governess," the housekeeper was saying. "Your family and any female friends are welcome to visit when they are in London. We don't expect you to lose all ties with your former life."

"I appreciate that," said Jenny, wondering how a person could speak such thoughtful words with absolutely no warmth in her voice.

"And you will have some opportunity to see a little of the city. You will be expected to accompany Celeste to church on Sundays, when she is physically up to it. On Saturdays she sometimes enjoys a carriage ride or outing in the park as well."

That answers my question about how my predecessor met her fiancé. It occurred to Jenny to inquire about the former nurse. Any observations she could give regarding the girl's condition would be extremely helpful. She set her empty cup back on the tea table and cleared her throat. "The nurse that I'm replacing . . . I assume I will be able to speak with her before she leaves?"

"I'm afraid that will be impossible," the housekeeper answered. "Miss Templeton left today, shortly before you arrived. She kept a log of Miss Harrington's seizure activity—no doubt you will find that helpful."

"I would find it very—" Jenny jumped in her seat, her words cut off by the sound of the door slamming against the wall. A stormy-faced young woman burst into the room, clad in the black and white of a servant. Her red hair, shorter than Jenny had ever seen on a woman, stuck out like a lion's mane from the crown of her head to her quivering chin. "I ain't gonna stay one more minute in this house!" she spat out, shaking the lace cap she held in her hand.

Mrs. Ganaway was on her feet in an instant. "Amelia, you may not come in here making a scene like this," she said in a tone that was still strangely bereft of emotion.

"The little monster ought to be strapped ten times a day! The brat cut off my topknot when she was supposed to be napping!"

"When she was napping? Weren't you supposed to be watching her?"

The girl's face grew even redder, but she tightened her jaw and folded her arms. "I dozed off for just a minute! It ain't a crime to be sleepy!" With a sob, she added, "My looks is ruint!"

Glancing up at the ceiling, Mrs. Ganaway took a step toward the door. "Who is with her now?"

The housekeeper's moderate tone of voice made the maid's words sound even more frenzied."Who's with her? That poor old-maid gov'ness, that's who! I expect if she had anywhere better to go, she'd be gone, too!"

Mrs. Ganaway's hands went to her full hips. "I take it that you wish to terminate your employment here?"

The maid blinked her eyes at the woman in front of her, then cocked her head. "Termi . . . ?"

"Are you *resigning?"*

"Aye . . . and right this minute!"

"All right," Mrs. Ganaway sighed. "Go to Mr. Palmer's office and ask for a character letter. Then wait there until your things are sent to you. I won't have you gossiping about Miss Celeste to the other servants and turning them against her."

The maid broke into a contemptuous grin. "Turn them *against* her? Beggin' your pardon, missus, but they was turned against the brat long before I set foot in this place." Suddenly she noticed Jenny. "If you're here lookin' for a job, miss," she said, wagging a finger at her face, "you'd better guard your life. The monster'll be loppin' off somebody's head one of these days!"

"That's enough, Amelia."

With a swish of skirts the maid turned and stomped out of the room as quickly as she had entered. The housekeeper then turned to Jenny, embarrassment in her pale blue eyes. "Mr. Harrington won't allow me to dismiss anyone without a letter of reference," she said as if she felt compelled to explain. "He has a fear of one of our former servants ending up in a workhouse . . . or worse, because she can't find another position."

"That's very generous," Jenny said, although she couldn't help thinking that the maid would probably rather have her hair than a reference.

"Yes. Unfortunately, the servants all know this—so they don't think twice about resigning over any little incident."

Any little incident? Jenny cringed inwardly at the thought of someone shearing off most of her hair while she slept. "Do you lose many servants?"

The housekeeper shot her a glance of pale blue steel. "Some people are not cut out to work with children. We'll take our tour now, if you've finished your tea."

Minutes later, Mrs. Ganaway was leading her through the dining room and to an airy morning room at the center of the house. The first thing that caught Jenny's eye was a large portrait above the fireplace. The woman staring back from the canvas had thick dark hair, striking eyes of Nordic blue, and most interestingly, a smile that suggested she was on the verge of laughter from some private joke. Jenny turned to the housekeeper. "Mrs. Harrington?" she said in a hushed voice.

"She died in childbirth, when Miss Celeste was born," Mrs. Ganaway said, standing beside her to look at the portrait. Finally some emotion had found its way into her voice. "She was very beautiful . . . and lively."

Jenny nodded. "I can see it in her face."

After dabbing at her eyes with her apron, the housekeeper stepped away from the portrait. "It was Mrs. Harrington's great uncle, Sir Joseph Paxton, who designed this house in 1860. Ill health precluded his supervising much of the work, however. Perhaps you have heard of him. He was the architect who designed the Crystal Palace built in the fifties."

Jenny wondered at the expression that had come over the woman's face. It was obvious that she loved this house. "I have heard of him," she nodded, then pointed up to the windows set over the French doors in the east wall. "Every room is so light and airy."

"Yes. Sir Paxton used glass and wrought iron extensively."

"I've also noticed a Greek influence throughout the house."

Mrs. Ganaway looked grudgingly impressed. "You have studied about Greece, Miss Price?"

"My father was there for a short time. I loved to hear him tell about his travels."

"Mr. Harrington has traveled extensively as well," said the housekeeper. "He even captained a ship for a number of years. But Miss Celeste doesn't seem interested at all in hearing about anything that doesn't concern her directly. It's quite sad, if you ask me."

Surprised that this forbidding-looking woman would confide in her, Jenny mumbled something to the effect that perhaps the child would be more interested in other people as she matured. "Most children outgrow that preoccupation with themselves," she added, parroting something she had read during her studies.

"One can only hope so," Mrs. Ganaway replied. But she didn't look convinced.

4

THE tour of the great house culminated inside an impressive one-and-a-half-story conservatory, complete with a screened aviary in the center. After Jenny had a few minutes to admire the canaries, the housekeeper suggested that it was time for her to meet Celeste. They used the servants' staircase just outside the conservatory and across a hallway from the back entrance to the dining room.

"We're using this staircase because it's closer," Mrs. Ganaway explained as they walked up the stairs together. "But you may use the main staircase as well, especially if you're with Celeste. By the way, she's not allowed to be on the stairs by herself, just in case . . ."

Upstairs, Mrs. Ganaway pointed out that this level of the house was divided into two parts. "Mr. Harrington's quarters and the guest bedrooms are in the east section," she said, stepping aside to give Jenny a view of a long balcony. Jenny recognized the French doors of the morning room underneath and wondered why she hadn't noticed this upper level while downstairs. Two bedroom doors to her right were separated by the landing of the great marble staircase, and several feet farther, the balcony disappeared into another hallway.

"The nursery quarters are in this wing of the house." The housekeeper was walking down the hallway to the left. "This leads to the schoolroom and Celeste's bedroom," she said, motioning toward a door on the immediate right. "The rooms at the end of the hall you will share with Miss Barton. Your bedroom opens up to the schoolroom, as does Celeste's. The lavatory also opens into both bedrooms, and the sitting room is behind your bedroom. That's where your meals will be brought."

"I'll do my best to look after Celeste," Jenny assured the woman. "I've been reading everything I could find on epilepsy ever since Miss Nightingale told me about this assignment."

"That is reassuring," Mrs. Ganaway answered without emotion, but there seemed to be some doubt in her eyes as she hesitated at the door. "I had not expected anyone so young, but with the shortage of trained nurses, one cannot afford to be choosy." Without further ado she took the knob in her hand and opened the door to the schoolroom.

Jenny followed with her shoulders sagging just a bit. On her first day at nursing school, she had been made painfully aware that some of the other students felt resentment because of her young age. She had worked hard to gain their respect, studying into the wee hours of the morning and making superior marks. Now, it seemed, she was going to have to prove herself again.

The cheerful colors of the room lightened her spirits immediately, as did the idyllic scene in front of her. A child seated on a short stool in front of a toy dollhouse had turned to stare at her with curious dark eyes. On a sofa just a few feet away from the girl, a woman closed the book in her lap.

"Miss Celeste?" Mrs. Ganaway said. "Your new nurse is here."

The girl stood and brushed at a fold in her jonquil poplin

skirt. "Are you a friend of Miss Templeton?" she asked, tilting her oval-shaped face.

"Miss Templeton?"

"The nurse you're replacing," the housekeeper reminded Jenny. "I don't imagine so, Miss Celeste."

"Actually, we've never met," Jenny answered. She gave the girl a sympathetic smile. "But I hope you won't miss her too badly."

Celeste shrugged her shoulders and glanced over at the other woman, who was now standing. "Miss Barton and I shall miss Nurse Templeton very much. But we are both too mature to blame you for her having left. These things happen."

"Ah . . . thank you," said Jenny, caught off guard for a second. Could this polite, articulate young lady be the same "monster" who lopped off the maid's hair? And if so, was Mrs. Ganaway going to just pretend the offense never happened? *Surely not,* she thought. *Perhaps she saves major discipline matters for Mr. Harrington to handle.*

The woman who had been reading stepped forward and held out her hand. She had plain features but intelligent green eyes. "My name is Elaine Barton."

"Miss Celeste's governess," put in Mrs. Ganaway as the two shook hands. To Miss Barton, she said, "If you would show Miss Price the rest of the nursery quarters, I have things to tend to downstairs."

Without waiting for a reply, the housekeeper turned and left the room. The governess regarded Jenny with a shy smile. "Your trunk was brought up just a little while ago. You must be tired from traveling—would you like to rest for a while?"

"I'm not that tired, but I would like to change from this dress." What Jenny really longed for was a hot bath, but she would have to wait until bedtime for that. The odor of cinders from the train still clung to her dress and skin, and she had no doubt that her hair smelled just as bad.

At that moment Celeste, who had been standing with her hands clasped behind her back, wrinkled her nose. "You smell like smoke."

"You can smell it, too?"

When the girl nodded, Jenny couldn't resist feigning a helpless shrug. One thing she had absorbed from her stepfather, besides an interest in traveling, was the principle that opportunities to laugh should be taken advantage of whenever prudent to do so. "It's the cigars, I'm afraid."

Celeste's mouth dropped open. *"You* smoke cigars?"

"A nasty habit, I know, but almost impossible to quit."

The girl said nothing for several seconds, but then her brown eyes narrowed. "You're joking, aren't you?"

"I'm afraid I am," Jenny confessed. She looked over at the governess, who was trying to cover a smile behind her hand. "Another habit that's hard to quit, I'm afraid."

Miss Barton looked as if she were about to reply when Celeste said in a bored tone, "It wasn't a very funny joke." With that, she sat back down on her stool and turned around to her dollhouse. "If you want to go look at your room with Miss Barton," she said over her shoulder, "I'll be fine in here."

The room that Jenny was to share with the governess was larger than she had anticipated, and extremely well appointed. Two mahogany beds with graceful fretted tops sat at opposite sides of the room. Separate wide chests of drawers, armoires, and even dressing tables gave each occupant more than enough storage space. Roses, Jenny's favorite flower, trailed down the wallpaper above the wainscoting, and on the floor stretched a rug of mauve, green, and burgundy. Tall windows let in sunlight through Balmore lace curtains and raised blinds. In a corner of the room to the left of the fireplace stretched a dressing screen covered with Oriental silk.

"Don't be hurt by her bluntness," Miss Barton said softly, after Jenny had changed into a starched uniform and apron behind the dressing screen. "She speaks that way to everyone."

Jenny frowned at her own lack of judgment. "It was a silly joke."

"I thought it was funny." The governess smiled again. "You certainly had me wondering, Miss Price."

"Please call me Jenny."

"Only if you'll call me Elaine."

Jenny sent her an appreciative look as she began to unpack her trunk. "I was trying too hard to make her like me."

"Which is exactly what everyone does when they first meet her . . . myself included. I'm certain you will get along just fine."

Jenny wondered if she had imagined some doubt shading that last sentence, but before she had time to consider it further, the governess began telling her about Celeste's schedule.

"Mr. Harrington feels that if her routine is kept basically the same, she has less chance of having a seizure."

"That seems reasonable."

Elaine excused herself, leaving the room to see about the girl in the nursery. When she returned seconds later, she continued. "Breakfast is at half past seven. By the way, all our meals are brought up to the adjoining sitting room. Celeste has her meals with us unless her father is at home. In that case, she joins him in the dining room."

The arrangement did not surprise Jenny. It was common knowledge that governesses and children's nurses dined separately from other servants, usually in the nursery with their charges. Hers was a lonely occupation—and not just because of mealtimes. The servants consigned to the endless chores of scrubbing, polishing, and carrying often resented and avoided those employees who enjoyed easier labor and more status.

"When does she have her lessons?" Jenny asked, shaking the wrinkles from a gown.

"Weekdays, from eight to eleven. An hour for lunch, and then another hour of lessons. She naps then, from one to two."

"And then her schooling resumes?"

The governess shook her head. "Four hours a day, no more. Then she spends an hour or so playing with some of the servants' children." As if she felt the need to explain, Elaine added, "Mr. Harrington believes that playtime is good for the child. Tea is at four, supper at seven, bedtime at eight. On Saturdays we go to the park or zoo . . . again, if Celeste feels up to it. I suppose you're aware that we are expected to accompany her to church on Sundays?"

"Of course." Mrs. Wardroper had already told her that. "I would wish to go myself anyway. By the way, which church?"

"St. Mark's, near Holland Park. You can hear the bells on Sunday mornings."

"Is the worship service—"

"The intensity of Celeste's lessons is the only thing that isn't set in stone," Elaine continued, leaving Jenny's unfinished sentence hanging in the air. She glanced at the door that opened into the schoolroom and lowered her voice. "I'm not allowed to push her further than she's willing to go. Many a lesson consists of my simply reading to her . . . sometimes she pays attention, sometimes not."

She had met the governess less than an hour ago, but Jenny could recognize the sadness in her voice. She hung a uniform in the armoire and smiled at the older woman. "You wish things were different?"

Elaine smiled back and shrugged. "It's not her fault." She opened her mouth as if about to say something else, but closed it and bent to pick up a pair of slippers from the bottom of Jenny's trunk.

"Surely you don't blame yourself."

After a moment's hesitation, she said, "I sometimes wonder if a more capable teacher could hold the child's attention longer." Elaine handed the slippers over to Jenny, seemingly embarrassed for having confessed so much.

Jenny didn't know what to say. She had no clue as to Elaine's teaching abilities, though it stood to reason that if Mr. Harrington had gone to the trouble of approaching the foremost authority on nursing in the world, Florence Nightingale, to find a nurse for his child, surely he had taken like measures to find a proper governess. "I'm sure the health problems have a lot to do with her attention span. Seizures do drain a person's energy."

"Yes." Elaine gave her an appreciative smile, then glanced back at the door. "Speaking of Celeste, I had better go see about her again. She's not to be left alone for long."

"I'll go," Jenny offered, closing the lid to her empty trunk. "After all, I'm officially part of the household staff now."

"All right," said the governess. "I'll stay in here and read for a while and allow you to become better acquainted."

"Just pray that I don't forget and make another joke."

Elaine smiled, but her green eyes were serious. "You'll do fine."

Jenny walked into the schoolroom and over to where Celeste still played with her dolls. She waited at the girl's shoulder for her presence to be acknowledged. When it was not, she cleared her throat and said, "I had a dollhouse like this when I was your age."

Celeste nodded but still did not turn around. "Where is it now?"

"I gave it to my sister before leaving for nursing school."

Again the girl nodded, then reached up into the dollhouse nursery to transfer a tiny baby doll from a toy pram to a crib. "My father bought this one for me."

"Mine was a gift from my father as well," Jenny said, slipping down on one knee beside her. She touched a quilted satin bedspread, about the size of a handkerchief, in one of the bedrooms. "I never liked to play with dolls until I received my dollhouse."

Finally Celeste looked at her, her brown eyes curious. "Why didn't you like dolls before then?"

"Well, I never had any toys of my own until my father married my mother." Quickly, so as not to confuse the child or give her the wrong idea, Jenny added, "My real father died when I was nine."

"So the father you have now is actually your stepfather?"

Jenny shook her head. "He adopted me legally after he married my mother, so I call him my father, too."

"I see." In a sitting room on the bottom floor of the dollhouse, two dolls representing the father and mother of the porcelain family were seated stiffly on a miniature stuffed settee. The girl picked up the mother doll and put her in a rocking chair in the nursery. "My mother died," she finally said, rocking the doll slowly in the chair.

A lump came to Jenny's throat. "I know, Celeste. I'm so sorry."

"Did you cry when your real father died?"

"Yes, I did."

"I still cry for my mother sometimes. Even though I've never met her."

Celeste turned to her with such a look of sadness that Jenny had to restrain herself from drawing the girl into an embrace. She had already learned from her failed attempt at humor that the child didn't appreciate familiarity from a virtual stranger, and she was determined not to make that mistake again. She did, however, say gently, "It's always hard to lose someone. But it'll get easier to cope with as you grow older."

The girl's dark eyes were glistening now. "Did it for you?" she whispered.

Jenny nodded. "It did."

Celeste swallowed audibly and turned her attention back to the doll in the rocking chair. "When my father marries Miss Beryl, maybe I won't think about my mother so much. Just like it was better for you when you got a new father."

Jenny still knew practically nothing about Mr. Harrington's personal life, so the news of an impending wedding was a surprise. It was good to see that the child seemed to anticipate the event. "When is your father getting married?" she asked.

"In five months. January." A smile, the first that Jenny had seen, brought a dimple to the girl's right cheek. "I can't wait to have a real mother. Miss Beryl is the prettiest lady in London."

"I'm sure she is."

The girl nodded in agreement, but the smile disappeared as quickly as it had come, leaving in its place a wistful expression. "I just wish I could see her more often. She hardly ever visits when Father is away—she has to take care of her mother."

"Then she must be a very nice person."

"Yes. And she loves me so much."

"I'm sure she does, Celeste." The bond of empathy for this

motherless child had grown stronger with each passing moment of their conversation, so much that Jenny finally reached out to touch the girl's shoulder. I'm glad you have someone like her."

Celeste's face was radiant. "Thank you, Miss Price," she said, and Jenny decided that the hysterical maid who'd come downstairs earlier had been mistaken. After all, she *had* admitted to falling asleep. Anyone could have come through the door and been gone in seconds, while the child slept unaware.

"Do you know how to play draughts?" the girl asked suddenly.

"Draughts?" Jenny smiled. "Of course. My family plays it all the time. Would you like to play?"

"I would love to." Celeste pointed toward a small teakwood table set in front of a window, with a matching bench on either side. Carved into the top was a checkered board. "My father bought the set in India."

"It's lovely," Jenny said as she got up from her knee.

Celeste went over to one of the benches, pulled out a drawer, and began drawing out stacks of circular black and white pieces. She handed a stack of white pieces across to Jenny. "I always take black. Do you mind?"

"Not at all." Listening to the child chatter about how much she enjoyed playing games, Jenny began setting the round pieces on their proper squares. She was pleased that a friendship with Celeste seemed to be fast forming, and after such a doubtful start. *Miss Nightingale . . . God was leading you after all,* she thought. She could always go to Canada later, but this child obviously needed a friend—at least until her father remarried.

The child across from her moved a black piece diagonally to another square and smiled. "I always start first, too."

"Well, it's your game," Jenny said, moving her own piece. It crossed her mind that it might be good to allow the child to win, at least this first time, but she decided against it. Again she remembered the cold shoulder she had gotten with her attempt at humor. A child as intelligent as Celeste would be alert to any obvious move to curry her favor. "I want to warn you, though, that I come from a family of cutthroats where draughts is concerned."

The girl moved another piece and looked up at her with a bemused expression. "You have pirates in your family?"

Jenny smiled at the image of her parents, sister, and brother with eye patches, gold hoop earrings, and swords. "No, I mean that the game is taken seriously at my house. We show no mercy."

"Well, I always win."

"Oh? Then you must be a cutthroat, too."

Celeste shook her head and returned Jenny's smile. "No, I just always win."

Five moves later, Celeste moved a piece next to one of Jenny's, leaving an open space behind hers. Jenny saw a chance to leap and took it, then collected the black piece she'd captured and set it on her side of the table.

Celeste frowned. "I didn't mean to move there."

"You didn't? But once you take your hand away, you have to stay in the same square."

"Well, I didn't mean to move it away." She looked up at Jenny and held out a hand. "Let me have it back."

After a moment's hesitation Jenny shrugged and handed the piece over to her. "If you wish. But you should be careful about moving your hand next time." They arranged the pieces back to their previous positions, and then Jenny looked around for another move.

"You could put it there," the girl offered, pointing to an open square adjacent to one of her black pieces.

Jenny squinted a wary eye at her and moved somewhere else. "I wouldn't care to do that, Celeste. That would give you a double leap."

The child was silent for a while, staring at the board. Jenny thought she was contemplating her next move, but then she looked up and said, "*Miss* Celeste."

"What?"

"You're supposed to address me as *Miss* Celeste. All the other servants do."

"You're joking," Jenny said, but even as she spoke she could see that the girl was deadly serious. The brown eyes that had had such a warm color minutes ago seemed cold as marbles as they regarded her from across the table.

"I'm an employee here," she told the girl in a tone she hoped was both gentle and firm. "But I'm not a servant."

"My father pays you, so you have to do as I say."

"Your father pays me to see to your health," Jenny said, her voice still level. "Not to be your slave."

Celeste's lips turned down into a frown. "You're supposed to keep me from getting upset. If you know anything about epilepsy, you know that I'm not supposed to get upset. Even Miss Templeton knew that. She may have been stupid, but she always allowed me to win at draughts."

Jenny blinked, realizing that all of this anger was because the girl hadn't gotten over that first loss at the game board a moment ago. "Always allowed you . . ."

"Miss Barton lets me win, too. And *they* address me as Miss Celeste."

Straightening, Jenny stared numbly across at the girl. How

had their relationship, so promising only minutes before, deteriorated so quickly? She took a deep breath, held it, then said, "No one likes to lose, Celeste. But it was only one leap . . . you still have a chance to win the game."

"Does that mean you'll allow me to win?"

"No, it doesn't mean that at all. How can you enjoy playing a game if you know you're going to win every time?"

"I like winning!" the girl seethed, her finger jabbing at the empty square on the board where she had tried to get Jenny to move her game piece. "I demand that you call me Miss Celeste, and that you move here!"

"I just can't do that," Jenny answered, alarmed at the intensity of the child's anger. She had never actually taken care of a patient with epilepsy, but as Celeste had mentioned a moment ago, the girl wasn't supposed to be getting upset like this. Yet how could she sit here and allow a child, even an afflicted one, to demand absolute obedience?

"You *will* do it!"

Jenny rose from her bench. "I think you need to rest for a while."

"I've already had my nap!" Celeste screamed. With her arm she raked the pieces from the game board onto the carpet. "And I want you to go away so Miss Templeton can come back!"

Elaine Barton appeared in the doorway of the schoolroom. "What's wrong?" she asked, her eyes on Celeste.

Shaking her head, Jenny turned back to the girl. "She needs to calm—" She didn't get the chance to finish her sentence, for the child in front of her let out a little cry, arched her back, and toppled from her bench to the floor.

Immediately Jenny was down at her side. "All right," she soothed, pushing the girl's bench away so that she would not bump her head. She looked up at the governess, who now hovered over them. "Please move this table, too."

After doing so, Elaine headed for the lavatory. "I'll get a wet towel."

"Good idea," Jenny said as she turned the girl, now pitching her arms in short, spasmodic jerks, to her side. With one hand on Celeste's shoulder, she pulled a folded clean handkerchief from her apron pocket and carefully pushed it between the girl's teeth, so that she wouldn't damage the inside of her mouth. *What have I done?* she thought as her heart pounded against her ribs.

When Celeste finally lay still, Jenny bathed her face with the towel the governess had brought back. "Are you all right?" she asked the girl after a little while.

Celeste opened her eyes and stared up at Jenny. She looked fragile and weak, and her oval face was pale as chalk. "My head hurts."

"Would you like me to put you to bed?"

She closed her eyes and did not answer for a while, and Jenny wondered if the girl would drift off to sleep. Just when she was trying to decide if she should pick the girl up and carry her to her bedroom, the child looked up at her again and mumbled something.

"What did you say?" Jenny asked, lowering her head.

"I want Miss Barton to put me to bed . . . not *you.*"

~

"There is always an adjustment period whenever two people are going to be spending so much time together," Mrs. Ganaway was saying from behind the desk in her office. "I'm sure Miss Celeste was just testing you. Perhaps you shouldn't have been so strict right away."

Jenny could only sigh and shake her head. It had been drilled into her head daily while at Saint Thomas's that nurses should strive to be credits to their noble calling, and here she was involved in strife on the first day of her first assignment. But could she have acted any differently with the girl? When did allowing oneself to be bullied make a good professional of any occupation?

"You're suggesting that I should have let her win after she demanded that I do so?"

"What would it have hurt? It's just a game, and she's a sick child."

"She's well enough to know the difference between right and wrong."

"It is her father's duty to teach her that, not yours or mine."

Jenny rubbed a vein that had started throbbing between her eyebrows. Canada had never seemed so attractive as it did at this moment. "And when Mr. Harrington is absent, his daughter is allowed to terrorize the household?"

"Terrorize? You have been in this house less than one day. How dare you suggest—"

"What about the maid who had her hair shorn?"

To Jenny's surprise, Mrs. Ganaway covered her face with her hands. "Oh, I don't know," she moaned, her voice finally filling with emotion. "Miss Celeste shouldn't have done that, but how could I have prevented it? I can't stay up there and watch her constantly."

Jenny wondered how she had ever felt intimidated by the woman in front of her. Surely Mrs. Ganaway's position as housekeeper depended upon keeping peace in the household.

It was clear that she was trying to keep both her employer's daughter and the servants content, and it appeared that the two forces had been at odds for some time.

"None of the upstairs maids have been here longer than a year," the housekeeper continued, dabbing at her nose with a handkerchief. "If Miss Celeste doesn't like one, which is *always* the case, it's just a matter of time before the maid is gone. She treated Miss Templeton so wretchedly that it's a wonder she stayed as long as she did."

Panic filled Mrs. Ganaway's red-rimmed eyes, and she sent a pleading look across to Jenny. "You're not going to resign, are you, Miss Price? It was just a bad start, but things will get better."

"Resign?" Jenny shook her head again. "I'm obligated to stay here for two years." A shudder caught her shoulders. Two years now stretched out before her like a lifetime. *Two years minus one day. Lord, could Miss Nightingale have been mistaken about your calling me here?*

"You're going to stay, then?"

"This is where I've been assigned. I would be a failure if I left."

Relief washed over the housekeeper's face. "Thank you, Miss Price. I shall speak with Celeste and ask her to try to be more tolerant."

"And *I,"* said Jenny, getting to her feet, "will start sleeping with a nightcap over my hair."

5

LATE Monday afternoon, Logan Fogarty wiped the sweat from his forehead with a sleeve, then got back to sharpening the blades of the mower. His muscular arm moved the whetstone along the metal in rapid motions; all the while his attention was focused on a scrap of paper he had tacked on a wall of the gardening cottage.

> *The Frankfurth Barrel Pump is the best ever made! Uses include washing windows, sprinkling the lawn or garden, or as a fire extinguisher. Brass nozzle, warranted not to leak.*

The advertisement had been pasted on the side of a pump that had arrived at the Harrington estate just this morning with a wagonload of other gardening and hardware supplies. Logan squinted at the letters while keeping up the steady rhythm of his work.

He had figured out the first word, *the,* weeks ago. *Frankfurth* came easy too, only because he had overheard one of the other gardeners say that Mr. Horton had paid extra for the Frankfurth barrel pump, because of the warranty. Once he'd reminded himself that the first letter of the third word was a *b,* it only stood to reason that the word was *barrel.* Understanding a word always gave him great joy, for then he was able to sound out the letters it contained, thereby helping him to decipher other words.

Repeating the word *barrel* carefully under his breath, Logan turned his attention to the next letter in the word. *"A,"* he told himself . . . only it obviously wasn't pronounced the same as the *a* in *daisy,* a word he had gleaned from studying a seed packet. It had been so discouraging to learn that many letters of the alphabet took on different sounds in different words. *Why can't they all be like the* s, he wondered. *Salt, soil, brass . . .* As far as he could tell, that letter always made the same sound.

"Look here! The dummy's at his studies again."

Cheeks burning, Logan turned his head slowly to the left. There slouched George and Healy, two of the five gardeners employed at the estate.

"Gonna be prime minister one day if he keeps at it," George said, tipping his hat with mock respect. He was the tallest of Mr. Harrington's yard servants, and probably the most handsome to the young lasses, Logan figured.

Healy was holding his sides at his friend's wit. "Why not? We got a Jew holdin' that position now!" He had two missing upper front teeth, so the word *position* came out in a spray of saliva.

"Rather 'ave a Jew!" George hooted, throwing a cuff at Healy's shoulder. "Micks can't do nowt but grow potatoes and get drunk."

"Ain't no difference between 'em to me . . . they both is awfully fond of lightin' candles."

"That's enough!" a voice cut into the revelry. Mr. Horton, the head gardener, stepped through the open doorway of the cottage. Taking his pipe from his mouth, he pointed the stem at the two jokesters. "Leave him alone."

They sobered up immediately, and George lowered his eyes to the stone floor. "We was just—"

"You weren't pickin' up the tools out by the vegetable garden is what you were doing. Now get back to work!"

When the two gardeners had scrambled outside, Mr. Horton walked over to the corner and eased himself down to crouch in front of the mower. Logan didn't know how old his supervisor was, but the man's gray hair and leathery skin suggested at least two decades more than Logan's thirty-three years. Though his arms were almost as muscular as Logan's, gout prevented him from doing any but the lightest manual chores. It was obvious that this distressed Mr. Horton greatly, even though, as head gardener, he wasn't expected to do any of the actual labor.

The man switched his pipe to his other hand and ran a thumb lightly against the blade that had just been sharpened. "I believe I could shave my face with that, Mr. Fogarty," he said. "You've been a right fine worker these two months."

"Thank ye, sir." Logan felt more at ease around Mr. Horton than he did around anyone else. The older man was quick to show appreciation for a job well done, and he didn't make sport of Logan's thick Irish brogue, as the other grounds servants did. Whenever they were nearby, Logan used as few words as possible. For that he had been labeled a dummy.

"You know, you could take on both of those jackals if you had a mind to."

Logan's head snapped up. "Sir?"

The man drew a whiff from his pipe and grinned. Logan had never felt a desire to smoke, but the aroma of the tobacco was pleasant, and it brought on a stab of homesickness he had thought he would never feel.

"I'm saying that if you ever get tired of the name-calling,

I'll be happy to go find somethin' to keep meself busy while you teach them some manners." His grin widened. "Though it would be a fair sight to see, I'll warrant."

Embarrassed by the warmth he could feel in his cheeks again, Logan worked faster. In the old days, he would have made gristmeal of George and Healy at the first insult. The ability to fight and brawl, and to nurse a grudge for years, was the legacy his father, Ryan Fogarty, had handed down to his five sons. That, and a hatred of any authority, including the church.

His father's dad had been just as bad, perhaps even worse, or so he had heard. The senior Fogarty had been killed in a knife fight outside a pub long before Logan came into the world.

During Logan's youth, being raised in such a volatile atmosphere had seemed natural, simply because he had no knowledge of anything else. Other families in Dublin had shunned the Fogartys because of their hot tempers and antagonism toward the parish priest, so he had seen little that he could hold up in comparison.

Only years after Logan immigrated to England did he realize that his family had been the exception, not the norm. From there, he began to wonder which particular incident had been the source of his family's ill temper. It had to have been something terrible and traumatic, for surely somewhere back in his ancestry there had been a Fogarty or two who hadn't considered every man his enemy.

Those bitter days were over now for Logan. Hard and unnatural as it was to turn the other cheek, he would continue to do so as long as God gave him strength of will.

"Learning some new words?" Mr. Horton said with a nod toward the paper on the wall.

Logan blushed even deeper. "Aye, sir."

The head gardener grinned. "Nothing wrong with that. I wish I'd learnt to read way back when."

"Ye can't?"

"Not a word, except my own name. Can't even recognize my dear wife Annabell's name on paper."

"Then how . . ."

"How do I write out orders?"

Logan nodded.

"Well, I don't. I just tell Mr. Palmer what I need, and he makes 'em out for me. You don't have to be able to read to be a good gardener." He glanced at the scrap of paper again and winked at Logan. "Maybe one day I won't have to climb those stairs up to Mr. Palmer's office to get my orders written. I'll just come to you. But then, once you learn reading, you'll likely be setting out for a better job."

With that, the man left, and Logan set to work on another blade. He was too shy to tell Mr. Horton that he couldn't imagine any better job than being a gardener. Why, the aroma of tilled, dark soil had no match—unless it was the smell of leaves after a rain. He would never lose the awe that came from the sight of a green sprout timidly edging up out of the ground where he'd planted a seed just days earlier.

Logan's desire to read had nothing to do with his occupation. It had originated the Sunday he had staggered in from the rain and onto a back pew of the Metropolitan Tabernacle at Vauxhall, South London. Though the pastor, a Charles Spurgeon, was a great distance away in that huge auditorium, he seemed to fix his eyes upon Logan alone while he opened a book he called God's Word. Sharper than any sword, the words pierced through the gin stupor that Logan had been in for days. A new and unfamiliar thirst took hold of Logan in that place. Before the service was over, his thirst was quenched by the Living Water.

He had been a gardener at the elderly Sir Willmore Kirkley's estate on Borough High Street at the time. Instead of wasting the leftover of his scant salary on gin, as in the old days, he began saving his pennies and bought his own Bible. He proudly carried the book under his arm to church every Sunday and kept it the rest of the time on the top of the dresser, where he could see it.

When the baronet passed away and the eldest son discharged most of the staff, Logan was out of work for almost a month. Doors on both sides of the Thames were closed to him almost as soon as he opened his mouth to speak, for most Londoners harbored a deep prejudice against the Irish.

Finding this position at the Harrington estate had been nothing short of a miracle. In desperation he had applied for work at the docks . . . along with at least fifty other men that day. When he, like most of the others, was turned away, an Irishman he had struck up a conversation with had told him that a domestic agency on Oxford Street could help him find gardening work. With great hope, Logan had gotten directions and set out to apply.

A man in gentleman's garb had happened to be on the stoop of the agency, just about to open the door, and Logan had opened it for him. The gentleman turned out to be Mr. Palmer, Graham Harrington's steward. Logan found out later that Mr. Palmer was married to an Irishwoman and harbored no prejudices.

Logan had been happy to find a small chapel on Campden Hill Road, here on the north side of the river, though he would always have fond memories of Mr. Spurgeon's church. And one day, when the congregation rose at the beginning of the service to read a Bible passage aloud, Logan Fogarty's Irish brogue would proudly join in.

6

THE next morning Celeste acted as if Jenny didn't exist. *She should be on the stage,* Jenny thought, for the child had an uncanny ability to appear as if she were looking right through her. Celeste also ignored her attempts at conversation, until Jenny gave up trying. If it were not for Elaine's assurances that things would likely get better, she didn't know how she could have borne being treated in this manner.

When the girl was down for her nap that afternoon, the governess suggested to Jenny that they take a walk. "You need a change of scenery," she said, "and you haven't gotten a chance to see the gardens yet. If you wait for whenever Celeste wants to go, it may be never."

"She doesn't like to play outside?" Jenny asked on their way through the morning room.

"Not very often. I hate to say this, but she's a bit on the lazy side. And Mr. Harrington doesn't really insist that she exert herself, either."

"Why?"

Elaine held open one of the French doors. "I'm certain he fears it isn't good for Celeste's health for her to do anything she doesn't want to do. He's terrified of her seizures, according to Nurse Templeton."

They stepped onto the gray brick terrace, bordered on two sides by lilacs and sweet-scented viburnums. The way to the lawn and main garden lay through a wooden arch festooned with fragrant rambler roses, their white petals starting to turn a yellowish color.

"I want to show you my favorite place," Elaine said as they passed under the arch. "You can see the river. . . ."

"Listen!" Jenny said, halting and touching her companion's sleeve.

The governess raised her eyebrows but was still. Jenny tilted her head. Faint strains of a masculine tenor wafted delicately through the leaves of a stand of young crab apple trees up ahead.

"Can you hear what he's singing?" she whispered to Elaine.

Elaine shook her head and gave a conspiratorial wink. "Let's get closer."

Jenny assumed the singer was a great distance away, because of the softness of the tune. But soon after passing the crab apple trees, the two caught sight of a brawny, fair-haired man about twelve feet away on his knees at a bed of Japanese anemones. He was hard at work pulling up weeds with both hands. His singing, though still soft and low, held an unmistakable Irish accent.

Come, follow me by the smell
Here's delicate Onyons to sell . . .

Jenny and Elaine looked at each other. "He might not appreciate our spying on him," Elaine said softly, though her lips were smiling.

"Can we go another way?" Jenny whispered back.

For this is ev'ry Cook's opinion,
No sav'ry dish without an Onyon . . .

The governess gestured for Jenny to follow her, but before they could turn to leave, the man glanced sideways and froze. Even at that distance, Jenny could tell that his cheeks were reddening.

Elaine nudged her side. "Let's go."

But to Jenny it seemed rude, now that they'd been caught, just to walk away. She nodded to the gardener. "Just admiring your singing, sir."

A look of shock crossed his face, and he returned to his weeding with a vengeance.

"This way," Elaine said, tugging at her arm. They circled around the anemone bed and walked along the shrubbery bordering the rose garden until they reached a line of apple trees bordering the Harrington property.

"Why do you think he was embarrassed?" Jenny asked, now that they were out of earshot. "He had such a lovely voice."

"From what little I've seen out here of that particular gardener," Elaine answered, "he seems to be a bit of a loner. That was the first time I've heard him make a sound."

"Do you think we should go back and apologize for spying?"

Elaine shook her head. "I think the man would just as soon be left alone." Changing the subject, she pointed southeast to the River Thames in the distance, clear of fog for a change and webbed with rigging.

"It's lovely up here," Jenny breathed.

"I coaxed Celeste into having part of our lessons in this spot one day. She seemed bored by it all, though."

Jenny sighed at the reminder of the child, then felt a touch at her arm.

"Celeste treated Lucille Templeton wretchedly, too," said Elaine. "You mustn't take it personally."

"Why doesn't she treat you that way?"

"She does at times. But you're brand-new bait, if you'll pardon the expression. She hasn't yet figured out how far she can push you."

"New bait." A sudden breeze lifted some strands of hair from the coil at the back of Jenny's head, and she made a futile effort to tuck them back in. "You mean like a mouse being toyed with by a cat."

"Somewhat," Elaine replied with an amused smile.

"Well, you know that the cat kills the mouse after it plays with it for a while," Jenny said half-seriously. "Should I be watching my back?"

The governess shook her head. "I don't think you have to worry about your back. But . . ."

Jenny lifted an eyebrow. "Yes?"

"Well, you *may* want to keep wearing your nightcap for a while."

Jenny smiled. For all her plain appearance, Elaine Barton had the kindest, most sympathetic voice she'd ever heard. The warmth of the woman's green eyes gave off a magnetism Elaine most likely was unaware of, and her thick auburn hair, tied at the nape of her neck with a ribbon, was simply beautiful. "Thank you," Jenny said to the governess. "I'll remember that."

They both looked out toward the river again. "I believe I could see St. Thomas's Hospital if not for the fog."

"Did you enjoy nursing school?"

"Very much. How about you?" Jenny asked. "Where were you educated?"

"My grandmother sent me to a boarding school in Manchester, and then to Bedford College here in London."

"Your grandmother? You were an orphan?"

"Since I was three. My parents were missionaries in India—they were murdered by Sikhs. A servant smuggled me to a British post, and I was sent to live with my grandmother in Essex."

Jenny's hand went up to her cheek. "Oh, how terrible!"

"I don't remember anything about it," Elaine said almost lightly. Folding her arms, she turned from Jenny to look at the river again. "Nor do I remember their faces. My grandmother has a portrait of my parents that was painted shortly after their wedding. That's all that is left of them. I don't even know where they're buried . . . if indeed they *were* buried."

One of the things Jenny had learned at St. Thomas's was that a nurse who wants to endure in the profession must harden herself to suffering. But the thought of the young couple being martyred, possibly in the hearing of their young child, was too much for Jenny. She found herself blinking away tears. "At least you know where their souls are," she managed over the lump in her throat.

Elaine turned back to Jenny, her green eyes mildly appraising. "I shouldn't have told you about that. I've gone and made you sad."

Jenny's apron pocket was empty, so she turned up the hem of her apron and wiped both eyes. "I'm glad you've still got your grandmother," she sniffed after a moment.

"My grandmother no longer claims me." Before Jenny could respond, the governess motioned toward the house. "Celeste will be waking soon. We should be returning to the nursery." The tone of Elaine's voice indicated that she no longer wished to discuss her family, and Jenny mutely fell into step with her and started for the house.

"Celeste isn't supposed to sleep past two o'clock," the governess said, her voice lighter this time. "If she does, she won't sleep well at night. Her little playmates will be up there soon."

"Her playmates?"

"For want of a better term. Three of the servants' children. Mr. Harrington feels that Celeste should spend some time with other children every day. It isn't good for a child to have only adults for companionship."

The two walked back upstairs and through the nursery to the girl's bedroom. Celeste's deep breathing could still be heard. A maid, wide awake and wearing a cap knotted under her chin, slipped out of the room when they entered.

"Miss Celeste?" Elaine said softly, walking around to the side of the bed.

Jenny caught up with her. "May I?" When the governess raised a puzzled eyebrow, she explained. "It's really my duty to do that, and I'd like to try for a new start with her."

Elaine smiled her understanding, and when she had left the room, Jenny touched the girl's shoulder. "It's time to wake up . . . Miss Celeste." The words were extremely difficult to force out of her mouth, but she decided it was up to her, as the adult, to go the second mile. A peace treaty was what she was after, and any agreement of peace between two equally matched opponents called for concessions from both. *But I refuse to sit and purposefully lose at draughts. That can be Celeste's concession.*

Jenny touched the shoulder again, and the girl opened her eyes, then turned her head on the pillow, looking over at the door that opened up into the schoolroom. "Where is Miss Barton?"

"I wanted to wake you myself."

"But I don't want . . ."

"I was wondering if we could start all over again," Jenny continued. "I would really like to be your friend." She swallowed, then added, "And if it will make you happy, I will address you as *Miss* Celeste."

Celeste sat up in bed and stared at her. After a moment, a dimple appeared in her right cheek. "What about draughts? Are you going to allow me to win from now on?"

Jenny considered this again and then shook her head. "The pirate in me just wouldn't allow it . . . Miss Celeste. Can you understand?"

"I suppose," the girl shrugged, as if it didn't really matter anyway. "But I'm not going to ever want to play draughts with you, if that's the case."

"Then I suppose I'll just have to live with that," Jenny replied. Glancing at the blue delft clock on the chimneypiece, she added, "Don't you need to get dressed?"

"Yes. Will you help me back into my dress?"

"I'll even braid a ribbon through your hair, if you like."

The girl tossed her sheets aside and slid out of the bed. "How do you know how to do that?"

"My younger sister, Nicolette," Jenny answered, picking up Celeste's blue gingham dress from where it lay at the foot of her bed. She eased it down over the girl's head. "I used to braid her hair all the time. She has the most beautiful dark hair . . . almost the color of yours."

After the last button was fastened, Jenny led the child over to a dressing table set against the wall. Celeste chose a blue satin ribbon to match the trim on her dress. Quickly Jenny gathered up the sides of the girl's hair and pulled them back to the crown of her head, then began braiding, threading the ribbon through at the same time. "You'll look like a Greek statue," she said, tucking the remaining ends of the ribbon underneath the last turn of the braid.

Celeste smiled and peered at herself from all angles in the mirror. "Will you comb my hair this way when my father comes home?"

"Of course," Jenny answered. A wave of relief washed over her; Elaine's words of assurance were finally coming true.

They walked into the nursery together, just as a housemaid took a hesitant step through the opposite doorway. She was even more slender than Jenny and wore the typical black alpaca and white lace, with streamers flowing from her neat little cap. Jenny would have guessed her to be no older than seventeen. At the sight of Celeste, her eyes lowered. "Miss Celeste?"

"Who are you?" Celeste demanded, her arms folded and eyes narrowed.

"M-me?" the young maid said, flustered. "I'm Gerdie, miss."

"You're new, then?"

The girl's cheeks reddened. "Just this morning, miss."

"Well, what do you want?"

"I-I'm to ask if you're ready for the other children."

"Make sure their hands are clean," Celeste said after giving a nod. "I won't have them touching my things with dirty hands."

"Yes, miss." The maid disappeared, and seconds later an older housemaid entered the room, followed by a boy and two girls. They were wide-eyed and quiet, their shoes moving noiselessly across the carpets. The three had to have been standing just outside the door as the younger maid spoke with Celeste, yet not even a whisper had drifted in from the hallway.

Celeste took charge immediately. "You, Charles," she said to the boy, a blond-haired lad of about nine. "Bring the benches from the draughts set over to my study table. I want to play whist first."

Without a word the boy obeyed, setting the stools at the ends of the table so that there were now four places to sit. The two girls, both with freckles and brown hair, held hands and hung back timidly, waiting to see which chair Celeste would choose before taking seats themselves.

"I'm going to fetch a book from my room," Jenny said to Celeste when the children had finally seated themselves.

The girl ignored her and started passing out cards to the other children. "It's my game, so I'll go first," were the last words Jenny heard her say before leaving the schoolroom.

Elaine was gathering up a needlepoint basket when Jenny entered the room that they shared. "I was just coming to join you out there," the governess said. "I take it that the children have arrived?"

Jenny nodded. "They're rather quiet, aren't they?"

"'Mute with fear' would be more appropriate."

"Whose children are they?"

"The girls are sisters—their mother is a downstairs parlor maid; I'm not sure if her name is Aida or Ida. The boy belongs to Mertice, one of the scullery maids. He runs errands for the cook when he's not in school . . . or 'playing' with Celeste."

"School?"

"Mr. Harrington insists that any servants' children under the age of twelve go to school. He even pays the fees."

"You mean there are other servants' children besides those three?"

The governess thought for a second and then nodded. "Two or three others, I think, but Celeste wants nothing to do with the ones that are too young." Her green eyes cut a glance at the door, then she added, "That may be a good thing. A younger child might not understand the necessity of following the little general's orders."

A sound of gleeful triumph could be heard in the nursery. Celeste had obviously won her first round. The noise reminded Jenny that her place was in there watching the child. Excitement could bring on a seizure almost as quickly as anger. Gathering up a copy of *Far from the Madding Crowd* by Thomas Hardy, one of the books her parents had sent back with her, Jenny walked with Elaine into the nursery.

They sat side by side on the sofa. While the governess got busy with her needlework, Jenny tried to concentrate on her book and not on the farce going on in front of her. The faces of Celeste's three young visitors were painful to watch. Their expressions went beyond eager-to-please to a sort of desperation. No doubt each child had been reminded often by a fearful mother that her position, and hence the family livelihood, was at stake.

Celeste tired of whist after a while. Leaving her chair, she walked over to her toy chest and brought out a box of miniature ninepins and a wooden ball. "Set these up," she ordered the oldest girl, who looked to be around eleven years of age.

At ninepins, the children's sabotage of their own efforts was more than obvious. They clapped and stretched their lips into congratulatory smiles whenever Celeste won a match, as if it were the most wonderful thing that could happen to them.

And Celeste, who had to realize that she was practically being handed points on a silver platter, gloated every time she won a match and laughed scornfully at the other children's losses.

But the little general soon became bored with this, too. "I want to play with my dolls now," she told the children. A second later Celeste had her back to her guests as she sat at her dollhouse, humming to herself. Apparently accustomed to this form of dismissal, the children slipped soundlessly out of the nursery.

Jenny peered down at the open book in her lap. She hadn't gotten past the second paragraph; she had been too caught up in the goings-on in front of her. "Has it always been this way?" she whispered to Elaine.

"It makes you want to be a child again, doesn't it?" the governess murmured sardonically, her eyes still on her needlework.

"Actually, it makes me want to throw up."

Elaine looked at Jenny, the suggestion of a twinkle in her eyes. "I think you and I are going to be good friends."

7

As usual, Logan Fogarty ate his supper in silence while the rest of Mr. Harrington's employees filled the servants' hall with jests and gossip. When he was finished, he pushed away from the table and left without speaking to anyone, but he did send a solemn nod to Dudley, one of the other gardeners.

The stars were beginning to appear in the evening sky when Logan walked out to a covered gazebo set among the Chinese junipers and yews. After lighting the nearest gas lamp, he sat down on one of the benches, pulled from his pocket the book Dudley had lent him, and practiced the words that he had already been taught this week. They were all small words, no more than three letters each. Some he had already known, but Dudley had promised that they would gradually build to longer words.

He wondered why he hadn't thought of this idea sooner. He could learn so much faster with a tutor. Worth every penny it was, to come closer to his dream of reading his precious Bible.

It would be easier to study indoors, where May beetles weren't attracted to the lantern, but Logan couldn't bring himself to be humiliated by the rest of the gardeners. He had warned Dudley that if the others found out, he would stop paying for his tutoring, so Dudley had agreed to keep it quiet.

Hearing footsteps in the grass behind him, Logan turned to look over his shoulder.

"It's me, Fogarty," came Dudley's voice, and the lanky young gardener stepped into the light of the lantern.

Logan slid over to make room for him. "The others?"

"Playin' cards in the room," Dudley answered in a tone that suggested that he would like to be doing the same. He sat down on the bench, and Logan caught a whiff of the gin on his breath. "Are you ready to start?"

"I'm ready." Logan held the open book out between them. "I was tryin' to figure out this word," he said, pointing to the page and spelling the letters out loud. "E-x-p-a-t-r-i-a-t-e." He then sounded out the syllables slowly and looked up at Dudley. "Am I sayin' it right?"

Dudley stared at the printed letters for a second. "That were right."

"What does it mean?"

"Mean?" Logan's tutor glanced at the page again. "We're supposed to stay with the little words fer now." He pointed to the word *the*. "Now, read this one for me."

"But I'm wantin' to know what it means."

"Well, all right," Dudley sighed. He scratched his head, looked at the word one more time, and replied, "It's one o' them diseases."

"Diseases?"

"You know, like dropsy. My uncle had it, back durin' the war. Makes you horrible sick."

Satisfied, Logan nodded and pointed to another long word. "What about—"

"Now, you can't be changing the order of yer learnin', Fogarty," Dudley said, wagging a stern finger. "You got to crawl before you can walk."

"But I already know—"

"If you want me for yer teacher, you've got to do it my way." He turned the page, ran his finger down the length of it, and pointed out another word. "Now, what's that say?"

Logan looked down at the word. Swallowing his disappointment, he replied, "Cup."

~

Jenny lay in bed and tried to will herself to sleep. She had been so exhausted last night from the rigors of her journey and her first day in the Harrington household that she could barely remember turning down her covers. But tonight the unfamiliarity of the mattress, the pillow, even the entire place caught up with her. After at least an hour of tossing and turning, Jenny got out of bed, pulled off her nightcap, and felt for her robe and slippers.

She could hear Elaine's steady breathing from the bed across the room. With her long hair hanging down her back, she quietly collected the flowered cardboard box that held her writing materials.

Remembering at the last minute that the door to their tiny sitting room creaked, Jenny decided to use the schoolroom instead. She closed the bedroom door behind her, then in total darkness felt her way to the study table and the overhead lamp. It took her a few seconds to find matches in one of the shallow drawers of the table, but finally she had some light.

Dear Mother and Father, Jenny wrote, and then began telling them all about her arrival at the Harrington household and the events of the past several days. *Please pray for Celeste,* she wrote at the top of her second page. *There is such a sadness about her. In spite of her possessions and the power she has over the household, she seems like an orphan child.*

She chewed at the tip of her pen and began to wonder about Mr. Harrington. Elaine had told her that business kept him away from London about half the time. Surely that had something to do with Celeste's behavior. How could a child help but feel abandoned when her only parent was away so often?

With a sigh Jenny refilled her pen from the inkhorn. She was finally becoming sleepy, but she decided to finish her letter so that she could post it in the morning. Her family would be wondering about her first nursing position.

Her ears perked up at a sound coming from Celeste's bedroom. With a start Jenny realized that she had been hearing it for the past several seconds without it registering in her weary mind. Now she recognized that it was the girl's voice.

She dropped her pen and got up quickly, not even worrying about the inkblot that stained the paper. Taking the lamp from its hook, she went to the girl's room and opened the door. Moans were coming from the bed, and Alma, the middle-aged housemaid who had been assigned to watch the girl, was wringing her hands at the bedside.

Jenny crossed the area and gently nudged the maid aside. "Celeste," she said, touching the girl's cheek. "You're having a bad dream."

Celeste blinked her eyes open and looked up at Jenny. Her lashes were clumped together with tears, and it seemed to take her a couple of seconds to realize who was standing over her. "What?" she murmured.

"You were having a nightmare."

A mixture of relief and confusion washed across the girl's face. "It was a dream?"

"Yes, it was." Jenny smiled at the ashen-faced housemaid, who still stood next to her. "You did fine. I'll stay with her for a while. Why don't you take a nap on the sofa in the schoolroom?"

The maid looked tempted, but unsure. "Won't I get in trouble, ma'am?"

"Not if I take your place. Just leave the lamp here on the night table."

When Alma was gone, Jenny pulled the Windsor chair closer to the bed. It was hard and uncomfortable, which was probably no accident. Whichever maid was assigned to watch the child at night was given most of the afternoon to nap, but still, the long, lonely night watch could induce slumber, especially in the quiet hours of the approaching dawn.

"Would you like me to put out the lamp?" she asked Celeste, who now lay on her side watching her.

"Not yet."

"You're not still frightened, are you?"

There was a long silence, and then, "A little."

"Then we'll keep the lamp on for a while." She got up and turned the lamp's wick down low to conserve what little oil was left, then sat back down again. "Now, why don't you tell me about that dream?"

The girl drew a shuddering breath. "Tell you about it?"

"If you'd like to. Sometimes when we talk about the things that frighten us, we see that they're not so terrible after all."

"Well, this *was* terrible." After another shudder, she said, "It was the cat from my book."

"Which book?"

"Alice's Adventures in Wonderland. There's a cat whose eyes glow in the dark. . . ."

"The Cheshire cat."

"That's the one. Only this one had long teeth, too, and it followed me everywhere I went. It was waiting for a chance to bite me."

"No wonder you called out," Jenny said sympathetically.

"I called out?"

"Didn't you know?"

Celeste shook her head on the pillow. "I remember trying to call for help, but I couldn't make my voice loud enough for anyone to hear me."

"Well, we heard you." Jenny stood again and pulled the counterpane over the girl's shoulders. "And there's no cat here. Why don't you close your eyes and think about pleasant thoughts."

"Will you tell me a story?"

Stifling a yawn, Jenny said, "All right. What kind of story would you like?"

"One that's not about cats," the girl answered right away.

"Have you heard the story about stone soup?"

"No."

Suddenly the light in the room flickered for several seconds, sending bizarre shadows across the bed. The girl gasped when the room was plunged into darkness.

"Nothing to be frightened of," Jenny reassured her, reaching up to pat her arm. Then she leaned back against the hard rail of the chair and said, "But there was once a soldier returning from a war who *was* afraid."

"What was he afraid of?"

"He was afraid that he would starve before he could make it home to his dear family. He was terribly hungry, you see."

"Why didn't he buy some food?"

Jenny shook her head in the darkness. "Because he had no money with which to buy some."

"What did he do?" the girl asked.

"Are your eyes closed?"

"Now they are."

"Well, the soldier came across a cottage, where a stingy man and woman lived. . . ."

Jenny stretched the story out for as long as possible, her own eyes getting heavier and heavier as she spoke. At last she was rewarded with the sound of Celeste's even breathing. She decided to wait a little while before leaving, just to make certain that the girl didn't wake up again. The maid would probably appreciate another thirty minutes or so of sleep, too.

She woke up hours later. The room was laden with an early morning chill, and every joint in her body ached from sleeping awkwardly in the chair. Wincing as she got to her feet, she stretched her arms and looked over at the girl. Celeste still slept, her face illuminated by the feeble light that seeped in through the windows. Her expression looked almost angelic in repose.

Jenny straightened the child's covers and backed away from the bed. She would rouse the maid from her long nap in the next room and try to get an hour of comfortable sleep before it was time to start the day. At the door she paused and turned around for one last look at the girl. *She needed me last night,* Jenny thought. *And I was able to help her.* The thought gave her an immense feeling of fulfillment.

She woke Alma, then her soft slippers padded soundlessly on the carpet on the way back to her room. Even though she knew it was silly to do so, she stole a hand behind her back to make sure that her long hair was still there.

8

TWO days later, Celeste came into the schoolroom from the lavatory. "Did you know you left this on the cupboard?" she asked Jenny while dangling a gold chain from her fingers.

Jenny's hand went automatically to her neck. "I must have left it in there after my bath last night." Setting aside her book, she rose from the sofa and fastened the locket around her neck. "Thank you for bringing it to me," she said to Celeste. "I shouldn't have left it lying about."

Celeste nodded and dropped down on the sofa. "I didn't see Miss Barton in the sitting room or her room."

"She just left," Jenny explained, taking her seat again. "She needed to buy some pencils and other school supplies."

"Ugh." The girl wrinkled her nose. "School supplies."

"You don't want to be illiterate, do you?" Jenny scolded playfully.

"Well, *someone* has to," Celeste replied with a grin. She had yet to mention her dream of the night before last, but Jenny was encouraged by the subtle change in her attitude.

"Where did you get your locket?" the girl asked.

"My mother and father gave it to me when I graduated,"

Jenny replied, leaning closer so that Celeste could read the inscription. "It's the most special thing I've ever owned."

"Was it because they were proud of you for becoming a nurse?"

"They weren't proud of me for becoming a nurse. The gift was because they were happy for me, and they wanted me to have something to remember the occasion by."

By this time Celeste's brown eyes were wide. "They didn't want you to become a nurse? Is that why they weren't proud?"

Jenny had to smile. "I'm sorry. . . . I've confused you. They were *glad* that I became a nurse. But my parents have told me that they were proud of me ever since I was a child. I didn't have to earn their approval by becoming a nurse, because I already had it."

Celeste frowned thoughtfully. "Even when you did bad things?"

"They were disappointed in me when I did bad things, but I always knew that they loved me in spite of them. And because I knew I had that love, I felt sorry whenever I disappointed them. It made me try harder to do what was right."

"Well, my father is never disappointed in me," the girl boasted. She affected a smug look that seemed oddly strained to Jenny. "He's proud of me all the time."

"Of course he's proud of you."

"Mrs. Ganaway says Father will be back from Liverpool any day now. He always brings me gifts when he comes home."

"I know you'll be glad to see him." Jenny smiled.

"Miss Beryl is proud of me, too. She thinks I'm the nicest girl she has ever met."

There was a knock on the door, and Reanna stood in the doorway to ask if Celeste was ready for the children to come in and play with her. Jenny could see the boy Charles peering timidly around the servant's shoulder.

Celeste thought for a second and then shook her head. "I would rather play with my dolls today," she said, jumping down from the window seat. "The children are becoming such dreadful bores."

Jenny winced, knowing that the boy had heard. But another glance through the doorway at the relief on his face told her that he hadn't minded a bit.

~

"Hudson is feelin' poorly today," the boy explained as he sat in the driver's seat of the curricle with the reins in his hands.

"I see." Elaine stepped from the front walk onto the bricks of the carriage drive. She looked up at the boy, who appeared to be no older than Celeste, despite the jaunty angle of his cap. "And so you're to be my driver."

He flashed her a defensive look. "I'm fourteen. I'm old enough."

"So you are." Walking around the front, she paused long enough to pat the neck of one of the two horses. She stopped at the other side, held her beaded bag in the crook of her arm, and waited.

The boy looked puzzled, cocking his head at her. "Are you ready?"

Elaine merely smiled and lifted a hand. After several seconds had passed, he flushed crimson, tied off the reins, and scrambled down the other side.

"Thank you," she said when the boy had helped her up to the seat. "What is your name?"

"Albert."

"I'm Miss Barton."

His reply was a disinterested grunt. Elaine managed to suppress a smile as the young driver gave the reins a snap; then she asked over the squeak of the metal axles, "Do you know Wickam's, on Kensington High Street?"

He merely nodded, his eyes on the road in front of him.

"I can usually find everything I need there."

Another nod.

Elaine turned her head to study the young lad. From under a misshapen cap peeked a thatch of rust-colored hair, and freckles had sprinkled themselves liberally across his face. When he gave her a sideways glance—most likely wondering why she was studying him—Elaine could see that his eyes were green, like her own.

"Have you been working for Mr. Harrington for very long?" she ventured again, when the carriage paused at an intersection.

"A couple of months," was his clipped reply.

"And yet you seem to be well acquainted with the streets of London."

The boy nodded a third time. Elaine decided to take the hint and leave him alone. The streets were clogged with vehicles, so she had a long time to sit in silence. When the curricle came to a stop at a post just a few feet past Wickam's, she got out by herself without waiting to see if Albert would help her.

Inside the store, Elaine had to wait several minutes until a shop assistant was free to gather the supplies that were on her list, then parcel them with brown paper and string. *I hope the boy hasn't decided to drive off,* she thought on her way out the front door.

"I say, miss . . . can you spare a couple o' bob for somethin' to eat?"

Elaine almost bumped into the man. Unshaven and smelling of alcohol and filth, he swayed toward her and held out a hand with blackened fingernails.

Ignoring him, Elaine drew her parcel and bag closer and attempted to pass. The next thing she knew, he had her fast by the sleeve.

"How's about a copper, then?" His words were carried on a wave of stenchful breath. "I'll warrant you got money in that bag."

"I don't give away money for gin," she said crisply, trying to pull away. "Now, let go of my sleeve."

"Dearie me!" the man mocked, throwing his other hand up to his cheek. "Who says anything about gin?"

Elaine became self-consciously aware that passersby were darting glances in her direction. Some even stared boldly. While sympathy was evident on most faces, none stopped to offer aid. With feigned bravado, she said, "I shall have to call out for the police if you don't unhand me."

"All I wants is—"

From out of nowhere Albert appeared. "Let go of the lady, you blatherin' sot!" he snarled, jabbing at the man's arm with a finger.

"What?" The drunk let go of Elaine's sleeve and turned his head to gape at this annoyance. "Go to yer mummy, little brat!" He balled up a fist to swing, but quick as lightning, Albert ducked down and grabbed one of the man's legs. With a surprised grunt, the man lost his balance and toppled, arms windmilling, to the cobblestone street.

"Come on, let's go!" Albert tugged at Elaine's arm. She

went willingly, not daring to glance back at the howls of fury from behind her. When they reached the curricle he helped her up without hesitation, then hopped up on the other side and gave a sharp snap to the reins.

Neither spoke while the carriage moved down Kensington High Street. When two blocks had passed, Albert pulled the horses over in front of a furrier's shop. "Are you all right, miss?" he asked, studying Elaine with worry in his young eyes.

Elaine felt a cold drop on her chin and realized that she was crying. She dug a handkerchief from her bag and blew her nose. "I'm being childish," she sniffed. "I've just never felt so helpless before."

"He was a mite pushy, wasn't he?" the boy agreed. He glanced back over his shoulder. "He's gone now."

She let out a long breath. "Good."

"Next time I'll walk with you . . . if I ever drive you again."

Smiling at his gallantry, Elaine said, "I *could* request that you be my driver every time I go shopping."

Albert returned her smile. "I'll bet if you ask Mr. Ramsey, he'd let me. Not the coach, maybe, but I can handle this little rig right fine."

"And so you can. You enjoy driving, do you?"

"Oh, I could drive all the day."

He picked up the reins and softly clucked at the horses. The street was still heavy with traffic, but Elaine didn't mind so much now, for the boy interested her. In spite of his "street urchin" cockiness, he obviously possessed a tender side. He had had some schooling, too; she could tell from the way he spoke.

"Do you live at the estate?" she asked carefully, so that her curiosity wouldn't cause him to become tight-lipped again.

"Over the stables with the grooms. Where do you live?"

"My room is in the nursery quarters. I'm Miss Celeste Harrington's governess—that's why I'm buying school supplies."

"I heard about her," he said, giving her a sympathetic look.

Elaine chose not to comment on that, but changed the subject. "And where did you receive your education?"

"School."

"Which school?"

A curtain seemed to fall across his face. "Just a school," he grunted, then gave his total attention to the horses in front of him.

Even though the rest of the trip was spent in silence, the boy was quick to help Elaine out of the carriage when he brought it to a stop outside the Harrington house. When she thanked him, he doffed his cap at her and grinned. "Remember . . . just ask Mr. Ramsey if you ever want me to drive you somewhere again."

Elaine met Reanna at the bottom of the servants' staircase. The maid carried a feather duster that she had obviously just put to use upstairs, for she held it away from her body, out of sneezing range. She gave her usual polite nod and was about to pass when Elaine spoke her name.

"Reanna . . . ?"

The maid stopped and peered up from her diminutive height. "Yes, miss?"

"Do you know a stable boy by the name of Albert?"

"Albert?" A slight smile touched Reanna's lips. "I sees him in the servants' hall every meal."

"Does he ever mention where he comes from?"

She shook her head. "The boy's not bashful about talkin' to folks . . . once he gets used to them, that is. But he don't say much about where he used to live. Stanley—he's one of the groomsmen—says that Mr. Ramsey says Albert ran away from one of them orphanages up in Sheffield. They was gonna apprentice him to a soapmaker or somewhat like that."

Elaine nodded in response and started up the stairs. She couldn't imagine anyone with as much spunk as Albert seemed to possess being content with making soap. *I would have run away, too.*

9

I FEEL like going somewhere today," Celeste told Elaine and Jenny Saturday morning. They had just finished breakfast at the small mahogany dining table in the sitting room, and Gerdie, the new servant, was picking up the dishes. "The zoo, perhaps."

"Are you sure you're up to it?" Jenny asked. The girl had suffered a seizure right before bedtime last night, and Jenny had sat up with her for a long while afterwards.

"I feel fine."

"Why don't we make it a picnic?" Smiling, Elaine pushed back her chair. "I'll run down to the kitchen and ask Mrs. Willis to pack us a hamper of sandwiches."

When she was gone, Gerdie extended her hand to take Celeste's half-full glass of milk from the table, then hesitated. "Are you finished, miss?" she asked timidly.

Celeste nodded. "And when you go to the kitchen, tell Cook we would also like for her to pack some biscuits and—" She broke off abruptly, letting out a squeal and jumping to her feet. "Watch what you're doing!"

Her face white as chalk, the maid stared with horror at the empty glass on its side at the edge of her tray. "I'm sorry, miss!"

She practically slammed the tray down on the table, tore off her apron, and approached Celeste. "Here, let me—"

"Just get away from me!" the girl seethed, holding the skirt of her robe away from her body. Her face was as red as Gerdie's was white. "You stupid skivvy!"

Jenny could stand it no longer. "Miss Celeste!" she said, getting to her feet. "Stop that right now!"

Both maid and girl turned to gape at her.

"It was only an accident. You've no right to talk to her that way."

Celeste's eyes grew wide. "This is my house, and I'll talk any way I like!" She turned her anger on the trembling maid. "You do anything like that again, and I'll be talking with Mrs. Ganaway about you!"

Uttering a small cry, Gerdie turned and ran from the room, leaving the tray on the table. Jenny could hear the maid's sobs trailing through the schoolroom. She looked at Celeste to see if the sound affected her. Apparently it hadn't, for the scowling girl was dabbing at her robe with a napkin.

"You were about to change your clothes anyway," Jenny said, making an effort to tone down the anger in her voice. "She's not much older than you are. Why did you have to threaten her like that?"

Celeste stopped fussing with her robe and turned a puzzled eye at Jenny. "Threaten her?"

"What you said about telling Mrs. Ganaway."

"But that wasn't a threat. I gave her one more chance. I believe I was quite generous."

That's very gracious of you, Jenny thought. "All this fuss over some spilled milk?"

The girl shrugged. "I don't care for her attitude. Now she knows she needs to straighten up around me."

"Her attitude?" Jenny shook her head. "She's too nervous around you to have any kind of attitude . . . which is probably why she spilled the milk."

Folding her arms, Celeste stared at Jenny with defiance in her dark eyes. "And what does this have to do with nursing?"

Jenny's mouth parted. "I beg your pardon?"

"You were hired to be my nurse, nothing more. This has nothing to do with you." The girl tossed her napkin on the table and started for the door. "I'm ready for you to help me change my clothes now."

Mute with frustration, Jenny helped Celeste change into a white lawn dress, then tied a white ribbon into the girl's hair. She said a little prayer for Gerdie under her breath and hoped that somewhere in the house, someone was comforting the poor girl.

When Celeste was dressed, Jenny went into her own room to change from her robe into a fresh uniform. *A walk through the park will be good for this soreness,* she thought as she eased her arms into her sleeves. The next time she sat up with Celeste, she would be sure to bring a pillow or two to ease the inhospitality of the hard chair.

~

The day was pleasantly warm, not hot, and Regent's Park was thick with people. Groups of white-aproned nurses were pushing prams, while bowler-hatted gentlemen and ladies of all ages occupied themselves with meandering, laughing, flirting, and gossiping.

Soon after being helped from the coach, Jenny, Elaine, and Celeste set out on one of the busy footpaths. "This way!" motioned the girl, rolling her eyes impatiently but obeying when Jenny cautioned her not to run. Near the entrance to the Zoological Gardens, they came upon a man selling lemon ices from a pushcart.

Half a dozen thirsty children were queued up in front of the cart. Before taking a place at the end, Celeste turned to her governess and held out a hand. She stood there, frowning, while Elaine fished in the bottom of her bag for halfpence. When the coin was in her hand, the girl closed her fingers around it and turned around without a word of thanks.

"Is that your own money you're spending?" Jenny asked Elaine while they waited for Celeste.

Elaine shrugged. "It's only halfpence."

"Does she do this often?"

The governess glanced away evasively. "It's bad for her health to become upset."

"And it's bad for her character to be allowed to practice extortion."

"Extortion? That's a rather harsh word."

"That's exactly what it is. Give her what she wants, or she'll have a seizure. The girl knows exactly what she's doing."

"Would you rather watch her have a seizure right here?"

Jenny had no time to answer, for Celeste was coming back toward them now. "I want to go to the monkey house first," she declared, with still no word of thanks to the provider of her treat.

They went from one exhibit to the other, with Celeste in the lead. At eleven-thirty, Elaine pointed out a lovely spot to picnic along a bank of the canal where the shrubberies were bright with flowers. "I'll go fetch the hamper from the coach," she told Jenny and Celeste. "Go ahead to the parrot walk, and I'll have everything laid out by the time you join me."

Jenny turned to the girl and crooked her arm. "Shall we, Miss Celeste?" she said with mock formality. She didn't really expect the girl to take her arm, for the small sickly child of last night had once again been replaced by her bolder twin.

But to Jenny's surprise, Celeste linked her slender arm around her own. With good humor she pointed ahead and answered, "To the parrot walk, Miss Price!"

The shrieks of the parrots could be heard well before their colorful plumes could be seen. A wire, suspended between trees, held up at least two dozen hanging perches where the birds preened their feathers and conversed loudly with each other. Jenny and Celeste watched from the edge of the crowd.

The most popular parrot, judging by the reactions of the onlookers, wore a coat of green feathers, except for his crown of red. Whenever he took the notion he would call out, to the delight of the people watching, *"A sadder and a wiser man . . . he rose the morrow morn!"*

"Why is he saying that?" Celeste asked Jenny at her side.

"It's from Samuel Coleridge," Jenny answered. "From *The Rime of the Ancient—"*

"Oh, look!" Celeste interrupted. She stood on tiptoe and pointed over Jenny's shoulder.

Jenny turned to her right. Several feet away, a man held a T-shaped pole high above the crowd, and on the crosspiece perched several colorful papier-mâché parrots. "They're pretty," she remarked, turning back to Celeste.

The girl wasn't there.

Jenny spun back around toward the peddler, and sure enough, Celeste was weaving her way through the crowd to him. "Celeste!" she called, but the girl either hadn't heard or chose not to stop.

Quickening her steps, Jenny caught up with her and put a hand on her sleeve. "You shouldn't run off like that—"

But Celeste shook off Jenny's hand and approached the parrot man. "How much are they?"

"For you, pretty miss?" the peddler coaxed, obviously recognizing a sure mark. "A mere sixpence. Worth twice that!"

"I want the green one," she told the man, pointing to the lone bird that resembled the most popular live one in the exhibit.

"Good choice! She's the last one."

As the man lowered the display to remove the toy, Celeste finally turned to acknowledge Jenny's presence. "They cost sixpence."

"I beg your pardon?"

"Sixpence," she said, holding out a hand while turning her eyes back to the toy.

Jenny tightened her jaw . . . and her grip on the beaded reticule at her side. What had happened to simple manners? Did the child really assume that she would meekly surrender her own money on demand? "I'm sorry, but I would rather not."

The girl turned back around and cocked her head. "What did you say?"

"I don't care to give you sixpence," Jenny said, her voice polite but firm.

Celeste's eyes widened in disbelief. "But I *want* that parrot."

"Then you'll have to bring your own money next time."

First aiming a scathing look at Jenny, the girl turned toward the distant canal bank, where Elaine was most likely arranging their lunch. She seemed to be considering whether she would have time to find the governess and be back before someone else purchased the green parrot.

Obviously she decided that she did not have time, for her tactics underwent an abrupt change. Turning back to Jenny, she stretched her lips into an artificial smile and held out her hand again. "Miss Price, may I please have sixpence?"

"I'm sorry, Miss Celeste, but you may not."

"But I said *please!*"

"And I said you may not."

The child's smile disappeared, her tone taking on a threatening edge. "I wouldn't want my father to be angry at you. You might just find yourself dismissed."

Jenny had enough money in her bag to buy a dozen toy parrots, but she could not in good conscience allow the child to manipulate her this way. If she had to spend the rest of her two-year obligation scrubbing bedpans and washing bandages in the basement of some crumbling hospital in Calcutta, she would do that before giving an inch more of ground to this tyrant.

"No."

A gentleman and two small children had drifted over to look at the peddler's wares. "Look at the green one!" one of the children called out to her father.

Celeste's expression changed from anger to panic. "It's only sixpence," she whispered forcibly. "You can get Mr. Palmer to repay you. Hurry and give me the money before someone else buys it!"

Steeling herself, Jenny leaned closer to the girl. She whispered, slowly and deliberately, "Not even if it only costs a half farthing."

"I *hate* you!" Celeste spat, her cheeks turning crimson. The peddler and his three other potential customers turned puzzled looks in her direction.

Alarmed, Jenny berated herself silently for getting the girl so upset. Surely she could have refused in a more tactful manner. "Miss Celeste," she said in as calm a voice as possible. "Miss Barton has a nice picnic ready for us. Let's go join her."

"I wish you would go away and never come back!"

Just buy her the toy before she has a seizure! Jenny told herself. *You can remind her to bring her own money next time.* But something inside her would not allow her fingers to loosen their grip on her bag.

Before Jenny could wrestle further with a decision, Celeste let out a cry and pitched to the ground. Jenny was down at the girl's side in an instant, drawing a handkerchief from her pocket. "Is there anything I can do?" a gentleman asked as a number of people gathered around to watch.

"Please fetch someone for me," she answered as she held Celeste's twitching and heaving shoulders. After giving the man Elaine's description, Jenny demanded that the curious group of onlookers back away and give the girl some air.

Elaine appeared just as Celeste's spasms had finally ceased. "What happened?" she asked, dropping to her knees at Jenny's side.

"I wouldn't give her money for a toy," Jenny answered. Suddenly she felt wetness on her own cheeks and realized she had been crying. She had caused two seizures in less than a week. Had she been unreasonable with the child? Was sixpence worth all of this trouble?

Glancing back at the vendor with the toy parrots, she noticed that he held the display up in the air again to take advantage of the crowd that had gathered. The green parrot, however, was gone.

"I'll go fetch Mr. Reeves and Mr. Hudson," Elaine said,

getting to her feet. Before leaving, she touched Jenny's shoulder. "It's not your fault."

Reeves carried Celeste, drowsy and complaining of a headache, back to the coach. Inside the moving coach she slept again, with her head on the governess's lap—Jenny had known better than to offer to hold the girl herself.

Her stomach churning with misery and uncertainty, Jenny watched as Celeste slept. Even Elaine's consoling smile did not help her feel any better about herself.

10

"THAT'LL be six bob, sir," the driver said, grabbing the satchel from the boot of the carriage. He eyed the steps leading up to the portico. "Carry it inside for an extra florin."

Graham Harrington put his umbrella under his arm and held out the fare, plus a threepence tip. "I'll take it." He reached for the luggage, and with a shrug of his shoulders the driver hopped back into the box of his carriage.

The satchel was light for its bulky size. Years ago Graham had realized it was easier to keep a small wardrobe in Liverpool than to worry with copious amounts of luggage every time he made a business trip. The laundress at L'hotel Jolie Vue maintained his clothes with great care, so Graham had to carry only the barest necessities back and forth.

Celeste must have wanted to go to the park, he thought, turning up the brick path that divided the huge front lawn. That would explain why Reeves hadn't appeared the instant the carriage drove up. Graham sometimes wondered if the footman stood at a front window on the days he was due to arrive. Often Mr. Palmer had admonished Graham to allow one of his own carriages to wait for him at the train station, but he enjoyed the liberty of not being held to a schedule.

He was never certain how much work awaited him in Liverpool, or how long it would take.

Graham hadn't always spent so much time traveling, and he knew in the back of his mind that it was unnecessary to do so now. His office manager, Jacob Wallace, was more than capable of running the business by himself. After all, *he* had been the one who taught Graham the ropes years ago. But ever since Theresa's death, it seemed that burying himself in business was the only way Graham could cope. As long as he kept his mind occupied with charts and ledgers, there was no time to grieve for his precious wife.

And no time to spend with the child left to him. His neglect of his daughter harried Graham with tremendous feelings of guilt, but the die had been cast years ago. Right after her birth, the girl had been whisked away to the nursery, and Graham had allowed it to be so. What did he know about raising an infant?

The times he did visit little Celeste upstairs, he was only a disruption to the routine that more capable hands had set. His visits grew further and further apart, and the nursery became the only room in his house where Graham Harrington felt like an intruder.

When the child was diagnosed with epilepsy at the age of five, Graham became terrified of losing her, too. The death of his wife and his parents had already taught him the fragility of life. He could no longer take for granted that the girl was being cared for properly, but laid down strict rules to Mrs. Ganaway. Celeste was to be watched around the clock. More important, she was not to be allowed to become upset.

Graham also realized the need to spend more time with Celeste when he was home, though he never did so without having a nurse at least within fetching distance. He had captained a ship, had even battled pirates once, but the seizures rendered him completely helpless, feeling less than a man. A bitter thought assailed him constantly: *Theresa would be so ashamed of me.*

He was halfway across the front lawn when the distant sound of horses' hooves upon cobblestones caught his ears. Turning, he switched the satchel to his other hand and waited.

~

Jenny stared at the face of the unconscious child across from her, again so innocent looking. *What would Miss Nightingale have done?* she wondered. Her mother and father had taught her that a person's character was infinitely more important than physical attributes. And she believed it, with all of her heart. The question was, did she have the liberty to assume that Mr. Harrington would feel that way?

She had been hired because of Celeste's epilepsy, and for no other reason. Was she overstepping her bounds by attempting to change the way the child behaved? As the coach turned up the Harrington carriage drive, she leaned back in her seat and thought about how attractive scrubbing bedpans and washing bandages seemed at the moment.

As soon as the wheels under them slowed, Celeste's head lifted from Elaine's lap. The girl yawned, raked a venomous look over Jenny, then leaned forward to peer out of the window. "My father is home?" she asked her governess with a wistful voice.

The door opened as soon as the vehicle stopped, but instead of seeing Reeves, Jenny found herself staring into the face of a complete stranger. Almost *a stranger,* she corrected herself, for she could see Celeste's brown eyes in the masculine face. *Mr. Harrington.*

"Someone said the prettiest girl in England is in here!" he said, grinning while holding out his arms.

"I *knew* it was you!" Celeste bolted into his embrace and laughed as she was spun around in his arms. "And you're the handsomest man in England!"

"Well . . . if you insist," he chuckled.

"What did you bring me?"

"And who says I brought you anything?"

"Ha! You know that you did!"

Reeves came around to help Jenny and Elaine from the coach. "I'll stand up for you," the governess whispered once Jenny was on the ground at her side. "You were right. The girl shouldn't demand money from people, especially her father's employees."

"Please don't," Jenny whispered back. It was comforting to know that she had an ally, but that was all she could accept from Elaine. "I can't have you losing your job, too."

Mr. Harrington put his daughter back on her feet, put his bowler hat on her head, and turned in Jenny's direction. He stood probably no taller than five-feet-ten, but his erect posture and authoritative bearing gave the illusion of greater height. His hair was much lighter than his daughter's, with gold flecks that shone in the sunlight and a touch of gray about the temples. Elaine had told Jenny that Mr. Harrington had captained a ship before taking over his father's shipping business. And he looked the part, too, with his tanned complexion and lines about the eyes, and the overall ruggedness of his face.

"I take it you're Celeste's new nurse," he said to Jenny,

after a polite nod to Elaine. "Miss Price is your name, isn't it?" His smile was casual and friendly, but she wondered how quickly it would fade when Celeste told him what had happened.

He was waiting for her to speak, and Jenny returned his smile with a tentative one of her own. "Yes, sir."

"I'm grateful that you were able to come. Miss Nightingale spoke very highly of you."

"She speaks highly of all her students," Jenny answered. Some morbid instinct made her dart a glance down at Celeste. Standing hand in hand with her father, the girl was studying her, as if trying to make up her mind about something. Jenny forced her attention back to her employer. "Miss Nightingale brings out the best in people."

His smile grew broader. "Well spoken, though I'm positive you're being too modest."

"She is being modest, Mr. Harrington." This was from Elaine, still at her side. "Miss Price is an extremely capable nurse."

Then it happened. Celeste peered up at Jenny, then pulled at her father's arm. "I had a seizure at the zoo."

"At the zoo?" Graham Harrington's eyes filled with alarm. "You mean today?"

Now it's coming, thought Jenny, bracing herself. *What will Miss Nightingale think about a nurse who couldn't even last a week?*

The girl nodded, her lips turning up into a sweet smile. "Miss Price took good care of me. She's just an angel. I can't imagine what would have happened if she hadn't been there!"

Letting out a long breath, Mr. Harrington shot Jenny a look of gratitude, then bent down to scoop his daughter up in his arms. "It's off to bed with you, then."

"But you just got home!"

He was already walking up the steps. "We'll catch up after your nap."

Elaine and Jenny followed Mr. Harrington and Celeste upstairs to the nursery wing. In the bedroom, Elaine helped Celeste remove her dress while Jenny turned down the covers. When Mr. Harrington had tucked his daughter in with a kiss on her cheek, he asked Jenny to speak with him in the schoolroom.

"Are you keeping a record of her seizures?" he asked after pulling the door shut.

Jenny nodded. "I'm continuing the notebook Nurse Templeton left."

"How many has she had since you came here . . . was it Monday?"

"Yes, sir. She has had three." It was on Jenny's tongue to tell him that she herself had caused two of the seizures, but she just couldn't make herself say the words. *Anyway, perhaps it won't happen again,* she dared to hope. After all, there had been moments in the past few days when she and Celeste had gotten along fairly well.

Jenny couldn't fathom why Celeste had spoken well of her to Mr. Harrington after being so angry at the zoo—except that maybe her father's presence had a stabilizing effect on her personality. Perhaps she and Celeste would not be locking horns again while Mr. Harrington was in residence.

"Keep me informed," he was saying. "I should be home for at least two weeks." Thanking her for taking such good care of his daughter, he turned to leave. "Oh, by the way . . ." he said from the door. "Please tell Miss Barton that Celeste will be having supper with me in the dining room this evening, if she is up to it."

Jenny smiled. "I'm sure she will be, Mr. Harrington."

"Is everything all right?" Elaine said when Jenny walked back into the room they shared.

"I suppose. Mr. Harrington believes I'm a ministering angel."

The governess looked amused. "And so you are."

"I don't know *what* I am any more. At the zoo I thought Celeste hated me. When she complimented me to her father, I couldn't believe it. Why would she do such a thing?"

Shaking her head, Elaine said, "If she were any other child, I would hope that she had a sudden attack of conscience."

"Then you don't think she meant it?"

Elaine sent her a wry smile. "I have a feeling there is more to this than meets the eye. But I've been wrong before. Let's hope I'm wrong this time." She got up from her chair. "I left our picnic in the park. Are you as hungry as I am?"

"Ravenous," Jenny answered. "It's a shame all of that food went to waste."

"Oh well, perhaps some needy soul came across it. Why don't we go down to the kitchen and look hungry until Mrs. Willis takes pity on us?"

Mrs. Willis, after some token grumbling, managed to produce two bowls of potato soup and some buttered bread at the kitchen worktable. When Jenny and Elaine returned to the nursery after their meal, Celeste was sitting up in bed.

"I'm hungry," she said, stretching. Before anyone could say anything, the girl turned to Alma, who had started stealing toward the door. "Get me something to eat."

"That's not necessary," Elaine said. "We brought you up a tray—it's in the sitting room. The soup should still be nice and warm."

Celeste slipped out of bed without a thank you and waited for the governess to bring her dress over. As Elaine complied, Jenny locked eyes with her over the girl's head, then stepped closer.

"How do you feel, Celeste?"

The girl frowned and brushed a pillow feather from her cheek. *"Miss* Celeste, you mean."

"Of course. Miss Celeste."

"I feel as well as can be expected."

The two women went with the girl into the sitting room to keep her company as she ate. Celeste's temperament seemed to improve once she had a meal inside her. She even went so far as to ask Jenny's opinion about which dress she should wear to supper tonight with her father.

Again, Jenny shot a bemused glance at Elaine. "You look nice in any of your dresses," she replied, smiling, "but the yellow one you were wearing when we first met was particularly becoming."

"It does look nice." The girl nodded. "I've got a yellow ribbon that matches it. You may braid it in my hair now."

Shooting an "I'll be next door if you need me" look toward Jenny, Elaine left the room. Jenny followed Celeste into her bedroom, then pulled out the bench at the dressing table. When the girl was seated, Jenny picked up a brush and began pulling it through her hair. For several seconds Celeste studied her in the mirror with no discernible expression in her brown eyes.

Then she let out a weary sigh—a strangely adult sound coming from the lips of a twelve-year-old—as if she sincerely regretted the course of action she was about to take. "Are you wondering why I didn't tell my father about your making me upset today?"

"Yes," Jenny answered, the brush motionless in her hand.

Celeste arched a questioning eyebrow. "What did you say?"

"I said yes. I would like to know."

"Yes, *miss,*" the girl corrected with a haughty voice and lift of the chin. "You forget to whom you're speaking."

So, Elaine was right after all, Jenny thought. Hardly able to believe any child, even Celeste, would speak to an adult this way, she swallowed her pride and said. "All right. Yes, miss."

Celeste opened a drawer, dug out a yellow silk ribbon, and handed it over her shoulder to Jenny. She wore just the hint of a smile, and it was plain to see that she was enjoying herself.

"I didn't tell Father because he would have dismissed you if I had."

"Why should that matter to you?" Jenny asked as she began work on the chestnut curls again.

Celeste shrugged. "On the way home, I thought that it didn't matter. But then I told myself that if Father dismisses you, he'll only get someone else to take your place."

"That should make you happy."

"It might if I knew *exactly* who would be next. I couldn't bear to have another stupid woman around like Nurse Templeton. Even though she allowed me to win at draughts, she never stopped talking unless she was writing a love letter or reading her magazines."

"How terrible for you."

Celeste either didn't notice or chose to ignore the sarcasm in Jenny's voice, for she continued. "The nurse before Miss Templeton was too fat. I don't like to be around fat people."

"And the one before that?" Jenny said through her teeth.

Celeste cocked her head as if trying to remember, then

shook her head. "I think her name was Miss Donnerly. She made me nervous."

"How so?"

"The woman laughed every time she spoke. You know, a little `hee-hee' at the end of every sentence. I would cringe whenever she talked, just knowing that her silly giggle was coming."

"And how did you get rid of her?"

Celeste didn't offer a denial—in fact, her dark eyes sparkled, and she hugged herself. "It was easy. I told Mrs. Ganaway that Miss Donnerly was a drunk and that she slapped me."

"You mean you lied."

"Well, of course. I had to," the girl said with wide, unblinking eyes. "Do you think she would have been dismissed if I had said I hated her giggle?"

The braid finished, Jenny tucked the ends of the ribbon into a section at the nape of Celeste's neck. "I'm curious," she said as the girl admired herself in the glass. "Why would you assume that the next nurse wouldn't be an improvement over me? You and I have already had a couple of clashes."

"She possibly could be better, but I'm tired of risking it," Celeste replied frankly. She picked up a silver mirror from the top of the vanity and swiveled around on her stool to admire the back of her head in the glass. "Sometimes you aren't so bad. And I like your stories and the way you braid my hair."

Celeste lowered the hand mirror and looked up expectantly at Jenny, as if waiting for her to express gratitude for the compliments. When none came, she shrugged and added, "Besides, we're going to get along perfectly now."

"We are?" Jenny said without emotion.

"Yes," the girl replied. "Because *now* you know what can happen if you don't do as I say."

"You mean, you'll tell your father and I'll be dismissed."

"Yes. Father doesn't like for people to upset me."

"And all I have to do is obey your every command."

Celeste's forehead creased for a few seconds. "I suppose you don't *have* to let me win at draughts if you're so dead set against it. But I'm getting weary of having to argue with you about other things."

"Such as my not handing over my money at the zoo."

"That's right. I'm certain that someone has bought my parrot by now. I'll never forgive you for being so stingy, when you could have simply asked Mr. Palmer to give you back your precious money when we got back here."

Jenny shook her head and sighed. How could she make the girl see that the problem wasn't the price of the toy but her assumption that she had only to hold out her hand and others would fill it?

"Why are you staring at me like that?" Celeste demanded.

"Because I will *never* allow you to demand money from me."

"It was only sixpence. You act as if I asked for the crown jewels."

"It doesn't matter how much it was." Jenny managed to keep her voice level, though she could feel her temper rising. "If I wish to be robbed, I'll walk down Pottery Lane alone at night."

"That's the silliest thing I've ever heard!"

"Oh, I've heard sillier things."

Celeste's brown eyes turned wary. "What sillier things?"

"I've heard of a twelve-year-old girl who assumed that everyone else was put on this earth to be her slave."

"You're saying stupider things than Nurse Templeton!"

Jenny lost the battle with her own temper and shot back, "Well, brace yourself, because I'm just getting started." Gathering momentum, she folded her arms across her chest. "From now on I will not address you as *Miss* Celeste. Not ever. I'm a trained nurse, not a servant. And if you want me to braid your hair, you will come up to me and say, `Miss Price, would you *mind* braiding my hair?' Is that understood?"

The wide-eyed girl gulped a big breath and slung the hand mirror sideways. It hit the wall and shattered. "I can't believe you're talking to me like this!"

"And *I* can't believe how good it feels to do so!"

There was a sound at the door. They both looked up to see Elaine standing there with her mouth open, an expression of disbelief on her face. "What is going on?"

Celeste burst into tears. "She's saying horrible things to me!"

Without looking at Jenny, the governess came closer. "You have to calm yourself, Miss Celeste."

"I'll calm down after I've spoken with my father!" the girl sniffed. She jumped up from the bench, and Jenny moved to the side to allow her to pass.

"Wait!" Elaine called, but Celeste was already heading into the schoolroom.

"You had better go with her," Jenny said.

"What happened here?"

She hung her head. "I'm afraid my temper got the best of me again."

"We'll talk later," the governess said on the way to the schoolroom. "She can't be running around by herself in that state."

Jenny flinched at the sound of the other schoolroom door

slamming, then took leaden steps over to the room she and Elaine shared.

She pulled her trunk from against the wall and set about packing her things. Her immediate problem was how she would get to the train station. Would Mr. Harrington allow one of his drivers to take her there, or would he be so furious that she would have to try to find a hansom herself? She shuddered at the shock that would be on her family's faces when she showed up on their doorstep. They would understand, she knew, but surely her mother and father would feel some disappointment in her.

She took one of her uniforms from the wardrobe, but a disturbing thought froze her steps on the way to the trunk. She couldn't go home! She had agreed to a two-year period of service in exchange for her education. She was still bound by that agreement. If she couldn't fulfill her obligation here, then she would be assigned elsewhere.

The idea of admitting her failure to Miss Nightingale was worse than facing her family. *Oh, God,* Jenny prayed, her heart sinking like a stone in her chest. *If this was indeed your plan for me to come here, I've gone and ruined it!*

11

JENNY looked up at the sound of someone clearing her throat. Mrs. Ganaway stood in the doorway, hands clasped in front of her ample body. "I thought you were going to try to be more patient with the girl," she said with an injured air.

Jenny sighed. "I suppose patience is not my strong suit, Mrs. Ganaway. But I really did make an attempt to get along with her."

"Well, it's no matter now. Mr. Harrington would like to see you in his office."

"Couldn't I just leave?"

The housekeeper shook her head, and this time she looked truly sad. "You'd best come along, Miss Price. If it's any consolation, you're not the first to have this happen. I'm sure you did the best you were able."

In silence they walked downstairs, through the great hall, to a door opposite the front parlor. Mrs. Ganaway gave a soft knock.

"Come in," came a masculine voice from the other side.

Jenny stood back while the housekeeper opened the door. "Miss Price is here, Mr. Harrington."

"Please ask her to come in."

"Yes, sir. Will you be needing me as well?"

"No, Mrs. Ganaway."

The woman turned and put a hand on Jenny's shoulder. Immense regret showed on her careworn face. "I'll have someone finish your packing for you, dear."

"Thank you," Jenny whispered, her eyes growing moist. When the woman was gone, she walked with stiff dignity into Graham Harrington's office. He looked up at her from behind a massive oak desk, then got to his feet.

"Please close the door," he said, then motioned toward a chair in front of the desk. Jenny took the chair, surprised that Celeste wasn't in the room.

"I had Miss Barton take my daughter out into the garden," Mr. Harrington explained, as if he knew what she was thinking.

Hands folded in her lap, Jenny nodded.

"I'll get right to the point," the man said when he had sat down again. His brown eyes were serious. "This is only your first week here, yet my daughter has told me some things that are quite disturbing."

Jenny fought the urge to lower her eyes. She had decided on her way downstairs that she would readily admit to being wrong, but that her only crime had been a lack of patience, not larceny or murder. Raising her chin with a cool stare in his direction, she replied, "I'm sure she has, Mr. Harrington."

"I must admit to being surprised. You were so highly recommended."

"And because Celeste is your daughter, you believe her." Jenny stated this as a fact, not a question.

"She's never been one to lie to me."

"Well, sir, I suppose there is nothing more to say." Jenny rose to her feet. "If I could trouble you for a carriage . . ."

Obviously startled, he lifted a hand. "Please wait, Miss Price. I would like to hear your side, too."

"You would?"

"Of course. Only a fool makes a decision before he has heard all of the facts."

"I appreciate that," she said, lowering herself back into the chair.

Mr. Harrington was watching her thoughtfully, and Jenny realized that he was waiting for her explanation. "I suppose it was a mistake for me to be assigned here," she began. Her own voice sounded weary in her ears, and she wished she could just leave. "But I would like you to know that I did make several attempts to befriend your daughter."

"It doesn't sound that way to me."

Jenny uttered a deep sigh. "I can't defend myself until I know what I've been accused of, Mr. Harrington."

He nodded, as if that were a reasonable request. "Did you tell Celeste a frightening story one night about a cat, after she had warned you that she was prone to nightmares?"

Jenny's mouth fell open. "She told you *that?*"

"Yes. Do you deny it?"

"Of course I do! Please send for Alma, the maid who watched that night, and she'll verify it."

Mr. Harrington's expression turned a shade unsure. "Actually, Miss Barton also said it was untrue."

"She did?"

"Yes. But Celeste believes that you two are conspiring against her."

Jenny couldn't believe her ears. "Miss Barton and I have only known each other for six days. Why would we conspire against a twelve-year-old girl?"

The line between his eyebrows grew deeper. "Celeste must have imagined it all, then. But what about the incident at the zoo?"

"There was, indeed, an incident at the zoo. And I seem to remember your daughter telling you shortly afterward that I was a wonderful nurse."

He absently ran a hand through his shock of light-brown hair. "Yes, that's true."

"Let me ask you . . . why would Celeste refer to me as 'wonderful' if I had mistreated her during our outing, or had terrorized her with stories of cats?"

"I thought we already settled that, Miss Price. Celeste was mistaken about the story. She has a very active imagination."

"Mistaken?" Leaning forward, Jenny gathered the courage to press her point. "Within the space of three hours your daughter has referred to me as an ogre and an angel. Both can't be true, Mr. Harrington. And you don't think she would tell a lie?"

"She told me that you struck her at the zoo, Miss Price!"

"I have never struck any child in my life," Jenny said with quiet forcefulness. "I simply refused to hand over the sixpence that she demanded of me."

His face reddened. "Surely she was asking to borrow—"

"Demanded, Mr. Harrington!"

"All right then, that was wrong of her. But I don't see why you couldn't have appeased her, out in public like that. You would have been repaid, and I would have spoken with her about it as soon as it was brought to my attention."

"And what if she had demanded that I buy her a pony? You would have wished me to appease her then as well?"

"Of course not!" Graham Harrington got to his feet, the veins standing out on his temples. "If you knew anything about children, *Miss Price,* you would know that most of them don't understand the concept of money!"

"And if *you* stayed here long enough to get to know your daughter, *Mister Harrington,* you would realize that a twelve-year-old who threatens to have someone dismissed if she doesn't pay up understands the concept of money all too well!"

His jaw dropped and he gaped at her silently. After several seconds he asked in a quiet voice, "Is it possible that you misunderstood her?"

The tinge of hope in the man's question was obvious, but Jenny had to be truthful. "Absolutely not."

~

Graham Harrington sank wearily back to his chair. *I've been a blind man,* he thought, rubbing his forehead.

For the past five years or so, Graham had noticed there were new faces among the servants almost every time he came home, particularly those servants who had to deal directly with his daughter. He pushed aside, however, any possible connection between this and Celeste's behavior. Mrs. Ganaway had never complained about the girl, he rationalized. But he had ignored the fact that the housekeeper needed her position and would likely never complain.

Graham looked at the young nurse. Miss Price seemed ill at ease, but she sat there regarding him with intelligent gray eyes. At the risk of her job, she had found the nerve to speak some harsh words to him. *Harsh, but true. I've ruined my daughter.*

"Mr. Harrington?" Miss Price finally ventured.

Still mute with self-recrimination, he merely stared back.

"I shouldn't have said the part about your not being here,"

she continued, her gray eyes suspiciously moist. "You have a business to oversee."

"No, I appreciate your honesty," Graham replied with a bleak voice.

The young woman shifted in her chair. "But it wasn't my place to lecture you."

"I wish someone would have had the courage to do so a long time ago." Graham paused to collect his thoughts for several seconds. "When Celeste's mother passed away, I should have stepped in to fill the void. I assumed nannies and nurses could better teach the child how to become a woman."

"We can't take your place, Mr. Harrington," Miss Price said gently. "And we can't teach her anything at all if we live in constant fear of being dismissed."

Her words were painful to hear, but he needed to hear them. He frowned and said, "And I've blamed the high turnover of servants here on their lack of understanding for a sick child."

"It's not my place to say so, but perhaps that's the problem."

"What do you mean?"

"The 'sick child,'" she answered. "Celeste isn't *sick*. She's a perfectly normal girl who sometimes has seizures."

"But we cannot just ignore the reality of her condition." A picture flashed across his mind of his child thrashing about on the floor . . . and of himself helplessly wringing his hands while calling out for assistance. He shook the thought away. "She has limitations that other children don't have."

"Of course she has. But they aren't so drastic that she can't overcome them."

How does a little girl overcome a monster? he wondered, but he kept silent.

"Ever since I was told of this assignment, I've been reading about epilepsy," Miss Price continued, her gray eyes eager now. "Are you aware that George Frederick Handel had epilepsy? He lived for seventy-four years, Mr. Harrington, and I would say that he overcame his limitations."

Graham raised an eyebrow. "Seventy-four years?" Somewhere in the far recesses of his mind, he caught sight of a glimmer of hope. "Please . . . continue."

~

Father, help me to make him understand what I'm trying to say, Jenny prayed silently. She opened her mouth to go on, but her mind still scrambled for the right words. *And help me to understand as well,* she added quickly.

"Every activity in this house seems to revolve around not upsetting your daughter," she said with as much tact as possible. "Is that the way you were raised?"

"Of course not," Mr. Harrington replied, a bit of irritation in his voice. "But I didn't have epilepsy. It isn't good for her to be upset. The likelihood of a seizure becomes far greater."

"But Celeste should be learning not to *allow* things to upset her. That's what other children have to do. Self-control isn't something we're born with; it must be cultivated."

"So you're suggesting we purposely make her angry?"

Jenny shook her head. "Of course not. What I'm suggesting is that you treat her as a normal child. Don't try to shield her from the normal frustrations that all children have to go through. Take, for example, the servants' children that she plays with. Playtime would be a golden opportunity for Celeste to learn so many things. Such as self-control, as I just mentioned. Patience, too . . . and the joy of putting others ahead of herself. But the children are so intimidated by her that they allow her to win at everything they do."

"Surely not."

"Everything, Mr. Harrington. They barely dare to speak in her presence, unless it's to congratulate her for 'winning' still another game. What's worse, Celeste is aware of what is going on, and still she gloats over them."

A pained look crossed his face. "That isn't good for any child's character. Why hasn't anyone told me about this?"

"Why do you suppose, Mr. Harrington?"

He winced. "What do you suggest I do about it?"

"Start with telling the children that they don't have to fear for their mothers' positions if they play to win," was Jenny's immediate reply. "Celeste will learn how to control her anger when she loses, and when she does win at something, she will have the satisfaction of knowing that it was earned. I believe she'll enjoy playtime even more, once she gets used to playing fairly."

For a long time he just sat there staring at his long fingers. "I like that idea," he finally said. "In fact, I'm going to do that right away. Would you have Mrs. Ganaway round up those children and their mothers?"

"I will," Jenny answered, getting up from her chair. At the door she paused and turned back to face Mr. Harrington. He was still looking at her, with a respect in his expression that had not been there when she first walked in. For some reason her old timidity came flooding back, and she wondered how she'd had the nerve to advise him on how to raise his child.

Mr. Harrington raised an eyebrow. "Was there something else, Miss Price?"

"I just . . . does this mean you're not dismissing me?"

"Dismissing you?" The corners of his mouth turned up just

a bit. "Indeed I'm not, Miss Price. We have some character building to do."

~

Jenny found Mrs. Ganaway in the morning room. The woman could not hide her surprise when Jenny stood in front of her. "You're still here?" she gasped.

"For now."

Relief flooded her pale blue eyes. "I said a prayer for you."

"That must be why I'm still here, then," Jenny said with a grateful smile. When the housekeeper had left to do Mr. Harrington's bidding, Jenny returned to her room and started unpacking. After a few minutes Elaine came through the door.

"It's true then," she said, smiling. "You weren't dismissed!"

Jenny raised an eyebrow. "Were you that certain I would be?"

"Well, Mr. Harrington seemed quite furious when he sent for you."

"I imagine he was, considering the things Celeste told him." After folding an apron, Jenny set it aside and walked over to give the governess a quick embrace. "Thank you for speaking up for me."

Elaine looked embarrassed but pleased. "You would have done the same for me. Besides, you should have heard some of the stories the girl invented."

"I was told. By the way, where *is* Celeste?"

"Her father sent for her just a little while ago." Elaine walked over to Jenny's open trunk and took out a blouse. "It seems that I'm spending a great amount of time lately helping you unpack," she said with good humor.

Jenny smiled. "Here's hoping that this is the last time for a while."

12

THE unpacking was finished by the time Celeste walked into the nursery an hour later, escorted by one of the housemaids. She ordered the maid to leave, then stood in the doorway of Jenny and Elaine's sitting room, an uncharacteristically meek expression on her face. "I would like to ask your forgiveness for my rude behavior today," she said stiffly.

"Why, of course." Jenny infused as much warmth as possible into her tone. "I would like for us to become friends, Celeste."

At the sound of her name without the title she had demanded, the girl's eyes flashed fire for a brief instant. Then she gave a somber nod and stepped into the room. "And my father and I would like to invite you to have supper with us this evening." She held out an envelope.

Exchanging a surprised glance with Elaine, Jenny opened the envelope and drew out a sheet of fine vellum paper.

Dear Miss Price,

I would like to apologize that our first opportunity to become acquainted was under such unpleasant circumstances, and I would like to start over. Would you be so kind as to join

Celeste, my fiancée, Miss Courtland, and myself at seven in the dinng room?

Sincerely,

Graham Harrington

"How very kind of your father," Jenny said, lowering the paper. Suddenly the thought crossed her mind that Elaine had not been included in the invitation and would be having a solitary meal here in the nursery. "But perhaps—"

"I would enjoy some time to myself," Elaine said, as if reading her thoughts. "I insist that you go."

An hour later, Jenny and Celeste walked downstairs to the dining room together. Not certain what she would be expected to wear, Jenny had decided to play it safe and put on a fresh uniform and cap. At the last minute she coiled her hair up at the nape of her neck, hoping that most of it would still be in place by the evening's end.

Celeste still looked lovely with her braided hair and yellow dress. Her spirit was sunnier too, and on the way down the stairs she chattered about how excited she was to have her father back home and to see Miss Beryl again.

"They aren't here yet," the girl said with a touch of disappointment as they entered the dining room. They stood to one side, near a black marble fireplace topped with a large gilt-framed mirror, so that the serving maids could finish setting the table.

Jenny had been in the dining room only once, during her tour of the house with Mrs. Ganaway. The room had an atmosphere of comfortable formality. A ponderous mahogany table dominated the center of the room, and above it hung a crystal chandelier. Twelve chairs surrounded the table, their padded seats covered with William Morris tapestries of green and rose. Underneath the table stretched a wide rug of moss green, with leaves of a deeper shade. At one end of the room, flanked by two ferns, stood a large ornate mahogany sideboard with a mirror.

"I don't suppose *you* have ever been in such a nice dining room," Celeste said, feigning a yawn.

Jenny ignored the condescension in her tone. "It is a lovely room."

"Are we late?" Mr. Harrington entered the room, wearing black tails with a velvet collar and cuffs, and a white, high-collared shirt. A woman who looked to be about Jenny's age stood clinging to his arm.

"Miss Beryl!" cried Celeste. She ran over to the woman and was caught up in her embrace. "I'm so glad you came!"

"Wild horses couldn't tear me away, dear," she answered in a throaty, eloquent contralto. The speaker was no less attractive than her voice. High delicate cheekbones, soft coppery curls cascading from an amethyst-studded comb, and a lithe figure covered in a violet silk gown combined to make Jenny feel suddenly dowdy in her plain uniform.

"I've got something for you," the woman continued, holding out a flat white box.

"For me?" Celeste practically snatched the box away, but the woman didn't appear to mind. Tearing off the lid, Celeste brushed aside a layer of tissue and held up a pair of white kid gloves. "Just like a real lady's!"

"From Paris." Mr. Harrington's fiancée smiled. "The buttons are real pearl."

Celeste embraced the woman again while her father beamed at them. All the while Jenny clasped her hands behind her back and wished she had politely declined the invitation, for she felt like an intruder upon this little family scene. *A dowdy intruder,* she thought, coveting the privacy that Elaine was enjoying upstairs.

Mr. Harrington picked that moment to take notice of her. "I'm sorry, Miss Price," he said, taking a step in her direction. "I haven't introduced you to my fiancée, Miss Courtland."

Jenny managed a smile and extended her hand. Too late she realized the social error of doing so, for a flash of shock registered in the woman's eyes. Still, she shook Jenny's hand after an almost imperceptible hesitation.

I've got to remember my station, Jenny told herself, feeling her cheeks go warm at the slight rebuff. Even though she wasn't a servant, as long as she was a household employee, she was not to be considered on the same social level as Mr. Harrington and Miss Courtland. It didn't matter that her parents were well-off or that she was well educated.

"This is Miss Price," Mr. Harrington was saying to his fiancée, seemingly unaware of the undercurrent of tension between the two women.

"I'm so glad you could join us," said Miss Courtland. Her topaz eyes appraised Jenny coolly, and a hint of a smile played at her lips.

"Why don't we all sit now?" Mr. Harrington motioned to where Reeves stood waiting to pull out the chairs. "I'm starving for something other than hotel food." When Miss Courtland and Celeste were seated in opposite chairs adjacent to the head of the table, and Jenny next to Celeste, he took his place at the head of the table. A serving maid began dishing turtle soup from a huge tureen at the sideboard, and another brought the bowls over to their places.

"How was your stay in Liverpool?" Miss Courtland asked Mr. Harrington over the clink of china.

"Busy, as usual," he replied, dabbing his mouth with his napkin. "But I was able to get so much accomplished that I'm hoping to stay home for at least a month this time." He shot a meaningful glance at Jenny. "I have recently realized how important that is."

Jenny smiled. It was good to see that Mr. Harrington was serious about getting more involved in his daughter's upbringing. While she wouldn't ever wish to repeat the scene at the zoo or its stormy aftermath, the resulting change in Mr. Harrington's priorities had made them worthwhile. Mother had told her many times that God could always bring good out of adverse circumstances, and once again, she was right. The future looked promising now, when it had seemed so bleak just hours ago.

Jenny lifted her soup spoon, then from the corner of her eye noticed that Miss Courtland had stiffened. Puzzled, Jenny looked at the woman. The cool appraisal that had been in those elegant eyes just moments ago had sharpened into overt hostility.

Still, a smile flitted over her lips as she lowered her spoon. "Miss Price," she said with her throaty voice, "how long have you been nursing?"

"This is my sixth day," Jenny answered, all the while wondering what she had done to offend Miss Courtland.

"Only six days?"

"Miss Price studied at Florence Nightingale's school," Mr. Harrington told her. "She was recommended very highly by both Miss Nightingale and the doctor in charge of her studies."

"How interesting. And now you're finally able to apply your studies to practice."

Jenny gave the woman across from her an uncertain smile. "We spent a lot of time with the patients at St. Thomas's Hospital, to give us some practical experience as well as text studies."

The maids collected the soup bowls and brought around the second course, a lobster salad, while Miss Courtland turned her attention to Jenny again.

"You must be a very special nurse," she said with an effusiveness that did not match the cool expression in her eyes. "Graham has never invited one of his . . . employees to dine with us."

"It was very kind of him," Jenny answered warily. She was acutely uncomfortable at this attention from someone who obviously disliked her but who just as obviously had no intention of letting the others at the table know it.

"I haven't had the opportunity to get acquainted with Miss Price," Mr. Harrington said from the head of the table. Jenny looked up just in time to catch the warning glance he sent in his fiancée's direction. So he *had* noticed! The undercurrent of tension in the room increased, and again she wished she had opted to stay upstairs and dine with Elaine.

"I must admit I'm very pleased that Miss Nightingale was able to choose someone so perfect for the position," Mr. Harrington continued. "Her intuition is always right on the mark, I've heard."

"Actually, she leaves the choosing to God," Jenny corrected tactfully. She hadn't intended to take over the conversation, but it seemed important to clarify this fact and give God the credit due him.

"You don't say?"

"When she informed me that I was being assigned here,

Miss Nightingale said that her every decision was `bathed in prayer.'"

"No wonder she has accomplished so much."

Celeste, who had looked bored while the conversation revolved around Jenny and Miss Nightingale, changed the subject. "I've missed you, Miss Beryl."

Miss Courtland beamed at the girl. "And I've missed you too, my sweet darling!"

"Why didn't you visit me when Father was away?"

"Oh, I wanted to so much," she sighed. "But there are so many things to do to prepare for this wedding! Why, I've had to go to Paris twice to be fitted for my trousseau. And you know how Mother demands so much of my attention."

"I understand," Celeste said, but to Jenny the young voice seemed colored with a hint of sadness. "Anyway, when you and Father get married, I'll be able to see you every day."

"Every day, you sweet child!"

As the evening wore on, Miss Courtland told some amusing stories about some of the people in her social circle, liberally sprinkling in the names of lords and ladies, dukes and duchesses. Jenny even found herself smiling at the story of a hapless baronet who mistook one Lord Hurlbert for a footman.

After a dessert of raspberries and cream, Jenny thanked Mr. Harrington for the evening and rose to excuse herself. It wasn't polite to leave right after a meal, of course, but surely the three of them would want to have some time together.

But Mr. Harrington would not hear of it. "First you must all come with me," he said, getting to his feet as well. "I've something to show everyone in the library."

Celeste and Miss Courtland each took one of his arms. Jenny followed them through the morning room and into the library. This had been her favorite room on the tour, because it reminded her of her parents' bookstore back in Bristol. The walls were of deep teal, grained to look like leather, set above mahogany-paneled wainscoting. Paintings and maps on the wall, exotic statues and art objects lent a museum quality to the room. Best of all were the heavy bookcases, filled with hundreds of books, and a large, masculine desk. Jenny decided that she could easily spend every day here and never grow bored.

Mr. Harrington had apparently noticed the awe in her expression, for he turned to her with an amused smile. "Do you like my library, Miss Price?"

"Very much, sir," she replied.

"Then you are welcome to come here anytime you like, you and Miss Barton. The room needs to be put to use more than it is. These books are begging to be—"

"What did you want to show us, Graham?" Miss Courtland cut in, linking her arm through his again. She did not look at Jenny.

"Do you remember my telling you about the shipment I was expecting from China?"

"Of course," she purred.

"One of my associates, Pascal Sauville, was on this trip. He has a good eye for genuine artifacts, and occasionally makes a purchase for me." He walked over to a Pembroke table against the wall and pointed to a wide porcelain vase. Six inches tall and bright yellow in color, it was decorated with various designs of green dragons. "It's a leys jar," Mr. Harrington explained, picking it up. "From the Ming dynasty."

Miss Courtland's eyes lit up as she made her way to the table with a fluid motion. "It must be worth a fortune!"

"It wasn't cheap. The shopkeeper knew what he had in his possession."

Not bothering to step closer, Celeste gave the jar a quick glance and said, "I've got much nicer things than that in my room."

Mr. Harrington laughed. "It's the age of it that makes it so valuable, Celeste . . . and more than that, the rarity. This particular piece comes from the early sixteenth century, and there are very few of them in existence."

"Are you going to sell it?"

"I'd like to keep it here for a while. Perhaps one day I'll donate it to the British Museum."

"You're going to have to find a better place than on that table to keep it," Miss Courtland remarked, shaking her head. "Perhaps a glass cabinet with a key. *Anyone*—" she darted a glance at Jenny—"could walk away with it."

"I trust the people who work for me," Mr. Harrington said, setting the jar carefully back on the table.

"How can you, when you have so many coming and going?" Miss Courtland turned to Jenny again, this time letting her gaze linger. "Have you ever seen such a frustrating man, Miss Price?" she said with a conspiratorial smile, as if they had been confidants for years. "Every time I'm here, it seems Celeste has a new nurse. He can't keep up with his own servants."

"Beryl!"

Jenny felt a deep flush creep up her neck, but Miss Courtland simply turned innocent wide eyes to her fiancé. "All right, I suppose I'm exaggerating a bit. But you do keep the agency busy, you must admit."

"Miss Price is not a servant," Mr. Harrington said in a

voice shaded with irritation. "And she wouldn't be here if she weren't trustworthy."

Miss Courtland put a slender hand up to her cheek. "Of course! How insensitive of me." To Jenny, she said, "Forgive my slip of the tongue, dear."

Jenny caught the smile of amusement that played about the corners of Miss Courtland's lips. Obviously, it was there for her benefit alone. Well, she had just about had enough of Miss Beryl Courtland and her condescending ways.

She turned to Mr. Harrington. "I must go now. Thank you for inviting me to supper."

"I'm glad you could join us. I'll bring Celeste upstairs shortly."

With a curt nod at Miss Courtland, Jenny made her escape.

~

When Jenny arrived back at her room, Elaine looked up from the book she was reading. "Are you all right?"

"Of course," Jenny answered. She had no desire to go into the details of the covert snubbing she had received from Miss Courtland.

"Your cheeks are flushed."

"Are they? It must have been the walk up the stairs."

Elaine gave her an affectionate smile. "And you such an old woman. How was the meal?"

"The food was very good," Jenny said evasively. Taking her nightgown from its hook inside the armoire, she walked behind the screen and began to undress. "I'm sorry you had to eat alone."

"I enjoy being alone sometimes," Elaine's voice came over the screen. "Don't you?"

"Actually, I do."

"Alma came to see if your church clothes for the morning needed pressing, so I picked out the lavender gown with the lace. I hope you don't mind."

"Of course not," said Jenny, pulling the nightgown over her head. "Thank you. I would have picked that one myself." She hooked her uniform dress over her arm and walked around the screen. "What do you plan to wear?"

The governess fixed her eyes back on her book. "I haven't decided. Now, if you'll excuse me, I'd like to finish this chapter before we turn the lamp out."

Elaine must be feeling poorly, Jenny thought, if she was ready to go to bed this early. "Is there anything I can do?"

Elaine lowered her book and looked up at her. "About what?"

"About whatever is ailing you."

After several seconds of silence, she answered, "There is no cure for what ails me, Jenny. Nor do I wish for one."

Tossing her uniform on the chair by her bed, Jenny walked slowly over to the foot of Elaine's bed and sat down. "Why do I have a feeling that you're not talking about a physical ailment?"

"Because you're very astute," Elaine sighed, though the tone of her voice was not angry. "And because I obviously have a loose tongue." Before Jenny could respond to that, Elaine closed the book in her lap. "On second thought, I'm a bit sleepy. Do you mind if we turn off the lamp when you've washed up?" There was a finality to her tone that did not invite questions.

"Well, if you ever need a friend to talk with about it, you have one here."

The governess didn't answer, but a look of gratitude filled her green eyes.

Jenny was just coming out of the lavatory when Celeste appeared in the open doorway. "I'm ready for my nightgown," she said to Elaine.

"Why don't you stay in bed?" Jenny told the governess. Turning to the girl, she said, "You don't mind if I help you dress, do you?"

Celeste motioned back over her shoulder. "You can't. My father is waiting to speak with you."

"I'll help her dress," Elaine said, already out of bed and tying her wrapper.

Wondering if Mr. Harrington had changed his mind about her staying in his employ, Jenny pulled on a dressing gown and went into the schoolroom. Celeste's father stood just inside the room. He was still wearing his evening clothes . . . and an uncomfortable expression.

"Mr. Harrington?" Jenny said as she approached. "Is something wrong?"

He shook his head, though it seemed that his discomfort increased. "I would like to apologize for Miss Courtland's slip of the tongue. Referring to you as a servant was certainly not intentional."

It flashed across Jenny's mind that Miss Courtland had known exactly what she was saying, but she didn't say so. "It's quite all right, Mr. Harrington."

Instead of looking satisfied, Mr. Harrington shifted on his feet and cleared his throat. "And one more thing."

"Yes, sir?"

"What she said . . . about anyone possibly stealing the vase. She wasn't implying that you would do such a thing."

Jenny nodded. "I appreciate your telling me that."

Now that the chore of setting things straight was over, he seemed relieved. "Very well then, I bid you good night." He started to turn toward the door, but instead looked back at Jenny again, a question filling his brown eyes.

"Mr. Harrington?"

"Nothing," he said with a slight shake of his head. "Just . . . thank you for understanding."

13

SUNDAY morning Jenny watched absently out the coach window as she tugged at her pearl-gray gloves. She imagined she could actually feel the curls straightening under her straw hat. Why she had allowed Elaine to coax her into putting a curling iron to her hair, she had no idea.

It was such a bother, worrying about what to wear. Since her days at nursing school, she had become accustomed to simply donning a fresh uniform every morning and pulling her hair back into a chignon. She felt self-conscious dressed any other way.

To add to her discomfort, Mr. Harrington had looked at her with something akin to surprise in his expression when she, Elaine, and Celeste had met him in the foyer just minutes ago. Now she could feel him watching her out of the corner of his eye as he sat there holding his daughter's hand.

Jenny hadn't even thought to ask what Nurse Templeton wore to church. Maybe a uniform would have been more appropriate, more befitting her station. But surely Elaine wouldn't have picked out a dress for her if she was expected to wear a uniform.

But apparently Jenny's choice of wardrobe was not on Mr. Harrington's mind. When she finally dared to look across at him, he cleared his throat and said, "My parents were the first of my family to attend Saint Mark's, so we don't have a box in the sanctuary, just a family pew."

Was he embarrassed, apologizing ahead of time that they wouldn't be seated in the grand manner? "Saint Jude's, the church my family attends in Bristol, is so small that it doesn't even have family pews," she offered. "People just sit where they wish."

"I like that idea." He nodded thoughtfully. "Every step we take is governed by too many rules of order. It would be nice if our churches were more democratic, at least where seating is concerned. After all, God is no respecter of persons . . . neither should we be." Mr. Harrington turned to Elaine, who had so far not said a word. "What do you think, Miss Barton?"

The governess gave a strained smile. "I agree with you, Mr. Harrington."

"Even at Saint Jude's," Jenny said, "most people end up in the same spot Sunday after Sunday anyway."

Mr. Harrington's smile broadened, causing his dark eyes to crinkle at the corners. "That would likely happen at any church, even if family pews and boxes were done away with. We British are creatures of habit." After a pause he went on, with no trace of rancor in his voice. "Not being members of the peerage also has something to do with our seating arrangement. Father was a dockworker before he ventured out into business for himself."

Jenny nodded and looked down at her hands. She hoped her expression hadn't betrayed the thought that flashed through her mind: For all his humble beginnings, Mr. Harrington certainly looked as regal as any duke or earl. He wore a black coat and trousers of fine milled cloth and a silk paisley waistcoat. His gold medallion stickpin and top hat spoke of his knowledge of the finer things—whether purchased with "old" money or "new."

Jenny glanced across at Celeste. She just sat there, her hand wrapped around her father's arm. Her new kid gloves went well with her ivory sateen-and-lace dress and matching bonnet. If the girl had the least hint of a smile on her oval face, she would have looked adorable.

"There it is . . . Saint Mark's." Mr. Harrington leaned forward to point out the window. Jenny could see the steeple of the cathedral rising above the houses about a mile away.

Finally Celeste decided to speak. "Father," she said, her lips drawing into a little pout. "I don't see why Miss Beryl can't come to church with us."

"I've explained that to you before," he answered gently. "Miss Beryl's family has gone to Saint Paul's for generations. It would be disrespectful to her mother and her other relatives for her to change until she's married."

The pout deepened. "Well, why can't you get married sooner?"

"Planning for a wedding takes time, Celeste. Just be patient. Besides, you'll see Miss Beryl at lunch today."

At last a smile came to the girl's face. "She's having lunch with us?"

"As she does every Sunday when I'm home," he teased gently.

The service was much more formal than Jenny was used to at St. Jude's, but she found the presence of God just as strong. She sat between Celeste and Elaine, sharing a *Book of Common Prayer* with the governess.

Jenny watched Celeste from the corner of her eye. Perhaps

the girl was finally becoming resigned to having her around. Then she reminded herself that on several occasions she had already tried to figure out what Celeste was thinking. And she had been wrong every time.

~

". . . And so I marched right up to Mrs. Farnsworth and told her that it was crude of her to allow her daughters to snipe at each other in public." Celeste watched as Mrs. Herbert Courtland struggled with her roast beef and tried to talk at the same time. Her big ruby-drop earrings jiggled with every word. "Why, Mrs. Gifford said she could hardly enjoy the theater last week, with those two practically performing Punch and Judy in the same box!"

Seated across the dining room table from Miss Beryl's mother, Celeste found the conversation boring, but the jiggling earrings were entertaining. She picked up her napkin to dab delicately at her mouth, the way Miss Beryl had done moments ago. *Everything* Miss Beryl did was graceful and refined, and Celeste's favorite daydream was growing up to be an elegant lady like her. The way Miss Beryl was now smiling at her father did not even make Celeste jealous, for the woman smiled just as sweetly at her. Life was going to be so much fun when she finally had a real mother!

". . . and *I* told Mrs. Farnsworth, 'Courtney and Denise will never find husbands if they don't learn some manners.' Of course she was furious at me, which goes to show you where her daughters' tempers come from . . . *n'est-çe pas?"*

Celeste was less enthusiastic about acquiring Mrs. Courtland into the family. In fact, the very thought of such a woman moving into the house with them caused her to shudder. That was the plan, too, for she had once overheard Miss Beryl tell her father that the taxes and servants' wages were becoming an immense burden for her mother.

Actually, Celeste had eavesdropped on that particular conversation. It had taken place in the conservatory the last time her father was at home. She was quite skillful at slipping around the house when she was supposed to be in bed, especially when Amelia used to watch her during her afternoon naps. Celeste regretted cutting the maid's hair, for the others were now more keen about staying alert during their nap and nighttime vigils.

"I would be glad to help your mother with the expenses." Her father's voice had drifted through the door that Celeste had eased open an inch.

"You are so generous, Graham!" Miss Beryl's elegant voice said. "But it isn't just the expenses. Mama would be so lonely without me living there with her. She practically lives her whole life through me, you know."

There was a pause, and then her father spoke again. "That's what concerns me. Once we're married, your mother shouldn't be doting over you as much."

"And she won't!" Miss Beryl protested. "Besides, if it weren't for Mama, we wouldn't be engaged."

"How is that?"

"I would have given up on you coming out of your shell years ago, but Mama refused to allow me to give up. And just think of how good it would be for Celeste to have two women to look over her."

Two women to look over me, Celeste thought. The very idea made her lose her appetite.

"Celeste, dear, is something wrong?"

She looked up to find Mrs. Courtland peering at her through the lorgnette she wore on a chain around her neck. By now Celeste knew that the concern on the woman's face was an act. Mrs. Courtland didn't care for her at all . . . not as her daughter did. Whenever Mrs. Courtland was around, she was constantly telling Father things like, "Now you and Beryl should have some time alone. I shall keep Celeste company. . . . We're great companions."

The truth was, Mrs. Courtland was not a great companion to anybody. Miss Beryl constantly asked her about her thoughts, her favorite things to do and such, but Mrs. Courtland only knew how to chatter on about her own life. She sprinkled her sentences with French phrases as though she were a duchess appearing at court, even though her husband, like Celeste's grandfather, had made his fortune in trade.

"Nothing is wrong," she said in answer to Mrs. Courtland's question.

The older woman seemed satisfied with this answer, for she immediately jumped to another subject. "The leys jar, Graham," she said, "you simply must allow me to show it off."

Celeste's father smiled indulgently from the head of the table. "What do you have in mind, Mrs. Courtland?"

"Tea . . . in your library, for some of my friends?"

"Whenever you like. Just give Mrs. Ganaway some notice so she can plan the refreshments."

"Oh, wonderful!" she exclaimed, her earrings bobbing. "I'll even contact *The Times'* society editor. Surely this would be a newsworthy occasion."

Wishing that Mrs. Courtland would be quiet for a change, Celeste noticed Miss Beryl looking at her and sent her a smile. Only because Miss Beryl made her feel so special had Celeste put up with her mother and had not tried to break up the engagement.

After dessert was finished, Celeste turned to her father. "Wouldn't a walk in the garden be lovely?" She wasn't particularly fond of the outdoors, but she wanted to head off any attempt by Mrs. Courtland to steer her away from her father and Miss Beryl. They would have plenty of time for the two of them to be alone once they married. Her father had just returned yesterday, and she was in no mood to be excluded from his company.

"I'm sorry, dear," Father said as he stood to pull out the chairs for the ladies. "But it's time for your nap."

"Do I have to take one today?" Celeste whined, even though she knew it was useless to argue. Her father would not budge in matters that concerned her health.

Sure enough, he nodded. "I'm afraid so. But when you wake up, I'll take you for a ride."

Mrs. Courtland placed a pudgy hand on Celeste's arm. "When you're my age, dear, you'll appreciate taking naps."

Celeste shrugged away from the unwelcome touch and gave her best imitation of a sweet smile. "When I'm your age," she said brightly, "I'm sure I'll appreciate just being alive."

But the sarcasm was lost on Mrs. Courtland. She clapped her hands and tittered, *"C'est exacte,* you bright child!"

They left the dining room and walked into the hallway. Father was reaching for a bell cord to ring for an upstairs maid when Miss Beryl looked at Celeste with sympathetic eyes. "Why don't you allow me to escort her upstairs this time, Graham? That is, if Celeste wouldn't mind."

Celeste smiled and was about to reply that she wouldn't, when the elderly Mrs. Courtland stepped between them.

"Wouldn't it be better if *I* tucked her in, dear?" she offered, her earrings bobbing to and fro. "You two have hardly had any time alone since Graham returned."

Celeste bit her lip to conceal her fury, then noticed with relief that Miss Beryl was shaking her head. "I would like to spend a little time with my soon-to-be daughter. I'll catch up with you and Graham in the garden."

~

"Why don't you have tea with Beryl and me tomorrow morning?" Mrs. Courtland asked Graham as they paused in the garden to admire a bed of lavender sweet-alyssum. "Say, ten o'clock?"

"Thank you for the invitation," Graham answered, "but I've not spent a lot of time at home lately."

"You have to eat," persisted the older woman. "And it would mean so much to Beryl."

Graham glanced back at the terrace doors. Beryl obviously intended to take her time helping his daughter get settled for her nap. They got along so well together, and for that he was thankful. But no one—not even a future stepmother—could make up for a father's presence. At last he turned back to Mrs. Courtland. "I'll already be leaving Celeste when we go to the theater tomorrow night."

"You're such a good father," Mrs. Courtland gushed. "Why don't you bring the dear child with you?"

"Well, her studies . . ."

"Surely she can skip her studies for one day. And you'll have her back in time for her nap."

Graham wondered absently if his fiancée's mother could talk Oxford into running the Cambridge colors. He stifled a sigh.

"Very well, Celeste and I will be there at ten. I will have to bring along her nurse too, of course."

"But of course. I will have some of my maids keep her company in the kitchen."

The offer was made with no insult intended, and Graham hadn't thought twice, on previous dinings out, about the nurses having meals in the kitchen. Indeed, Miss Templeton had seemed to enjoy a camaraderie with Mrs. Courtland's maids—something about a mutual fondness for serialized stories.

But he felt an uneasiness about asking Miss Price to do the same thing. The arrangement now seemed demeaning, and he wondered why he had ever agreed to it before. But would Mrs. Courtland agree to changing the routine, in her own house? *She'll have to,* he thought.

He gave a charming smile to his future mother-in-law and patted the arm she had hooked through his. "You know, I would feel much more comfortable if Celeste's nurse were in the same room whenever she's away from home. You just never know . . ."

After a second Mrs. Courtland caught on and bobbed her head in understanding. "*Si vous voulez,* Graham! Then the nurse should dine with us."

~

After Father and Mrs. Courtland had gone into the garden, Miss Beryl offered her hand to Celeste and walked her over to the staircase. "Let's sit here and chat for a while," she said.

"Here on the step?"

Miss Beryl nodded and glanced up at the top of the stairs. "Just for a minute."

"All right." Celeste's heartbeat quickened. *Miss Beryl must have a secret to share!* Celeste prided herself on being a good secret-keeper. Occasionally Miss Beryl would ask questions about various people that Father had contact with and would ask Celeste not to tell anyone that she had asked. "Your father needs both of us to look out for him," Miss Beryl had said more than once. "But we mustn't tell him that, because men are like proud little boys. They like to think that they can take care of themselves."

Celeste lowered herself to sit on the bottom step, and Miss Beryl did the same, her rose-colored sateen skirts billowing about her ankles. "Did that new nurse go with you to church this morning?" she asked, leaning closer.

Celeste nodded, her excitement dying down a bit. How could any good secret involve Miss Price? She was only someone who worked for her father.

"Where did she sit?" Miss Beryl was asking.

"On the other side of me. Just like Miss Templeton used to."

"What did she and your father talk about in the coach?"

Celeste shrugged. "Seats at church, or something boring like that."

"Has she spent any other time with your father?"

"Other time? Father just got home yesterday. Why?"

"Just wondering." Miss Beryl stared off into space for a moment, a wrinkle appearing between her eyebrows. She turned back to Celeste. "What do you think of her?"

What do I think of her? Celeste wasn't quite sure herself. "Yesterday I hated her. But sometimes I don't think she's so terrible. Why are you asking so many questions about Miss Price?"

"Oh, I just like to make sure you're being well taken care of." Miss Beryl smiled, reaching out a slender finger to brush aside a stray lock of hair from Celeste's forehead. "After all, I only want the best for my future daughter."

"I can't wait!"

"Nor can I, dear." After a glance up the stairs again, Miss Beryl got to her feet and held out a hand to help her. "Now, not a word to anyone about our conversation," she whispered, giving a conspiratorial wink.

Celeste smiled and put a finger to her lips. "Not a word."

14

AT half past eleven the next day, Jenny sat across from Mr. Harrington and Celeste and breathed a sigh of relief as the barouche made its way back home. She had survived her first—and perhaps last—social engagement at the Courtland estate.

The tea, held in the Courtlands' bric-a-brac-infested dining room, had been a rather strained affair. At first Jenny had wondered if she were the cause, but that seemed not to be the case. Miss Courtland and her mother were both polite, if not overly warm to her, and of course paid most of their attention to Mr. Harrington and Celeste.

But there had been some kind of unspoken tension between mother and daughter. It had been well masked by smiles and the latest gossip and probably not even recognized by the other two guests . . . but Jenny had been exposed to enough tension in her early years to recognize it.

"Did you enjoy the meal, Miss Price?"

Jenny turned her head to find Mr. Harrington watching her. She had not enjoyed the past hour and a half at all, but surely there was *something* good she could say about it. *The Veau aux Truffes,* she reminded herself, then smiled and answered, "The food was quite delicious."

He smiled back and responded, "Yes, quite."

Jenny recalled something that Solomon had written, about it being better to dine simply but in a peaceful atmosphere than to feast where there was contention. *Next time I'll offer to have my meal in the kitchen,* she thought. She was certain that Miss Courtland wouldn't mind.

~

"Are you ready for the children now, Miss Celeste?" Gerdie asked at the door Monday afternoon.

Celeste, just up from her nap, gave a bored nod. "Check their hands and send them in."

"This I have to see," Elaine whispered to Jenny, who sat beside her on the sofa. Jenny had informed the governess that the children had been told not to deliberately lose any of the games, and Elaine had expressed doubts that the children could break out of their timid molds.

"Mr. Harrington was quite adamant that they should try to win," Jenny reminded her in a low tone. "He even told their parents as much."

"Old habits die hard," Elaine answered back as the children filed silently into the room. "And their mothers know enough about Celeste to make them cautious."

Sure enough, Elaine's words were prophetic. Jenny could see no change in the children's behavior. If anything, they were more timid. When one of the girls "accidentally" sent her ball rolling more than three feet from the ninepins, Jenny could bear to watch no longer.

"Celeste," she said, getting to her feet. "May we talk in your room?"

"I'm rather busy here," the girl replied as she aimed the wooden ball at the set of ninepins.

"Just for a second?"

"Oh, all right!" Celeste answered in a martyred voice and lowered the ball. "Don't touch any of my toys," she warned the children before following Jenny into her bedroom.

After closing the door, Jenny turned around and said in a low voice, "Did your father talk with you about playtime?"

Celeste tilted her head thoughtfully. "Let's see . . . it's possible that he did. . . ."

"I don't mean to criticize, but aren't you supposed to be sharing the victory a bit?"

"That's not what Father told me."

"Well, what *did* he tell you?"

Celeste was quiet for a few seconds, as if mulling over in her mind whether she cared to answer. Then she shrugged her shoulders. "Father informed me that the other children were going to play according to the rules and not allow me to win every time."

"But you're winning every game."

"I know," she said, raising her eyebrows innocently. "Disobedient little wretches, aren't they?"

Jenny didn't appreciate the girl's attempt at humor. "Perhaps you should reassure them that you won't be angry if they play to win."

"I don't recall Father saying that I had to do that," the girl answered with a haughty lift to her chin. "Now if you'll excuse me, I have guests."

It was useless to argue any further. Jenny opened the door and walked back over to the sofa. This time, Celeste gloated even more exuberantly whenever she won a game, making sure to send a pointed look in Jenny's direction. Finally Jenny leaned closer to Elaine and said, "I'm going to fetch my book."

The governess nodded. "Bring mine, too."

Celeste tired of the children before the hour was up, and she sent them away. When tea was brought to the sitting room, she told Elaine that she would be having supper upstairs with them as well. "Father and Miss Beryl are going to the theater," she sighed.

"Do you know what they're going to see?"

"*Trial by Jury*. It's something called an operetta."

"Gilbert and Sullivan," Elaine said. "I read about it in the newspaper."

The girl sighed again. "I wish I could go, too."

"You will one day, when you're older," Jenny consoled. But the child was still in her haughty mood and chose to ignore her.

~

"I wonder if Prince Edward will be in attendance this evening," Mrs. Courtland mused out loud for the fourth time, peering with her opera glasses across the darkened Royalty Theater as the orchestra warmed up in the pit below. "*Voyez-vous?* There are only three people seated in his box so far, and none of them look familiar."

Graham Harrington, seated between his fiancée and future mother-in-law, answered through clenched teeth. "I don't know. Perhaps he was here opening night." Mrs. Courtland would undoubtedly spend the better part of the evening scouting the audience, frequently asking if he recognized so-and-so. Sometimes she would lean so far over the box railing that he would have to keep a hand ready to grab her, lest she tumble headfirst to the floor below.

"If only you would have gotten tickets for Saturday night," the woman sighed. "I can't see anyone important here."

"Mama," came the cool voice at Graham's right. "Graham wasn't sure that he would be home Saturday."

Graham shot his fiancée a smile. She looked beautiful tonight in a gossamer satin gown gathered at her shoulders and with her coppery hair piled up in rhinestone-sprinkled ringlets. How fortunate he was, being engaged to someone who could bring beauty back into his life and guide Celeste along the path of womanhood. *I should have proposed four years ago.*

He blamed the fact that he didn't on his own hardheadedness. Beryl had been only nineteen when he was introduced to her at a wedding. Graham had found her lovely then, but the pushiness of her mother, hovering at her side and dropping not-too-subtle hints about his need for a wife, had frightened him away.

Graham was grateful to Beryl for persevering over the years, when she could have easily married any of the suitors who hovered around her like moths around a lantern.

Finally he had realized that he would never find the kind of love that he had shared with Theresa. Perhaps that kind of love was only meant to be experienced once in a lifetime. Still, he had an obligation to provide Celeste with a mother. For himself, he needed to do something about the loneliness that had plagued him since the death of his wife.

A small voice in the quiet of night sometimes accused him of being unfair to Beryl. In his own defense, Graham had never professed to love her. It didn't seem to worry Beryl. She wore self-confidence as comfortably as she wore silks, and she seemed sure that the affection he had for her would one day grow into love.

Beryl smiled back. "Mama is interested in people," she

whispered. "I appreciate your patience with her. She has such few comforts at her age."

The voice from the other side wasn't finished. "Well, Graham could have ordered the tickets and then *made a point* to be back in London," Mrs. Courtland droned on. "What's the use of owning a business if you can't do as you please?" A hush descended upon the gathering as the curtains began to open, but Mrs. Courtland was on her feet, waving her fan. "Oh look, *s'il vous plaît!* I can see Mister Gladstone sitting there!"

"Mama, please . . ."

Graham tried to ignore them both and concentrate on the chorus of jurymen, barristers, and attorneys on stage in the opening scene.

Hark, the hour of ten is sounding:
Hearts with anxious fears are bounding,
Hall of Justice crowds surrounding,
Breathing hope and fear—

"Mr. Harrington?"

Graham turned to find an attendant holding the red velvet curtain to one side. "Yes?"

"Begging your pardon, but I've a message for you."

"I'll return shortly," Graham whispered to Beryl. Rising from his seat, he went through the opening in the curtain and let it fall behind him.

"Here you go, sir," said the boy as he handed over an envelope. The lamps in the corridors behind the boxes were turned down during the performance, but the nearest one shed enough light so that Graham could see the writing on the outside of the envelope. *Palmer's handwriting,* he thought. His steward wouldn't disturb him at the theater unless there was an emergency. Tearing into the envelope, he prayed under his breath that nothing was wrong with Celeste.

From bias free of every kind,
This trial must be tried—

"What is it, Graham?"

He looked up to find Beryl holding back the curtain. "I have to leave now. Palmer has sent another carriage for me. You and your mother may take my coach after the play."

A gloved hand went across his sleeve as Beryl stepped closer. "What is it, dear?"

Graham closed his eyes against the stinging tears. "One of my employees in Liverpool . . . Jacob Wallace. He died last night. I'll have to get ready to go there in the morning."

"That's terrible," came his fiancée's melodious voice. There was a short pause, and then she said, "But why do you have to leave? There really is nothing you can do, is there?"

He opened his eyes and looked at her. "Jacob was a good friend, too. I'll need to see that his wife is taken care of and find out about the funeral arrangements. I don't much feel like watching the play now, anyway."

"Of course you don't," the woman before him sympathized, but there was a slight edge to her voice.

Graham had heard that tone of disapproval before. The first few times, it was simpler to allow Beryl to have her way. Now it was beginning to annoy him. "Beryl, what's the matter?" he asked somewhat testily, stuffing the envelope into his waistcoat pocket.

She folded her arms, her pretty face a mask of irritation. "You haven't been back three days, and now you're off to Liverpool again. Don't you have workers who can handle things like this?"

"He was my friend, Beryl," he said in a flat tone. "Bid good night to your mother for me." He turned, and the baritone strains of a love song accompanied his footsteps down the corridor.

When my first old, old love I knew,
My bosom welled with joy;
My riches at her feet I threw—
I was a lovesick boy. . . .

~

Just before bedtime that evening, Celeste had a seizure. Jenny tended to her as normal, then told the maid that she would like to sit up with the girl for an hour or so, to make sure that she was all right.

"I'll work on some needlepoint next door. Just tell me when you're ready for me," Alma said, leaving the door open as she went into the schoolroom.

Turning the lamp down low, Jenny sat on the edge of the bed and bathed the girl's face with a damp cloth.

"My head hurts," Celeste complained after a while, her voice fragile.

"Where?" asked Jenny, leaning closer.

When Celeste indicated her forehead, Jenny began to massage lightly with the tips of her fingers. "Does that feel better?"

"Better. Don't stop doing that."

"I'll keep it up until you're good and asleep."

"Will you tell me a story, too?"

After a moment's thought, Jenny said, "Have you heard the story about the princess who wanted to join the circus?"

"Is it a good one?"

"One of my favorites. But first you have to close your eyes."

Celeste gave a wan smile, and the dimple in her cheek appeared. "Do you ever tell stories to people with their eyes open?"

Jenny laughed. "Not very often."

She started the story, weaving in extra characters and incidents to stretch it out longer. When she finished, Celeste appeared to be sleeping, so she moved her fingers from the girl's forehead and eased up off the side of the bed. She got up quietly and started to slip out of the room. Before she could reach the door, Celeste's sleep-laden voice came from behind her.

"Miss Price?"

She turned around. "Yes, Celeste?"

"I'm sorry I lied about you to Father . . . after the zoo."

"I forgive you, Celeste." Jenny walked back over to the bed and touched the girl's forehead. "Does your head still hurt?"

The only answer she got was the steady breathing of the sleeping child. Some strange, maternal emotion welled up inside of Jenny, and she found herself bending down to kiss the girl's cheek. *You poor motherless baby.*

She turned toward the door again, but was startled to find Mr. Harrington standing in the doorway, his face a curious mixture of tenderness and surprise.

"I—I thought you were at the theater," Jenny whispered, noticing that he was still dressed in his evening clothes.

"I had to leave early," he whispered back. "Is she asleep?"

"Yes, she just fell asleep. Did you want to say good night?"

He looked disappointed. "I don't suppose I should wake her."

"She really should rest. She had a seizure right before bedtime."

A stricken look came across his face. Peering over Jenny's shoulder at the bed, he asked, "Is she all right now?"

"Yes, of course."

"Then I'll say good-bye to her in the morning."

"You're going away?" Jenny asked. After the words were out she wished she hadn't spoken them. It was really none of her business.

Mr. Harrington stepped back from the doorway into the schoolroom and turned to Alma, who had put her needlepoint aside and was sitting there expectantly. "You may sit with her now." To Jenny, he said, "May we talk in the library?"

The house was dark and quiet as Jenny followed the light of Mr. Harrington's candle. Most likely all of the servants—except for Alma, holding vigil in Celeste's room—were asleep. Because he carried the light, Mr. Harrington walked through the library door first. He stood at the open door and waited for Jenny to follow, then used the candle to light a lamp in the library. When she could see the whole room, Jenny found her eyes automatically drifting to the table where the Chinese jar had been displayed. Her heart lurched in her chest when she realized the jar wasn't there.

"I decided to lock it in a cabinet," said Mr. Harrington, as if reading her mind. Motioning with his hand, he said, "See?"

Just a few feet from the table sat a walnut cabinet with glass doors that hadn't been in the library the last time she'd been there. Jenny walked closer, then noticed with relief the jar sitting by itself on the top shelf. *Miss Courtland must have convinced him,* she thought.

She felt relieved, recalling how, in this very room, Miss Courtland had insinuated that she might be capable of stealing it. If it ever turned up missing, she would always feel as if she were suspect.

"If only it could talk," came Mr. Harrington's voice from behind her.

Turning to look at him, she said, "Sir?"

"The jar," he said with a nod toward the cabinet. "I wonder how many hands have held it, and what their stories are."

Jenny understood. "My father owns a musket that was used in the war with the American colonies. When I was a child I would hold it and try to imagine what sort of soldier might have used the gun, and if he made it back safely from the war."

"Very likely some homesick boy," Mr. Harrington said, then gave Jenny a reassuring smile. "If the musket made it all the way back to England, then it's likely your soldier made it home safely, too." He motioned toward a pair of leather chairs in the far corner. "Do you mind if we sit?"

With the light shining on Mr. Harrington's face, Jenny noticed that his expression was solemn, even grave. *What have I done?* she wondered as she took one of the seats. Whatever was wrong had to be serious, if he had left the theater over it.

"My steward, Palmer, sent a message to my theater box," he said, as if reading her mind. "I have to prepare to leave for Liverpool first thing in the morning."

"Is your business in trouble?"

He shook his head. "Worse. My most valuable and trusted employee in that office has passed away. Jacob Wallace was his name. My father hired him when I was still a boy."

"I'm so sorry."

Mr. Harrington accepted her condolence with a grim nod. "Jacob was the person who taught me to read shipping charts. I could go to him with any question." His dark eyes glistened in the light of the lamp. He seemed to need to talk, so Jenny sat back in her chair and listened.

"Having my business divided between London and Liverpool is hard. But I never had to worry about the Liverpool end when I was here at home. Jacob had—" His voice broke. "Integrity. He was my friend."

"I'm sorry," seemed to be all Jenny could say.

Mr. Harrington drew a handkerchief from his pocket and wiped his eyes. "I didn't mean to burden you with this."

"It's no burden, believe me."

He took a deep breath and let it out. "Anyway, I'll be catching the first train out of London in the morning. But I'm glad we have this chance to talk, because I don't know how long I'll be gone."

"Yes, sir?"

"I've been thinking more about what you said, about my daughter needing to learn self-control for her own good. My father died when I was in my early twenties, but he had treated me like a man for years, and I was able to take over the business and the household. I won't always be around to shield Celeste from life's frustrations. It's important that she develop some strength of character."

"She can do it, Mr. Harrington. Celeste is a bright child."

"Has she played with the servants' children since we spoke last?"

Jenny cringed inwardly. Failure was hard to admit, coming

on the heels of her assurances that their plan would work. "This afternoon, Mr. Harrington."

"And?"

"The children are still too intimidated by her."

"That's too bad," he said, shaking his head. "But we have to keep trying."

"I think so too."

Sighing, he ran his fingers through his short hair. "I really meant what I said about staying home more, but this is something over which I have no control."

"Of course not," Jenny agreed. "When you return . . ."

"I don't want to wait that long. I've already wasted too many years allowing my daughter's strong will to warp her character." His dark eyes took on an apologetic expression. "I would like you to take charge of this matter until I get back. In the morning I will inform Mrs. Ganaway that you have total authority over affairs concerning my daughter while I'm away."

The idea of having that much responsibility over someone else's child was frightening to Jenny. "Are you sure? Miss Barton has known her longer—"

"Positive, Miss Price. And now more than ever." A slight smile lit his face, though his face was still haggard. "I saw you kiss her cheek up there. You care about her, don't you."

His words came out more as a statement than a question, and Jenny nodded. "I didn't realize how much until today."

Staring across at her, Mr. Harrington lapsed into a thoughtful silence. There was a tenderness in his expression he seemed to be unaware of. Jenny was grateful for the dimness of the room, for she could feel a disconcerting flush spread across her cheeks. What was he thinking about? And why was it affecting her this way?

As if catching himself then, he blinked, straightened in his chair, and said, "I know you'll do what's best for her."

"I'll try my best, Mr. Harrington."

"I'll speak with Celeste in the brief time I'll have before I leave, but she's not had to account for her actions for twelve years now. I don't expect she's going to make it easy for you."

I don't expect so either, Jenny agreed silently. "I appreciate the confidence you—"

"Is everything all right, sir?" came a female voice from the doorway. Jenny and Mr. Harrington both looked up at the same time. Mrs. Willis, the cook, stepped into the room holding a candle and wearing a brown flannel wrapper, rag curlers peeking out from her nightcap.

"I hope we didn't wake you."

She shook her head. "I was having trouble sleeping, so I'm on my way downstairs for a bit o' warm milk. May I fetch you anything from the kitchen?"

Mr. Harrington gave Jenny a questioning look. "Miss Price?"

"No, thank you."

"Nothing for me either," he said to Mrs. Willis, "but thank you for asking." The cook was just turning to leave when a doorbell sounded from the front of the house. "I'll get that, sir," she said with a sideways glance at her employer.

Eyeing her wrapper and slippers, he made a move to get to his feet. "But I'll be glad to—"

"Just keep your chair, Mr. Harrington," she said, motioning with a plump arm for him to stay put. She left the room, but Jenny could hear her grumbling down the hallway, "Anybody knocking on a person's door this time o' night deserves to be greeted by a nightcap and curlers."

Jenny couldn't help but look at Mr. Harrington and smile. "Mrs. Willis is her own person," he said softly, returning her smile with one of his own.

"I hope it's not more bad news, coming this late."

"I didn't even consider that."

A single set of footsteps rang against the tiles of the hallway, growing louder with each beat. Jenny suddenly felt as if she were intruding into Mr. Harrington's business. "Perhaps I should leave."

"Please stay. I'll need to walk you back upstairs with the candle anyway."

Jenny was about to say that she could find her way alone when Miss Courtland came through the open doorway. "Your cook told me that you were in here," she said, walking toward his chair. The lamplight made a shimmering reflection against the folds of the gossamer gown she was wearing, and Jenny thought she had never seen Mr. Harrington's fiancée look more stunning. "I could tell you were angry when you left—"

At the sight of Jenny, she froze in the middle of the room. "Am I interrupting something here?"

When he recovered from the surprise, Mr. Harrington's face creased with weariness. "Why did you leave the theater, Beryl?"

"I'd say it was a good thing that I did," she replied evenly. Her topaz eyes seemed to catch the flame from the light as she turned back to Jenny and demanded, "What are you doing here with my fiancé?"

Stunned by the fury on the woman's face, Jenny stammered, "I—I just . . ."

"Miss Price is employed in this house, Beryl." Mr. Harrington got to his feet. "She has every right to be here."

"I thought her job was to take care of Celeste upstairs. Now I see why you had to rush back here!"

"That's ridiculous."

"Then why were you—?"

"Enough, Beryl!" His expression turned as stormy as hers. "I'll not be called to account for the way I run my household. And I won't put up with your dropping in to check up on me."

"That wasn't why I—"

Jenny found the nerve to get to her feet. Without a word to either of them she started across the room.

"Miss Price?"

At the door, she turned at the sound of Mr. Harrington's voice.

"Please don't leave," he said.

"I would really rather be upstairs now."

"Please." He walked over to his fiancée. "Miss Price and I were discussing Celeste," he said, his voice terse. "And you owe her an apology."

The room grew thick with tension as Miss Courtland stared back at him with a decidedly inelegant pout on her lips. Then she seemed to wilt under his gaze. Turning, she cleared her throat and focused her eyes somewhere around Jenny's chin. "I ask your forgiveness for . . . overreacting. It was most unladylike of me."

"I understand," Jenny answered with as much graciousness as possible.

Miss Courtland's lips then stretched into a forced smile, and Jenny knew instinctively that it was there only for Mr. Harrington's benefit. "Planning for the wedding has put me under a tremendous strain lately."

"I'm sure that can be stressful."

"Isn't she a dear?" The woman turned back to Mr. Harrington and gave a helpless shrug. "I feel so silly, bursting in like that."

Weary of having to stand there making insincere small talk, Jenny bade both of them good-night.

"Wait. Please take this," Mr. Harrington said, walking over to the lamp table to relight the candle. Jenny studied the pattern on the carpet to avoid having to chat with Miss Courtland while she waited. When Mr. Harrington approached her with the candle, she noticed the exhaustion on his face. In spite of her deep embarrassment, she felt a surge of sympathy for him.

She held out her hand for the candle. "Thank you."

"Thank you," he answered with a quiet voice. For a brief second it seemed as if he were about to say more, but then his eyes darted away. "I'll speak with Celeste in the morning."

~

When the sound of Miss Price's soft footsteps had faded away, Graham turned to Beryl and frowned. "What in the world were you thinking of?"

She rushed over to put a hand on his arm. "I—I don't know," she replied, her eyes pleading. "I left the theater because I was worried that I'd made you angry. And then when I walked in here and found you together, I . . ."

"I believe you've hurt Miss Price deeply. And for the second time, no less."

A tear trailed down her cheek. "It's just that you don't realize how many women in London would give anything to trade places with me," Beryl sniffed. "I don't know how I could bear it if I lost you."

"You're not going to lose me," Graham assured her gently. At the same time he wondered why the touch of the hand resting upon his arm suddenly felt unbearably heavy.

15

TUESDAY afternoon, while Celeste was at her lessons, Jenny sat on the sofa in the tiny nursery sitting room and reread the letter she had just received from her mother.

> *I thought I had gotten used to your being away while you were at nursing school, but I find myself listening for the sound of your footsteps in the room upstairs.*

Jenny pulled a handkerchief from her pocket and wiped her eyes. *I miss you too, Mother,* she thought, then read on.

> *Of course we will keep the little Harrington girl in our prayers. Have patience, dear Jenny. God can change even the most stubborn hearts. Look what he did for your mother!*

She had no doubt that her mother would pray for Celeste—every day, just as she prayed for others. It was hard to imagine Mother being anything other than the virtuous woman she was now. Perhaps it was the memory of that past that caused her to be such a strong believer. Hadn't Jesus said in the Bible that whoever is forgiven much, loveth much?

Perhaps there is hope for Elaine, too, she thought. When she answered the letter, she would be sure to ask her parents to pray for the governess, as Jenny had been doing herself. There was a deep root of bitterness in her friend, a bitterness that only showed itself on rare occasions. Jenny had begun to suspect that Elaine was angry with God. It might be because of her parents' death, but Jenny sensed that the source of the anger went even deeper than that.

The letter contained a postscript from her father, telling her how much he missed her organizational skills in the bookstore. *If you ever grow tired of nursing, you always have a job here.*

Ever grow tired of nursing? Holding the letter to her chest, Jenny thought back to last night, when she had been able to keep a child from hurting herself during a seizure, and then soothe her to sleep afterward. There might be times in the future when she would question her calling, but she was positive that it was meant for her from the day she was born.

Not that it's going to be easy, she thought to herself. Last night the girl had been so sweet. But this morning, after speaking with her father, Celeste had treated her with a thin veneer of politeness that did not match the challenge and resentment in her dark eyes.

"Jenny?"

She looked up at Elaine, standing just a few feet away. "Oh, I'm sorry," the governess said. "I didn't realize you had a letter."

Jenny tucked the pages back into their envelope and smiled. "It's quite all right. I've finished reading it."

"Gathering wool?"

"Enough for a coat or two."

Elaine smiled. "Celeste is down for her nap. I wonder if you fancy a walk to the stables. I haven't been out to see the horses in months."

"I would enjoy that."

As they headed downstairs, Elaine asked Jenny how she planned to carry out Mr. Harrington's request to teach Celeste some self-control.

"I'm not sure yet," Jenny replied. "She obviously resents my having charge over her."

"An understatement."

"Do you think it would do any good for me to speak with the children who play with her?"

"Didn't Mr. Harrington already do that?"

"Well, yes."

Elaine thought for a few seconds and then shook her head. "You have to understand the thinking of people who have been in servitude all of their lives. The master of the house reigns supreme."

"But Mr. Harrington is the master of the house."

"Not in those children's minds. Their master is Celeste, whom they see almost every day. She terrifies them . . . and terrifies their mothers, too."

"Then I'll have to pray for another answer," Jenny said deliberately.

Elaine pointed. "The stables are in this direction." They strolled to the opposite side of the house from the formal gardens, where the stables were located next to a hedged pasture enclosed by a fenced paddock. The musty, sweet smell of hay, wood, and horses grew stronger as Elaine and Jenny got closer.

Jenny would never admit it to anyone, for she was certain that she alone felt this way, but she had always liked the aroma of horse stables—perhaps because it reminded her of home.

Her father had two carriage horses, and she had always enjoyed bringing them apples and bits of celery from the house.

Mr. Harrington owned five carriage horses, two drays, and two colts. They were all in the pasture save a magnificent shire, alone in the paddock. The two women walked over to the pasture gate and tried, without success, to entice one of the colts to come closer by holding out clumps of grass they had pulled from the base of the fence post.

"His name's Lancelot." The voice came from behind, and a stable boy joined them at the gate. He looked to be about Celeste's age, short and wiry, with freckles and reddish-blond hair peeking out from under a cap.

"Albert!" Elaine smiled at him.

The boy doffed his cap and grinned. "You talk with Mr. Ramsey yet?"

"I'm sorry, I haven't needed to go shopping again. But I won't forget."

He shrugged good-naturedly. "Mr. Palmer let me drive him to the tobacco store this morning. Nobody grabbed *his* sleeve, though."

"I should hope not," Elaine replied, still smiling. "I would like you to meet Miss Price." To Jenny, she said, "This is Albert. He works in the stables."

The boy lifted his cap again. "Pleased to meet you." Turning to extend an arm over the top rail, the lad made a clucking noise with his tongue. The colt trotted over to them, and once it had pulled the grass from Jenny's hand, it was joined by the second colt.

"The black one's Triton. Go ahead and pet them if you like," the boy urged. "I've got to go back to work."

Jenny and Elaine alternated between feeding the colts grass

and stroking their silky coats. Finally the animals tired of this and went back to join their mothers.

"That was fun," Jenny said, brushing her hands together, as they turned back in the direction of the house. "It was nice of the boy to help us out."

Elaine nodded. "He drove me to buy supplies last week. Seems to be a scrapper for someone so young."

They passed close to the paddock, and Jenny went over to examine the lone occupant. The horse was a powerful-looking animal, his coat almost entirely red except for a white star between his eyes. "I wonder why he's not with the others?" she said, stepping up to the fence.

"I've never seen this one before, but perhaps there's a good reason," Elaine cautioned. "I wouldn't get too close."

"I'll stay behind the fence," Jenny said, already pulling up a clump of grass. "He reminds me of a horse my father once had. Wellington was his name. . . ." She held the grass between the top and middle rail, and imitated the clucking noise that the boy had made. The horse stared at her for a second, then started walking toward her.

She felt a hand on her arm. "Jenny . . ."

"You're hungry, aren't you, fellow?" Jenny cooed, ignoring Elaine's warning as the horse came closer. "Some nice green—"

The horse was only inches away when Jenny felt two arms encircle her waist and give a hard pull. Caught off balance, she stumbled backward and fell on top of someone she suddenly realized was not Elaine.

"I'm sorry, ma'am!" Albert cried. He scrambled to his feet and tugged at Jenny's arm. "That horse bit off one of Tom's fingers yesterday! He's meaner than Judas!"

With the help of Elaine and the stable boy, Jenny got to her feet. She gaped at the animal, who stood watching with something suspiciously resembling disappointment in his expression.

Albert turned back to the horse and shook his finger. "Shame on you, frightening the lady like that! If you were mine, you'd be on your way to the glue factory!"

"Why does Mr. Harrington keep a horse like that around?" Elaine asked, her face blanched.

"He won't be around much longer." The boy shook his head. "He was just bought three days ago, but he's going back in the morning. Nobody knew he was a biter."

Automatically curling the fingers of both hands into her palms, Jenny took another step backward. "Thank you for stopping me," she said over the sound of her blood rushing through her ears.

Two groomsmen came running out from the stables, but they retreated when Elaine assured them that Jenny was all right. "I'm sorry about the grass on your dress, ma'am," Albert told her.

Jenny looked down at her uniform. Sure enough, grass and bits of dirt clung to the fabric. She smiled and held up a hand. "Better than losing a finger."

After the boy left for the stables, Jenny and Elaine started back for the house. "What do you know about our young hero?" Jenny asked Elaine.

"Only that he came from an orphanage up north."

"An orphanage?" Jenny's heart went out to the boy. "He seems so young."

"He's fourteen. He told me that right away." They walked on in silence for a few minutes. When they had almost reached the house, Elaine whispered, "Isn't that Mr. Horton coming this way?"

"Where?" asked Jenny, but before the governess could answer she had spotted a man limping his way purposefully toward them, a pipe perched between his teeth. "And who is Mr. Horton?"

"The head gardener. He looks as though he'd like to speak with us." Elaine stopped walking and called out, "Good afternoon, Mr. Horton."

"And a good day to you too, Miss Barton," said the man as he got closer. "I figured you to be in the garden this time o' day."

"We decided to visit the horses instead." Mr. Horton had finally reached them, and Elaine put a hand on Jenny's arm. "I don't believe you've met Miss Price. She is Celeste's nurse."

The man tipped the bill of his cap and smiled. "Haven't had the pleasure yet, Miss Price."

Offering her hand, Jenny said, "I take it that you're the one responsible for the lovely grounds."

"I thank you for the compliment." The gardener beamed as they shook hands. "But I've got help." A wry look came upon his face, and he mumbled, "Some better than others, I'm afraid."

Mr. Horton turned to Elaine. "Do you mind if I have a word with you?" Giving an apologetic shrug to Jenny, he said, "It's kind of a private matter . . . but I shan't take long."

"Take as long as you like," Jenny said, smiling. "I'll go on up to the nursery."

~

Mr. Horton took a puff from his pipe as he watched Jenny walk away, then turned back to Elaine. "Sorry to send the miss away." The words came out with a haze of smoke. "But it's about one of my gardeners, the Irishman. Most likely you've seen him around here?"

"Yes," Elaine answered. The memory of the big, muscular man singing about "Onyons" came back to her, and she suppressed a smile.

Shifting on one foot, the gardener said, "Well, you see, it's come to my attention that Mr. Fogarty—that's his name, Logan Fogarty—has been payin' one of the other gardeners for readin' lessons. Only Dudley, his 'steacher,' can barely read his own name. I hate to see the good man waste his money like that."

"Are you asking me to tutor Mr. Fogarty?"

Mr. Horton broke into an appreciative grin. "I reckoned you for a smart woman, Miss Barton. That's what I'm askin'."

She opened her mouth to speak, but he went on as if anxious to head off any denial. "He'd be payin' you the same money he's been payin' Dudley. You could teach him out here in the garden this time every afternoon."

Elaine considered the opportunity. With the need to save for her old age, having another source of income was always welcome. "But what about his work? How can he take off for an hour every day?"

"I talked with Mr. Palmer about it this morning. Mr. Fogarty works twice as hard as my other gardeners, so he's due a little time off. And when the man learns to read, it'll save my old legs the trip up the stairs to have my orders made out. I'm just being practical."

Elaine gave the man a smile. "And kind, too."

He waved away her compliment, but looked pleased. "Then you'll be agreeing to do this?"

"How badly does Mr. Fogarty want to learn to read?"

"More than I've seen a man want anything, Miss Barton. You should see him studying his scraps of paper."

In Elaine's mind that settled it. To again teach someone who actually *wanted* to learn would be a joy. "When would he like to begin?"

"Well, that's another matter," said the man, easing back his cap to rub his forehead. "You see, I wanted to talk with you first."

Elaine raised an eyebrow. "You mean you haven't spoken with him about me?"

"He doesn't know that I know about his tutorin' with Dudley. But Dudley gets talkative when he's in his cups, so it's not a secret anymore."

"How do you know Mr. Fogarty would want me to tutor him?"

"Once I tell him Dudley can't read, that'll settle it." Mr. Horton pursed his lips thoughtfully, then mumbled, as if to himself, "I'll have to keep the other gardeners busy elsewhere, or they'll come around to torment him."

"I beg your pardon?"

He blinked and then smiled at Elaine. "Logan Fogarty will meet you at the gazebo tomorrow at this time. I guarantee it."

~

An hour after Elaine had returned to the nursery, Jenny was seated in Mr. Palmer's office, across the desk from the steward. "What may I do for you, Miss Price?" asked the bespectacled man.

Suddenly Jenny wondered if she should have given this notion more thought and surely some prayer. But she plunged ahead. "I would like to ask your permission for one of the stable workers to play with Celeste for a little while every day."

Mr. Palmer looked as if he had something stuck in his throat. "I beg your pardon?"

"Albert is his name. Do you think he would mind?"

"Whether he minds or not isn't the issue," said Mr. Palmer. "He's paid wages to work at whatever he's ordered to do. I'm at a loss to understand why you want him, though. Shouldn't Miss Harrington play with girls?"

Jenny shook her head. "Celeste needs someone who would not be so intimidated by her. Yet someone who is kind as well."

"And you suppose Albert is all that?"

"I have a feeling that he is."

"I like the boy, too, or I wouldn't have let him talk me into hiring him," Mr. Palmer said. "But I want to warn you, he hasn't come from the sheltered background that Miss Harrington enjoys."

"I've heard that he ran away from an orphanage."

"And has spent the last year living on the streets of London."

"I think Celeste would like him," Jenny persisted, "once she got used to him."

The steward gave a shrug and then pushed away from his desk. "Mr. Harrington says you have full authority in these matters. I'll tell Ramsey to send the boy up to the nursery every . . ." He paused and peered over his spectacles. "Afternoon?"

"Afternoon." Jenny got up to leave. "And thank you."

The man smiled. "I hope it works."

~

"I can't believe you've asked Albert to play with Celeste," Elaine said to Jenny. The two of them, dressed in their nightgowns and robes, were playing dominoes at the tea table in the nursery sitting room.

Jenny scanned the dozen or so dominoes already in place and answered, "We've got to try something. And he hasn't got parents to order him to kowtow to the master's daughter."

"Well, I wish you luck," said Elaine.

"Thank you." Looking up at her friend, Jenny said in a voice she tried to keep casual, "But I don't believe in luck. I would rather you prayed for me."

Elaine stared back, her green eyes unreadable. "You'll have to settle for my wishing you luck."

Jenny suddenly lost all interest in dominoes. "What's wrong, Elaine?"

"There is nothing wrong. Are you going to play?"

"I don't feel like it any more." Jenny sat back in her chair. "This is so frustrating."

"You don't like dominoes?"

"No. It's frustrating not to be able to talk with you about spiritual matters."

"Why must we discuss spiritual matters?"

"Because they're important to me. Yet you withdraw whenever I mention anything about prayer, or God."

"Perhaps I wish to keep some things private," Elaine said without a trace of anger in her voice.

"That's just my point. People who know the Lord enjoy talking about him. At least the people I've known."

After a long silence, Elaine sighed. "All right, Jenny. I suppose we need to talk."

"Do you feel bitterness toward God because of your parents' deaths?"

"Not at all." The governess absently balanced a domino

on the back of her hand. "I suppose I've enjoyed our short friendship too much."

"What do you mean by that?"

"I mean you're going to hate me when I tell you—"

"I could never hate you," Jenny cut in to protest.

"I'm an atheist."

Jenny's mouth gaped open. *"What?"*

"I realize the concept of not believing in God is horrible to someone like you. My grandmother even disinherited me because of it."

"You're serious? You aren't a believer?"

"I'm not."

"But you attend church."

Elaine shrugged. "How many people would hire me to tutor their children if I professed to be an atheist?"

"Your parents were missionaries!"

"If they had been surgeons, I would not automatically have become one unless I studied medicine myself."

"But I daresay you would be at least a little *interested* in medicine," Jenny persisted. "Have you never tried to find out about God for yourself?"

Elaine's expression hardened. "My grandmother plunged into that task willingly. She had me on my knees constantly, trying to appease God. Most of the time I had no idea which serious infraction I had committed to make him so furious at me. When I was nine years old, I decided that I could not believe in such a God."

Jenny had never heard of such a thing. "But surely your grandmother told you how much God loves you."

"Of course. But I never perceived any sort of love from the way she spoke. When I contracted smallpox and almost died . . ."

Her voice broke, and she looked away for a second. "She told me that God was punishing me for being such a wicked child."

Getting to her feet, Jenny walked around to Elaine's chair and sat on the arm. She reached out a hand and put it on the governess's shoulder. "She was wrong, Elaine. Forgive me for speaking ill of your grandmother, but it was cruel of her to behave that way."

"Oh, it was silly of me to bring it up." Elaine wiped at her eyes, obviously embarrassed for having confessed so much. "I'm grateful to her for taking me in. She could have sent me to a foundling hospital. And it's all in the past now, anyway."

"It's not in the past. It's affecting you right now, by making you bitter against God."

"I'm not bitter against God, Jenny. I simply do not accept his existence. . . ."

"And *I* simply don't believe that."

"Believe what you wish," Elaine said. She gave Jenny a questioning look. "You know I would be dismissed if Mr. Harrington found out."

Jenny nodded. Elaine was right; most likely that was exactly what would happen.

"I've never tried to influence Celeste to my way of thinking . . . *never.* Just because my faith was robbed, I wouldn't steal a child's."

Jenny had listened to enough tutoring sessions by now to believe her. "Mr. Harrington won't find out from me," she assured the governess. "Not unless he asks me directly, you understand."

"I appreciate that. And now, at the risk of sounding rude, I must tell you that I'm not going to want to discuss this any more."

"Why?"

"Because I don't want you or anyone else attempting to convert me."

"That's going to be hard," Jenny admitted. "If you could only know how good God really is—"

Elaine held up a hand, and Jenny's words were left hanging in the air. "I'm glad your faith makes you happy," said the governess, with a trace of something akin to envy in her voice. "Perhaps one day I would be interested in hearing about it."

"But not at this time," Jenny finished dully.

"Not at this time."

16

THE next morning, Albert Hollis was shoveling manure from a cart to the fertilizer pile in back of the stables when Mr. Ramsey strode toward him. Flanked by two grinning groomsmen, the head of the stables also sported a wide smile.

"Got a little chore for you this afternoon." The man's words were followed by a chorus of snickers from the grooms, Butch and Stanley.

"Yes, sir?"

"Mr. Harrington's little girl has invited you to play."

Albert smirked at what was obviously the latest attempt at a prank. As the runt of the stable workers, he was often subject to practical jokes. "Is that so?" he replied, leaning on his shovel.

"Little Miss Harrington needs a playmate, so Mr. Palmer says. You're to go up to the nursery every afternoon from now on."

Albert shook his head. Something was wrong here. Mr. Ramsey was grinning, but he looked as if he was telling the truth. And Butch and Stanley seemed to be enjoying themselves just a little too much. Albert narrowed his eyes suspiciously. "You *are* just foolin' me . . . aren't you?"

"No, kid," Mr. Ramsey said, hooking his thumbs through his stays. "Even I couldn't have come up with a joke *this* good."

Albert's spirits took a plunge. "Every day, sir?"

"Unless her nurse tells you different."

"Do I have to?"

Mr. Ramsey nodded. "Cheer up, lad. It's more pleasant than shoveling muck, ain't it?"

"I'd rather shovel muck."

"What's the matter, Albert?" asked Butch. "Too good to sit and play dolls with Mr. H's daughter?"

"Maybe you need to shut your mouth," Albert grumbled back at him. He usually took the jesting in good stride, giving back as good as he got. But this was . . . serious.

"Touchy today, ain't we?" Stanley hooted. "Maybe he's afraid the girl will make him wear a dress!"

Amid gales of laughter, Albert gave a pleading look to Mr. Ramsey, but the older man was too busy laughing to rescue him.

"Chin up, Albert!" Butch exclaimed when he could catch his breath. "Just think . . . if the girl takes a liking to you, maybe she'll marry you when you grow up." He spread his arms in the direction of the manure cart. "Then all this will be yours."

"And you'll be tellin' us what to do! That oughter be worth a little tea party in the nursery every afternoon," Stanley added.

"All right, that's enough," Mr. Ramsey finally scolded, though his face was still beet-red from laughing. "We've had our fun. Now it's time to leave the lad alone and get back to work."

After the men scattered, Mr. Ramsey turned back to Albert. "One thing more," he said, lowering his voice. "The young Miss Harrington wouldn't like her playmates smellin' of muck, so you're to have a bath and change your clothes every day."

He raised his eyebrows at the boy's grime-stained work pants. "You *do* have some clean clothes upstairs, don't you?"

"Yes, sir," Albert sighed. At least Stanley and Butch were not around to hear this latest order.

"Well, good then," Mr. Ramsey said. "In the meantime, let's put that shovel back to work."

~

The question of whether to tell Celeste ahead of time about the new playtime arrangements had kept Jenny tossing and turning for a good part of the night. As she changed from her nightgown into a clean uniform, she decided she would wait until it was absolutely necessary. No use in giving the girl another reason to sulk all morning.

The door opened a few inches, and Elaine stuck her head through the doorway. "Are you dressed?"

"I just need to brush my hair," Jenny answered. "I didn't mean to oversleep, but I had trouble falling asleep last night."

"It's not late at all," Elaine smiled. "Breakfast is here." She opened the door wider and held it open so that Gerdie and Reanna could bring the trays through the bedroom and into the sitting room. Celeste followed, still in her nightgown and yawning.

Quickly Jenny ran the brush through her long hair and joined the others in the sitting room. Toast and marmalade, tea and milk, and a platter of bacon and eggs were arranged on the table, filling the small room with a savory aroma.

"Good morning," she said to the others as she took her place at the table. Only Elaine returned the greeting. Celeste did not even look at her. After the moment of silence and bowed heads, they began to serve their plates.

"Has Father sent word about when he's coming home?" Celeste asked Elaine around a mouthful of toast.

"No, Miss Celeste. He only just left yesterday morning."

The girl turned to Jenny with a baleful expression. "I suppose you're happy about this."

"About what?" Jenny asked, her teaspoon of sugar poised in midair.

"Having the right to order me around. What is it you'll be having me do today, Miss Price . . . shine your shoes?"

"Miss Celeste!" Elaine exclaimed. "You shouldn't say—"

Jenny held up a hand. "That's all right, Elaine." To Celeste, she said in her most reassuring tone, "You have every right to wonder. Change is frightening."

The suspicion in the girl's tone turned to bravado. "I'm not frightened of you."

"And you shouldn't be." Giving a sigh, Jenny decided to go ahead and tell the girl about Albert's pending visit. "I think you're going to like him," she finished.

"A *stable* boy?"

"A hard worker." Jenny bit her lip and went on. "And I would appreciate it if you would allow Albert to address you as 'Celeste.'"

Celeste stared at Jenny as if she had just suggested that she allow the boy to kiss her cheek. "Why?"

"Well, to be truthful, he can't feel comfortable around you if he feels he has to bow and scrape."

"And to be *really* truthful," the girl said with a hint of a smile, "you want me to play with the boy because he won't feel comfortable about allowing me to win."

Jenny's mouth opened with wonder. How could a child who did so poorly at her studies get to be so bright? Celeste was waiting for her answer, so she replied, "Well, yes," but her voice sounded tinny and weak.

Celeste said nothing after that, just studied the eggs on her plate while Jenny held her breath. Finally, the girl picked up her fork and began to eat. "This bacon is quite good."

A few minutes later, while Celeste brushed her teeth in the lavatory, Jenny helped Elaine set out the schoolbooks. "Why do you think she didn't stay upset?" she asked in a low voice.

The governess straightened and gave a wry smile. "New bait."

~

After the school lessons were finished and Celeste was in bed for her nap, Elaine took a beginning reader from one of the shelves in the schoolroom. "I'll be back in about an hour," she said to Jenny.

Jenny smiled and held up a book. "I'll do a little reading of my own."

"I'll miss our walks together," Elaine said hesitantly. She had confided to her new friend about Mr. Horton's request and explained her need to save money for her old age. "But I really should put away as much money as possible."

"That's important," Jenny reassured her. "Now go, or Mr. Fogarty will wonder what happened."

Elaine went on down to the gazebo, taking a seat on the closest bench. She was a bit early, but she had half expected Mr. Fogarty to already be here. She fingered the spine of the *Norcliff Beginning Reader* and wondered if the gardener had decided against being tutored by a woman. Closing her eyes, she took in the scent of a rose-laden breeze and the sound of pigeons fussing over a nest in the eaves of the roof. Presently she heard footsteps in the grass. She turned in their direction and found the Irishman approaching the gazebo with an air of uncertainty.

"Mr. Fogarty, I presume." She smiled in an effort to put the man at ease.

He stepped up into the gazebo and stood awkwardly a few feet away from her bench. "Miss Barton?" he said in a timid Irish brogue.

Elaine held out a hand. "We've never formally met, have we?"

After a moment's hesitation, he stepped forward and shook her hand. "I thank ye for . . ." He gave a helpless shrug and motioned toward the book she was holding. "This."

"Perhaps we should begin now," Elaine said, scooting to her right a bit so he would know he was expected to sit beside her. When he had settled on the bench, she opened the book and held it between them. A drawing of a boy, happily holding a piece of bread, dominated the page. "I will have to see what progress you've already made on your own, Mr. Fogarty. Would you mind reading the words under the picture for me?"

He nodded and took a corner of the book with his work-roughened hand. "The . . . lad . . . will . . . h-a-v-e." His brow furrowed, he worked his lips for a second and then turned to Elaine. "Have?"

Smiling, Elaine nodded, aware that she had been holding her breath as he analyzed the word.

"The lad will have . . . jam . . . on . . . his bread."

"Very good," Elaine said, but Mr. Fogarty was shaking his head.

"I'm knowin' that last word was *bread* because of the picture," he told her. His blue eyes were filled with self-disgust, as if he had cheated in some way. Glancing back at the book, he asked, "Does every page have pictures?"

Elaine could see his point, and she admired his determination to learn without taking shortcuts. "From now on, I'll cover them with my hand," she offered.

He gave her a quick look of gratitude, which unsettled her a bit. She wondered why, and then realized that she had never, to her recollection, sat this close to a man. Ashamed of herself for her schoolgirlish thoughts, she concentrated again on her tutoring. With each page she turned, Logan Fogarty was obviously eager to attack any words that he had not already learned. "Up . . . on the . . . hill . . . t-h-e-r-e . . . there . . . l-i-v-e-d . . ."

Glancing at her watch later, Elaine was surprised to find the hour almost over. The man beside her had read almost half the book. She had had to assist him with very few words, and only after he had exhausted all efforts to figure them out for himself.

"It's time for me to go back inside, Mr. Fogarty," she told him. "We can read the rest of the book tomorrow."

He looked disappointed, but nodded his understanding. Getting to his feet, he reached into his shirt pocket. "I'm grateful to ye for teachin' me, Miss Barton."

"I would prefer if you wait until the end of the month to pay me."

"But the month's almost half over."

"Just add up the days at the end of each month." Suddenly Elaine flushed at her own insensitivity. Of course it would be easier for him to pay every day. Why had she taken it for granted that he could add monetary sums, when he could barely read? "Or if it would be easier for you, I can tell you how much . . ."

"I can do figurin', Miss Barton," he said quietly, then held out a hand to help her to her feet. His actions were nothing more than a courtesy, but Elaine felt herself blush when his great hand closed over hers.

"Of course you can." She tucked the book under her arm, and they walked to the entrance to the gazebo together. She murmured something to the effect that he would very likely finish the book during the next lesson.

For the first time, the tension in his face seemed to ease, and he smiled. "That would be a fine thing. Then what will we read?"

"Something without pictures," Elaine said, smiling back.

17

THE kitchen and servants' hall were the only rooms in the house that Albert had ever seen, so it was with wide eyes that he followed the maid Reanna through the house to the servants' staircase. Just as they got to the landing at the top of the staircase, a lady came out of a door to his left and closed it behind her. Albert recognized her as the same pretty lady who had almost gotten a finger bitten off yesterday, a Miss Price.

The lady walked over to the landing and thanked Reanna, who turned and went back down the stairs. "I wanted to talk with you in private," Miss Price said in a soft voice after glancing over her shoulder at the door she had just come through. "I was just heading downstairs. . . . I didn't expect you to be so early."

Albert clutched his cap in his hands. With a hopeful note in his voice he said, "Should I come back later?"

"No, being early is good." She smiled and held out a hand. "I don't remember if I told you yesterday, but I'm Miss Price, Celeste Harrington's nurse . . . who still has ten fingers, thanks to you."

Albert relaxed a bit at her friendliness, though he still dreaded the thought of playing dolls with a girl. If his salary wasn't so decent for someone his age, he would be out looking for another position this very minute.

"I don't know what you've been told, but we would appreciate your spending some time with Celeste. She has several games that you might enjoy."

"Games?" He relaxed a bit more. "Not dolls?"

"Just games. Do you know how to play any?"

"Yes, ma'am. Lots of games." The only good thing about the orphanage was that every Saturday the children had been allowed to play games. And having spent a year living by his wits on the streets of the city, he had played all sorts of other games with other street urchins. Most had involved dice and money, but he was certain that wasn't the kind of game Miss Price had in mind.

She looked pleased at his answer; then her expression turned serious. "I suppose you've heard that Celeste has epilepsy."

Albert nodded. He had heard it from someone in the servants' hall. The thought of a little girl having a fit right in front of him brought back his discomfort.

"I'll be with her all the time, so you don't have to worry," Miss Price said, as if she could hear his thoughts. "And you mustn't let her condition, or the fact that she is Mr. Harrington's daughter, frighten you into allowing her to win the games. Just play as you would with anyone else."

Albert followed Miss Price into a room that was a cheery version of the school he had once attended, except for the shelves laden with toys and knickknacks. A girl, seated on a small sofa, put down a doll and stood.

Albert had seen Mr. Harrington's daughter only three times in the two months that he had worked here, and always from a distance. She was prettier than he had imagined and not much shorter than he was. But though he was wearing his good clothes, the way she was looking at him made him feel as if he still had on his smelly work pants.

Miss Price turned and laid a hand on his shoulder. "Celeste, this is Albert . . ."

"Hollis," he finished for her.

She smiled. "Albert Hollis. And of course you know this is Celeste Harrington."

He bobbed his head at the girl, and she gave him a superior nod.

"You are already acquainted with Miss Barton."

Albert was glad Miss Barton was there. She wasn't pretty like Miss Price, but her smile was nice, and he found himself sending a cautious smile back.

The girl turned to take a tin box from one of the nearby shelves. "Do you know how to play jacks?" she asked with a raised eyebrow.

"Yes, miss."

"Miss?" said the girl, raising an eyebrow in the direction of Miss Price. "You and I are to be playmates. You must address me as Celeste."

"I don't know if—"

"I insist." The girl then walked over to the far corner of the room and indicated that he was to follow. "We'll have to play here," she said, nodding down at the thirty inches of polished wood floor. "The ball won't bounce properly on the carpet."

She sat down on the floor with her back to Miss Price and Miss Barton, and Albert took his place in the corner across from her.

"You're my guest, so I think you should begin," said Celeste, a little louder than Albert thought was necessary. When he hesitated, she nodded. "Go ahead."

Closing his hand around the tin jacks, he let them fall close by on the floor. He was about to bounce the ball to pick up a jack when he noticed the girl across from him wince, as if in pain.

"Are you—," he began, but she put her finger up to her lip and glanced over her shoulder.

"I have these spells sometimes," she whispered. "But I don't want to worry Miss Price, or she won't let me play." She indicated that he should go ahead and take his turn.

He had snatched up three jacks, one at a time, when the girl winced again. "Don't stop," she said when he held the ball still. With a brave smile, she added, "You were so nice to come and play. . . . Don't mind me. Have you a handkerchief in your pocket?"

Albert nodded and started to bring it out, but Celeste shook her head. "You don't need it now. But if I should have a seizure, be sure to put it between my teeth or I may bite my tongue off."

"Bite your—"

"Don't worry. It likely won't happen if you're quick with the handkerchief." She sighed. "Just watch your fingers, though. I would feel bad if I accidentally nipped you."

The next turn he missed . . . on purpose, but here she was being so nice to him while feeling so sickly.

~

"I have to confess I had my doubts," Elaine murmured to Jenny ten minutes later, as they watched the children from the sofa. "But they seem to be getting along very well."

"I had more than my share of doubts, too," Jenny answered quietly. "Especially when she acted so charming a little while ago."

"Well, she admitted to being bored with the other children."

Jenny nodded. "Mr. Harrington will be—"

"That's my fifth win in a row!" Celeste exclaimed, jumping

to her feet in the corner of the room. Her voice dripping with disdain, she turned to Jenny. "I thought you said this stable boy could play games! Posh! A baby could play better than he does!"

Jenny and the boy scrambled to their feet at the same time. The boy stood in the corner like a trapped deer, his face contorting in anger. "She—," he began, then clamped his mouth shut.

"Celeste, did you order him to allow you to win?" Jenny asked through clenched teeth as she walked in their direction. There was no doubt in her mind that something was amiss. She had watched the girl play jacks with the servants' children, and Jenny knew that Celeste was a lukewarm player, a result of never having had to struggle to win.

"I did not!" the girl retorted smartly. "Just ask him!"

Albert's nostrils flared as Jenny approached. "This girl is crazy!" Snatching his cap from the floor, he slapped it on his head, crossed the schoolroom, and was gone.

Jenny didn't know whether to give chase or scold Celeste. Celeste was closer, so she chose the latter. "What did you tell that boy?" she seethed.

Celeste raised her eyebrows, her expression one of misunderstood innocence. "Why, I didn't tell him a thing, Miss Price." Glancing at the door, she shook her head and with a tone of disapproval added, "Touchy sort, wasn't he? But I suppose some people just can't face up to losing."

"Well, that settles it." This came from Elaine, who had set aside her book and was standing.

Jenny and Celeste both turned to look at the governess. "What do you mean?" asked the girl, but Elaine just ignored her and headed for the door.

"Miss Barton," the girl persisted. "Where are you going?" A hint of worry filled her voice.

At the door Elaine paused and looked back at them. Her green eyes were charged with fire. "I'm going to fetch that boy. Playtime isn't over yet."

~

At the bottom of the stairs, Albert paused for a second to decide which way to go. He had been so full of anxiety when he followed the maid through the house that he hadn't paid attention to the route they had taken. Now he found himself a few feet from a door that he was fairly certain would take him through the kitchen area.

He jerked it open, then saw rows of bookshelves and realized he had gone in the wrong direction. This room was obviously a library, and he could see no passage to the kitchen area. He turned to make his way back to the staircase. When he got there, Miss Barton was just stepping down from the last step.

"Albert, I want to speak with you," she said in a voice that killed his instinct to run.

"Yes, ma'am?" he said, snatching his cap from his head.

"Why did you allow Celeste to win at jacks?"

He tightened his lips. "She tricked me, ma'am. She looked in a bad way, and I thought she would get sick."

Miss Barton closed her eyes for a second. When she opened them, she said, "Yes, she tricked you, Albert. And then she laughed at you."

Albert clutched his cap tighter in his hands. "Yes, ma'am." He had hated being the object of the girl's ridicule, but he hoped Mr. Harrington's daughter had had enough sport at his expense and would never want to see him again. "Can I go back to work now?"

"Your work is upstairs for now, son," she said, not unkindly.

"I don't want that awful girl laughing at me!"

Miss Barton leaned closer, the corners of her mouth turning up into a smile. "She won't laugh if you play to win. You can do that, can't you?"

Albert nodded. Mr. Harrington's daughter had played so badly at jacks that he had to work hard at losing. He could beat her at anything.

"Well then," Miss Barton said, holding out a hand. "Let's go."

Reluctantly, he took the hand she offered and ascended the staircase with her. At the nursery door, Miss Barton gave his hand a squeeze and ushered him inside. "Celeste, Albert has returned to play with you," she said when the door closed behind them.

The girl, who had returned to her dolls, stood, and Miss Price watched from the sofa with a look of surprise. The girl glanced at her nurse and then her governess, then shrugged with what looked like resignation. "Do you know how to play draughts?"

"Yes."

"I always go first. And I always get the black pieces."

He shrugged. "I don't care."

She motioned him toward a draught table and benches, and Albert's sagging spirits lifted a bit when she handed him a stack of white pieces. He had cut his teeth on a draughtboard. And this time when the pained look crossed her face, he ignored it. Within minutes he had captured a stack of her black pieces.

The girl said nothing as they played on, but once in a while he would catch her dark eyes watching him with an unreadable expression. Then, when there were two black pieces left on the board, she put her hand to her heart, let out a cry, and pitched off her bench to the floor.

The nurse was at her side in a second. Albert didn't know what to do, so he got up and backed away from the scene. Was the girl going to die right here in front of him?

After what seemed like hours, Miss Price scooped the now-limp girl up in her arms and took her off to another room. Miss Barton made a move to follow, then stopped and put a hand on Albert's shoulder. "You didn't cause this, you know."

He shoved his hands in his pockets and looked at his feet. Of course he had caused it! She had even warned him, and he had thought she was trying to trick him.

"She has had seizures for most of her life, Albert. And she has known you for less than an hour."

"Thank you, ma'am." He felt some relief at those words. "May I go back to the stables now?"

"Of course."

"Do I still have to come back tomorrow?"

She looked unsure, then nodded. "Unless you hear otherwise."

~

"I take it that Albert is gone?" Jenny asked, coming back into the schoolroom where Elaine was putting the draughts game back in order.

"Yes," the governess answered. "Is she asleep?"

"I believe so." She went over to the bell cord and pulled. Less than a minute later, Gerdie was at the door.

"You rang, miss?" she asked Jenny.

"I did. Would you sit with Celeste while she takes a nap?"

"Another nap, miss?"

"She had a seizure."

When the maid had closed the door to Celeste's bedroom

behind her, Jenny turned to Elaine. "I think she was pretending," she said in a voice barely above a whisper.

Elaine's eyebrows rose. "You do? Why?"

"Have you ever seen anyone's lips when they're trying hard not to smile?"

"Yes. Do you mean . . . ?"

"Twice, I caught her lips twitching."

"You didn't say anything?"

"I'm no match for Celeste when it comes to her seizures. You know how anxious her father is about them. What do you think he would say if Celeste claimed that she had a seizure and I didn't take her seriously?"

Elaine set the remaining draught pieces on the table. "What are we supposed to do?"

"I don't know," Jenny sighed. "It appears that she has won this one. At least today." She smiled at Elaine as she changed the subject. "I never got the chance to ask about your tutoring session with Mr. Fogarty. Did it go well?"

"Extremely well," Elaine answered. "He *wants* to read. I feel like a real teacher again."

~

When Celeste had recovered from her "seizure," Jenny approached her in the schoolroom. "Would you mind if we took a little walk?"

The girl looked over at Miss Barton, who was at the study table writing out lesson plans. "All of us?"

Miss Barton looked up and smiled. "Why don't you two go on without me?"

"How does the terrace sound?" asked Jenny. "It's nice and cool out there this time of day."

Celeste gave a resigned shrug. "All right." Silently they moved together down the stairs and through the house. When they passed through the morning room, the girl stopped in front of the portrait of her mother.

"Do you think I look like her?"

"Oh, very much so," Jenny answered, coming over to stand next to Celeste.

The child sighed, her voice wistful. "She doesn't even know what I look like."

"You don't know that for sure, Celeste. Perhaps your mother is watching you from heaven."

"Would God allow her to do that?"

Jenny paused before answering. "God is very kind. I don't think it hurts to believe that he would."

"I'll ask him tonight, just to be sure."

"You pray?" Jenny couldn't help the surprise in her voice. She assumed the child was too young to be concerned with spiritual matters, yet she herself had become a Christian at the age of ten.

Celeste looked embarrassed. "Sometimes I forget . . . especially if I've done something . . ."

"That you shouldn't have?"

"Yes."

Jenny had to smile. "You know, God forgives if we ask."

"I know." The girl sighed again and looked down at her feet. "It's just that I seem to have to ask a lot."

Touched, Jenny was relieved to know that the girl had a conscience. It was on the tip of her tongue to ask, with as much gentleness as possible, why she felt compelled to do so many things that required later repentance. But Celeste motioned toward the terrace doors.

"I'm ready to go outside now."

The afternoon sun hung low in the sky when the two settled on a wrought-iron bench. Jenny faced Celeste and said, "I have the feeling that you still don't understand why I invited Albert up to play."

Celeste merely turned away to trace the scroll pattern on the bench.

"Celeste?"

"I know why you did," the girl answered, her face still turned from Jenny. "But I just don't like him."

"You hardly know him. Don't you think you should give him a chance?"

"Why should I? I already had friends to play with, and you made them go away."

"They weren't your friends, Celeste. They're nice children, but they were too terrified of you to give you the kind of friendship you need."

The girl turned toward Jenny again and was opening her mouth to answer when a soft noise sounded from behind.

A tall, lanky man stood only four feet away with a pail in one hand and shovel in the other. Two eyes, fringed with thick lashes, traveled from the top of Jenny's head to her shoes. "Didn't mean to startle you, ma'am."

"That's all right," Jenny said.

"Just mulchin' around the plants." His thin lips stretched into a knowing smile, and his voice took on an ingratiating quality that made Jenny's skin crawl. "Got to mulch 'em if they're to grow proper."

Jenny nodded, then turned back to Celeste. "Albert is close to your own age. You probably have a lot in common."

Celeste yawned. "Such as?"

"Well, you both love games, for one—" The noise came again, this time closer and to Jenny's left. She looked up to find the same gardener standing there with the same leer across his face.

"Beggin' your pardon again, ma'am," he said. "I ain't ever seen you around here before. Are you the new nurse?"

"Yes," Jenny replied, her voice tinged with the irritation she was beginning to feel. "Miss Price. Now if you don't mind . . ."

"Yer a pretty little thing to be a nurse, ain't ye?" He took another step closer. "I'm George Welby. You like to go dancin' sometime?"

"What?"

"Dancin'. The ladies all tell me I'm a real good dancer."

Too shocked to answer, Jenny looked over at Celeste. The girl was bent over, her face buried in both hands, her shoulders shaking with suppressed laughter.

The voice went on, undeterred. "I'm sure I could teach you a thing or two if you'd—"

Jenny grabbed Celeste's hand and jumped up from the bench, practically dragging the child back through the French doors. They headed through the morning room and hallway at a rapid pace, but when they reached the bottom of the steps, Celeste balked.

"Wait, Miss Price," she pleaded. The girl was holding her side with her other hand. "Hurts."

Realizing then how fast she had been going, Jenny stopped and gaped at the girl. "Oh dear . . . are you all right?"

"It's just my side," Celeste answered before dissolving into another fit of giggles.

Jenny guided the girl to the bottom step. "Sit down here

until you feel better." Celeste complied, taking rapid shallow breaths and rubbing her side. Seconds later, she looked up at Jenny and grinned.

"Would you like to go dancin', pretty miss?"

Frowning, Jenny snapped, "It wasn't *that* funny."

"Yer a pretty thing for a nurse, ain't ye?"

Jenny opened her mouth to deliver a sharp retort, when a picture of the scene crossed her mind. "He was rather forward, wasn't he?"

"But you never know . . . he *could* very well be a good dancer," Celeste snickered, then clutched at her side again.

Suddenly the absurdity of the situation hit Jenny, and within seconds the corners of her mouth were twitching "You're right about that," she said to the girl.

Celeste's eyebrows shot up. "About what?"

"I'll never know."

The two burst into giggles, so much that Jenny had to sit down on the bottom step with Celeste. When they finally recovered enough to walk up the stairs together, Jenny wiped her eyes and whispered, "If I allow you to beat me at draughts once in a while, will you forget all about this?"

Celeste broke into another grin. "Sorry, Miss Price. This is better than winning at draughts."

18

ARE you really going to have Albert up again today?" Elaine asked Jenny the next morning.

"I think it's the best thing to do," Jenny answered, combing her hair at her dressing-table mirror. Her talk with the girl yesterday had likely been in vain, especially after being interrupted by the gardener, but she could see no other option.

"Even if she refuses to have anything to do with him? She already railed about the boy at breakfast, and you certainly can't *force* her to play with him."

"You're right. But I'm not ready to admit defeat just yet." With a half-smile and a pointed look at the governess, Jenny continued. "I spent a good deal of time last night in prayer about the situation."

Elaine sent her a good-natured smirk. "And I suppose you have the answer."

"I believe so. I just need a minute alone with the boy before he comes up to the nursery."

"And just what do you plan to do?"

Jenny smiled slyly. "I plan to see if he has ever played draughts with a pirate."

~

"You won't lose your job, even if Celeste gets angry."

Miss Price's words were both a reassurance and a torment to Albert as he followed the nurse up the stairs. After the sleepless night he had spent worrying about being fired, the reassurance came as a relief. He liked being with the horses at the Harrington estate, and he felt sure that if he worked hard enough, he could be a regular driver one day, just like Hudson. He also appreciated the fact that he never went to bed hungry and had a decent bed to sleep in. It had been a miracle that he had come across this position, and the likelihood of his finding another at his age was remote.

The torment came from knowing he was still expected to spend every afternoon in Celeste Harrington's company. Better to be with Butch and Stanley, even if they did call him "brat" and occasionally dunked him in the water trough.

Miss Price paused to give him another smile at the nursery door. In the schoolroom, Albert saw Celeste sitting on a stool by the large dollhouse, and Miss Barton in a chair. The governess looked up from her needlepoint. "Good afternoon to you, Albert," she said, smiling.

"Good afternoon, Miss Barton." Celeste hadn't turned from her dollhouse yet, so Albert waited.

"Celeste?" said Miss Price, walking closer to the girl. "Albert is here. Would you like to play?"

There was no answer from Celeste as she continued to move her dolls from one room to another.

Relieved, Albert expected Miss Price to send him back to the stables. But the nurse simply turned back to face him. "Albert, I would enjoy a game of draughts with you."

He blinked and glanced over at the draughts set.

"You don't mind if we use your set, do you Celeste?" Miss Price asked the girl. Stony silence was the reply, so the nurse shrugged and walked over to the set. "I want to warn you, Albert. I intend to win."

In spite of his eagerness to get back to his familiar job at the stables, Albert found himself intrigued by the challenge. Shoving his cap into his back pocket, he went over to pull out a bench for Miss Price. Fifteen minutes later, he had three of her game pieces in a stack on his side of the board . . . and she had three of his.

"Jenny, I believe you've met your match," Miss Barton said, setting down her needlepoint. She got up and brought her chair over to the draughts set.

"Well, the game isn't over yet," answered Miss Price, a little furrow of concentration between her eyebrows. Brightening, she moved her piece diagonally to a promising spot.

Albert was pleased that the nurse had fallen for the trap he had arranged and took the opportunity to make a double leap. The surprise in Miss Price's eyes was gratifying, yet he felt sorry for her because she had been so friendly. Pointing to one of the pieces on her side of the board, he advised, "You could move there and—"

She put a finger to her lips, the furrow growing deeper. "Don't help me, Albert. When I win this game, I don't want you and Miss Barton to say that I cheated."

"I wouldn't say that!" he protested, then realized the nurse was teasing him. For the first time this afternoon, he smiled. It made no difference that the girl hated him, now that he knew she couldn't have him discharged. She was just a spoiled brat who didn't ever have to worry about herself, much less anyone else.

While Miss Price was contemplating her next move, he glanced over her shoulder at Celeste. The girl sat rigid as a statue at her dollhouse, but it seemed from the back that her posture had changed. Was she listening to them as they played? For just a second Albert felt sorry for her. She seemed so small and lonely against the backdrop of the huge dollhouse, and—

"Albert?"

He blinked and looked at Miss Price.

"It's your turn."

A quick glance at the board told him she was still following the strategy she had played since they started the game. He made a move that would force her to a certain square, thereby setting himself up for another double leap.

The game was finished ten minutes later. "I wish we had time to play again," Miss Price said, leaning happily back in her chair.

Miss Barton raised an eyebrow. "Even though you lost?"

"Ah, but the chance to watch a genius at work was worth losing."

Albert felt his cheeks grow warm with a mixture of embarrassment and pleasure. "I'm not a genius at all."

"You're too modest, Mr. Hollis."

"You know," Miss Barton remarked offhandedly as she helped gather the game pieces, "I'm rather good at draughts myself."

"Then you two should play tomorrow," said Miss Price. "I'll be your audience."

"Perhaps." Miss Barton glanced to her left, at Celeste's back. "But if anyone *else* would rather play, I certainly wouldn't mind stepping aside."

Celeste made no comment, but, her spine stiff as a ramrod, sat with her back to them all.

~

The next day, when Elaine had left for her tutoring session with the gardener and Celeste was down for her nap, Jenny thought about taking a walk in the garden. A picture of George, the gardener, came immediately into her mind, and she opted instead to take advantage of Mr. Harrington's offer to use his library. There were still several unread books in the bundle her parents had sent with her, but the idea of browsing through shelves and shelves of books again was inviting.

Father often said that you could know a person's character by what he liked to read. On her way downstairs, Jenny found herself wondering what character assessment she would make about Mr. Harrington. *Strong head for business . . . self-assured . . . except where it concerns his daughter.*

Jenny had often thought about their last conversation just three days ago, before he left for Liverpool. It was flattering that Mr. Harrington put so much stock in her advice concerning his daughter. Frightening, too—what if she was wrong? *Lord, keep me walking in your wisdom and not my own,* she prayed silently.

Jenny was just reaching for the knob on the library door when it was pulled open from the other side. A little cry sounded, then Beryl Courtland stood in front of her. "Oh, Miss Price!" she breathed, her hand over her heart. "You startled me."

Jenny's heart pounded rapidly. "I'm sorry, Miss Courtland. I didn't realize anyone was here."

"We're seeing about the final arrangements for Mother's tea,"

Miss Courtland said with a nod over her shoulder, where Jenny could see an older woman conversing with Mrs. Ganaway. "You can't take for granted that servants will carry out your plans exactly as you've instructed." Her pretty features arranged themselves into a disdainful expression. "Especially Graham's servants. He allows them far too much latitude, in my opinion."

If a subtle insult was intended, Jenny chose to ignore it. Something told her that there was no chance of this woman ever liking her, much less accepting her as an equal. Staying as far away from her as possible seemed prudent, although she didn't know how that was going to be possible once Miss Courtland became mistress of the house. "I hope you have a pleasant tea," she said politely before turning to leave.

"Miss Price."

Jenny turned back around. "Yes?"

"I was just going up to the nursery to speak with you." Jenny waited for her to continue, and the woman frowned thoughtfully. "We really should have Mr. Harrington install a bell for you. What does he do when he wishes to have a word with you?"

The insult was in no way subtle this time, and Jenny swallowed the sharp retort on the tip of her tongue. "Perhaps you should ask Mr. Harrington."

Miss Courtland went on as if she hadn't heard. "It is hardly fitting for him to have to send someone upstairs to fetch you, when he has so many important things on his mind."

"What do you wish to speak with me about, Miss Courtland?"

"Oh, yes." The woman's perfect features brightened. "Mother would like Celeste to attend her tea this afternoon. Would you have her dressed appropriately by four o'clock? Something in pastel with a bit of lace would be appropriate."

"I'll have her down here at four," Jenny answered.

"Perfect! By the way, I don't think it's necessary for you to attend the tea with her. As long as you're upstairs where we can find you if she has a seizure, I don't think we'll have to worry." Giving Jenny a curt nod of dismissal, the woman turned and went back into the library. The door closed behind her with a final click.

Staring at the closed door, Jenny clenched her jaw and entertained a brief mental fantasy of taking a casual stroll into the library and telling Miss Courtland that for all her beauty and refined ways, she had the graciousness of a pig!

~

"Light," read Logan Fogarty, after staring at the last page of the reader for several seconds. He looked up at Elaine. "Just like *night,* except for that first letter there."

Elaine nodded. "And *fight, sight,* and *right."*

The gardener's face lit up. "So if we put a *b* and *r* together in front, it would say *bright."*

"Very good. Try the *f* and *l* now."

Without hesitation he answered, *"Flight."*

"Can you think of any more with two letters together?"

He was quiet for a long time, his brow tensed in concentration, and Elaine began to wonder if she should have given him such a difficult challenge. She was opening her mouth to assist him when Mr. Fogarty held up a hand. "Please don't be helpin' me," he said gently, his brow still furrowed. After a span of several more seconds, he turned to her and smiled. *"Fright, plight, slight.* And one every gardener should be knowing—*blight."*

Elaine smiled back. "Right."

On her way back to the house when the hour was up,

Elaine marveled over the almost childlike eagerness with which Mr. Fogarty approached his lessons. Very unexpected from a man so muscular and rugged looking. *A gentle giant,* she thought, and as she walked through the morning room, she found herself wondering if he had a wife. Immediately she chided herself for the thought. Whether he was married or not, he was her student, nothing more.

And he's not blind.

~

"Oh, you *have* to braid my hair!" Celeste exclaimed when Jenny told her she was invited to Mrs. Courtland's tea in the library. As soon as the words were out of her mouth, she amended them. "I mean . . . will you please braid my hair?"

Jenny smiled and helped the girl slip on the dress she had worn this morning. "I believe we have a little time before Albert gets here to do that. But let's save putting on a fresh dress until after playtime." She spoke the words casually, hoping Celeste wouldn't raise a fuss.

But the girl made no comment at all concerning playtime. "I wonder if you could weave in two ribbons at the same time?" Celeste said on the way to her dressing table. "My pink dress has white lace, so what about pink and white ribbons?"

"I believe I could do that," Jenny answered, disappointed in the girl's continued indifference toward Albert. "But if you have a bit of white lace, that would look even nicer."

"Lace *and* ribbon?"

"We could try it."

The dimple appeared in Celeste's right cheek as she fished around in the top drawer of the dressing table. "I can't wait to see how it looks!"

Jenny picked up the brush and set to work on the girl's hair. She decided that, even though her earlier effort had been ignored, she had to take advantage of Celeste's rare good mood. "Wouldn't you like to play with Albert today, Celeste? He's very nice."

The dimple disappeared. "I would rather play with my old friends."

"But you said more than once that they were boring."

"They let me win, though."

Jenny parted the girl's hair into three sections at the crown of her head. "Why is that so important to you?"

"It just is," was the clipped reply. Changing the subject, Celeste held up a pink ribbon and white strip of lace. "Tell me when you want me to hand this to you."

Elaine came through the door from the schoolroom. "I didn't realize it was so late."

"It's not late," Jenny told her. "Celeste woke up a few minutes early." She wanted to ask the governess how the tutoring session with the Irish gardener had gone, but she had a feeling Elaine wouldn't want to discuss it in front of Celeste.

"Ribbon and lace braided together?" Elaine said, coming closer.

"Just an experiment. Celeste has a tea to attend this afternoon."

"It looks rather nice together." The governess smiled at Celeste in the mirror, but the girl's face was strangely expressionless. "You must be wearing your pink dress to the tea."

Jenny nodded, her fingers continuing to braid the girl's hair. "She's going to look—"

"It makes me feel smart," Celeste cut in, her face still without emotion.

Trading puzzled glances with Elaine, Jenny leaned closer. "What did you say, Celeste?"

A small frown worked its way onto the girl's brow. "I feel smart whenever I win at games."

Jenny set down the brush and sighed. How could she explain to this child, whose brown eyes now followed her every move, that lasting feelings of worthiness couldn't come from manipulated success? "Don't you know how bright you are?" she asked in a gentle voice.

Celeste looked unsure, but answered, "Miss Beryl tells me all the time how smart I am."

"Well, there then," said Elaine. "Don't you believe her?"

"Of course," was the girl's immediate answer. "Miss Beryl never lies to me."

There was a knock on the schoolroom door. "That must be Albert." Elaine headed for the door.

"Good afternoon, Albert." Elaine's voice drifted in from the schoolroom.

"All finished," Jenny said to Celeste. Impulsively, she gave the girl's shoulders a squeeze. "Miss Courtland is right," she whispered. "You're very bright."

"Yes," Celeste whispered back. In the glass, her dark eyes locked on Jenny's for a moment. The spell was broken when she reached for the new hand mirror on the dressing-table top. "I look nice," she said, studying her hair from different angles.

"I'm glad you like it."

"I do." Celeste gave her a small smile. "But I'm still not going to play with Albert."

Sure enough, today's playtime was almost identical to yesterday's. Celeste played with her dollhouse, keeping her back to Elaine and Albert at the draughts table. Jenny was disconcerted to find that Elaine was a much better draughts player than she was. Still, the stable boy was winning.

She wondered if Albert got any enjoyment out of the sessions. It hadn't even occurred to her to ask if the boy would want to play with a twelve-year-old girl every afternoon. Could he be bothered by Celeste's cold shoulder?

Jenny looked over at the girl. Celeste still sat at her dollhouse, yet had hardly played with her dolls during the ongoing draughts game. She wondered about the girl's admission that she needed to feel that she was smart. True, Celeste was a lukewarm student, but obviously not from any lack of ability on her part. As much as Jenny disliked Miss Beryl Courtland, it was good to see that she was doing something positive with the girl

Or was she? Jenny's mother, always with a perceptive eye for the empty phrases and flattery that seemed to be in vogue these days, was fond of saying, "He who compliments everyone compliments no one." It stood to reason that a child who was praised for every little thing she did would after a while begin to doubt the flatterer's words.

The door from the hallway opened, and Doris, one of the downstairs maids, stepped into the room. "Beggin' your pardon, but I've got letters for Miss Celeste and Miss Price," she said, handing them over to Jenny.

Celeste was at Jenny's side in an instant. "It must be from Father!" she exclaimed.

"I believe so," said Jenny, handing the letter to the girl. Celeste tore open the envelope and took out a single sheet. Her face glowed with happiness as she read the words out loud.

> *My darling daughter, I pray every day that you are doing well. I miss the dimple in your cheek, and I long to pick you up and spin*

you around. I hope to return to London on Tuesday or Wednesday. Remember to listen to Miss Price and Miss Barton. Your loving father.

"I'm going to put this in my box with my other letters," the girl said as she disappeared into her room.

Jenny smiled at Elaine and Albert, then looked down at the envelope still in her hand. *Miss Jenny Price* was written in a masculine, orderly script.

"Perhaps we should continue our game now," Elaine said to the boy.

Celeste came out of her bedroom and over to the draughts table. "Aren't you going to read your letter?"

"In a little while," Jenny replied, slipping it into her apron pocket. Even though the letter likely contained some employer-to-employee instructions, it was addressed to her alone, and she felt uneasy about reading it out loud.

"I read mine to you," Celeste said with a bit of a whine, but when Jenny just smiled at her, she shrugged and went back to her dollhouse.

When Albert was gone, Elaine said, "I'll help Celeste get ready for Mrs. Courtland's tea. Why don't you go into the other room for a while?"

Jenny smiled appreciatively at her. Touching the envelope in her pocket, she went into the sitting room, took a seat on the sofa, and opened her letter. The contents were on a single sheet, like Celeste's, and written in the same masculine hand.

Dear Miss Price,

It was necessary for one of my employees to make a trip to London to retrieve some papers, so I asked him to deliver these letters.

Jacob Wallace's widow is holding up well. She is a strong Christian woman whom I believe you would admire.

My business here should be concluded by the seventeenth, and I look forward to learning if you have had any progress with Celeste. I am aware that her will has been strengthened by years of overindulgence, and that you likely have a battle on your hands. I regret that I am not present to assist you with this, but I am presently making arrangements that will allow me to spend more time at home.

My prayers are with you constantly, Miss Price.

Sincerely,

Graham Harrington

Jenny reread the letter, then slipped it back into her apron pocket. *My prayers are with you constantly.*

For a brief moment, Jenny wondered if she had done anything with the girl that would make Mr. Harrington proud. She had had no success in coaxing Celeste to play with Albert. On the other hand, she had not thrown a temper tantrum since her father had left. Would Graham Harrington view that as progress?

Keep praying, Mr. Harrington, she thought. *We all need it.*

19

"I HOPE you have a lovely time," Miss Price said after escorting Celeste to the open library door. Too anxious about her appearance to pay her nurse any mind, Celeste nodded and reached to touch the braids at the back of her head. Miss Beryl met her as soon as she walked into the library. Her father's fiancée smelled like jasmine and looked exquisite in a peach-colored gown of soft fabric that floated about her like a cloud.

"My dear Celeste!" she cried, opening her slender arms to embrace her. "You must come and meet all of Mother's friends!" Miss Beryl took her by the hand and introduced her to at least a dozen women, most of whom seemed to be as old as Mrs. Courtland. They were all standing, gathered in a loose circle around the table where the leys jar now sat. Mrs. Courtland brightened upon seeing her, spouting phrases in French as she kissed both of Celeste's cheeks.

For the rest of the afternoon the older woman ignored her. Celeste preferred it that way. She stayed at Miss Beryl's side, and when it was time to sit and have refreshments, Celeste took a chair next to her. Soon the women drifted into little groups so that they could indulge in the real purpose of their gatherings, which was to find out or pass along the latest gossip.

Even Miss Beryl participated, turning away from Celeste so that she could talk with two haughty-looking older women. Both of them wore rouge and had hair piled high upon their heads. Celeste supposed the women were Mrs. Courtland's sisters, or best friends. She munched on shortbread and little sandwiches and was rapidly growing bored, when Miss Beryl turned back to her. "Are you having a good time?"

"Yes," she lied. She tried to think of something to talk about that would interest Miss Beryl so that she wouldn't turn away and talk with the other women again. "Father will be home Tuesday or Wednesday," she said brightly.

It worked, for Miss Beryl gave her an indulgent smile. "Are you sure about that? I thought he would be away for at least two weeks."

Celeste nodded, wishing she had brought the letter downstairs with her. "He sent me a letter today. Miss Price, too."

The smile faded from Miss Beryl's face. "Your father sent a letter to Miss Price?"

"It was hardly fair of her to keep it to herself. After all, I read mine out loud."

After a few seconds of silence, Miss Beryl motioned toward the door and whispered, "Why don't we slip away to the conservatory for a chat? I doubt if anyone would notice our absence."

Celeste could barely contain her excitement. After pausing at the tea table to grab a handful of biscuits, she followed her father's fiancée out of the library.

The conservatory was Celeste's favorite room, next to her own. In the winter it was always deliciously warmer than the rest of the house, and now, in late summer, the abundance of greenery caused the temperature to remain cool. They walked inside and admired the canaries for a little while, then sat down on one of the white cast-iron benches.

"Would you like a biscuit?" Celeste asked, digging in her pocket.

Miss Beryl smiled and shook her head. "You go ahead and have them." Then she asked Celeste if she remembered what time the letters arrived.

It only took a second for her to figure it out. "About half past two. Albert was still there."

Miss Beryl frowned. "I went home to change my clothes about that time. It seems that if a letter had been sent to me, I would have received it soon after that."

"I don't know." Celeste chewed slowly. Maybe she shouldn't have mentioned the letters. Perhaps Miss Beryl was hurt because she didn't receive one. Celeste felt panic beginning to rise up in her. Surely Miss Beryl wouldn't be angry and call off the engagement! "Father must be very busy in Liverpool."

The effect was not what Celeste had desired, for Miss Beryl's lips tightened. "Yet he had time to write to your nurse."

"I don't think it was a long letter. Mine was only a page. He's very busy—"

"Yes, I know," she snapped. As soon as the words were out, Miss Beryl gave her an apologetic smile. "I didn't mean to lose my temper at you, dear. I'm just a bit concerned about your Miss Price."

"Because she has a letter from Father?"

"Oh, not because of that." She clutched her gloved hands together in her lap and sighed.

"Miss Beryl?" Celeste touched her arm.

"I'm sorry, dear. Perhaps we should return to the library. I'm not very good company for you right now."

"I shouldn't have mentioned those silly letters," Celeste worried out loud. The unhappiness in Miss Beryl's face made her want to cry.

"Oh, please don't blame yourself." Miss Beryl gave Celeste a sad smile, then reached over to pat her hand. "I have been worried ever since that nurse came here."

"You have?"

After still another sigh, she said, "Do you remember the night that Miss Price had supper with us?"

"The day I went to the zoo. Father's first night back."

"That's right. Well, when he came for me in the coach, all he could talk about was how bright the new nurse was. It seems they had a heated argument, but then your Miss Price convinced him that you weren't being raised properly."

Celeste's mouth fell open. "Miss Price said *that?"*

"Didn't you know?"

She shook her head, but at the same time she realized that soon after Miss Price came, Father had asked the servants' children to stop allowing her to win when they played. He had put the nurse in charge before leaving this time, too. Not even Mrs. Ganaway had ever had that much authority over her. Why hadn't she made the connection before?

"And do you recall when your father took us in the library to look at that jar?" Miss Beryl's eyes were blazing now. "All I did was refer to *her majesty* as a servant, and your father scolded me afterward. It was a mere slip of the tongue, yet he overreacted as I've never seen him do before. How could I have known? When I was a child, we treated my nursemaids no differently than the rest of the servants!"

"Father was angry at you because of Miss Price?"

"Yes, but that isn't my main concern." The anger in her

face turned to sadness as she looked straight into Celeste's eyes. "It's *you* I'm worried about. Your father has never given any of your former nurses as much authority over you as he has Miss Price. I believe she's looking forward to the day when she can have complete rule over you."

Celeste couldn't help the laugh that burst from her lips. "Miss Price? Why, I could have her sent away tomorrow if I really wanted to!"

"But didn't you want to have her sent away the day you argued at the zoo?"

"Well, yes . . . for a little while. But I was angry."

"And yet your father kept her on. And plans to do so indefinitely, it seems." Miss Beryl tilted her elegant face to study Celeste. "But then, perhaps you don't *mind* having Miss Price as your nurse?"

"Of course I do," Celeste answered right away, because that was the answer Miss Beryl seemed to want. But then she remembered Miss Price telling her that she was bright . . . and seeming to mean it! She braided her hair, and she even laughed with her after the encounter with that awful gardener. Life had not been so boring since Miss Price had come.

True, she had been given more authority than any other nurse had been given, but so far the only major change Miss Price had made was to invite Albert up to play. Though Celeste felt compelled to fuss about the boy's intrusion into her playtime, she *had* been getting terribly bored with the other children. And Albert was rather . . . interesting, even if he was only a stable boy.

"Celeste?"

She looked up at Miss Beryl, who was now dabbing at her eyes with a handkerchief. "You don't have to worry about me," Celeste said, reaching up to touch her shoulder. "Miss Price hasn't been *that* terrible."

Miss Beryl winced and was quiet for several seconds. When she finally spoke, her voice was uncharacteristically flat. "There is . . . something else that disturbs me."

"There is?"

After a sigh and another pained look, she said, "I wasn't going to mention this, but I strongly suspect that the reason Miss Price wants to have control over *you* is that she hopes to use you to ingratiate herself with your father."

"Ingratiate?"

"She wants to look good in his eyes so that he'll want to marry her instead of me."

The very idea struck Celeste as hilarious, but it was obviously not funny to Miss Beryl, so she restrained a laugh. "Miss Price? Why, she isn't nearly as pretty as you."

"She's pretty enough. And she is *here* all of the time. In fact, I came across them chatting cozily in the library before your father left."

"But Father is engaged to you."

"We aren't married yet, dear. And Miss Price has that wide-eyed, unsophisticated air that men like your father find themselves attracted to."

"But why?"

Miss Beryl frowned again. "Remember my telling you once that men are like little boys? They swagger around like pretend soldiers and are only too happy when they come across some modest little milksop of a woman who pretends to need rescuing."

The description of a milksop didn't seem to fit Miss Price, but nonetheless Celeste nodded in agreement. Miss Beryl knew far more about these things than she did.

"I hate burdening you with this, dear, but London is full of women whose goal is to marry a wealthy man like your father." She paused for a breath, then turned sad eyes upon Celeste and said with a broken voice, "I do believe your Miss Price has designs upon him."

A tumble of confused thoughts and feelings assailed Celeste—chief among them, an acute sense of betrayal that Miss Price was not what she seemed. Had all of the concern the nurse professed for her welfare been just an act? Guilt surged through her too, for not having recognized the hurt that Miss Beryl was feeling.

"What should we do?" she asked over the lump at the back of her throat.

Miss Beryl dabbed at her eyes again. "I suppose there is nothing we can do but hope that your father will realize what kind of woman Miss Price really is." Taking a long breath, she added, "The sad thing is, most men are blind to women like her."

"Then we'll tell Father, and he'll send her away."

"Oh, we can't do that," Miss Beryl said with a quick shake of the head. "Unfortunately, that would only make your father think I'm jealous, which would just make Miss Price look even more attractive to him. Surely we can think of something else."

The answer came to Celeste then, and she wondered why she hadn't thought of it sooner. And it was in her area of expertise, which made it all the more appealing. "What if she were to leave on her own?"

Miss Beryl was looking at her with new interest on her face. "Whatever do you mean?"

"What if Miss Price were so unhappy that she couldn't stand it here anymore?"

"You mean . . . you would do things to her?"

Celeste began to feel like a heroine from one of the novels that Miss Barton was always pressing her to read. "I could," she replied with a little smile.

To her surprise, Miss Beryl shook her head. "I simply cannot suggest that you do that."

"Why not?"

"Because it would be wrong."

"But isn't it wrong to try to steal someone's fiancé?"

Miss Beryl thought that over for a few seconds. "Even so, it's rather risky. It wouldn't work if Miss Price was aware of what you were doing. She would only go to your father."

"But what if she had no proof?"

"No proof?" Shock, mixed with admiration, filled Miss Beryl's dark-blue eyes. She picked up Celeste's hand and squeezed it. "You're a clever girl . . . do you know that?"

~

Jenny had never had the time or the patience for needlework, but she enjoyed watching Elaine's progress on her tapestry panel. Flowers of all colors stood out against a dark-blue background. "What will you do with it when you're finished?" she asked the governess.

"A pillow, I believe," Elaine answered. "Of course I shall have to work on the other side when I've finished this one."

They sat in the nursery sitting room—Jenny in the chair, and Elaine on the settee. Celeste had been gone to the tea for over an hour now, but they knew not to expect her back anytime soon.

"You should save it for when you get—" The thoughtless words were out of Jenny's mouth before she could stop herself.

Her cheeks grew warm at her own insensitivity. It was highly unlikely that the governess would ever marry, and they both knew it. Jenny lowered her head, wondering if an apology would make matters worse.

"Jenny," came Elaine's soft voice from the sofa. "You don't have to be embarrassed."

"I didn't mean . . ."

"I know." The governess squinted at the needle she held in front of her eyes. "A long time ago I accepted the certainty that I will remain a spinster for the rest of my life." Once the needle was threaded she asked if Celeste had mentioned any plans for Saturday, two days away.

"She hasn't mentioned anything so far," Jenny answered. It was obvious that Elaine had changed the subject in an attempt to lessen the embarrassment Jenny felt over her flippant remark, and she shot the governess a grateful glance. "How was your second tutoring session with Mr. Fogarty?"

Elaine did not look up from her needlework, but a smile played at her lips. "Mr. Fogarty. It's so rewarding to teach someone who wants to learn."

"You love teaching that much?"

"As much as you love nursing."

"Sometimes I don't even like nursing . . . much less love it," Jenny confessed. "Other times I think I'm the most blessed woman in the world."

"It's the same way with me about teaching."

The sound of a door opening and closing came from the schoolroom. "Go ahead with your needlework," Jenny said, stretching as she got to her feet. "I'll see if Celeste is back." She walked through their bedroom and into the schoolroom to find the girl showing Miss Courtland some of her dolls. The two looked up at her, but neither said a word.

"Oh, I didn't realize you had company," Jenny said to Celeste. She gave a nod to Miss Courtland, then turned to leave. On her way back through the bedroom, she imagined she caught the sound of a smothered giggle. Jenny immediately dismissed the thought as ludicrous.

Later, Celeste drifted into the sitting room and dropped down next to Elaine on the settee. "I had such a lovely time!" she exclaimed. "When I grow up, I'm going to have at least one formal tea every week."

"Were there many guests?" asked the governess.

"Several. But I spent most of my time with Miss Beryl." Celeste then turned to Jenny, an enigmatic smile on her lips. "You can't imagine how fascinating she is. My father thinks she's the most wonderful lady in the world."

Jenny forced herself to look interested. Though there was a smile on the child's face, she was obviously trying to make some point. Jenny just didn't feel like trying to figure out what it was or why. "How lovely," she replied as politely as possible.

"He would never want to marry *anyone* else."

"Of course not."

After supper, Jenny took her bath while Elaine tucked Celeste into bed. She dried herself and put on a nightgown, enjoying the feel of the clean cotton fabric against her skin. With her hair bound up in another towel, she walked into the nursery sitting room, where Elaine now sat with a book.

"What are you reading?" she asked the governess as she pulled a comb through her damp hair.

"Around the World in Eighty Days."

"Ah, Jules Verne."

The governess raised an eyebrow. "You know it?" She shook her head. "Of course you do. I keep forgetting your family background. It must have been interesting to work in a bookstore."

"It was." Jenny yawned. "I didn't realize until now how sleepy I am. I shouldn't have washed my hair."

"You'll catch cold if you go to bed with it wet."

She yawned again. "I'll have to take that chance. I don't think I can keep my eyes open much longer."

"Well, bundle it up in a towel and go to bed then," Elaine said good-naturedly as she covered her own yawn with a hand. "You have me doing it now."

Jenny laughed and got to her feet. "I'm on my way." But she didn't go to the door right away. Instead she walked over to Elaine's chair and gave her shoulders a quick squeeze.

The governess blushed a little—obviously embarrassed, but pleased. "Why did you do that?"

"I just like you. You're quite pleasant to be with."

"So are you." Elaine gave her a shy smile. "I almost feel as if I have a sister."

Her heart warming at the compliment, Jenny bade her new friend good-night and started for the bedroom. As she drew back the covers of her bed, the thought occurred to her that she and Elaine could truly be sisters . . . if only they shared the same Father.

~

The next morning, Jenny woke to find her hair disheveled and limp from going to bed with it damp. While Elaine dressed behind the screen, Jenny sat at the mirror and arranged her hair into a chignon so that the stringiness would be less noticeable.

She put the last of the pins in her hair, then opened the top drawer of her nightstand to get her locket. The box was empty.

Her hand went automatically up to her neck. *Didn't I put it in here last night?* On the verge of panic, she rummaged through the drawer, and then the one beneath it.

"Jenny?" came Elaine's voice from behind the screen.

"It's me," she said, closing the bottom drawer. "I seem to have misplaced my locket."

"Were you wearing it before you had your bath last night?"

Jenny gave a relieved nod. "I'm sure I was. I must have taken it off in the lavatory."

The lamp was still burning in the windowless room. She glanced at the washbasin first, not really expecting to find it there or she would have noticed it when she washed her face and brushed her teeth. The open shelves of the linen cupboard were the logical place to look. After scanning every inch, she got down on her hands and knees to peer under the bathing tub. When the locket didn't turn up, she turned over the reed laundry basket in the corner and shook out every piece of clothing in it. Now the panic came full force, and she searched the room again.

On leaden feet Jenny walked back into the bedroom and came upon Elaine, on her knees peering under her bed. "I assumed you didn't find it when I heard you moving things around in there," the governess said as she got back to her feet. "Let's move the nightstand out and look behind it."

The search proved futile, and Jenny sat on the edge of her bed and wiped at her eyes. "I don't mean to be so childish about this, but it was a gift from my family."

"It will turn up," soothed Elaine, coming over to sit beside her. "We'll ask the maids to keep an eye out for it."

"Breakfast is here," trilled Celeste's voice from the open doorway. The girl walked through their bedroom to the sitting room with Reanna in her wake, carrying a tray.

"Let's go have a bite to eat," Elaine suggested. "Perhaps you'll think of where you left it. Celeste may even have seen it."

The girl seemed sympathetic, but said that she had no idea of the locket's whereabouts. "We had some trouble with mice once," she said, applying a liberal spread of butter to her bread. "Perhaps one took your locket to his nest."

"Perhaps," Jenny answered without enthusiasm, studying the girl's face.

"Why are you looking at me like that?" Celeste asked a second later, raising an eyebrow as she held the butter knife poised over her plate.

She could have taken it last week, but she brought it to me instead, Jenny reminded herself with a twinge of guilt. The toast felt like sawdust in her mouth.

After breakfast she and Elaine and even Celeste searched for the locket again. "It couldn't have walked off by itself." Elaine lifted a rug to peer underneath.

"Sometimes things turn up in shoes," said the girl, on her knees in front of Jenny's open armoire. "I once found some marbles I had been missing in the toe of one of my slippers. Turns out I had hidden them there and forgot about them."

Jenny dumped the contents of her reticule and then her cloth bag on her bed and fished through them in vain. "I appreciate your help," she said to Elaine and Celeste as she got to her feet. "But isn't it time to start your lessons?"

Elaine glanced at the clock on the chimneypiece and gave a reluctant nod. "You're right. It's time for school."

"Oh, I'd much rather do this than go to school," Celeste

spoke up from the bottom of Jenny's armoire. "Besides, it's best to look for things when you first notice they're missing."

In spite of her disappointment, Jenny was touched by Celeste's helpfulness. *Shame on you,* she scolded herself once more. *Suspecting a child.*

~

"I have done one b-r-a-v-e-r . . ."

Elaine held the open reader between them and waited, and sure enough, after a while Logan Fogarty looked up at her and said, *"Braver?"* When she nodded, he repeated the words he had just read softly to himself. "I have done one braver."

He looked at her again. "And what might a braver be, ma'am?"

"First finish the line, and you'll see."

Taking a long breath, Mr. Fogarty spelled out, *"T-h-i-n-g."* The Irishman stared at it for a while, then shook his head. "It can't be *ta-hing."*

"No," Elaine answered. "Remember that the *t* and *h* together make a separate sound."

Mr. Fogarty chewed on his lip for a bit. *"Thing. I have done one braver . . . thing."*

"Very good."

He turned to Elaine, a shy smile creasing the corners of his eyes. "Thank ye, ma'am. Have we time to finish the poem?"

A light rain was beginning to pelt the roof of the gazebo—Elaine knew that it could very likely turn into a deluge within minutes. A sensible woman would start for the house, but she found herself answering, "More than enough time."

They worked through the words together until he was sure

of all of them, and then he took the book from her hands, cleared his throat and read:

I have done one braver thing
Than all the Worthies did,
And yet a braver thence did spring,
Which is, to keep that hid.

When he was finished, he set the book on his knee. "It has a lovely sound to it. . . . What does it mean?"

"Well, it was written by John Donne. It has to do with modesty."

Mr. Fogarty picked up the book and studied it again. "Modesty. So he's sayin' that even though he did somethin' brave, it took more courage to keep it to himself?"

"Yes. Exactly."

"What sort o' brave thing did Mr. Donne do, that he didn't boast about it?"

"I'm not sure. It could be any act of courage." She thought for a second and said, "Such as, what you're doing now."

He looked surprised. "What *I'm* doing?"

"Learning to read."

"Ah, but it don't take courage to learn to read."

Elaine smiled and ignored the incessant patter of the raindrops overhead. "It takes courage to decide to learn anything. What if you were to fail?"

"It would about kill me," he answered right away.

"Some people refuse to attempt anything new for that very reason." Impulsively, she said, "You're a brave man, Mr. Fogarty."

The man beside her flushed and lowered his head, and Elaine wondered if he had gotten the wrong impression—that she was flirting with him. *What in the world were you thinking about?* she chided herself.

She was just about to apologize for her bluntness when Mr. Fogarty said, "Few around here would call me brave, Miss Barton."

There had been no self-pity in his voice, only the flat tone of a factual statement. Elaine recalled what Mr. Horton had said about the other gardeners making sport of this gentle man, and anger tightened her throat.

"Mr. Fogarty, there are those who attempt to accomplish things, and those who sit with their hands in their pockets and ridicule. Which of these has the most courage?"

He didn't answer her question, but gave her a grateful smile. "Thank ye, Miss Barton. I will remind myself of that every time it needs rememberin'."

Thunder rumbled in the distance, and the man peered with obvious surprise at the curtain of light rain that surrounded them. "My word, ma'am. I was so caught up in the readin' that I didn't pay the weather no mind."

Rising from the bench, Elaine walked to the edge. The spray felt refreshing on her face. "It's still not coming down very hard. I believe I can—" She felt a faint touch on her sleeve and turned. Mr. Fogarty was standing there, and he motioned toward the bench.

"Ye don't need to be gettin' wet, ma'am. We've some oilskins in the cottage. Would you mind waitin' here so's I can fetch one for ye?"

The offer was one that almost any civilized man would make to any woman, yet Elaine had had precious little experience with such acts of chivalry. Moved almost to tears by this act of consideration, she sat down and watched the big Irishman set out in the rain.

20

When Albert arrived at the schoolroom that afternoon, Jenny held her breath, waiting for the explosion. But Celeste actually seemed pleased to see the boy. "Hello, Albert," she said sweetly, glancing up at the sound of rain against the roof. "I hope you didn't get soaked out there."

The boy's startled eyes flitted to Elaine and Jenny. "I borrowed Mr. Ramsey's umbrella," he answered with just a bit of caution in his voice. Jenny couldn't blame him. Albert was learning, like everyone else who came in contact with the girl, just how short-lived her good moods could be.

"Would you like to play a game?" Celeste asked.

"You *want* to play with me?"

"Draughts, if you don't mind. And I wonder if you would be so kind as to teach me how to play as well as you do."

"I can teach you." The boy nodded.

"Good!" The two walked over to the draughts set, and the girl listened attentively to all of Albert's instructions. Jenny forgot her book and watched, delighted that Celeste seemed eager to learn. Elaine, beside her on the sofa, watched as well.

After a while, Celeste stretched her arms in front of her.

"This is great fun," she said to the boy, "but I feel like walking around for a bit. Have you ever seen our conservatory?"

"I haven't," he answered.

She got up from her bench and motioned for him to do the same. "You will love watching the birds." Then turning to Jenny and Elaine, Celeste smiled. "We shouldn't be too long."

"Take as long as you like." Jenny set her book aside and stood. "But I'll need to go with you."

The girl's smile wavered just a little. "Nothing is going to happen to me. If it does, Albert can come and fetch you."

Jenny could understand any child's desire to have some privacy with a friend. In fact, she often thought that Mr. Harrington's rule about having someone hovering over the child every minute of the day was going too far. And the likelihood of Celeste having a seizure during that short trip was remote. But there was a bit too much eagerness in her expression. What if she was up to something? A glance at Elaine told her that the governess was thinking the same thing.

"I'm sorry, Celeste. You'll have to allow me to tag along."

Elaine stood. "We can all go. I haven't been down there in a while."

"Oh, joy," Jenny heard Celeste mutter on her way to the door.

~

Celeste hurried through her supper in the nursery sitting room, causing Miss Price to remark that the air in the conservatory must have given her an appetite. She had agreed with all politeness, but in truth could barely stand to look at the nurse without clenching her teeth.

How easy it would have been to talk Albert into delivering the note! For all his skill at draughts, the boy was piteously gullible. But she had had no chance with the two women watching her every move.

"I'm going into the schoolroom," she announced as she pushed her plate away. Stretching her lips into a smile, she said, "I would like to play with my dolls alone for a little while before bedtime."

"All right," Miss Price said, smiling back. "We'll peek in on you once in a while, but we'll try not to disturb you."

"Thank you." When Celeste had closed the schoolroom door behind her, she grabbed a couple of her dolls and brought them to the study table. After another quick glance at the door, she drew out two folded pieces of paper and opened the first. Her own handwriting stared back at her.

Dearest George,

I think you are very handsome. Will you meet me at midnight on the terrace? Perhaps I would like to go dancing after all.

With warmest regards,

Miss Price

She would have to wait until tomorrow to find another way to deliver this first note. There was always the possibility that whichever maid sat up with her tonight would fall asleep, but she was too afraid of the dark to venture outside alone.

Sighing, she unfolded the second note, printed on a piece of coarse brown lining paper she had taken from the bottom of one of her dressing-table drawers. She smiled down at the sloppy, crude lettering.

Deer Miss Price

I fownd your loket but am afraid to bring it to you because they will think I stoll it. Will you meet me at 12 oclok tonite on the terace? Plese dont show anybode this note.

From a friend

Celeste frowned and took a pen and a bottle of ink from the desk drawer. Even as messy as the note was, it wouldn't do to have Miss Barton get hold of it. The governess was likely smart enough to take one look at the lettering and guess its authorship. With the pen Celeste underlined *anybode.*

If only Miss Beryl were here to see this, she thought, slipping the notes into envelopes. *Wouldn't she think I was smart!*

"Is everything all right in here?" Miss Price's voice came from the door. Celeste shoved the notes back into her pocket, picked up a doll, and turned to smile.

"Fine."

"Would you like a story at bedtime?"

Celeste was opening her mouth to decline the offer, but she did so enjoy Miss Price's stories. "Yes, I would like that," she answered instead. *I might as well hear them while I can,* she thought, surprised at the tug of regret that she felt inside. But she consoled herself with the thought of how happy Miss Beryl would be when Miss Price was gone.

~

Jenny came out of the lavatory Saturday morning to find Reanna standing in front of her dresser, peering into an open drawer. The laundry had been delivered Tuesday, so she wasn't quite sure what to make of the girl's activity.

"Reanna?" she asked, walking closer.

The maid looked up with a start, but did not seem alarmed when she saw that it was Jenny. "Oh, hello, Miss Price. Sorry to be in your way."

"Can I help you find something?"

"I hopes not, miss. If I finds it, I gets to keep the whole fiver myself."

"The fiver?"

"Didn't you know?" She cocked her head in the direction of Celeste's room, where Elaine was helping the girl dress. "Miss Barton promised us upstairs maids five quid to whoever finds your locket for you. I hope I finds it first, so's me and my sisters can make new dresses for the fair."

Jenny stood there, openmouthed. The girl obviously misunderstood her surprise, for now she was saying, "Don't you know about the St. Mark's fair? I wasn't here last year, but Alma tells me that the master gives the whole household the day off, and an extra half sovereign to spend on refreshments and the like!"

"No, I didn't," Jenny managed to answer.

"I s'pose you'll be wantin' to dress now," said the girl, turning toward the door. "But I'll be sure to come back later and look. That locket's as good as found, miss."

Jenny slipped a uniform dress over her head, wondering what to make of the maid's words. Elaine was saving for her future, had even agreed to tutor one of the gardeners for extra money, and here she was willing to give away a substantial sum for something she couldn't keep?

She was touched—and saddened. The more affection she felt for Elaine, the more she was reminded of her friend's lost spiritual condition . . . and the more she was aware of her own inadequacies. Surely a stronger Christian would have made Elaine understand her need for a Savior by now.

"Oh, you're up?" A voice cut into Jenny's thoughts, and she turned to the door. Elaine stood there in a jade dress that accented her eyes.

"I have been for a while," Jenny answered. She walked over to the governess and gave her a quick embrace. "Reanna was in here searching for my locket. She told me about the reward. Whatever made you do such a thing?"

"They weren't supposed to tell you about it," Elaine answered with a frown. "I just couldn't stand the thought of your family heirloom being lost like that."

"Well, if anyone finds it, I'll pay the—"

"No, you'll sit down right now and brush your hair, that's what you'll do. I don't want to go on about this all morning. Five quid is worth not having you mope around for days."

Jenny started. "But I haven't moped, have I?"

Elaine was already pulling out the dressing-table bench for her, a little smile on her face. "There is always that chance now, isn't there?"

~

In the schoolroom, Celeste listened to the muffled voices from next door as she paced the carpet. She had excused herself early from breakfast so that she could speak privately to Gerdie, but the girl hadn't shown up to clear the breakfast dishes yet.

Reaching her hand into the pocket of her robe, she touched the sharp edge of an envelope. It had seemed like a good idea to go ahead and put the gardener's note in an envelope, just in case Gerdie was a snoop and could read. She considered ringing for the maid, but what reason could she give Miss Price and Miss Barton?

Just then the doorknob turned on the door leading to the hallway, and the maid walked in with an empty tray.

"Gerdie!" Celeste exclaimed softly.

The girl looked frightened and lowered her head. "Yes, miss?"

With a glance back at the other door, Jenny brought the envelope out of her pocket, along with a coin. "How would you like to earn a florin?"

"A florin, miss?" The chin came up a bit.

"I'll give it to you right now." Celeste grinned and slipped the coin into the maid's apron pocket, along with the envelope. "Do you know George? He's one of the gardeners."

The girl gave an unenthusiastic nod.

"When you go for lunch in the servants' hall, I want you to give this to him. Don't let anyone see it . . . do you understand?"

"Do I have to, miss?" she asked, her lips quivering with timidity. "He's . . . a bad sort, that one. Mrs. Ganaway says that we maids ain't supposed to talk to him."

"All you have to do is slip him the letter."

"But what if he can't read?" Gerdie asked, obviously grasping for any straw.

Celeste paused. She hadn't even considered this. The gardener had seemed rather witless, come to think of it. "Then surely he'll be curious enough to have someone read it to him," she finally hissed. "But don't dare tell him who gave it to you, or you'll be dismissed before the night is up." Giving her most threatening scowl, she said, "Do you understand?"

The maid's face blanched. "I understand."

"Good!" Celeste glanced back at the door, then drew a folded piece of paper from her pocket. "And I want you to give this to Miss Price when you go in to clear the dishes. But you mustn't tell her that I gave it to you."

"But what if she asks me, miss?"

She had expected this question and had a ready answer. "Tell her you found it on the staircase and saw her name on the outside. You can read, can't you?"

The maid's head bobbed. "I can, miss."

"Then just do as I said." With another glance over her shoulder, Celeste motioned the maid over to the hallway door. "I want Miss Price to be alone when you give it to her. Leave the door open a crack and wait outside—you can go into the sitting room when you hear me come back in here."

Celeste turned and walked through Miss Price and Miss Barton's bedroom to the sitting room. Both women looked up from their teacups.

"I'm sorry to disturb your breakfast," she said in her most polite voice. "But, Miss Barton, would you mind coming into the schoolroom for just a minute?"

"I was almost finished anyway," the governess replied, getting to her feet. But before walking away from the table, she turned to Miss Price and said, "Now, what was that idea you said just came to you?"

At the door, Celeste tried not to look impatient when Miss Price sent back a mysterious smile. "It has to be a secret for now. First I have to see if it's possible. As soon as I finish my tea, I'll go see if arrangements can be made."

To Celeste, she said, "You haven't made any plans for today, have you?"

"No." Celeste shifted on one foot and turned to Miss Barton again. "Will you come with me now?"

"Of course." The governess followed her through the bedroom to the schoolroom. "Now, what is it I can help you with?" she asked, looking around the room as if she expected some sort of problem to manifest itself.

"I can't find that book you wanted me to read," Celeste said, louder than necessary as she motioned toward the shelves. "You know, that American book, *Little Women."* On cue, Gerdie came through the door and sailed through the room with her head lowered.

Miss Barton tilted her head. "You need it this very minute?"

Managing a wounded expression, Celeste answered, "Well, you've been telling me I should read it for a week now. I should think you would be pleased."

"All right, let's look for it." The governess walked closer to the rows of storybooks and peered at them for a minute. "Perhaps it got mixed with your schoolbooks. Have you searched there?"

"My schoolbooks?"

Gerdie walked back through the schoolroom again, this time with a loaded tray. She sent a quick nod in Celeste's direction.

"You know, it may be there at that," Celeste said. She peered underneath the study table and caught sight of the book . . . exactly where she had placed it only minutes ago. "Well, here it is!" she exclaimed and held the book up for the governess to see.

~

After reading the note twice, Jenny folded it and slipped it back into its envelope. *Why would someone be afraid to give the locket to me?* she wondered. For that matter, if someone were so desperate to return it and not be accused of stealing, why not simply enclose the locket in the envelope with the note?

Then she remembered Elaine's reward. *That has to be why.* Hearing footsteps coming from the other room, she stuffed the note into her apron pocket. *If this note is real,* Jenny told herself, *I don't want Elaine spending her own money to get my locket back.*

She was just getting up from the table when Elaine walked into the sitting room, flanked by Celeste. "Are you going to tell us what you're planning?" asked Celeste. There was a grudging anticipation in her expression, as if she hated having to ask but couldn't deny her own curious nature.

"I'm just about to see about the arrangements," Jenny answered. She went into her bedroom and slipped a starched apron over her uniform, tying the apron strings as she headed down the stairs.

Thirty minutes later she was back in the nursery schoolroom. "Put on your bonnets and let's go downstairs," she told Elaine and Celeste.

"The garden?" asked the governess.

"I can't tell you yet."

The excitement in Celeste's eyes faded. "I don't feel like playing in the garden."

"Not the garden," Jenny sighed, reluctant to give away her secret just yet. "Out front."

The three walked down through the house to the front door. Before opening it, Jenny wheeled around to face Celeste. "I want you to know that, as your nurse, I would never allow you to do anything that would hurt you. You know that, don't you?"

"I suppose," Celeste said impatiently. She stood on the toes of her slippers and tried to peer over Jenny's shoulder.

"But even crossing the street has its risks," Jenny went on. "The trick is to be careful, no matter what we're doing, and use common sense."

"All right," the girl sighed. "I'll be careful. Now open the door . . . please."

Jenny sent a smile laden with mystery to both Celeste and Elaine, then opened the door. There, right in front of the house, waited Mr. Harrington's curricle. Albert sat holding the reins to two placid-looking horses.

Again, Celeste looked disappointed. "I can go for a ride any Saturday. What's so fun about that?"

"The fun part is that you're going to *drive.*"

The girl's eyes widened. *"Me?"*

"Just around the carriage drive today, but for as long as you like."

"But what if I have a seizure?"

"We'll catch you," Jenny answered matter-of-factly. "You'll be seated between Albert and Miss Barton, or Albert and me. We'll take turns." She turned to Elaine. "Is that all right with you?"

The governess looked doubtful, but her eyes sparkled with interest. "I'll sit here on the front lawn and wait for the second turn."

Celeste walked over to the carriage, but hung back at the side when it came time for her to climb in beside Albert.

"Couldn't I sit between you and Miss Barton instead?"

"You enjoyed Albert's company yesterday," Jenny whispered back. "Why would you ask such a thing today?"

"I just don't feel like sitting by him."

"Well, if you want to drive, you'll have to. You've hurt that boy's feelings enough."

The old fire came into the girl's dark eyes, but the anticipation of actually driving was stronger, and she allowed Jenny to help her to the seat. Jenny got in beside her and smiled at Albert. "Ready?"

With a solemn nod, the boy handed the reins over to Celeste. The wide-eyed girl held them stiffly out in front, as if she were afraid they might bite her. "You just have to give them a little flick and cluck your tongue," Albert advised.

"Cluck my tongue?"

"Don't you know how?"

Celeste's chin raised to a haughty angle. "Of course I do." Then lifting the reins almost imperceptibly, she called out, "Cluck-cluck."

Jenny gave way to a burst of laughter. While Celeste sent her a smoldering glare, the boy next to her seemed to be struggling to suppress a smile.

"I don't think I want to do this after all," the girl seethed.

"Oh, let's not be so serious," Jenny admonished in a pleasant tone. "And allow me to show you how to cluck your tongue." Softly, so as not to stir the horses, she ran her tongue along the roof of her mouth to produce a clicking sound. "Now, just give the reins a little flick and try it."

With a look of intense concentration, the girl worked her mouth until the sound came out. She let out a little cry when the vehicle jerked forward. "Albert! What should I do now?"

"Just hold on till we reach the end of the drive," he advised. "Then I'll show you how to turn."

They went around the long semicircular carriage drive, stopping at the street to look for other carriages. When the way was clear, the horses turned to the right and walked several hundred feet to the other end of the drive. After four or five trips around, Celeste had relaxed considerably and was holding the reins in a more natural position. "How do I make them go faster?" she asked Albert.

Albert sent a panicked look to Jenny, who vetoed that idea right away. "It's Miss Barton's turn now," she said as they neared the front of the house again. "Stop when you get to where she's sitting."

Elaine took several turns with the children while Jenny sat on the steps. When it came Jenny's turn again, Celeste said, "Let's go to Hyde Park! I can take us there." On Saturdays, Rotten Row, on the south end of the park, was the favorite place for London's elite to show off their carriages and horses.

"You're not ready for that yet," Jenny and Elaine replied in unison.

Celeste's face fell. "What about Holland Park?" While much smaller and less prestigious than Hyde Park, it was only two blocks away.

"I don't think so," Jenny said as she climbed up into the seat. "There are four of us, and only room for three in here."

Elaine, standing beside the curricle, reached up to touch Jenny's hand. "I really would enjoy some time alone," she said softly. "Why don't you go on ahead?"

Jenny leaned down closer to the governess. "Do you think Mr. Harrington would mind?"

"I don't think so . . . not with you and Albert watching her like that. If you don't mind waiting a bit, I could go ask Mrs. Willis for some sandwiches so you can have a picnic. The ground seems to have dried up from yesterday, but I can send out a quilt as well."

"Oh, let's do that!" exclaimed Celeste. "We can keep going around the carriage drive until you get back."

"Are you sure you don't mind?" Jenny asked Elaine, but the governess had turned toward the house before she could even finish the sentence.

"I don't mind at all!" came Elaine's answer as she made her way up the front walk.

Celeste drove remarkably well the two blocks to Holland Park. She did not become flustered at passing vehicles, but kept her eyes steady on the street just in front of the horses. "I can't wait to tell Father about this!" she exclaimed, her cheeks flush with excitement.

Gratified to see the girl look so happy, Jenny could only hope that Mr. Harrington wouldn't disapprove. She would never compromise Celeste's health, and even now she sat poised to grab the girl should she have a seizure. Sitting high in the seat, she pushed back her bonnet and allowed the August sun to bathe her face. *Carpe diem,* she told herself, remembering her Latin from school. *Sometimes we have to seize the day!*

~

At Holland Park, Celeste tried to walk after Miss Price helped her to the ground, but she was alarmed to discover that her legs were weak. "Why can't I walk straight?"

Albert, tying the horses to a stout birch limb, answered for her. "You aren't used to driving, miss. It takes a lot out of you at first. You'll be all right in a minute."

Celeste giggled and took a couple of wobbling steps. "Looks like I've been down to the gin house!"

Miss Price froze with the picnic hamper on her arm. "Celeste!"

The shock on her nurse's face made Celeste laugh again. "Well, I seem to remember *your* telling jokes about cigars."

"I shouldn't have done that." There was pain in her expression now. "I've gone and set a bad example for you."

"Not at all. In fact, I can remember your saying something a little while ago that set a good example for me."

"I did?"

Celeste had to struggle to keep from giggling again. "Back at the house. You said `Let's not be so serious.'"

Miss Price gaped at her for several seconds, then began to laugh as she realized that she was being teased. Celeste found herself joining in, while Albert stared at the two of them with a bewildered expression.

They found a shady spot under the low boughs of an oak tree, and Miss Price spread the quilt. Later, as Celeste picked up sandwich crumbs from her napkin with the tip of her finger, she tried to imagine her father's face when he found out that she had driven the curricle. She stretched happily and wondered when she had ever had so much fun.

A pair of fashionably dressed ladies passed on the nearby path. Celeste sat up with a start, for one carried herself in a familiar way. On second inspection, Celeste noticed a cascade of dark brown curls from behind the lady's hat, and she sat back with a sigh of relief.

How could she have forgotten all morning that Miss Price was the enemy? What if that had been her father's fiancée on the path? She was glad that Miss Beryl hadn't been around to hear her laughing with the nurse. What would she have thought? Would she even have second thoughts about wanting such a disloyal child for a daughter?

At least she'll be happy when I tell her about the locket. The thought was some consolation. Miss Beryl would think she was so clever for having used her comb to push the locket into the narrow space between the bottom of her armoire and the floor. The piece of furniture was too heavy for the maid to move during the regular cleaning, and the space was too small to sweep underneath.

Did Miss Price even suspect that she had taken it from the lavatory? Whether she did or not, it didn't matter, for she had no proof. *And she'll never find it, either.* A nagging guilt hovered at the edge of her consciousness, but Celeste suppressed it. Nurses were in high demand, and Miss Price could easily find a better job somewhere else, where no one played tricks on her. In a way, she was doing Miss Price a favor.

"Albert, how did you become so skilled at draughts?" Miss Price was asking the boy.

Albert actually blushed, then answered, "We had contests on Saturdays at the . . . charity home. On weekdays I would practice different moves in my head."

"How long did you live there?"

"Since I was three, but I don't remember anything before that."

Celeste, overcome with sympathy for Albert, exclaimed, "You poor boy! You mean your parents are dead?"

His answer was a curt nod, then he got to his feet. "I'd better see about the horses."

It disturbed Celeste that the boy had looked so stricken. When he was gone, she asked Miss Price if she had been too blunt.

"No, of course not. You were very kind to show him some sympathy."

Celeste couldn't remember anyone *ever* telling her that she was kind. The words warmed her heart, and she wished she could hear them again. She looked up at Miss Price. "Do you really think so?"

"Yes, I do." The nurse smiled back at her, then got to her feet and brushed at her skirt. "I believe I should go speak with him. Would you mind packing up the hamper?"

"All right—" Forcing herself to remember her mission, Celeste closed her mouth and worked her face into a hard stare. "On second thought, do it yourself. I'm not your servant."

21

WHEN Logan Fogarty had finished washing the dirt from the potatoes he had dug this morning, he spread them in the grass to dry. The air was heady with the scent of damp soil, and the sun felt good through his shirt. He worked fast, whistling an old tune his mother used to hum in her rare happy times. By the time he had set out the last of the potatoes, the first were dry and ready to be sacked. He walked over to the dry spot by the gate where he had set the stack of burlap sacks, but they weren't there.

Scratching his head, he searched around the area, but to no avail. No one was in sight who could have taken the sacks, either. There was nothing to do but go to the gardening cottage and try to find out what had happened.

Inside the cottage, he found George and Healy sitting on opposite sides of a stack of burlap sacks, a deck of cards between them. "Well, if it ain't the dummy comin' to visit!" George smirked.

"Just put your callin' card in that silver tray over there," Healy piped in with a spray of saliva. "We'll 'ave the butler announce you directly."

His jaw tight, Logan glanced over at the stairs.

"If you're lookin' for Mr. Horton, he had to go to his cottage and get some rest." George shuffled the cards while shaking his head in mock sympathy. "The gout and all, y'know?"

"But we told him we'd carry on, like good soldiers," said Healy. "By the way, Mick, 'ave you brung the potatoes down to the cellar yet?"

"I need the sacks," Logan mumbled.

"Eh?" Pretending to have something in his ear, George cocked his head and hit one side with the heel of his hand. "I believe the dummy tried to say somethin'!"

A shadow fell across the doorway, and for an instant there was fear in the two gardeners' faces. But then Logan turned to find Dudley behind him, a pint of ale in his hand. The young gardener had never made sport of him like the others, so Logan was relieved to find an ally.

"I need the potato sacks," he said to Dudley, hoping the young man would reason with the other two.

But he shrugged and spat instead. "And I needed the money you was givin' me for readin' lessons."

Logan's mouth parted in surprise. Dudley had had to be talked into agreeing to the lessons in the first place and had actually seemed relieved when told very tactfully that they were over. Obviously George and Healy had teamed up to stir resentment in the young gardener.

The potatoes were not supposed to be out in the hot sun for too long, or they wouldn't keep the winter. With no hope of any support from anyone, Logan turned back to the two men on the sacks. His old nature, the one that threatened to reassert itself occasionally, urged him to bang their heads together like a pair of cymbals. He clenched his fists at his sides. Life would be so much easier if he didn't have to turn the other cheek constantly.

Immediately he felt shame for the thought. *You allowed them to nail you to a cross, Lord,* he prayed silently. *How can I be faithful if I'm not willin' to follow your example?*

All three gardeners were watching him with smug expressions. Though it was one of the hardest things he had ever done, Logan turned on his heel and left the cottage. The hair prickled on the back of his neck at the hoots and laughter inside the cottage, but he did not slow his pace. Circling around to the right, he went to the crates stacked against the back wall and loaded as many as he could into his arms. He would have to bring the potatoes to the cellar in crates, then transfer them to sacks whenever he had the chance to get them.

As he worked, he made sure to breathe a prayer for Mr. Horton. It was a shame that the other gardeners took every chance they could to shirk their duties. Mr. Horton was a decent man, but his illness prevented him from giving the supervision necessary for the likes of George and Healy.

From the corner of his eye he caught some distant motion. Straightening, he recognized Miss Barton on her way to the gazebo with a book under her arm. She was too far away to notice him, and even if she had, he would be too bashful to wave. Nonetheless he smiled at the thought of the patience she had shown during his lessons, and the comforting warmth of her voice.

~

As Celeste sat erect in the seat and steered the curricle back toward home, Jenny wondered at the change that had come over her. The girl had been so thrilled on the way to the park, but now she seemed almost bored with her new adventure. *Why did she even insist upon driving back?* she thought. Albert could have easily taken the reins again.

She sighed, causing Celeste to glance in her direction. The smile Jenny sent back was ignored. *Elaine was right,* she told herself. *I've got to stop assuming that I have this child figured out.*

~

Celeste opened her eyes when pain invaded her dream about horses and carriages. The dimness of the room told her that the hour was late in the afternoon, yet she couldn't remember lying down for a nap. Her head throbbed unmercifully, and she turned on her pillow to find Miss Price standing beside her bed.

The nurse put a cool hand on her forehead. "How do you feel, dear?"

In spite of her headache, Celeste remembered Miss Beryl and said, "I'm not *your* dear."

A look of pain briefly washed over Miss Price's face, but still she smiled. "Is it your head?"

Celeste winced. "Did I have a seizure?"

"You don't remember?"

"No."

"It happened in the schoolroom," Miss Price explained. "You were playing with your dolls."

She remembered just a little, then.

"Would you like me to rub your forehead?"

It was on Celeste's lips to say no, but then she remembered the cool touch of the nurse's fingers on her forehead. Surely Miss Beryl would understand. "Yes," she whimpered.

Miss Price immediately began massaging with her fingertips. "Would you like a story, too?"

Celeste shook her head and mumbled, "Hurts too much to pay attention." After a moment of thought she added, "But would you mind humming something?"

"Hum? You mean sing?"

"No words, just hum. You know, something that sounds soft."

"All right." Miss Price began humming a tune that Celeste vaguely remembered from church. The fingers on her forehead moved in little circles, and the tune was soothing. *This must be what it's like to have a mother,* she thought as she drifted back to sleep.

22

WHEN I was a girl, someone told me if I ate lots of pickles my hair would become curly," Jenny said idly, moving the peg three points ahead on the cribbage board. Now that Celeste was in bed for the night, Elaine and the nurse were involved in a game in the nursery sitting room. "I ate so many pickles that I can't stomach the taste of them to this day."

"Did it work?" Elaine asked, then gave a little laugh. "Well, I suppose that's a silly question. Your hair is still lovely though— nice and shiny. You'll be the envy of every woman in church tomorrow."

"I would hope that no one goes to church to envy someone else."

Why did I have to bring up church? Elaine scolded herself. She knew right then that she should switch to another subject, but she found herself saying, "I'm sure people go for all sorts of reasons."

"Elaine." Jenny looked up at her. There was no condemnation in her gray eyes, only sadness. "Do you really believe that?"

"Take me, for example. I'm every bit a hypocrite. I go only to keep my position here."

Setting her cards facedown on the table, Jenny leaned back on the sofa. "May I ask you one question?"

Elaine sighed. "Why do I have a feeling that this is going to involve religion?"

"Because you're very perceptive," the nurse answered. "Just one question?"

"All right. But just one."

"How can you go to church every Sunday and not believe in God?"

"You mean, why haven't the sermons affected me?"

"Exactly."

"It's quite simple." Elaine shrugged. "I simply don't listen." It was not entirely the truth, but she couldn't allow Jenny any encouragement or she would never stop trying to convert her. Many times she caught herself following the words of a sermon, envying the simple faith that the people seated around her seemed to possess. If only it were true—that there was a wise, benevolent deity who had the time to care for *her*. She wouldn't even mind the judgment part if she could be assured of the love.

"How is it possible not to listen?" Jenny was asking.

Elaine shook her finger in a mock scold. "Didn't we agree to just one question?"

"One more? Please?"

"All right." Elaine let out another sigh. "I daydream. I think about the week's lesson plans, books I've read . . . whatever strikes my fancy."

"In church?"

"Don't tell me you've never daydreamed in church before."

"Yes," Jenny admitted. "I've daydreamed in church sometimes. But it's not my usual practice."

Elaine shook her head. Jenny was a dear, but she could be so exasperating! "Well, it is mine. Now, if you don't mind, I don't feel like answering any more questions about religion." She laid her cards down with a flourish. "Ever."

Jenny straightened and looked across at her with serious gray eyes. "I will respect that, Elaine." Her tone was gentle, even loving, and Elaine immediately regretted her earlier flippancy. "But I wish to say one more thing." Before Elaine could open her mouth to protest, the nurse held up a hand. "This isn't a question, but something I've observed. Will you permit me to say it?"

Elaine settled back in her chair and folded her hands in her lap. Perhaps it was good to clear the air right now and have it done with, then the subject could be closed indefinitely. "All right," she answered in an even tone.

"You've told me that you're an atheist, and I'm sure that you believe it to be so. But you aren't."

"I'm not?" Elaine couldn't help but smirk. "What am I, then?"

"Someone who is angry at God." Jenny's serious expression did not waver. "And you can't be angry at someone you don't believe exists."

"And why would I be angry at God?"

"I don't know. Perhaps because of your grandmother, or your parents' deaths, or even that you caught smallpox as a child."

Elaine's jaw tightened. "That's ridiculous."

"Is it?" Raising an eyebrow, Jenny said, "Tell me . . . do you believe in Father Christmas?"

"Father Christmas? Of course not."

"Well then, do you purposely 'daydream' whenever you

hear little children talking about him at Christmas, as you do in church? Would you become defensive and angry if someone questioned you about him?"

Elaine shifted in her chair, conscious that the room was becoming uncomfortably stuffy. *Tell her you won't listen to any more of this,* she reprimanded herself. *Tell her she's getting too personal.* Yet how could she take issue with Jenny, the first person in a long time who seemed to really care about her? "You know the answer to that," she said evasively.

Jenny nodded. "Of course you wouldn't become angry, because you *know* with all your heart that Father Christmas doesn't exist. But whenever I speak to you about God, it seems to touch a nerve." Jenny seemed unaware that tears were now glistening in her eyes. "In the process of punishing God for whatever wrong you feel he's done you, you're punishing yourself as well. It saddens me because I know where all this bitterness will end."

Elaine blinked, then realized her own eyes were moist. "I don't care to continue this conversation," she said, getting to her feet.

Rising as well, Jenny wiped her cheek with the back of her hand and said, "If I've hurt you . . ."

"You haven't hurt me," Elaine said over her shoulder on her way to the room they shared. "I'm just tired and want to go to sleep." She froze in the doorway at the thought of Jenny standing there crying for her. Turning, she managed a half smile for her friend. "Good night, Jenny."

~

After the door closed, Jenny wiped her eyes again and wondered if she had been too aggressive. She certainly didn't want to chase Elaine even farther away from God. *Speak the truth in love,* echoed in her mind, one of the sayings from the Bible that her mother was fond of quoting. Yet had it done any good?

She could hear her mother's voice again. . . . *A seed can sprout in the hardest ground. Sometimes it just takes a little longer.*

Jenny waited until she was sure that Elaine was in bed before she went into their room. In the dim light of the lamp the governess had left burning for her, Jenny quickly gathered her book and nightgown, took a five-pound note from her purse, then walked over to the lampstand.

"Jenny?" came Elaine's voice from the sudden darkness.

"It's me," she whispered back. "I'm going to read for a bit."

"The light won't bother me if you'd like to read in here."

Smiling to herself in the dark, Jenny was relieved that there was no reproach in her friend's voice. "I plan to be up for a while," she answered. "The sofa in the schoolroom is comfortable." Actually, the settee in the sitting room was far more comfortable, but that room was out of the question. In order to leave at midnight she would have to come back through the bedroom and disturb Elaine.

She felt her way through the next room in the dark, then lit the lamp and settled down with her book to wait . . . wondering why this note writer couldn't have picked a more civilized hour to turn in her locket.

~

At the sound of soft footsteps, Celeste shifted on her pillow. She knew instinctively who was in the next room.

"You're still awake, miss?" Reanna asked from the Windsor chair, where the maid sat with her needlework in the dim light of the lamp. "Do you want me to fetch your nurse?"

"No," Celeste replied, turning to her side. "What time is it?"

"It's half past ten, miss."

Celeste closed her eyes and thought about her dolls, the parrots at Regent's Park, the new dress being made for her to wear. Anything to keep the image of Miss Price and George, that horrible man, out of her mind. But try as she might, she could not quiet the small voice that begged her to send for the nurse and confess her misdeed. She opened her eyes and looked over at the closed door. *Or I could tell her I had a nightmare. She would stay in here with me then.*

But what would she say the next time she saw Miss Beryl? What if Miss Beryl *asked* what she was doing to make Miss Price want to leave? Would she think that being rude and hiding a locket were enough?

Turning to her other side, Celeste pulled the pillow tighter under her neck and squeezed her eyes shut. There was always the possibility that her plans wouldn't work out. *Maybe Gerdie didn't even give him the note.*

~

Big houses seem so empty in the dark, Jenny thought as she walked away from the staircase on the ground floor. At least a dozen people were asleep under the same roof, yet she couldn't help but feel an eerie sense of loneliness . . . which wasn't helped by the misshapen shadows her candle threw against the wall beside her.

It's worth it to have my locket back, she reminded herself. *I'll never leave it lying about again.*

She slipped through the morning room, turned the latch on the French doors, and walked out to the terrace. The air was pleasantly cool and heady with the scent of green things, and so many stars shone overhead that Jenny blew out her candle. Feeling better than she had in the dark house, Jenny drew in a deep breath, sat down on the closest bench, and waited.

Presently she heard footsteps to her right. Turning, she was aware of the figure of a tall man in the distance, coming in her direction from the gardening cottage. Her hand went up to her neck. How would a *man* be in possession of her locket? *Could the catch have broken when I was out in the garden?*

Jenny became aware of the quickened pace of her heartbeat. *Something isn't right.* She jumped up from the bench and started for the house. The French doors of the morning room were only a few feet away—she was reaching out to take one of the knobs when a hand grabbed her arm, pulling her to a stop.

"Where are you goin', pretty miss?" came an oily, familiar voice close to her ear. "Forget your dancin' shoes?"

Jenny took a deep breath and turned to face the man she now recognized as George. "Do you have my locket with you?" she asked hopefully . . . just in case.

"Locket?" He grabbed her other arm, a leering smile creasing his face. "Don't know about no locket. How's about we take a little walk, you and me?"

"You didn't send me a note?"

"A note? You're the note sender, miss. And I'm right glad, I am."

A chill snaked down Jenny's spine, and she felt herself shrinking under his lecherous gaze. "I-I didn't send you any note."

"Turnin' bashful, are you?" the gardener crooned, his hands tightening around her arms. "Don't worry yerself, pretty miss . . . old George knows how to treat a lady."

Mute with fear now, Jenny struggled to get away. The

hands released her for an instant, but before she could turn and run, arms encircled her like a vise.

"So, you like to play games, huh?"

"Let go of me!"

"Not till we has our dance, love." A pair of lips came crushing down on Jenny's mouth, choking off her breath. In her panic she was vaguely aware of the sound of a door to her left.

"You leave her alone!" a woman's voice ordered.

The arms around Jenny loosed immediately, and the man backed away. Her knees weak, Jenny turned to find the governess standing there in her robe, a brass poker brandished threateningly over her shoulder.

"Elaine!"

Elaine shook the poker at George. "Get away from her!"

He held up both hands in a placating gesture. "But we was just—"

"Now!"

The next thing Jenny saw was George's back as he beat a hasty retreat. Letting out a cry, she fell into Elaine's arms. "Oh, thank God you came!"

"Now, now," Elaine soothed, patting her back. "He's gone now."

~

"How did you know I was out there?" Jenny asked the governess a few minutes later. She sat at the kitchen worktable while Elaine lit a match to kindling and set the teakettle on the stove.

"I couldn't sleep," the governess answered, looking through the massive cupboard for some tea leaves. "Ah, here they are," she said as she took down a tin container.

"Did I wake you, walking about in the schoolroom?"

Elaine shook her head. "The things you said to me . . ." Embarrassment crept into her expression. "Some of them made sense."

"They did?" Jenny perked up for the first time since her ordeal with George had started.

"Some of them, I said." Elaine brought two cups to the table and set them down in front of Jenny. "I heard you close the door to the hallway about midnight, so I got up to see what was going on. Your nightgown and book were there on the sofa . . . along with a piece of paper."

Jenny shivered and rubbed her arms. It seemed she could still feel the gardener's grip upon her. "The note."

"I didn't realize what it was until I had read a few words," the governess explained. "Or I wouldn't have snooped."

"Thank God you did!"

"Yes," agreed Elaine, folding her arms. "Because by then I had recognized the author."

"George, you mean."

"Celeste."

"Celeste?" Jenny felt her cheeks grow hot. "Are you sure?"

"I'm positive. And if we check all the drawers in the nursery, I'll wager we'll find some lining paper missing."

After a moment's thought, Jenny said, "George told me that I had sent *him* a note."

Elaine shook her head and moved over to the stove. "Our little princess has been busy, hasn't she?"

Unable to speak, Jenny watched her friend bring the kettle over to the table. After Elaine poured her tea, Jenny put both hands around her cup. The warmth was pleasant, unlike her thoughts. "How could Celeste do such a thing?"

"I don't know. I wouldn't have thought even her capable of anything so mean."

The girl is trying to get me to leave, Jenny realized. *She hasn't wanted me here from the first day.* Unlike the tantrum at the zoo, this incident had taken some advance planning. What other plots were going on in that twelve-year-old mind? She took a sip of her tea, then looked at Elaine. "I don't want to mention what happened tonight in front of Celeste."

Elaine looked up from stirring her tea, a frown of disapproval at her lips. "Why not? It's quite a serious matter. What if George would have . . . ?"

"This is something Mr. Harrington should handle. Besides, I don't care to listen to her denials."

"I don't see how she can deny it. We have the note."

"Please?"

"All right," the governess sighed. "But you're definitely going to tell her father."

"Yes," said Jenny, her voice dull. "And I'm going to tender my resignation at the same time."

Elaine set down her cup with a thud, then winced when some of the tea spilled onto her hand.

"Are you all right?" Jenny asked, reaching out for her hand.

"It was just a drop," she answered, waving Jenny's hand away. "I'm more in shock over what you said."

"I've got to leave, Elaine. I'm only making Celeste worse."

"That's not true." The governess leaned forward, her green eyes almost pleading. "I've seen moments when her behavior has been much better than before."

"Moments?" Jenny shook her head. "How bad can things be, when we're grateful for *moments* of proper behavior? I'm too young . . . too inexperienced." *And Miss Nightingale was wrong,* she added to herself.

"You care about the girl," Elaine persisted. "I can tell you do."

As furious as she was with Celeste, Jenny had to admit that the governess was right. The few times that Celeste had actually allowed her to come close, Jenny had felt a bond that stirred every maternal instinct she possessed. And that was another reason she had to leave. Those tender moments only made the hurt worse when the girl turned on her.

"But what are you going to do?" Elaine's voice cut into her thoughts. "Aren't you obligated for two years?"

"I'll just have to ask Miss Nightingale to assign me elsewhere." Jenny looked up to find the governess's eyes filled with tears. It had been an emotional night for both of them. Suddenly she felt drained, in need of sleep. Giving her best effort at a smile, she said, "I will miss our talks."

Elaine's face was a picture of sadness now. "Me too. Even the ones about religion."

"There is always the post."

"Yes," Elaine sighed. "There is always the post."

23

GOOD morning, Miss Price," Celeste said, taking a chair across from her at the breakfast table. "Did you sleep well?"

Jenny stopped buttering her scone and looked up at the girl She would have broken her resolve not to mention last night's incident had there been a smug look on Celeste's face. Instead, though, there was a curious mixture of anxiety and forced cheerfulness. "I slept very well," Jenny answered.

To her surprise, Celeste's face settled into an expression of relief. "That's good." Turning to her governess, the girl asked the same question.

"I slept well also," Elaine answered. She raised an eyebrow. "And how about you, Miss Celeste?"

The girl shifted her attention to the plate in front of her. "I had a bit of trouble falling asleep."

"Imagine that," Elaine murmured, ignoring Jenny's warning look.

Celeste darted a curious glance up at the governess, then flushed, her eyes going back to her plate.

Later that morning, the girl sat silently in the barouche all the way to church, and once Jenny caught her watching her with an anxious expression. She could almost feel sympathy for Celeste. *She's wondering if her prank worked, and if I suspect she had anything to do with it.* Very likely the girl's *chief* worry was that her father would find out.

The thought of Mr. Harrington brought a stab of disappointment. Jenny had so wanted to help the man with his daughter. Now she had failed . . . perhaps even made things worse. Would he be angry at her for resigning? *I won't be the first nurse to leave the Harrington household,* she rationalized. *He can always hire another one.* But the idea of someone taking her place brought a bit of uneasiness, so she pushed the thought from her mind.

. . . by grace the Comforter comes nigh;
and for thy grace our love shall be
forever, only, Lord for thee.

After the opening hymn, the congregation of worshipers at Saint Mark's took their places in the pews. Jenny sat next to Elaine, with Celeste on the governess's other side. Several times during the sermon Jenny darted glances at her friend from the corner of her eye, wondering if she was daydreaming, as she claimed. The last time she looked, Elaine sent a knowing wink in her direction, then turned her face attentively toward the vicar.

Jenny couldn't help but smile. *God, please don't give up on Elaine.*

~

"Miss Price . . . Miss Celeste is having a seizure!"

Jenny sat up in bed and blinked at the sight of Alma hovering over her. The last thing she remembered was telling Elaine that she was still tired from last night and was going to lie down while Celeste napped. She glanced over at the other bed. *Elaine said she wanted to walk in the garden.*

"Miss Price?"

The fog cleared from Jenny's mind, and she tossed the covers aside. "She had a seizure while she was *napping?*" she asked while following Alma to the girl's room.

"She wasn't asleep yet," the maid answered.

When Jenny reached Celeste's bed, the girl was on her side, moaning and pitching wildly. "Please get me a damp towel," she said to the maid. With one hand she drew the handkerchief out of her apron pocket and reached over with her other hand to steady Celeste's shoulder. Then something about the expression on the girl's face struck her. *She's pretending!*

But why? There was nothing to be gained by it, as when she faked a seizure to keep Albert from winning at draughts. It was so tempting to turn around and go back to bed, but until she could give her resignation to Mr. Harrington, she was still Celeste's nurse. She had been hired to treat seizures, not to determine if they were real or feigned.

"All right, Celeste," she soothed, slipping the handkerchief between the girl's teeth. With her other hand, she kept a firm pressure on Celeste's shoulder. "I'm here."

When Celeste had stopped thrashing, she opened her eyes, blinked a couple of times, and looked at Jenny. "My head hurts."

She was almost convincing, but not quite. *You'll have a new nurse to practice your dramatics on soon,* Jenny thought, resenting being jolted from a peaceful sleep.

"Will you stay with me?" came the small voice.

In spite of herself, Jenny found her resentment softening

just a bit. Breathing a quiet sigh, she said, "Do you really want me to?"

The briefest of smiles touched the child's lips. "Please?"

~

Seated on the ground at her favorite spot overlooking the Thames, Elaine heard someone whistling a tune, and then the sound of footsteps in the grass behind her. She looked over her shoulder to find Logan Fogarty stepping from between the apple trees.

"Oh! I'm sorry," he said, coming to an abrupt halt.

Elaine blinked at the blurred image. "It's quite all right."

"I'll be gettin' along, then," the big man said. But instead of moving, he hesitated for a moment, as if unsure of what to do, and then took a step closer. "Forgive me for askin', ma'am, but are ye cryin'?"

A lump welled in Elaine's throat. She shook her head, unable to answer.

"Here ye are." Drawing a handkerchief from his back pocket, he came over to her and squatted on the ground. "It's clean, ma'am."

Taking the handkerchief from him, Elaine wiped her eyes and blew her nose. "I'll wash it and return it," she croaked. "So silly of me."

"Everybody has to shed a tear now and then. It's naught to be ashamed of."

"I haven't cried like this in years," Elaine said, wiping her nose again.

"Well then, it's high time for it, don't ye think?" He sent her a gentle, shy smile. "Is there anything I can do for ye, ma'am?"

"No, thank you." Elaine took stock of the brown linen coat he was wearing. "Why aren't you working?"

"Why, it's Sunday, Miss Barton. Don't ye have the day off, too?"

She shook her head. "We . . . Miss Price and I are paid extra to work on Sundays. Some of the maids, too." Elaine didn't know why she was telling him this, but he seemed interested in what she had to say.

"Am I disturbin' ye, Miss Barton?"

"What?"

His big shoulders shrugged self-consciously. "If you're wantin' to be alone, I'll leave ye be. But if you're needin' company . . ."

I'm needing company, Elaine thought right away. She could never tell him that, in a million years. Instead, she said, "Have you been practicing your reading?"

"Every day," he answered, easing down to sit on the ground a respectful two feet away from her. "And sometimes late into the night. I've been thinkin' about that poem we read the other day."

"Do you like poetry?"

"I believe I like it right fine." His brow furrowed with recollection. "Can't say that I ever seen any till that one."

"Why, Mr. Fogarty, songs are simply poetry set to music. You've sung songs, haven't you?" As soon as the words were out of her mouth, she regretted them. Surely he didn't think she was making a jest about his singing in the garden that day.

Elaine sent a cautious glance over at the gardener. He was smiling back at her, a glint of good humor in his eyes. "Aye, ma'am. 'Tis an unfortunate Irishman who cannot carry a tune."

His smile was contagious, and Elaine found herself smiling back. "You can certainly carry a tune, as I recall."

"Thank ye, ma'am," Mr. Fogarty said, his expression a mixture of self-consciousness and pleasure. "Are ye feelin' better now?"

She nodded, but her smile faded with the remembrance of why she had come out here. "My friend Jenny Price—the nurse—is leaving here soon."

"I'm sorry."

"I haven't even known her for long. I don't know why I'm acting this way."

"How long you know somebody don't . . . doesn't . . . have anything to do with how ye feel about 'em."

Elaine nodded, and the ache returned to her throat. "I can talk honestly with her, and she doesn't judge me. For the first time, I almost feel that I have a sister."

"Now then," the Irishman said softly. "There I go makin' ye sad again."

His expression of sympathy was touching, but Elaine knew instinctively that the good-hearted man would have the same sympathy for a stranger, and the realization only added to her sense of melancholy. Touching her scarred cheek, she thought, *Must life always be so lonely?*

"Ye know, when I'm feelin' lonesome I find that it helps to pray."

Elaine looked up at him, a bit startled. "You feel that way sometimes?"

"Aye, I do at that. Many times. Would ye be wantin' me to pray for ye?"

I don't believe in God, automatically went through Elaine's mind, but then she heard Jenny's voice saying, *"You do believe . . . and you're angry at him."* Mr. Fogarty was watching her, so she shrugged her shoulders. She didn't know what she believed any more. "Here?" she said out loud, looking around her.

Logan Fogarty smiled again, his blue eyes radiating kindness. "God is everywhere, ma'am."

A week ago Elaine would have brushed him off with a polite "Thank you anyway." Now she felt painfully aware that something was missing inside of her . . . and had been missing for as long as she could remember. Was it God? That question was too overwhelming to consider at present, but how could prayer from this earnest man hurt anything? "All right, then," she answered, bowing her head as she spoke.

When the man didn't say anything right away, she looked up at him again. He hesitated, then said, "Do ye mind if we hold hands?"

"Hold hands?"

"We pray holdin' hands at my church. I kind of feel closer to God that way."

"You go to church?"

"Aye, ma'am. I'm a Baptist."

Elaine held out her hand, and he closed his great paw around it. "Oh, Lord," he began with a sincere voice. "We'll be askin' ye to look down on your servants and hear our prayer . . ."

Listening to this giant of a man humble himself to petition heaven for her, Elaine was moved as she had never been before. Mr. Fogarty spoke to his deity with quiet assurance, as if he were speaking to someone who stood nearby. And he prayed for *her.* Had anyone ever done that before? Right away Elaine knew the answer to that thought. *Grandmother and Jenny.*

So many people praying for me, she thought. *God, if you* do *exist, I'm certainly no stranger to you.*

24

"Now, let's give it another try, shall we? Just remember that the radius is *squared* in this case, not doubled."

The next morning, Jenny sat on the sofa in the schoolroom and listened as Elaine went over a mathematics lesson with Celeste. *I'm going to miss hearing that soothing voice,* she thought.

She had been certain that her decision to leave the Harrington household would dissipate the cloud that had hung over her for the past few weeks, but the opposite was true. In a near stupor she sat there, too drained even to look at the open book in her lap. She didn't notice Gerdie's presence in the room until the maid was standing in front of her.

"I was told to bring this up here," Gerdie said, holding out an envelope. Jenny thanked her and reached for the letter, but her spirits sagged even more. A letter from home was a reminder that she had yet to tell her parents of her failure. She was turning the envelope to tear open the flap when she caught sight of the name on the front.

"Why, this isn't for me."

Gerdie was gone now, so Jenny got up and brought the envelope over to the study table. She shook her head when Celeste reached out an expectant hand. "It's for Miss Barton."

"Me?" Elaine looked up, her pencil poised in the air. "Are you sure?"

Jenny smiled and handed over the letter. "It has your name on it."

"Stuart Northrop, Solicitor of Law," Elaine mused out loud, looking at the return address. "I don't recognize the name."

"Would you like to go into the other room and read it in private?" Jenny asked, but the governess was already tearing open the flap. She read the contents of a single sheet, then let it fall to the table.

"Miss Barton, what's the matter?" asked Celeste.

"My grandmother is dead."

Jenny's hand went to her heart. "I'm so sorry."

Elaine's voice was flat as she met Jenny's eyes. "It was her heart, the letter says. Her funeral is the day after tomorrow."

"Have you time to get there?"

"She lives . . . lived . . . on Mersea Island, in Essex. Two hours by rail at the most."

"You're going to go, aren't you?"

"Yes."

"We can help you pack," Celeste offered, already out of her chair.

Elaine gave the girl a wan smile. "Thank you, but I need some time alone right now." With that she got up and crossed over to the room that she shared with Jenny.

When the door closed, Celeste turned to Jenny, her eyes glistening. "Do you think Miss Barton will be very sad?"

"I'm sure she will," Jenny answered, too jaded by the girl's past actions to be touched by the sympathy in her young voice. "Perhaps we should see if someone could fetch a train timetable for her."

"Would you like me to ring for Mrs. Ganaway?"

"All right. She should be told that Miss Barton is leaving anyway."

Some thirty minutes later, Jenny eased open the bedroom door. Elaine was standing by her bed, packing clothes into a leather portmanteau. Her face looked splotchy, as if she had been crying. "Can I do anything to help?" Jenny asked.

"I've just finished," the governess replied. "I don't expect to be gone long, so I packed light. There will be nothing for me to do once the funeral is over."

"I'll let Mr. Fogarty know that his lessons are suspended for a while."

"Thank you."

"And you'll need this." Jenny stepped into the room and held out a printed timetable. "You can leave from Victoria Station at noon today, or at eight in the morning."

"I'll go today," Elaine said, taking the paper from her hand. "Thank you for seeing about that—it never even crossed my mind."

"Mrs. Ganaway said to ring for her, and she'll send someone around for your luggage."

Elaine nodded, toying with a small button on her sleeve in a distracted manner. "I don't know why Grandmother would request that I be notified of her death."

"You were her only family. Of course she would want you to know."

"Yes." She continued to work the button. "She said some harsh words to me when I last saw her. I returned them tit-for-tat, I'm afraid. Now I wish I had tried more to accommodate her. She was just a lonely old woman who had lost her only daughter."

"And you were a young girl," said Jenny. "We all have regrets, Elaine."

Elaine nodded, frowning. "The past is a painful pill to swallow sometimes."

"Only if you dwell upon it and make it a bigger pill than it has to be." Jenny knew that this was not the time to preach, but she couldn't stop herself from adding with all gentleness, "God can deliver us from the bondage of our past if we'll allow him."

The green eyes turned cold. "What regrets, Jenny? You with your perfect complexion and parents who dote over you . . . what regrets can *you* possibly have?"

"My . . . life hasn't been . . . ," Jenny stammered defensively, taken aback by Elaine's bitter tone. Then she noticed the hurt on her friend's face, and she reached out to rest a hand upon her shoulder. "I'm sorry."

"No, I am," the governess sniffed. "Forgive my sharp tongue. I'm just a bitter old spinster with no more family."

"You're a wonderful person, and my friend."

Elaine closed her eyes, seemingly taking comfort in those words, but when she opened them the change in her expression was startlingly abrupt.

"Jenny, I have to ask you something," she said, glancing at the mantel clock. "Would you please give Celeste one last chance?"

Jenny shook her head. "I'm not leaving because I'm angry at Celeste. I just believe that someone else would be better for her."

"You're exactly what she needs. And what about Mr. Harrington? He's depending on you to help him with her."

"Mr. Harrington doesn't need my help anymore. He realizes he needs to spend more time with her, and he plans to arrange his business so that can happen."

"*I* need you to be here." Elaine's eyes pleaded now. "This is so selfish of me, but I don't want to come back from burying my grandmother and find someone else taking your place. Will you please at least think about it a bit longer?"

Jenny opened her mouth to say that she would miss Elaine, but the words wouldn't come out. "I'll put off leaving until you return," she answered. "I would have to give Mr. Harrington some notice anyway. But I can't stay here any longer than it takes to find a replacement for me."

~

Celeste backed away from the door and eased her way back into her bedroom. *Miss Price is leaving?*

She sat down at her dressing table and stared at her own dark eyes in the mirror. *It worked.* Why was she so surprised? She had always managed to drive away anyone that she didn't like. Closing her eyes, she pictured the relief that would be on Miss Beryl's face when she found out the news.

But something was wrong. Why would Miss Price be so *adamant* about leaving—especially with Miss Barton begging her to stay—if her goal was to marry Father? Could it be that Miss Beryl was mistaken about that?

Her father's fiancée, after all, hadn't spent much time around Miss Price. It was easy to get a wrong impression of someone that you hardly knew. Celeste remembered the hatred she had felt for the nurse when Miss Price refused to allow her to win at their first and only game of draughts. She couldn't imagine feeling that way about Miss Price now, though they still locked horns occasionally.

For a second she considered reasoning with Miss Beryl, telling her about the conversation she had just eavesdropped upon. Then Miss Beryl would see that she had been wrong. But something told her right away that it would be pointless to try to change Miss Beryl's opinion. Besides, there was nothing she could do to persuade Miss Price to change her mind, not without confessing that she had been the sole instigator of the prank concerning George.

Celeste picked up her brush and began pulling it through her hair. Perhaps she could ask Father to make sure the next nurse he hired could style hair. Then she wouldn't miss Miss Price when she was gone. *And she'll need to know a lot of stories.* That, and how to massage her temples whenever she had a headache.

The image in the glass in front of her began to blur. Opening the middle drawer, Celeste brought out a handkerchief and wiped her eyes. *Someone who tries to tell jokes, too.*

~

"Mrs. Ganaway says Mr. Harrington should be home tomorrow," Mr. Horton said between puffs of his pipe. "She asks if you would bring her a cuttin' of roses for the library and some mixed flowers for the dining room."

"Aye, sir," Logan answered, reaching for the shears on their peg on the wall. He was used to this duty, picking out the flowers and greenery to fill vases in various rooms in the house. Mrs. Ganaway had caused him to blush one time over supper in the servants' hall by remarking about his knack of mixing just the right colors and shapes—but he had been pleased at the compliment.

He set out to gather the roses first. He would take single

cuttings here and there from bushes scattered all over the grounds, so as not to affect the landscaping. Early morning sunlight turned the dew that still clung to the grass into a velvety sheen, and honeybees were just starting to hover about the flower beds. As he did nearly every morning, Logan thanked God for the privilege of working in such a beautiful setting. Never would he take his blessings for granted, when there were so many unfortunates spending their workdays down in coal mines or in sweltering factory buildings.

From a bush by one of the fountains he cut two Golden Masterpiece roses.

". . . Anyways, he bet a whole bull that he could draw the nine o' hearts three times in a row . . ."

At the sound of Dudley's voice, Logan sent a quick glance to his right, then turned back to his work. Dudley and George were walking toward the side of the house with buckets and brushes, having been told to scrub the bricks of the front walk. George had been in an even fouler mood than usual lately, and Logan prepared himself for the taunts that were sure to come when they got closer.

"Hey, dummy!"

Logan clipped another rose, ignoring George's usual insult and Dudley's echoing guffaws.

"Pickin' flowers for your readin' teacher?"

"He that is slow to anger is better than the mighty," Logan reminded himself. Had it been just a coincidence that his pastor had spoken on that very subject this past Sunday?

From eight feet away George's taunts grew louder, bolder. "We always figured she was too ugly for any man to notice her . . . but come to think of it, she'd likely be the prettiest woman in *Ireland!*"

Logan dropped the roses and shears and turned to face the pair.

"I don't know . . . my cousin's old *dog* would likely be the prettiest wo—" Having finally come up with an insult of his own, Dudley clamped his mouth shut when Logan took a step toward them. The gardener sent a panicked glance to George and then held up both hands. "Now, Fogarty, we was just—"

"Miss Barton is a nice lady," Logan said through his teeth, taking another step.

The smug look on George's face faltered, but only for a second. "Don't worry yerself, Dudley," he said from the side of his mouth. "He ain't gonna do nothin'."

Dudley's face blanched as Logan continued to close the gap between them. "Maybe we'd better get to work," he said quickly, turning to trot off for the front of the house. For a second George looked as if he would turn and join him, but then he squared back his shoulders and glared at Logan.

Logan stopped just inches away from him and raised his fists. The temptation to grab the gardener around the neck was almost overwhelming. "Don't be sayin' things like that again," he seethed.

George stared back through narrowed eyes, but his lower lip had begun to tremble.

Suddenly Logan got a mental picture of how he must look in God's eyes, standing there making threatening gestures to a man who hardly weighed twelve stone. Was that behavior becoming of a Christian? *What am I doin'?*

It took all his strength, but he lowered his fists.

"I knew you didn't have it in you, Fogarty," George whispered, his thin lips stretching into a sneer. "How did such a big ox like you get to be such a coward?"

Logan lowered his eyes in shame.

"It makes me sick, just lookin' at you," George went on, growing bolder with Logan's backing down.

Suddenly Logan felt a glob of spittle strike his cheek. He clenched his teeth so hard that they ached, but he did nothing. George raised the scrub brush in his hand to his forehead in a mock salute, then turned and casually strolled away.

Logan wiped his cheek with his sleeve as he picked up the shears from the ground. Standing, he heard a noise behind him. The nurse, Miss Barton's friend, stood under the rose-covered arch at the end of the terrace. He could tell by the way she was poised there that she had seen and heard everything. "What do you want?" he heard himself growl, then instantly felt more shame, for the woman had done nothing to him.

She looked taken aback for a second, but then hurried toward him, retrieving a handkerchief from her apron pocket. "Here . . . use this," she offered in a calm voice.

He shook his head when she got close enough for him to take the handkerchief, but still she held it out to him. Not wanting to hurt her feelings, he took the square of linen and wiped his face hard, as if he could scrub away his shame along with George's spittle.

"I'll wash it for you," he mumbled, about to shove it into his pocket. He could not bring himself to thank her, for he wished with all his heart that she had not been there to witness his humiliation. Still, she did not seem put off by his lack of manners, and she reached for the handkerchief. "I'll put it with the other wash," she said. "I have more than I'll ever use anyway."

Logan nodded and was about to turn back to his work when the nurse went on. "Miss Barton just left for the train station. She wanted me to tell you."

He stared at her, baffled, and a heaviness settled in his chest. "She's gone?"

"Just for a few days." The nurse went on to tell him the reason for Miss Barton's departure.

"I'm so sorry." He shook his head. "Is Miss Barton—?"

"She took it rather hard. Her grandmother was the only living member of her family."

Logan let out a long breath. He understood how it felt to have no family. "I'll be prayin' for her."

The woman in front of him tilted her head to study him. "You're a believer, Mr. Fogarty?"

"Aye, Miss—"

"Price," she answered, and then a small smile came to her face. "Imagine that," she murmured, looking away as if talking to herself.

"Ma'am?"

Miss Price blinked and turned her gray eyes back to him. "She needs your prayers," she said, her tone becoming somber again. She was quiet for a moment, and it seemed that she would leave, but then her brow furrowed. "I don't wish to be rude, Mr. Fogarty, but why did you allow that man to spit on you?"

Logan was ready to turn back to his work so that she would leave again. Instead, he asked, "Are ye a believer, Miss Price?" When she nodded, he said, "Then ye know I've got to be forgivin' of others."

"But you don't have to allow them to bully you."

"Fightin' is wrong, Miss Price."

"Not when you have to defend yourself . . . or others." She folded her arms. "Or else why would God equip David to slay Goliath?"

"We're not to be angry," was all he could think of to say.

"As our Lord Jesus was when he threw the moneylenders from the temple?"

Logan gaped at her, unable to answer.

"If you don't stop people like that from bullying, they're only going to keep on doing it . . . and not just to you."

"I've got work to do, Miss Price," Logan mumbled. This time he turned away before she could say anything else.

~

"Henry II, great-grandson of the Conqueror, succeeded to the throne after a period of anarchy under King Stephen. . . ."

Seated across the study table from Celeste, Jenny listened as the girl read from her history text. Elaine hadn't been in the state of mind to assign any schoolwork before leaving this morning. When time came for the short afternoon session, Jenny had suggested that Celeste read over one of her coming assignments. The girl had not responded with great enthusiasm, having likely supposed she would enjoy a respite from her schooling, but to Jenny's surprise, she complied without a single argument.

". . . full title was King of England, Duke of Normandy and Aquitaine, Count of . . ."

The schoolroom seemed empty without Elaine's presence. She and Celeste had made occasional small talk earlier over lunch, but the girl seemed as preoccupied as Jenny was. Jenny wondered if Celeste still worried about the aftermath of her prank, or if the news of Elaine's grandmother had caused disturbing thoughts about death.

Whatever the cause, it seemed to drain her energy. After Celeste's nap, when Albert showed up at the door, she walked over to the draughts set and played a quiet game with him, not even bothering to complain when he won again. The boy sent occasional confused glances to Jenny and even offered to teach Celeste some more strategies of the game, but she merely replied, "Perhaps tomorrow."

Only later that evening, when Celeste had finished most of her supper in the nursery sitting room, did she hint at what was bothering her. "Do you remember that time we were talking about asking God's forgiveness?" she asked Jenny, idly making swirls in her dish of custard with her spoon.

"Yes," Jenny answered. She was tempted to add, "That was the day that George disturbed us on the terrace," but she didn't yield to the temptation.

Celeste nodded and lowered her eyes to her dessert. "If someone does something really bad and then asks God to forgive her . . . shouldn't other people forgive her as well?"

Settling back in her chair, Jenny asked, "What exactly did this person do?"

"Nothing specific," was the girl's hasty reply. "I'm just wondering."

"Well, was this person truly sorry for what she did when she asked God to forgive her?"

"Oh, *yes*."

Jenny smiled, touched by the unexpected earnestness in the child's tone. "In that case, I believe other people should forgive her, too."

Celeste's posture relaxed. "That makes sense to me."

"But if the person we're talking about *hurt* someone with her actions, she has a responsibility to ask whomever she has hurt for forgiveness."

"Even if she has already asked God to forgive her?"

"Yes, even so."

After a thoughtful pause, the girl asked, "Does that mean she would have to admit what she did?"

"I believe that would be necessary," Jenny said with a nod. "She couldn't just approach someone and say, `I would like to ask your forgiveness . . . but I can't tell you what I did.'"

"I see." Celeste's face assumed the anxious expression she had worn this morning, and she stared down at her custard again.

"Celeste?"

The girl's brown eyes met hers.

"Is there something you'd like to tell me?" Jenny asked in her most gentle tone.

"Tell you?" The girl's lips trembled slightly, and she shook her head. "I'm just curious about things, that's all."

25

WHY don't we spend playtime outside today?" Jenny buttoned the last button on Celeste's dress and walked to one of the open windows. The afternoon breeze, unseasonably cool for mid-August, bathed her face. "We could both use some fresh air."

The girl went to her dressing table and bent close to the mirror, eyeing her braids from all angles. "Is my hair mussed?"

"Just your bangs, a bit." Jenny walked to the table and picked up the brush. "Here, let me fix them for you. What do you think about going outside?"

"I'd rather not." The answer didn't surprise Jenny. Clearly, she was waiting for her father's arrival. Celeste had asked to have her hair braided right after breakfast, with ribbons and lace to match her favorite yellow dress. During her morning lessons she had been more distracted than usual, glancing at the schoolroom door at every hint of sound. She hadn't even been able to settle down at nap time until Jenny sat with her for a while and told her a story.

I hope Mr. Harrington doesn't wait until tomorrow, Jenny thought. His letter had said Tuesday *or* Wednesday. Celeste's anxiety charged the atmosphere in the nursery with tension, so much so that Jenny found herself glancing at the door once in a while herself.

Besides, now that she had made the decision to resign, she was eager to have it over and done with.

When she finished brushing Celeste's bangs, the two of them walked from her bedroom to the schoolroom. Just then a soft knock sounded at the door, causing Celeste to jerk her head in that direction. *"Father?"*

"That's Albert's knock." Jenny opened the door. Sure enough, the boy stood there, clutching his cap in his hands. "Come in, Albert," she said, opening the door wider. "I'm trying to talk Celeste into playing outside today."

"I don't want to muss my hair or dress," Celeste said from behind her. "But if I could drive the gig again—"

"I'd rather you wait until your father can go with you," Jenny turned to tell her. "I'm not sure how he's going to feel about my allowing you to drive. But we could have just as much fun playing croquet on the front lawn. And it won't ruin your hair or dress."

Ever since Jenny had arrived, a wooden croquet set had occupied a place against the wall next to a dappled gray hobbyhorse. Celeste had told her once that her father had bought the set in Belgium, but that it had never been used. At nursing school, Saturday afternoon croquet matches always brought a welcome respite from the pressure of studying and attending lectures. A little exercise would be a good remedy for the girl's jitteriness . . . as well as her own.

Celeste began to show a little interest. "The front lawn?"

"Why not?" The garden still had no appeal to Jenny, even though she could hardly blame George for what had happened last Saturday night. "There's plenty of open space to set up the ame."

"That means we would be able to see Father right away when he drives up."

"That's right." Jenny turned back to Albert. "Have you ever played croquet?"

"No, ma'am," the boy answered, eyeing the set against the wall. "But I've seen people playing it before."

"I've never played either," Celeste said with a doubtful tone to her voice. But as soon as the words were out of her mouth, she cocked her head at Albert. "That means we would be evenly matched, wouldn't it . . . if we're both learning the game at the same time?"

Jenny smiled. "I'll teach you."

Just then Gerdie came into Celeste's bedroom from the lavatory, where she had been cleaning the tub. She wiped her hands on her apron. "It's right easy to learn croquet, miss," the red-haired maid offered timidly to Celeste, while looking down at her hands.

"You've played?" Jenny asked.

A smile touched Gerdie's lips, and she raised her head. "Me and my sisters play almost every Sunday, when I go home for a visit."

"Then you must play with us. That way we'll have two teams. You can teach Albert while I teach Celeste."

"But I've got work to do," the girl protested. The excitement in her eyes, however, told Jenny she would welcome the interruption.

"I'll ask Mrs. Ganaway right now," Jenny said on her way to the door. "Help Celeste tie her bonnet, then go fetch one for yourself."

Jenny found the housekeeper in the dining room, organizing a large bouquet of flowers in a vase. When Jenny made her request, the older woman nodded. "Mr. Harrington said you're in charge where it concerns Miss Celeste."

There was no reproach in Mrs. Ganaway's voice—in fact, she even looked away from the flowers long enough to smile at Jenny. "I've had no complaints from the upstairs maids lately," she said with a meaningful glance up at the ceiling. "You've been a blessing to this house, Miss Price."

Jenny smiled her thanks and tried not to think about the housekeeper's reaction to her leaving. Thirty minutes later, Albert was driving the last of the wickets into the ground with a mallet.

Gerdie turned out to be quite a skillful player, and Celeste squealed with delight whenever her ball bumped a post. Albert even seemed to be enjoying himself, his face shedding its worried look for a while.

The sound of horses at the entrance of the carriage drive brought the game to a halt. "Father!" Celeste cried, switching her mallet to her left hand so that she could wave at the approaching hansom cab.

"What have we here?" he said, his face wreathed in a smile as he stepped down to the bricks of the carriage drive. He wore a gray suit that was a bit wrinkled from the trip, and he handed his satchel and umbrella to Reeves, who had just come out of the house for the luggage. After paying the driver, Mr. Harrington held out his arms for his daughter, catching her up in a gentle spin.

"I didn't know you knew how to play croquet!"

"I do now," she giggled. "Would you like to play?"

Mr. Harrington set her back on her feet and then smiled at

Jenny. "But you've already started the game," he said as he looked over at the arrangement of wickets and posts.

"Take my place, Mr. Harrington." Jenny held out her mallet. "I'll watch."

"Are you sure?"

"Of course. You and Celeste can be teammates."

Celeste's face lit up. "Oh, do play, Father!"

"Teammates? How can I refuse?" He shed his coat and handed it to Jenny, taking the mallet she held out.

Mr. Harrington turned to Gerdie and Albert, who now wore uneasy expressions. "You're Albert, from the stables, right?"

"Yes, sir." The boy nodded.

"Albert has been playing with Celeste in the afternoons." Gerdie was hanging her head as if she would like to shrink into the ground. Jenny stepped over to put a hand on her shoulder. "And Gerdie works upstairs. She came out here to help me teach Celeste and Albert how to play."

"Gerdie. You must have been hired right before I left." Mr. Harrington smiled at both servants to put them at ease, then held up his mallet. "Shall we have a go at the game? I warn you, I'm a bit rusty."

Jenny walked to one of the benches that lined the front walkway, then sat down to watch, holding the coat in her lap. Mr. Harrington played awkwardly for the first few strokes, but he seemed to be having fun anyway, even joking about his own lack of skill.

He and her stepfather would get along well, Jenny thought, for they both had the same self-deprecating wit. Did Miss Courtland appreciate her fiancé's sense of humor?

Absorbed in the game, Jenny felt something soft against her

face. It was one of his coat sleeves, and as she held the rich kerseymere cloth against her cheek, she inhaled the scent of wool mixed with smoke from the train. *Mr. Harrington is a fine gentleman,* she mused, *so kind and—*

Suddenly Jenny came to her senses and realized what she was doing. As if it were a snake that might strike at a moment's notice, she flung the coat to the bench beside her and, with cheeks burning, looked to see if Mr. Harrington or any of the children had noticed.

Apparently they hadn't, for the game was still going strong. Mr. Harrington had obviously warmed up—though too late, for Gerdie and Albert won in a close contest.

"Oh, let's play again!" Celeste exclaimed when the losing and winning team members shook hands. The sparkle in her dark eyes was a comfort to Jenny. *Perhaps I haven't failed totally with her,* she thought. After all, the girl had just lost a game, yet she wasn't sulking. Jenny sent up a silent prayer of gratitude: *Thank you, Lord, for allowing me to see this.*

Mr. Harrington smiled and reached over to tug playfully at the bill of his daughter's bonnet. "You're not tired?"

"Not one bit. And it's so lovely out here."

He turned to Albert and Gerdie. "What about you two?" When both servants returned eager, albeit timid, nods, he replied, "Then we'll play until dark, as long as you're up to it. But I'm going to need to bow out of the next game. Your father hasn't had a meal all day, and I'm hungry enough to eat a horse."

Celeste made a face. "Didn't you buy anything on the train?"

"The horse would have been more appetizing than depot meals." Turning to Jenny, Mr. Harrington said, "I'd like a chance to talk with you as well, Miss Price. Do you think it would be all right to leave Celeste here with Gerdie and Albert?"

Jenny could hardly believe her ears. The man who so feared for his daughter's health that he had maids sit with her while she slept, was suggesting that she play, unchaperoned, outside? Retrieving his coat from the bench beside her, she got to her feet and walked over to the group.

"I think she'll be fine," Jenny answered, "but are you sure you'll be comfortable leaving her out here?"

"We can sit in the front parlor, just inside the house," was his answer. "I'll send for a tray of sandwiches."

Celeste took her father's hand and peered up at him. The blissful flush on her cheeks had been replaced by a look of anxious dread. "I think Miss Price should stay here with me. You never know when I might have a seizure."

Mr. Harrington glanced at the house, his expression unsure. Nonetheless, he said, "I think we should try this today. Albert could fetch us in seconds if necessary. And we should be back out here by the time the three of you finish your game."

"But what if I . . . ," Celeste began, but then hesitated.

"Yes?"

She glanced over at the house. "I'll be fine."

"That's my girl." Mr. Harrington patted her shoulder and turned toward Albert. "Just don't let her overdo herself."

A wave of apprehension washed over Jenny. While she had hoped to be able to tender her resignation as soon after his return as possible, now that the opportunity was at hand, it filled her with dread. Would he be terribly angry at her for ruining his homecoming?

"How is Mrs. Wallace?" Jenny asked as the two of them walked the brick path toward the front of the house.

A shadow passed over his face. "Holding up well. She and Jacob have a large family, and they draw strength from each other. As I mentioned, her faith in God sustains her." Just as they reached the portico, he noticed that she was still holding his coat. "Here, let me take that. I didn't intend to have you carry it around."

Jenny fought to ignore the unsettling quickening of her pulse. "I didn't mind, sir."

Mrs. Ganaway had obviously been pacing the entry hall. As soon as the door closed behind them, the housekeeper hurried over to Mr. Harrington to take his coat and hat. "Welcome home, sir."

"Thank you, Mrs. Ganaway. I trust everything is going well?"

"Most well. May I do anything for you?"

"A tray of sandwiches would be nice." He turned to Jenny. "Enough for two?"

"I've had lunch, thank you. But tea would be lovely."

"Two teas." Mr. Harrington smiled at the housekeeper and added, "And please have some lemonade sent out to the children out front."

If Mrs. Ganaway was surprised that Celeste was allowed to play outside without her nurse, her expression didn't show it. Still, the corners of her mouth twitched slightly before she turned to make her way down the hall.

The front parlor was dimly lit and stuffy. Mr. Harrington directed Jenny to one of the Louis XV chairs opposite the sofa, then went behind them to pull open the drapes. Sunlight flooded into the room, and when he raised the window, the aroma of gardenias from the bushes outside wafted in on a gentle breeze. "Mrs. Ganaway has a fear of the sunlight ruining the fabric on the furniture," he said, taking the other chair, "so she keeps the curtains drawn when this room isn't being used."

"She cares deeply about this house, doesn't she?"

"It's good that you've noticed. Most people can't see past her rather unapproachable front." Mr. Harrington settled back in his chair and crossed his legs. "How did someone so young become so perceptive?"

"If I have any perception at all, I suppose God knew ahead of time that I would need it in order to be a good nurse," Jenny answered simply. "But I still make more than my share of mistakes in judgment."

"I find that hard to believe."

You won't find it hard to believe when I tell you everything, Jenny thought.

"I've had plenty of time this past week to think . . . and pray," he went on, his dark eyes leveled at hers. "I must confess to an occasional misgiving about having assigned you complete control of my daughter in my absence. After all, you haven't known her for very long."

"Perhaps your misgivings were right."

"No, they weren't. Do you realize how good it is to come home and find my daughter *playing* on the lawn? And she was so eager to have me play croquet with her that she didn't think to ask what I brought her."

He frowned slightly. "I've caught myself wondering more than once if she would be just as happy if I simply sent regular gifts."

"Surely you know she loves you."

"Of course I do. But I also know that I've got to stop trying to appease my conscience by giving her material things, and give her what she needs most . . . my time. You've taught me that, Miss Price."

Jenny shook her head. "For such a thing to happen so quickly, God had to have been working on your heart about this long before I came here."

He stared at a framed Manet on the opposite wall for several seconds, then looked back at Jenny and smiled. "There you are with that perception again. And speaking of spending time with my daughter, I wanted you to be the first to hear this . . . since you're the one who influenced my decision."

"Your decision?"

His face took on the expression of a young boy watching someone open a gift he had wrapped. "I'm going to sell the Liverpool end of the business. I have more than enough work here in London to keep me busy."

"That is wonderful news!"

"I knew you would think so. That's why I couldn't wait to tell you."

Jenny remembered what he had once said about his father starting the business from practically nothing. "It took a lot of courage . . . to make that sort of decision."

A shadow passed over his face. "My father worked hard to build the business, and the strain of it killed him before his time. I've come to realize that the quality of family life is far more important."

Jenny smiled as the full implication of his words sank in. "Celeste will be so happy to hear this."

"I hope so. Anyway, I'm going to wait and surprise her with the news when the sale is complete. It could take a year or so to find a buyer—I'll only sell to a company that will agree to keep my employees on at the same wages."

"Well, I for one am very proud of you, Mr. Harrington." Suddenly Jenny wished she could erase her silly words—as if the man would care what his daughter's *nurse* thought of him!

But Mr. Harrington smiled in return. "I'm glad, Miss Price. Very glad."

~

"Lemonade, Miss Celeste?"

Still concentrating on aiming her mallet, Celeste held her breath and swung. Her ball rolled along the grass in a straight line, but then arched wildly to the left to land three feet away from the second wicket. "Oh, posh!" she muttered.

"Would you like some lemonade, Miss Celeste?" Marline, one of the kitchen maids, had come from the back of the house with a tray.

"Yes, I would." Celeste walked over to take a glass, took a huge gulp of the lemonade, then turned to Albert and Gerdie, who were pretending not to notice. "Well, are you just going to stay there and die of thirst?"

With hesitant steps the two servants walked over to Marline and took glasses. "Thank you," they mumbled at the same time, obviously not used to being waited upon in such a manner. The maid poured refills for them, then departed. Celeste lowered her mallet to the ground and pointed to her ball. "I'm not playing very well right now. I think I should rest."

"Should I get Miss Price?" Gerdie asked, her expression anxious.

"No, but perhaps I should sit with Father and Miss Price for a little while."

Albert turned to squint at the house. "I'll walk with you."

"To the front parlor?" Celeste shook her head. "You two carry on with the game. When I get back we'll start another one."

"Are you sure?"

"I'm sure." She motioned that they should start, then waited until they had each taken a turn before turning to head for the house. Once she had reached the bottom step of the portico, Celeste turned to peer across the lawn. As she had hoped, Albert and Gerdie were wrapped up in their game and were not watching her.

She took soft, even steps over to the left side of the portico and, crouching down, carefully edged her way between the gardenia bushes and the house. She could hear her father's voice coming through the open window.

~

"Are you sure you wouldn't like a sandwich?" Mr. Harrington held up the half-eaten sandwich from the plate he had balanced on the arm of his chair. "This roast beef is quite good."

"No, thank you," Jenny replied, balancing her cup and saucer on her knee. "Am I making you uncomfortable by watching you eat?"

"Not at all," he smiled. "When I'm in Liverpool, I have most of my lunches at my desk . . . and there is usually a visitor on the other side."

Tell him now! Jenny told herself. "You must have a demanding schedule," she replied instead.

"Extremely demanding. I don't know how I've done it all of these years." Abruptly his expression turned wistful, and his dark eyes drifted toward the painting again. "Only one thing worries me."

"Worries you?"

"Celeste is twelve years old. Have I done irreparable damage with my past neglect?" His voice wavered for a second, so he stopped to clear his throat. "Will she be bitter when she gets older and realizes the only memories she has are of nursery walls and various servants?"

"She will remember that her father made arrangements just so that he could spend more time with her. That will stand out more in her memory than anything else."

"But her earlier years, when she needed me so much . . ."

"Children have a huge capacity for forgiveness, Mr. Harrington." Jenny leaned forward intently. "I assure you, your love and attention now will make up for a multitude of past hurts."

His eyes were questioning. "I have a feeling you're speaking from experience."

Jenny nodded.

"Please tell me about it."

"I don't know if I can," she replied. "I've never spoken about this to anyone outside of my family."

"Why?"

"Because I don't want anyone to think ill of my parents."

"Your parents?" Mr. Harrington shook his head. "I'm not in the position to judge any parent. And I will certainly keep whatever you tell me in strictest confidence."

After a moment of hesitation, Jenny said, "My mother abandoned my father and me when I was just a baby."

His mouth opened. "No!"

"Remember," Jenny said, still holding her empty teacup in her hands, "you said you wouldn't judge."

"You're right. Please forgive me."

"My father turned me over to an aunt and her family in Leawick. My father died—as a result of drinking—some years later."

"Did your aunt's family treat you well?"

"They fed and clothed me," Jenny answered tersely. "Not much more."

"I'm sorry to hear that. It's a wonder that you aren't bitter."

"How can I be, when I've been so blessed?"

Mr. Harrington lifted an eyebrow. "How so?"

"Mother became a Christian when I was ten, and she came back to Leawick for me. She treated me like gold and later married a wonderful man." Smiling, Jenny repeated herself. "I've been blessed. So you see, the memories I choose to dwell on are the good ones."

"But they can't erase the bad memories that you must have."

"No, they can't," she agreed. "But I look back at them now through a filter of love and forgiveness. Which is how Celeste will look back on her childhood . . . especially now that you plan to spend more time with her."

Mr. Harrington nodded thoughtfully. "You know, my first impression of you was that you spoke your mind too bluntly, not caring if the words stung." His eyes crinkled at the corners. "But you're very encouraging, Miss Price."

The compliment, which would have normally lifted Jenny's spirits, filled her with an acute sense of loss. *Now it's time,* she thought, and she squared her shoulders. "Mr. Harrington . . . there is something I must tell you—"

The rattling of the doorknob cut off her words, and suddenly the door swung open. Celeste, her face wet and splotched, headed for their chairs.

"Celeste—?" Mr. Harrington began, but then the child was in his arms.

"Don't let her leave!" she sobbed into his shoulder. "I'm sorry I did it!"

"There, there now. What are you talking about?"

"The locket! And I wrote those notes, too!"

Patting his daughter's back, Mr. Harrington raised a puzzled eyebrow at Jenny. "Do you know what she's talking about?" he asked over his daughter's sobs.

"I do," she answered.

"Your locket's in my room," came the muffled voice. "*Please* don't go away!"

Compassion overtook Jenny's first impulse to be skeptical. She got to her feet and walked over to Mr. Harrington's chair. Pulling her handkerchief from her apron pocket, she leaned down and touched Celeste's shoulder.

Celeste turned a tear-streaked face to her. "Will you stay here?"

All Jenny could do was dab at the girl's cheeks with the handkerchief. "You mustn't get so upset, now."

"Will someone please tell me what this is about?" Mr. Harrington looked from his daughter to Jenny, then back again.

"I did something bad to her," Celeste sniffed. She turned to Jenny. "But I'm sorry, Miss Price. Honest I am. Don't leave—please!" She gulped. "I love you, Miss Price. Please say you'll stay with me.

Jenny swallowed hard, then cupped the girl's chin with her fingers.

"I'll stay."

26

HERE it is," Celeste said, rising to her knees in front of her armoire with the gold chain dangling from her fingers. Her brown eyes were anxious as she handed it over to Jenny. "Just a little bit of dust, that's all."

Jenny closed her hand around the locket and turned to Mr. Harrington, who was standing at her side. "Everything is fine now. I'm so glad to get it back."

His expression as hard as granite, Mr. Harrington helped his daughter to her feet. "Everything is not fine. There's still the matter of punishment."

The girl paled in front of him.

"Your prank was unbelievably malicious. Whatever possessed you to do such a thing?"

Celeste looked down at the floor. "I wanted Miss Price to leave."

"But why?"

"I thought . . ." Tears welled from her red-rimmed eyes. "Something bad about her," she finished in a whisper.

"She's obviously been in torment about this for a while," Jenny said softly to the man beside her. "Don't you think she's been punished enough?"

"No, I don't. Not only did she take your property and trick you, but she almost caused that gardener to lose his job."

Jenny recalled Mr. Harrington's reaction, back in the front parlor just a few minutes ago, when Celeste had confessed her part in the meeting on the terrace. With a thunderous expression on his face, he had started for the door with the intent to fire George, until Jenny stopped him. "It wasn't his fault," she had insisted, catching up with him and putting a restraining hand on his arm.

She hadn't told him how George had forced a kiss upon her. Though the memory of it made her skin crawl, she still couldn't stand by and watch someone lose his position because of a prank. And for some reason she couldn't quite fathom, she knew that Mr. Harrington would have him dismissed immediately had he known the whole story.

Mr. Harrington's voice cut into her thoughts. "She involved that young maid too. This is just too serious to ignore."

"Are you going to spank me?" Celeste asked, her head lowered again.

He gave Jenny a quick helpless look, then shook his head. "I have never spanked you. I should have, a long time ago, for your sake. But you're almost grown now."

Jenny watched the girl's posture for a sign of relief, but there was none. *She wants to be punished,* Jenny realized. Her heart ached for Celeste, and she longed to ask Mr. Harrington again to go lightly with her.

"I believe if you spend the rest of your playtimes this week polishing the silver, you'll appreciate how hard people work for their belongings. And you'll see how important their positions are to them."

"Yes, Father."

Mr. Harrington let out a sigh. "I realize that's not a severe penalty, but I agree with Miss Price that you've punished yourself enough over this. But I want one more thing from you."

"Yes, sir?"

He reached out and placed his hand gently on the top of her head. With a smile and wavering voice he said, "I want you to tell me who is the handsomest man in England."

Celeste raised her head, her eyes glistening. "You are."

Mr. Harrington stooped to gather his daughter up into his arms, then turned to Jenny. She could see that his eyes were shining as well. "Would you mind doing me a favor?"

"Of course," she whispered with a dab at her own eyes.

He smiled. "Would you tell those two children outside that they may stop playing croquet whenever they wish?"

~

After supper, Celeste leaned against her father's arm as they sat on a sofa in the library.

"'Peggotty!' repeated Miss Betsey, with some indignation." Father read Miss Betsey's part in *David Copperfield* in a mock falsetto voice that brought a smile to Celeste's face. "'Do you mean to say, child, that any human being has gone into a Christian church and got herself named Peggotty?'"

Celeste put a hand on his arm. "But she didn't choose her own name. No one does."

Lowering the book, he looked sideways and smiled. "Miss Betsey is just exaggerating."

"Mr. Harrington?"

They both looked up at Mrs. Ganaway, standing in the doorway. "Yes, Mrs. Ganaway?" her father answered.

"Mrs. Courtland and Miss Courtland are here to see you, sir."

"Oh." Celeste's father was quiet for a moment, then he closed the book. "Please show them in."

"Shall I send for tea, sir?"

"Yes, I suppose you should." He turned to her when the housekeeper was gone. "We'll read again in a little while."

Celeste nodded her understanding, ignoring the surge of disappointment that she had just felt. How could she not be excited to have Miss Beryl come for a visit? *Mrs. Courtland is with her,* was the explanation she gave herself. Of course. If Miss Beryl had been *alone,* she would have jumped for joy.

Still, she found herself hoping that it wouldn't be too long before she would be back leaning against her father's arm and listening to him read to her.

Mrs. Courtland's voice could be heard trilling down the hallway, growing louder with each footstep. "There simply aren't enough hours in the day, Beryl! *J'ai encore beaucoup à faire . . .*"

Father looked at Celeste and shrugged, and for a brief moment she thought she could see that same disappointment in his eyes. "I suppose we should greet our guests."

No sooner had they gotten to their feet than Miss Beryl and her mother were ushered through the door by Mrs. Ganaway. After the housekeeper had left, Miss Beryl turned to Celeste and her father. "I hope you don't mind us popping in like this. We're just coming from dinner at the Langstons', some old friends of Mother's. Celeste had mentioned that you could be returning today, so . . ."

"Of course we don't mind," Father said, walking over to take her hand. He brought it to his lips, then smiled and nodded at Mrs. Courtland. "You're both looking well."

Celeste thought so too, at least where Miss Beryl was concerned. The pale green muslin she wore was simply cut, which only served to draw attention to her elegant figure. As for Mrs. Courtland, Celeste had to keep from smiling at the orange ruffles that tiered her skirt from the waist to the floor. *She looks like a pumpkin,* she thought. She glanced over at Father, who signaled at her with his eyes.

"I'm pleased to see you," she said, curtsying.

"Were we interrupting anything?" Miss Beryl asked Celeste. There was such a look of worry on her beautiful face that Celeste immediately forgave her. *Anyway, Father said he would read to me later.*

"No, Miss Beryl," she answered.

"Such a dear!" Mrs. Courtland exclaimed, though her eyes were on the leys jar in its cupboard. Her hand fluttered to her heart. "I just can't come over here without looking at that *beautiful* artifact."

Father smiled. "Would you like to sit down?"

Celeste knew that Miss Beryl would be taking the place next to her father, so she sat down in one of the chairs closest to the sofa. That left a comfortable overstuffed armchair for Mrs. Courtland. Miss Beryl was so amusing, telling about the peculiarities of the family she had just visited. After about twenty minutes, though, Miss Beryl looked over at her.

"I wonder if you and I might have a chat out on the terrace," she said with a smile. She lifted the white knotted silk reticule at her side. "I've something to give you."

Celeste was out of her chair in an instant. "Just you and me?"

"Just the two of us." She gave Father a little smile as he helped her to her feet. "You don't mind, do you?"

"Shouldn't you and Graham have some time together?" Mrs. Courtland cut in before Father could answer.

"We'll only be a minute," Miss Beryl said. She lifted an eyebrow at Celeste's father. "Graham?"

"Of course not," he replied. "Perhaps your mother and I will read some Dickens."

"Dickens?" Mrs. Courtland brightened at once. "Did I ever tell you that I saw Mr. Dickens at the theater. . . ."

~

The sun was low in the sky when Celeste and Miss Beryl walked out onto the terrace. As soon as they were seated on one of the benches, Miss Beryl took a small white box from her reticule and handed it to Jenny. "I saw this in a little shop on Mayfair Street this morning, and I just had to get it for you."

Celeste eagerly opened the hinged box. A small ivory cameo stared back at her, attached to a pink velvet ribbon.

"I know you're rather young for brooches," Beryl was saying as she watched her face, "but it would be appropriate to wear around your neck in the evenings if you have a dress-up occasion."

"It's beautiful," Celeste breathed, holding it out in front of her. "Thank you for getting it. May we go show Father?"

"Soon." She felt a hand rest lightly on her arm. "The main reason I wanted to come here tonight was to talk with you."

"It was?"

"Of course." Miss Beryl took the cameo from her and put it back in the box. "You don't want to handle the velvet too much or it will go limp. Do you remember our conversation the day Mother had guests here?"

Celeste nodded. "About Miss Price."

"How has she treated you these past few days?"

"Very well."

Miss Beryl looked down at her with a thoughtful expression. "You know you can trust me with anything, dear," she said, her voice warm with affection.

"I know." Celeste took a deep breath. Why was it that, even though she had *good* news to give Miss Beryl, she couldn't help feeling a strange dread that it would not be well received? "I hid Miss Price's locket and played a trick on her so she would want to leave," Celeste began. "And she was going to leave, too, only I decided I don't want her to."

She waited for an outburst from her father's fiancée, but Miss Beryl only nodded.

"You would like her too, if you could spend more time with her," she rushed on. "Miss Price had Albert teach me to drive the curricle, and she tells me stories. And she rubs my forehead when I've got a headache, and I don't even mind playing with Albert."

Celeste paused for a breath and looked up to see Miss Beryl watching her with an expression that she couldn't read. *I have to try to make her understand,* she told herself. It was important that her future mother, who could have the authority to hire and discharge servants, understand her need to keep Miss Price in her life. An idea came to her right away. "If you could only know how hard her life has been, you would feel sorry for her."

Miss Beryl raised an eyebrow. "Hard?"

"Terribly so! It almost makes me cry to think about it." The things she had heard through the open window were fresh on her mind, so Celeste repeated what Miss Price had told her father. At the end of the story she said, blinking, "Can you imagine how sad she must have been? Even though her mother came back for her, she lived ten years knowing that her mother didn't *want* her!"

"That *is* very sad," Miss Beryl soothed, putting an arm around her shoulders.

The expression of sympathy was encouraging to Celeste, and she smiled at the woman beside her. "I knew you would understand."

"Of course, darling. But tell me . . . when did Miss Price tell you this?"

"Well, she didn't, actually," Celeste hedged. "I overheard her telling Father."

"You did? When?"

"Today. They were in the front parlor, and I . . ." Shame caused her to lower her eyes. "I was listening outside the window."

"Do they know that you were listening?"

Celeste clutched the box in her hand a little more tightly. "No. I was supposed to be playing with Albert and Gerdie." She looked back up at Miss Beryl and whispered, "You aren't disappointed in me, are you?"

"I could never be disappointed in you," Miss Beryl reassured her with a little smile.

"Father would be, if he knew that I spied. I was going to tell him when I confessed about the locket, but then he was so angry. . . ."

The arm across her shoulders drew her closer. "Sometimes it's best not to tell everything that happens to us. You were right to keep it to yourself. Besides, it turned out for the good, didn't it?"

"It did?"

"Of course, darling. Now I realize that I was wrong about Miss Price."

Celeste sighed and felt her muscles relax. Why had she doubted that Miss Beryl would change her opinion of the nurse, when she was always so understanding? "You should come play croquet with us one day."

Miss Beryl smiled and gave her shoulders a squeeze. "I'll just have to do that, won't I?"

~

"May I go tell my father good morning before I start my lessons?" Celeste asked Jenny the next morning as they were finishing breakfast. "I'll only take a minute. He's likely in his office by now."

"Of course." Jenny laid her napkin on the table. "I'll walk with you downstairs."

As they walked down the staircase together, Celeste told Jenny about her father reading *David Copperfield* to her last night. "We're going to read a chapter every day after supper, and when we finish this book, we'll start another."

Jenny suppressed a smile. "How terrible for you. I'm so sorry."

Celeste paused on the step. "Terrible?"

"Aren't you the same lass who said she hated books?"

The dimple appeared in Celeste's cheek. "That girl was a brat, wasn't she?"

"Oh, I don't know," Jenny replied, taking Celeste's hand as they continued down the staircase. "She had her good qualities."

Celeste's eyes flashed some of the old sparkle, and she said with a wink, "I'll remember that when I'm polishing silver this afternoon."

When they reached the bottom of the staircase, Jenny let go of the girl's hand. "We do have to study," she reminded Celeste.

"I won't take too long."

Standing at the banister, Jenny watched the girl go down the hallway, under the dome, and to the left to stop at her father's office door. Celeste turned her head in her direction and smiled, then lifted her hand. Jenny could hear the soft knock, then a faint masculine voice. "Come in."

At the click of the doorknob, Jenny gathered her skirts and sat down on the bottom step to wait. *Two days ago, I was sure that I was leaving,* she thought. *Three days ago, I almost hated this child.* She fingered the gold locket that hung around her neck. How incredible that things would have changed so quickly!

Jenny closed her eyes and began to pray. *I can see your hand in this, Lord. When will I ever learn to trust you more?*

She was still for a while, and then it seemed that a great tide washed through her, filling her soul with a peace that brought tears to her eyes. A voice, inaudible but very clear, came from somewhere deep inside her. My child, you're learning even now.

"Thank you, Father," she breathed, then opened her eyes. A sound startled her out of her calmness—a man's voice, calling out for help.

Mr. Harrington! Jenny jumped to her feet and took off down the hall for his office. She burst through the door and found her employer kneeling on the floor in front of his desk, his daughter heaving and pitching in his arms. He gaped up at Jenny, his face blanched as white as his shirt.

"Help her!"

"Put her down on her side," she ordered. Reaching into her apron pocket for a handkerchief, she knelt on the other side of the child and started to ease it between the girl's teeth. Then she stopped and looked at Mr. Harrington.

"What's wrong?" he demanded.

Holding Celeste's shoulders with one hand, Jenny handed her employer the handkerchief. "You do it."

His eyes went wide. *"Me?"*

"Put it between her teeth. She may depend on you to help her one day, and you should know what to do."

"But—"

"Mr. Harrington, you *can* take care of her. She isn't going to die."

He looked down at his daughter again and up at Jenny. Then with hands that were visibly shaking, he bent forward and did as she had instructed.

"Good," Jenny said. "Now keep one hand there to keep the handkerchief from falling out, and put your other on her shoulder, as I'm doing." When he seemed incapable of motion, she reached for his hand and brought it over. "Like this."

They both knelt there, her hand holding his steady, until Celeste's seizure had diminished. At last the girl lay quiet, the ringlets about her forehead damp. "Should I take out the handkerchief now?" Mr. Harrington asked.

"Of course." Jenny realized that her hand was still covering his on the girl's shoulder, and she quickly moved it away.

Mr. Harrington let out a long breath. "She's all right now?"

Jenny nodded. "She just needs you to carry her to bed."

"All right." He scooped her up into his arms and got up from his knees. With Jenny at his side, he carried Celeste through the doorway and down the hall. Celeste's eyes fluttered open before they reached the staircase. "Father?"

He stopped walking and smiled down at her. "You're fine now. Your father is taking care of you."

Later, when the child was sound asleep and Alma positioned on a chair at her bedside, Mr. Harrington followed Jenny into the schoolroom. His face had returned to its usual tanned color, but when he looked at her there was something akin to wonder in his expression. "I should go back to work now."

"I'll look in on her every once in a while," Jenny told him, leaving the door to the girl's bedroom propped open.

"Thank you."

"I don't mind. I'll just get my book and—"

Mr. Harrington shook his head. "What I mean is, thank you for showing me that I didn't have to be afraid."

Jenny smiled, recalling the confidence that had finally been on his face when he carried his daughter upstairs. "You handled the situation quite well, Mr. Harrington."

Returning her smile, he lifted an eyebrow. "Why, I did, didn't I? After you calmed me down, that is."

He turned to leave, but had gone only a step or two when he turned back again to Jenny. "You know, you're quite remarkable, Miss Price."

It was a compliment that any employer would give an employee under similar circumstances. Jenny merely had to acknowledge it with the appropriate words. But to her utter embarrassment, she could only stand there groping for a reply. The worst part was, she could tell from his expression that he was aware of the turmoil going on in her mind. *He must think I'm an idiot!*

He folded his arms and leaned forward just a bit. "Are you all right, Miss Price?"

"Yes," Jenny finally managed, trying desperately to assume an expression of professional dignity.

"I have the feeling that I make you uncomfortable."

"Uncomfortable?" She realized she had been fiddling with her necklace, and dropped her hands to her side. "No, not at all." The stab to her conscience was immediate. Truthfulness had always been important to her, and here she was shading it. *Lying,* she corrected herself. *Forgive me, Lord.*

Mr. Harrington continued to watch her, and just the hint of a puzzling smile touched his lips. "Well, I'm glad to hear that. I'll be going now."

The door closed behind Mr. Harrington, but not before a scarlet flush had crept up Jenny's neck and heated her cheeks.

27

THE phylum Arthropoda includes the familiar insects, spiders, centipedes, millipedes, crayfish, crabs, and lobsters," Celeste read aloud during the next morning's study time. Marking her place with a finger, she looked across the study table.

"What is a crayfish?"

Jenny leaned forward to squint at the upside-down printing on the page from *The Study of Living Things*. "Are there no drawings?"

Celeste shook her head and pushed the open book across the table. "I looked on the pages before and after, too."

"Well, I believe a crayfish looks like a tiny lobster," Jenny replied after searching the same pages herself.

"How tiny? Like an insect?"

"I've never seen one, but I would suppose them to be about the size of a clothes-peg."

"What's a clothes-peg?"

"A clothes-peg is what you use to hang out the wash," came a male voice from behind Jenny. "You must get out of this nursery more often."

"Father!" Celeste exclaimed, looking up from her book. Jenny turned her head to nod at Mr. Harrington, standing in the doorway smartly dressed in a navy coat and fawn-colored pants.

"I'm in the mood to go for a ride," he said. "Can you recommend a good driver?"

The girl's mouth fell open. "Me?"

"You?" Taking his chin in his fingers, he pretended to consider this. "Well now, that's a possibility. . . ."

"Oh, please!" Celeste said, then her face fell. "My lessons," she sighed. "And at playtime I've got the silver to do. Today the trays need polishing."

Jenny looked down at the floor, struggling to hide her amusement at the mental picture of Celeste yesterday afternoon, her forehead creased with concentration as she scrubbed away at one cutlery piece at a time. *If only Elaine had been there to see it.*

Mr. Harrington nodded and put both hands in his pockets. "Well now, we can't rightly take you away from your important work on the silver. But what if we took a recess from your morning lessons . . . just for today?"

Celeste looked at Jenny eagerly. "Do you think that would be all right?"

"I think it would be lovely."

"There's room for three in the curricle," Mr. Harrington said, walking over to the study table. "We would enjoy having you come along, Miss Price."

Jenny marveled at the confidence her employer now possessed, concerning what should be done if Celeste were to have a seizure. *He isn't asking me as Celeste's nurse, but out of politeness,* she thought. Smiling, she thanked him anyway. "I've some correspondence I can catch up with."

He seemed disappointed. "The fresh air would do you good."

"Yes, Miss Price," Celeste urged, now standing at her father's side. "Why don't you come with us?"

Jenny was tempted to accept their offer, even if it only originated from courtesy. But then she remembered how she had stammered and flushed when Mr. Harrington complimented her. What was to prevent her from suffering another embarrassing attack of self-consciousness? She shook her head. "I'll be fine here. You two should have some time alone."

She helped Celeste into her bonnet and gloves and, when the two were gone, walked into her bedroom. At one of the windows Jenny moved aside the lace curtain a couple of inches. Minutes later she could see Mr. Harrington and Celeste walking out to the carriage house, where two of the groomsmen were hitching up the curricle.

She watched as Mr. Harrington lifted Celeste into the driver's seat, and for a brief moment she imagined herself sitting there with them as they rode through the streets of London. Celeste, of course, would sit in the middle, and the three of them would make pleasant comments about the weather and the sights that they passed. They would laugh at jokes that weren't particularly funny, because they were so caught up in enjoying each other's company. And every so often, Mr. Harrington would send her a look, over the top of Celeste's head, of such adoration. . . .

As soon as Jenny realized what she was doing, she let the curtain fall and backed away from the window. For heaven's sake, she was acting like a moonstruck schoolgirl! With determination, she turned to find something to do to keep her mind from straying to such thoughts again.

She took stationery and a pen to the study table in the schoolroom and sat down to write a letter to her parents. Ten minutes later she looked down at the blank page and realized she had been daydreaming. *What is wrong with me?* she asked herself.

Suddenly Jenny heard footsteps approaching the schoolroom door. It was probably one of the maids. She picked up her pen and turned her attention back to her letter.

"Is that any way to greet a friend?"

"Elaine!"

Elaine stood just inside the door, a weary smile on her lips and portmanteau at her side. "I was half afraid you wouldn't be here."

"It looks like I'll be here for at least my two years."

The governess's smile grew wider, and after they had embraced, Jenny took the portmanteau to the next room for her. "Do you think we could beg a crust of bread from the kitchen?" Elaine asked, tossing her reticule to her bed. "I know lunch is an hour and a half away, but my train left too early this morning for breakfast, and I couldn't stand the thought of—"

"Depot meals?" Jenny finished for her. She laughed and linked her arm through her friend's. "Let's go see."

~

"I was Grandmother's sole beneficiary," Elaine said as they sat on the sofa in the schoolroom a short while later. Celeste had not shown up yet, so Jenny assumed that she and her father would be going to a restaurant for lunch. "I still can't understand why anyone would be so forgiving, after the ugly things I said to her the last time I saw her."

"She must have loved you very much."

"Incredibly, she did. I wish I had known it before she died."

"Does that mean you'll be leaving here?"

Elaine shook her head. "I can't see how. Only about two hundred families live on Mersea Island, so the chances of my finding a position as governess are slim. And I'm told the parish school has employed the same teachers for years."

"Would you *have* to teach?"

"Teaching is my life, Jenny. Grandmother left a little over six hundred pounds, after the doctor and funeral expenses. A goodly amount to be sure, but not enough to keep up a house of that size for the remainder of my life." She sighed. "I hate the thought of selling the last tangible reminder of my family, but I suppose I'm going to have to consider it."

Elaine lifted a hand in a gesture of dismissal. "I'm too tired to plan for the future right now. But I do want to show you something." The governess got up and disappeared into the bedroom, coming out seconds later with an envelope. When she had sat back down, she handed it over to Jenny. "Read this."

"Are you sure?"

"I'd like you to."

Jenny opened the envelope, pulled out the folded paper, and straightened it with both hands.

My Dearest Elaine,

My physician tells me that my increasingly irregular heartbeat and lack of strength are not good signs, and that I should restrict my activities even more. I am taking his advice, but this morning performed one more duty, that of making my will. I have informed Mr. Abraham, my solicitor, not to contact you until I am gone. I could linger for years or go tomorrow, and I do not wish you to be burdened with the responsibility of watching me die. I am being well taken care of by my two servants, Martha and Alfred, and am comfortable.

The purpose of this letter is to beg your forgiveness for turning my back on you when you were a young woman. How can I blame you for your bitterness against God, when I am the cause? There is no excuse for the harsh way you were raised. All I can say in my meager defense is that when my daughter was murdered as a result of being in God's service, I became bitter myself. I did not have the courage to shake my fist at God, so I hid my bitterness under years of frantic service. You were not fooled by my false piety, were you?

I pray that as you read this, you will think of me not as the critical, unsmiling old woman that I was, but as a contented person who has made her peace with God. I go to be with him soon. When I am there, I will wrap my arms around your lovely mother and father and tell them that their daughter will also make her peace with God.

After all, there is no lying in heaven.

With undying love,
Grandmother

Lowering the letter, Jenny looked at Elaine and shook her head.

"I know," said Elaine, wiping her eyes. "I couldn't read it the whole way through the first few times without crying."

"I would like to have known her."

"So would I . . . the woman who wrote this letter, I mean." She took the page from Jenny's hand and put it back in its envelope. "Why didn't I swallow my foolish pride and visit her while I still had the chance?"

"Elaine, you thought she had disinherited you," Jenny reminded gently.

"I could have at least made an effort."

A silence stretched between them for several seconds, then Elaine cleared her throat. "Remember when you told me I wasn't an atheist, but was bitter at God?"

Jenny looked up at her. "I still believe that."

With a wry little smile, Elaine said, "I was so angry at you for that. But you weren't fooled, were you? Neither was my grandmother. And I think I've always known that, in the back of my cynical mind."

Feeling a surge of hope, Jenny said, "Does that mean . . . ?"

"That I believe in God? As you so bluntly put it last week, I have always believed in God. But my bitterness toward him is gone."

"Oh, Elaine!" Jenny breathed. "You've become a Christian?"

Elaine shook her head. "I took a giant step by discovering that God has been there all along, in spite of my self-imposed stupidity. But I have been too absorbed with my grandmother's funeral to sit down and give Christianity the consideration that it merits."

Her expression turned thoughtful. "But there has been this . . . *voice,* especially when I was trying to sleep. Not anything that I could hear with my ears, but . . ." She turned hooded eyes to Jenny. "My fatigue has me talking like a madwoman."

"No, not at all."

"You mean, you've heard it too—this voice?"

"Yes," Jenny replied, smiling. "And so has your grandmother."

28

By the time Alma brought the lunch tray upstairs, Elaine was in bed, too tired to stay awake long enough to eat a full meal. Jenny saved Elaine's apple and slice of plumcake so that the governess could have them later. Gerdie had just left with the dishes when Celeste burst into the schoolroom.

"Guess what? We had lunch at Miss Beryl's and—"

"Wait." Jenny put a finger to her lips and got up from the sofa to close the door. "Miss Barton is resting."

The girl winced. "Miss Barton is home?" she whispered. "How is she?"

Jenny nodded. "She's tired right now, but I believe she'll be all right. What did you want to tell me?"

Fishing in her pocket, the girl brought out an envelope. "Miss Beryl would like you and me to go to her house on the twenty-first—that's Saturday—for a garden party."

"Your father isn't going?"

The girl shook her head. "It's for ladies only."

Jenny started to ask why *she* had been invited, but then realized that Miss Courtland likely wanted her there in her capacity as a nurse.

"Aren't you going to read it?"

"Oh. Of course." Holding the almost transparent paper in front of her, she read the spidery script:

Dear Miss Price,

Celeste has become quite taken with you, and I can see why. Would you grant me the opportunity to start all over and become your friend?

The note went on to read that she would be having an intimate gathering of friends Saturday at teatime and that she would be honored to have Jenny present. The postscript read:

You surely must grow weary of your uniform. Why not dress up for a change? I have already instructed Mr. Harrington to allow you to do so.

"I just knew that Miss Beryl would like you once I talked with her." Celeste beamed. "You will go with me, won't you?"

"Of course." Jenny couldn't tell the girl that it was her duty as a nurse to go anyway, unless Mr. Harrington were to be present. At least with an invitation, she wouldn't be sitting alone in some empty parlor. *Considering the company, an empty parlor might be preferable!*

Immediately Jenny regretted the thought—how could she be so cynical when an olive branch was being extended to her?

"And I would love for you to help me pick out a dress," she said to the girl with a smile.

~

"I heard ye was back, ma'am." Logan Fogarty grinned up from the hedge that he was trimming, wiping his forehead on the sleeve of his brown fustian shirt. "But I didn't think ye was up to teachin' so soon."

Returning his smile, Elaine tucked the advanced primer under her arm. "I had a nice rest earlier, and Miss Celeste is napping now. I have the time if you can get away."

"Aye, I just have to wash me hands." A shadow crossed over his face. "I'm sorry about your grandmother, Miss Barton."

"Thank you. She was a good woman."

"Are ye sure ye wouldn't want to wait a week or so?"

Elaine shook her head. "I need to keep busy. I'll go on to the gazebo."

She sat alone for less than five minutes, then he appeared. He had changed into a clean shirt, a blue one, and suddenly Elaine realized that he had done so for her. *Why?* she asked herself. She was only his tutor.

"I been practicin'," he told her as she opened the book.

"Really? And what have you been reading?"

His blue eyes crinkled at the corners. "Saint Matthew, as much as I'm able to make out the words."

"Saint Matthew? You mean the Bible?"

He nodded, and Elaine thought, *Why am I not surprised?* She listened as he read a page in the primer without her assistance, and then another one. "You're doing well," she said, turning the page.

"Thank you, Miss Barton. All the credit's to your teaching."

She looked at him, seated beside her. "Mr. Fogarty, may I ask you a question?"

"Certainly, Miss Barton," he said, and Elaine wondered at the tenderness in his voice.

"Do you . . ."

He was waiting, but Elaine could not bring herself to voice

the words. She cleared her throat, and instead of asking *"Do you ever sense the voice of God?"* she said lamely, "Do you enjoy gardening?"

He looked a bit startled at the question, but then smiled. "Aye, Miss Barton. But I think I like readin' even more."

~

After several attempts to concentrate on the same stanza of "The Eve of Saint Agnes," Jenny closed the book of Keats's poetry. She tidied up the sitting room, then, finding nothing else to give her restless attention to, decided to walk down to the conservatory. She stopped in the door of Celeste's bedroom long enough to whisper to Alma where she would be if Celeste awoke from her nap, then she made her way to the stairs.

As the door to the conservatory clicked shut behind her, Jenny closed her eyes and took in an appreciative whiff of the greenery. When she opened her eyes again, she was startled by the sight of Mr. Harrington, seated on a bench. "Oh, I'm sorry," she said, taking a step back and reaching behind her for the doorknob.

"It's all right." His voice rose above the chorus of canaries. "Please, come in."

"I'll be happy to come back later." To her embarrassment, she found herself stumbling over her words. "Celeste is napping, and I thought I would . . ."

He was standing now, a bit of a smile at his lips. "Do come and sit. I would enjoy your company." Motioning toward the finches in their aviary, he amended, "That is . . . the birds and I would enjoy your company."

Jenny nodded and took a step forward. She hesitated then, not quite sure *where* she should sit, for the benches in the room were too far apart for conversation. Again, he seemed to sense her confusion and moved to the side to make room for her on his bench. "I don't really care to shout. There's more than enough room here for two."

Mr. Harrington remained standing until she had taken a place as close to the end as possible. When he took his seat again, a space wide enough to place a hat separated them, but still Jenny was acutely aware that she had never sat so close to him before.

"I met Miss Barton when she was on her way out to the garden," he said, his expression sobering. "She seems to be coping fairly well with her grandmother's death."

"I believe so," Jenny answered. "She's a strong person. Of course, there are always regrets when someone close dies."

"Especially when it comes unexpectedly."

Jenny could tell that he was referring to his wife. She thought of the portrait that drew her eyes every time she passed through the morning room. "What was she like?"

"Theresa?" Lifting his hands in a short, expansive gesture, he answered, "She was everything I ever wanted in a wife. Beautiful . . . graceful . . . godly . . ."

He was quiet for a moment, his eyes tender with recollection. "She was a voracious reader, too. But do you know what I admired most about her?"

Jenny recalled the expression on the face in the portrait. "I believe I do, Mr. Harrington."

"You do?"

"Her sense of humor?"

He gave her a sidelong look of disbelief. "Why . . . yes." Then he folded his hands in his lap and stared at them in silence for a while. "She had a keen wit, mind you—but never at the expense of others. And sometimes, even during the most solemn occasions, she would get a certain 'look,' and I knew something outrageous was brewing in her mind."

"How wonderful that the artist who painted her portrait was able to capture that expression," Jenny told him.

"You know . . . you're right." He nodded. "I have some photographs of her, but none bring out the humor as well as the painting does."

He turned to Jenny, and his expression became serious. "You remind me a little of her."

"I do?"

"Not at first, mind you, or when we argued about Celeste in my office. *Especially* when we had that argument. You reminded me more of . . ."

"What?"

A wry smile touched his lips. "Well, a bear, to be honest."

In spite of her nervousness, Jenny couldn't resist a retort. "As I recall, you did some growling yourself."

"That I did," he conceded good-naturedly. "I suppose there is a bit of the bear in all of us. Seriously though, I caught a glimmer of that same expression—the one Theresa used to have—on your face that time we had brunch with Miss Courtland and her mother. What outrageous thoughts were going on in your mind, Miss Price?"

Jenny shook her head. The occasion had been so unpleasant that she had gladly pushed it out of her mind afterward. "I can't remember having any outrageous thoughts."

"Are you quite sure?"

"I don't think—" She paused as the scene replayed itself in her mind. *Mrs. Courtland.* Showing off her French vocabulary, the woman had raved about the tenderness of the *Chien aux Truffes* that her cook had prepared. Jenny's knowledge of the French language was limited, but she had known that the correct name of the dish was *Veau aux Truffes,* or *Truffled Veal* . . . not *Truffled Dog,* as Mrs. Courtland had dubbed it.

"You remember it now . . . don't you?" he said. "I can see it on your face."

Jenny turned away from him and bit her lip to keep from smiling at the memory. She couldn't tell him what she was thinking. He might be offended, and at the very least it would be disrespectful to his future mother-in-law. "I would rather not say."

He reached for her chin and gently turned her face back to ward his. "Oh, come on, you're struggling to keep from laughing over it right now." He was grinning broadly as he took his hand away. "Be a good sport and tell me what was so funny."

In spite of herself, Jenny found herself grinning back at him. "I'm sorry, Mr. Harrington . . . but I would rather be a bad sport and keep this to myself."

Mr. Harrington cocked his head to study her, an amused glint in his brown eyes. "Well, then give me a hint. Would it have anything to do with a certain gourmet dish and the canine species?"

Jenny let out a horrified gasp. "You knew all along?"

"I'm afraid so," he replied, his grin even wider.

"Then why . . . ?"

"Why did I just torment you so?"

She couldn't help but laugh. "Yes!"

He joined in her laughter, then rubbed his chin while considering her question. "Actually, I don't know. It was beastly of me, to be sure."

"Beastly," she agreed, shaking her head in mild disbelief. "But unfortunately, I rather enjoyed it, so I can't promise never to do it again."

There was a silence then—the comfortable kind that sometimes comes when two people are enjoying each other's company. After a minute or two, Jenny decided it was time to allow Mr. Harrington the solitude he had come in here to find. Rising from the bench, she said, "I should go back upstairs now. Celeste will be waking soon."

He looked disappointed but got to his feet as well. "Thank you for visiting with me, Miss Price," he said as he held the conservatory door open for her. "It felt so good to laugh again."

~

I shouldn't have taken that nap, Elaine grumbled to herself that night as she punched her pillow into shape for the tenth time.

"Elaine?" Jenny's sleep-laden voice came from the darkness across the room.

"I'm sorry, Jenny. I've disturbed you with my tossing about."

"It's all right. Is there anything I can do?"

"Nothing, but thank you," Elaine replied gently. Jenny was, indeed, true to her calling as a nurse. "Now go back to sleep." She turned to her other side, closed her eyes, and made an effort to clear her mind, but the same thoughts kept coming back to rob her of sleep.

She stood at the graveside, listening to a vicar quote the twenty-third psalm, stunned by the finality of Grandmother's coffin being lowered into the gaping earth. A discreet distance away, two gravediggers leaned on shovels, waiting for the mourners to leave so that they could perform their morbid duty. It was obvious by their posture and motions that they were involved in a conversation that had nothing to do with the burial service taking place.

The sight was disturbing to her. Men who were strangers to her grandmother were about to shovel dirt on her grave, then go home to their mutton stews and suet puddings and never even wonder about her. Was that all there was to life? What had happened to the part of Grandmother who had laughed, loved, and even felt sorrow? Where was her soul?

Her soul isn't in that coffin with her, Elaine had told herself while standing at the graveside. And at that moment she had acknowledged the reality of God's existence.

Slipping out from under the covers, Elaine padded over to a window in her bare feet. She drew back the draperies, and she could make out the five stars of Auriga to the northeast. Could her mother, father, and grandmother see her? She could sense someone watching from out in that vast darkness.

The emptiness she had carried around for years intensified, becoming almost a physical ache. She touched the cool glass with her fingertips. *Is it you out there, God? Are you beckoning for me to come to you . . . be your child?*

It didn't make sense. Why would God want someone who had spent the better part of her life shaking her fist at him, even while denying his existence?

Please help me to understand, she prayed.

~

"I'm glad that's over with," Celeste said Friday afternoon as Jenny helped her into a clean dress. The girl had worn an apron while finishing the last of her silver polishing, but the sleeves of her lavender dress were smudged with hartshorn powder.

"Oh, I don't know," Jenny teased, buttoning the last button. "The kitchen maids are likely hoping you'll play another prank."

"What—," Celeste began, then caught on and smiled. "Your jokes are getting better."

"Thank you." Jenny smiled back. "I can imagine one person who'll be glad you're back to your regular playtimes again."

"Who?"

"Albert. I believe he was starting to enjoy playing with you."

Celeste shrugged, but she looked pleased. "Father said he would play croquet with us every afternoon next week. Albert and Gerdie too, if they like."

"Oh, I'm sure they'll enjoy that."

They both turned their heads toward the open door, where voices could be heard in the schoolroom. A moment later, Elaine appeared in the doorway. "Mr. Harrington would like to speak with all of us," she said.

He stood next to the study table, dressed in a tweed suit of Devonshire brown. One look at him told Jenny that he was going away. Had he changed his mind about staying home more?

Celeste had obviously caught the somber look in his eyes too, and she crossed the room to stand before him.

"Father?" she said in a worried voice.

He winced, as if the reminder of his paternal responsibility would make it even harder to give his news. "I have to go to Liverpool," he said, drawing her to him.

"Again?" She pulled back and frowned, and a little of the old whine came into her voice. "But you said—"

"I don't *want* to go. But I just received a message that my solicitor has found a buyer for the Liverpool concern, and he's eager to get it done with. It's a miracle that someone made an offer this soon."

Celeste's face clouded, and Jenny took a step forward. "Are you saying that this is your last trip to Liverpool?"

Mr. Harrington shot her a look of gratitude and offered his daughter a hopeful smile. "Don't you see? If I make this trip now, it will be my last. Then I can stay home in London all the time."

The girl tilted her head suspiciously. "All the time?"

He smiled. "You'll be positively sick of me after a while."

Celeste stepped into her father's embrace. "All right," she said. "But come back as soon as you can."

"As soon as I can."

~

"Why are you so quiet?" Celeste asked Jenny. Their barouche was passing in front of a row of terraced houses on Wimpole Street in Marylebone.

I don't want to go to Miss Courtland's garden party, Jenny was thinking. But she didn't say so to the girl. Instead, she asked evasively, "Are you sure my hat matches my dress?"

Celeste reached up to adjust a ribbon on the small straw hat that Jenny wore tilted forward. Jenny didn't have a hat to match her sea-green dress, so Celeste had suggested changing out the ribbons on one of her older hats. "You look very nice," she said at last.

Jenny smiled in appreciation. "And so do you." In her blue-sprigged muslin dress with a softly pleated underskirt, the girl looked more like a young lady than a child.

The carriage stopped in front of Mrs. Courtland's house. Reeves helped Jenny and Celeste down and escorted them to the door, where a maid took Jenny's fabric bag and led them down the hallway and through the back door.

A brick terrace, bordered with potted ferns and statues of cherubs, was the scene of the gathering. Half a dozen wicker chairs had been arranged with the cast-iron terrace benches into an intimate grouping on one side. Ten fashionably dressed women, all seeming to be within five years of Jenny's age, stood about in chattering groups.

From one of these groups, Miss Courtland stepped back and looked in their direction. "My dear Celeste!" she cried, hurrying toward them. She looked exquisite in a bustled silk gown of pale blue, with a feather-bedecked straw hat tilted forward over her coppery curls.

Celeste went into her arms, and the chatter on the terrace died down to scattered murmurs. After a quick embrace, Miss Courtland turned her to face the other guests, putting her gloved hands on the girl's shoulders. "I don't think all of you have met the girl who will soon become my daughter," she announced, smiling proudly. "This is Celeste Harrington."

Smiles and nods greeted Celeste, and the chatter resumed. Mrs. Courtland, whom Jenny hadn't noticed until now, burst into a gushing of French concerning Celeste's beauty and talents.

Just when Jenny was wondering if Miss Courtland had invited her here so that she could snub her publicly, the woman turned and touched Jenny's arm. "And this is Miss Price," she announced to the gathering. "One of my new friends."

The wording of her introduction surprised Jenny. Had Miss Courtland introduced her as "Celeste's nurse," there would have been an immediate barrier between herself and the other women present. For one thing, the reputation of nursing still suffered somewhat from the days before Florence Nightingale, when nurses were recruited from the dregs of society and drunkenness was rampant in the wards. But whether the work itself was respectable or not, for these society women it was inappropriate for an upper-class woman to *have* a career—any kind of career.

Jenny was not ashamed of her occupation, and she would have preferred to be honest. Still, she found herself appreciating her hostess's obvious effort to help her fit into the group more comfortably.

"I'm so glad you could come, Miss Price." Miss Courtland was smiling at her now. "I want you and Celeste to meet my friends." Linking her arms with both of them, Miss Courtland led them around to each clique. The other guests were warm and inquisitive, especially wanting to know how Celeste felt about getting a new mother soon. When the girl beamed and answered that she couldn't wait, it caused a ripple of laughter throughout the gathering.

Two more ladies arrived, and after the new introductions were made, Miss Courtland asked each of her guests to take a seat. Four crisply uniformed maids began circulating with trays of tea, cheeses, crab cakes, small sandwiches, and biscuits. "You two must sit near me," she told Jenny and Celeste. She led them to wicker chairs on either side of her, making sure that they availed themselves of all the treats offered them.

Miss Courtland, Jenny noticed while sipping her tea, had an incredible knack for keeping the conversation going and making sure that the more reticent guests took part.

"Captain Matthew Webb is the young man's name." Miss

Dirks, one of the guests, answered Miss Courtland's question about a man who intended to swim the English Channel.

A murmur ran through the group, and then a woman dressed in willow-green silk mentioned that her husband had introduced her to a Captain Webb at a soirée. "I'm quite certain he's the same man."

"Tell me, was he incredibly handsome?" asked another guest, causing another bit of laughter.

"I can't remember."

"That means he wasn't," someone piped up, and the laughter increased.

"But he's a brave one, that's for certain," insisted the woman in green. "Just think about the waves. The last time we took a boat from Dover, I became dreadfully ill." The speaker lifted her eyebrows. "And what about sharks?"

Assorted gasps and murmurs met this last question. "No doubt there's some woman he's trying to impress," someone said. "That's the only reason a man would do something foolhardy like that."

"Well, whatever his reason, he still has courage."

"I agree." Miss Courtland held out her cup when a maid came near with the teapot. "Courage is not so rare as we think. People perform acts of bravery all around us, and we don't even notice most of the time."

"Do tell?" A young woman with maroon ostrich feathers on her hat sent her an amused smile. She had been introduced to Jenny as an old friend of Miss Courtland's. "Such as . . . plan for weddings?"

Miss Courtland threw back her head and laughed, and the others joined in. Even Jenny found herself smiling, and her opinion of her hostess went up several notches. Hadn't Father said that the ability to laugh at oneself was one of the most noble virtues? Still smiling, Jenny looked over at Celeste. The girl grinned back at her with a knowing expression, as if to say, *Now you see how wonderful she is?*

"That's not what I mean, and you know it," Miss Courtland said when the laughter had died down. She stopped talking and beckoned to one of the maids, a young girl whom Jenny had noticed earlier hovering on the edge of the gathering. It had seemed strange to her that, while the other servants busied themselves taking care of the guests, this one had nothing to do but watch Miss Courtland.

When the maid stood by her chair, Miss Courtland then turned to Celeste. "Darling, I want to order you a special dress for the wedding when I make my last trip to Paris. Please go upstairs with Anna and allow her to take your measurements."

The girl looked excited at the prospect of a new dress, but she motioned at the half-empty plate in her lap. "Now?"

"It shouldn't take too long; we'll save your plate. I meant to have it done the last time you visited and forgot." She turned to the group with an apologetic smile. "I've been so forgetful lately, with all of the—" she gave the woman with ostrich feathers a mock scowl—"*wedding* plans."

With a shrug the girl got up and followed the maid. When the door had closed behind them, Miss Courtland picked up the same topic of conversation. "*My* idea of courage is overcoming the almost impossible obstacles in life."

"And you've had to overcome so many," her friend teased.

She smiled and shook her head. "No, I haven't. But I know someone who has." Her topaz eyes were serious when she turned to Jenny. "My friend, Miss Price here, for example."

Jenny looked at her, puzzled, while another murmur went through the group.

"You see, what I didn't tell you was that Miss Price is a nurse . . . trained under Florence Nightingale. She's an inspiration to young ladies everywhere."

Miss Courtland paused to send an admiring glance Jenny's way. Jenny sent back a tentative attempt at a smile, for despite her hostess's apparently noble intentions, being singled out in such a manner was embarrassing.

"It was just a matter of keeping up with the lessons," Jenny explained, aware that every eye was studying her like an insect under a microscope. "Nurses graduate from Saint Thomas's every year."

"Ah, but how many had such a tenuous start in life? How many were abandoned by their mothers when they were mere babies?"

Jenny gasped and spilled some of the tea on her dress.

"Oh, dear!" Miss Courtland said, watching Jenny dab at the wet fabric with her napkin. "I certainly hope I didn't embarrass you. I've just been enthralled with you ever since I heard about your hardships."

"I would rather not—"

"Why, I can't imagine anything worse than having your mother leave you. But then having your father put you off on relatives, and then drink himself to death!"

A chill caught Jenny between the shoulders. She stopped worrying with her dress and sat there, mute, as the voice beside her droned on, sounding as if it came from a deep tunnel.

"You don't have to be ashamed of your heritage, dear," Miss Courtland went on, giving Jenny a smile that contradicted the venom in her eyes. "It has nothing to do with the woman you've become."

Then, turning to the others, she made a magnanimous gesture in Jenny's direction and said with a voice as smooth as velvet, "Why, look at the way Beethoven started out. His father was a drunk, too, and his mother no better than a common—"

"That's *enough!"* Jenny shot to her feet, sending the wicker chair toppling to the bricks behind her.

"Oh, dear!" Miss Courtland exclaimed, her hand up to her chest. While her mouth gaped with shock, there was a definite glint of triumph in her eyes. "I certainly didn't *intend*—"

"You certainly *did,"* Jenny seethed through her teeth.

She turned, ignoring Mrs. Courtland's confused, "Miss Price . . . *vous en etes faché*?" and hastened to the back door. One of the maids hurried to hold it open before she reached it. Once inside, Jenny did not wait for the maid to catch up and show her through the house or even fetch her bag.

Waiting carriages lined both sides of the street. Jenny went straight to the barouche, and without waiting for assistance, gathered her skirt and climbed into the back seat. "Please take me to Mr. Harrington's."

The driver and footman exchanged confused glances. "But Miss Celeste . . . ?"

"The party still has an hour to go. You'll have time to come back for her after you take me there."

Jenny sat rigid, her fingers splayed on each side of the seat to keep her balance during the jostling ride. *How could the woman be so hateful?* she asked herself. Jenny had never felt more humiliated, more shamed, more *betrayed*.

The last thought made her catch her breath. Although the very remembrance of Miss Courtland's smug face made Jenny almost nauseated, the woman had simply performed in keeping with her true nature, as would a scorpion or snake. The woman hadn't betrayed her. . . .

But someone had.

Jenny had told her story to only one person. Someone she trusted. Someone she cared for.

And now, ironically, only after his betrayal could she admit to herself just how much she cared for Graham Harrington. She had fallen for her employer—her *engaged* employer, she reminded herself—and now she must suffer the consequences.

29

WHAT do you mean, you're leaving?" Elaine demanded, watching openmouthed while Jenny threw clothes into her trunk. "You said you were going to stay."

The nurse turned a swollen, splotched face to her. "I want to go home."

"Why? You've worked miracles with Celeste—"

"Celeste." Jenny hesitated for a second, raising Elaine's hopes that she was reconsidering. But then she bent and began gathering shoes from the bottom of her armoire. "Please tell her good-bye for me," came her muffled voice. "I hate leaving the child without a nurse, but you've helped me enough with her seizures to know what to do. Her . . . father can hire someone else when he returns."

"Won't you tell me what happened? Did Miss Courtland say something to you?"

Jenny dropped the shoes on top of the dresses in her trunk. "I can't talk about it."

More befuddled than before, Elaine tried to reason with her. "You'll ruin your career. Your obligation is for two years—"

"I'll write Miss Nightingale when I get home. She can send

me another assignment by post . . . if she hasn't lost all confidence in me."

Elaine shook her head and walked over to touch her friend's sleeve. "Jenny, please don't leave like this."

"I have to." The lid snapped into place with a loud *thud.* "I'll see if Albert is ready with the carriage," she mumbled to herself on the way to the schoolroom. Before Elaine could make a move to follow, Jenny made an abrupt stop at the door.

"Elaine." She turned around, arms folded across her chest. "I may never see you again."

"I know," Elaine whispered, her throat suddenly tight.

Jenny crossed the room and took her by the shoulders. Her gray eyes blazed with something resembling madness. "I've been meek and cowardly concerning your spiritual condition, but I don't want to live the rest of my life with you on my conscience."

"What?"

"Jesus Christ went to a cross for you, laid down his life for you, and you act as if it means *nothing.*"

Elaine's hand went to her heart. "Jenny!"

"Well, don't you?"

"Y-yes," she faltered. She would have cut anyone else off cold for speaking to her in such a blunt manner, but she couldn't think of doing that to Jenny now. "But not anymore. I've . . . been considering becoming a Christian."

"Why should salvation be something that has to be considered? Do it now."

"Now?"

"Before I leave here. Then I can sleep nights."

Elaine tried to back away. "Some things can't be rushed, Jenny."

"And why not?" Jenny's grip on her shoulders tightened. "If you were drowning, and I begged you to hurry and grab the lifeline, would you accuse me of rushing you?"

Weary of being pressured, Elaine opened her mouth to retort that Jenny's analogy was simplistic. The fresh tears in her friend's eyes stopped her . . . along with the longing that suddenly welled up in her chest. "I'm . . . not sure how," she admitted.

Jenny released Elaine's shoulders, took both of her hands, and held them between her own. "It's not hard. Just *ask.*"

Swallowing, Elaine voiced her true concern. "What if God doesn't want me?"

"He wants you, Elaine. He tells us in the Bible that *whosoever will* may come."

"But what should I say?"

"You know what to say. You've heard it all your life."

Elaine thought for a long minute, then swallowed again. "I want to ask him to forgive me, and to save me."

"Then do it now," Jenny urged.

"All right . . . I will," she whispered, trembling. She bowed her head, and in the quietness of the room prayed under her breath, *Lord God, I want to be your child.*

Not until Elaine actually prayed those words did she realize how much they meant to her. The God she had denied for so long was opening his arms to her, giving her the opportunity to become his child. It was almost too incredible to think about.

Please forgive my sins and save me, in the name of your Son, Jesus Christ.

Lifting her chin, Elaine marveled that the empty place in her heart could be filled with a peaceful calm within those few seconds. The next thing Elaine knew, she was being caught up in Jenny's arms. "You can't imagine how I feel at this moment," Jenny said, her eyes shining.

"I'm sure I can't." Elaine smiled back at her. "I can't quite imagine how *I* feel at this moment."

Jenny laughed. *"Happy* would likely be the word for both of us."

Cautiously, Elaine asked, "Happy enough to stay?"

"I can't." Jenny stepped back, her expression clouding again. "But I'll write to you. Maybe not right away, but . . . when I'm able."

"When you're able," Elaine echoed sadly.

"And tell Celeste that I'll write to her, too. Be sure and tell her I love her."

"I'll tell her." Trying to muster another smile, Elaine said, "Be careful of strangers on the train."

Jenny returned a weak smile of her own. "I want to thank you for being my friend."

Elaine nodded sadly. "And thank *you* for leading me to God."

~

Ten minutes after Jenny left, Celeste came stomping into the schoolroom. "Where is Miss Price?" the girl demanded.

Standing in her bedroom doorway, Elaine gaped at her. "You don't know?"

"All I know is that Hudson said she came back here."

Elaine crossed the room and took the girl by the hand. "She's gone, Celeste."

"Gone?" The girl shook her head, her dark eyes unbelieving. "But she was with me at Miss Beryl's house just a little while ago. How can she be gone?"

"I wish I knew. Did anyone say anything to her?"

"You mean, something ugly?"

Elaine thought about Beryl Courtland and nodded grimly.

"Not at all," was Celeste's adamant reply. "In fact, everyone was quite pleasant to her." The girl pulled her hand away and with Elaine following, walked to the doorway of the bedroom. "This has to be a mistake. Are you sure she—"

When Celeste saw the open door of Jenny's empty armoire, she stopped talking . . . and began to cry.

~

"I don't feel like going to church without Miss Price here," Celeste said in a listless voice. She watched in the mirror as Elaine tied a ribbon in her hair.

"I'm going to miss her being with us, too. But she would have wanted you to go . . . both of us."

"I still don't understand why she had to leave. I thought she wasn't angry at me any more."

"Oh, Miss Celeste," Elaine said with a sad voice. "I don't know why she left, but Miss Price wasn't angry at you. She loved you."

Mr. Palmer and his wife, a petite woman with red hair and an Irish accent, met them at the coach. Celeste supposed that her father's steward was nervous about her not having a nurse in attendance. In fact, he mentioned to Miss Barton as they rode in the coach that he hoped to hire another as soon as possible.

"I don't want another nurse," Celeste told him. "I want Miss Price."

Mr. Palmer and Miss Barton only looked at each other.

Later, after Celeste had taken her nap, Alma came up into

the nursery and announced that Celeste had a visitor down in the front parlor—Miss Courtland. Miss Barton walked with her as far as the front hallway, and then said she would wait for her in the library.

"Darling!" Miss Beryl beamed, getting up from her chair when Celeste walked through the doorway. "I just felt so lonesome for you today that I thought I would pay you a call.

Celeste went into her arms and broke into sobs.

"Why, whatever is wrong?"

The soothing voice and the hand patting her back should have comforted Celeste, but she cried all the more. Miss Beryl took a handkerchief from her bag and led her to the settee.

"I keep expecting Miss Price to walk into the nursery," Celeste said between breaths as her face was being wiped.

"Why, of course you do, dear."

Celeste could only shake her head. Miss Beryl stared at her for a second, then arched both eyebrows. "Miss Price *is* up there, isn't she?"

"No," Celeste sniffed.

"Where is she?"

"She went home. To Bristol."

"Bristol? When?"

"After she left your party. She only came here long enough to get her trunk, and I don't even know why." Celeste took the handkerchief from Miss Beryl and wiped her eyes again, then went on. "I don't even have her address so I can write and ask her to come back."

"Oh dear," Miss Beryl said, sinking back into the cushions with her hand over her cheek. "I didn't think I had made her *that* angry."

Celeste tilted her head, puzzled. "You?"

Miss Beryl bit her lip and nodded. "I didn't want to tell you this, but when you were inside the house with Anna . . ."

"What happened?"

After a sigh, she went on. "Miss Price said something that wasn't very nice."

"About what?"

"Well, dear," Miss Beryl sighed again. "About you. I didn't want to tell you this, but I overheard Miss Price telling one of my other guests that she thought you were . . ." She closed her eyes, as if the memory was still painful for her. "A spoiled brat."

"No!" Celeste cried.

"I wish it weren't true. Well, of course after she said *that* about you, I rather lost my temper and demanded that she apologize. That was when she stormed through the house and left."

"I can't believe she would say that about me."

Giving her the tenderest of looks, Miss Beryl combed her fingers through Celeste's hair. "You're still too young to understand that people are not always what they seem."

As Miss Beryl went on about how, in time, Celeste would forget about Miss Price entirely, the melancholy that Celeste had felt since yesterday welled up unbearably inside of her. As she felt a tear trail down her cheek, she wished with all of her heart that she could undo the damage she had caused by hiding Miss Price's locket and writing those awful notes.

30

MRS. Ganaway says that it may take at least a fortnight to get another nurse," Elaine told Logan Fogarty on Monday afternoon, after he had completed his reading lesson. A month ago, the thought of having to take over the nursing duties, even temporarily, would have filled her with panic. She had been surprisingly calm and collected, though, when Celeste had had a seizure yesterday evening.

"I'm sorry your friend left," he said. His blue eyes stared at her with sympathy. "She was a fine person, Miss Price was."

"You've met her?"

Mr. Fogarty nodded. "She told me about your grandmother."

"Jenny could be rather frank at times, but I admired that in her."

"Aye," the man agreed, smiling. "I was on the receivin' end of her frankness."

"You were?"

He looked down and began tracing the embossed letters on the cover of Mark Twain's *The Innocents Abroad,* Mr. Fogarty's first assigned novel. "She set me to wondering if I've been doin' some wrong thinking about . . . somethin'."

"About what?"

His cheeks flushed. "It would embarrass me to say, ma'am."

"Then don't say." He sent a grateful look her way. Elaine sighed. "Jenny used that frankness to lead me to become a Christian before she left."

Mr. Fogarty's blue eyes creased at the corners. "Glory be, Miss Barton!" he exclaimed, studying her face. "What a grand thing to hear!"

"You mean you knew that I wasn't?"

The smile eased from his face. "Have I offended you, miss?"

Elaine shook her head. "Not at all. But I'm curious."

"Well, it's not anything of my doin'," he said gently. "It just seemed to me that God was always puttin' you in my prayers."

"You mean you've prayed for me?"

"Aye, Miss Barton." His face creased into another smile. "And it's becoming a habit, it is. I'll likely keep doin' so, if you don't mind."

Elaine stared boldly at the man next to her and wondered how any man so rugged could be so tenderhearted. "I can think of no one I would rather have praying for me," she heard herself say.

A silence stretched between them, until Elaine became flustered and lowered her eyes. Mr. Fogarty cleared his throat a few times, then asked if Elaine had heard of the Saint Mark's fair. "I've heard some of the others say that it's a decent bit o' fun."

"Now that you mention it," Elaine told him, "I arrived here last year only a week after the fair had ended."

"Would you be of a mind to go with me?"

Elaine couldn't believe her ears. Was this man actually asking to be her escort? *He's just being kind because Jenny left,* she told herself. But before she could reply that she appreciated his kindness, but didn't plan to go to the fair, he gave her an anxious look.

"I've got a better suit of clothes than the ones I wear for workin'."

There was no sign of false modesty in his voice. He was sincerely afraid of embarrassing her. She gave him a shy smile. "I would enjoy going with you, Mr. Fogarty."

A hopeful eyebrow rose. "You truly would, ma'am?"

"No matter what you're wearing."

~

"Celeste isn't awake yet," Elaine said when she answered Albert's knock on the schoolroom door that afternoon. "Reanna said she had a hard time falling asleep, so I'd like to give her just a little longer."

The boy nodded, his cap in his hand. "I'll come back," he said, backing out of the doorway.

"There is no need for that. By the time you got to the stables, you'd have to come right back." Elaine motioned toward the study table behind her. "Why don't we visit while we wait? There is something I would like to discuss with you anyway."

Following her into the room, Albert hurried around to pull out a chair for her at the school table. She thanked him for his chivalry, remembering how the lad had had to be prompted to help her up into the curricle. When he had taken the chair across from her, Elaine folded her hands on the table and began. "I don't know if Celeste will feel up to playing today. Miss Price is no longer employed as her nurse, and she's been quite despondent about it."

The boy gave a solemn nod.

"I do appreciate your coming up here to play," Elaine said, even though she knew that the boy had no choice in the matter. "Perhaps if you offer to show her some more of your strategies at draughts, she might take an interest."

"Yes, ma'am," he answered, glancing at the door to Celeste's bedroom. After a slight hesitation, he offered, "I learned a long time ago that keeping busy helps."

"You mean the orphanage in Sheffield?"

He looked surprised that she would know about his past, then nodded. "Sometimes new boys would spend most of their days crying. But the lessons and the chores helped keep their minds off their families. *Most* of the time, it did," he amended. "There was still some sniffling goin' on at night sometimes."

The thought of orphaned boys weeping in their beds evoked a strong tug of sympathy in Elaine. "Were you lonesome there, too?"

"No, ma'am."

"Not at all?"

"I don't even remember my parents." He shrugged. "I might have stayed longer if they hadn't tried to apprentice me to a soapmaker."

Elaine couldn't help but smile. "I take it that you're not interested in soap."

"Soap?" A wry grin came to his freckled face. "Only after I've mucked out the stables."

The door to Celeste's bedroom opened, and the girl walked into the schoolroom, followed by Reanna, who had obviously helped her to dress. "Why, good afternoon, Albert," she said brightly, walking over to the table. "It's so nice of you to visit. Would you care to paint with my watercolors?"

The boy sent a puzzled glance to Elaine, as if to say, *I thought you said she was upset?*

Later over supper, Elaine commented on the change in Celeste's behavior. The girl had chattered brightly as she and Albert painted, even bursting into giggles occasionally over his description of the practical joking between the groomsmen. "It's good to see your spirits have lifted," she told the girl.

"Why, Albert makes me laugh," Celeste answered, pulling the crust from her slice of bread. "I used to think he was dull, but he's actually quite witty." Giving a contented sigh, she locked eyes with Elaine and said pointedly, "I rather like not having a nurse. I wonder if Father would consider not hiring another one?"

Elaine watched the girl turn her attention back to the food on her plate. Celeste was taking great pains to show that she no longer cared that Jenny was gone. But why the effort, when it was so obvious that the child was carrying around a great hurt inside? Even the nonchalant smile seemed pasted on. "Is there anything you would like to talk with me about?" Elaine finally asked.

Celeste stopped chewing and raised an eyebrow. "About what?"

"I believe you know."

"Are you referring to my former nurse?"

Elaine nodded.

"Why, I simply realized that she never cared about me," the girl answered. "Therefore, I no longer care about her."

"How in the world can you believe Miss Price didn't care about you?"

"Quite easily. But since I no longer *care* about her, I also have no desire to discuss her." She further demonstrated her dismissal of the subject by picking up her fork and knife to make a great show of fussing over her roast quail.

"As you wish," Elaine said, placing her napkin on the side of her plate. "But I want to remind you that one of the last things Miss Price said before she left was that she loved you."

Celeste lifted her chin. An uncertainty crept into her expression for just a moment, and then her features hardened. "I don't want to hear that name ever again."

Late that night Elaine lay in bed and prayed, still in awe of the privilege she had of communicating with God. *Please give Jenny peace over whatever is tormenting her now. And help Celeste not to feel so much bitterness.* She was about to say 'Amen,' but then another thought came to her. *One more thing, Lord. If the idea that has been in my mind all evening has truly come from you, please show me some sign.*

~

Then said David to the P-h-i-l-i-s-t-i-n-e . . .

Holding his Bible close to the lamp on his bedside table, Logan ran his finger under the word again, remembering what Miss Barton had told him about the *p* and *h* together. "Fill-iss-tyne," he murmured.

Thou comest to me with a sword, and with a spear, and with a s-h-i-e-l-d . . .

He stopped again, then recognized the word and continued.

But I come to thee in the name of the Lord of h-o-s-t-s . . .

With the unfamiliar words that Logan had to decipher, it took him thirty minutes to finish reading the story of David and Goliath. He closed his Bible afterwards, extinguished his lamp, and stared at the dark ceiling above his bed for a long time.

~

"We received the book you ordered, Mr. Berthold." Behind the counter of Price's Bookstore, Jenny handed the leather-bound collected works of Eduard Mörike to an older gentleman with a thick, graying mustache. "May I wrap it for you?"

"Nein, danke schön." The customer cradled the book lovingly in his arms as if it were a dear child. "I carry it just as it is." He drew a crumpled one-pound note from his waistcoat pocket and handed it to Jenny, then smiled as she counted out his change.

"It has been a long time since I see you in here, Miss Price. For how long are you back to stay?"

Jenny smiled and answered, "For only a little while." As Jenny watched the man walk out of the shop, she could hear her father uncrating the remainder of the shipment on the other side of the curtain.

Father had offered to buy her two-year obligation by sending Saint Thomas's the money that it cost to train her, but Jenny had gratefully declined. She had sent a letter to Miss Nightingale on Monday, just two days ago. She had no idea how long it would be until she received a reply, but she suspected there would be no time wasted in assigning her elsewhere. Even though Miss Nightingale would be disappointed in her, there was still a heavy demand for nurses in Great Britain.

Due to circumstances beyond my control, I find that I can no longer fulfill my duties in the Harrington household. I am willing to serve in any other situation that you deem appropriate, had been the succinct wording of Jenny's letter. She could only pray that Miss Nightingale would not demand an explanation. How could she possibly admit that she had fallen in love with her employer? And how could Miss Nightingale, whose first love had always been nursing, understand the pain of betrayal she still felt?

True, Mr. Harrington had never professed any affection for her . . . nor had she expected him to. But she *had* expected him to keep the confidence that she had entrusted to him and not to repeat it for the amusement of his fiancée.

The bell above the door signaled another customer entering the shop—actually, a group of three women. Helen, the shop assistant who had worked for her parents from the beginning, was busy waiting on someone else, so Jenny left the counter to see if she could be of assistance. She was grateful for the opportunity to keep her mind occupied with something other than the people of the Harrington household.

~

Minutes after Graham Harrington's return from Liverpool Wednesday afternoon, he sat across his desk from Mrs. Ganaway and listened to the news of Miss Price's resignation.

"You mean she gave no reason for leaving?" he asked, incredulous.

The housekeeper's face was grim. "None to me, Miss Barton, or anybody else. Just packed up and left."

"How did Celeste take it?"

"You would have to ask her governess about that, sir. But she seems to be fine now."

Graham ran his hand through his hair. He had expected more from Miss Price than to leave whenever she became bored with her position. Immediately he chided himself for the thought. *This isn't like her . . . and she loved Celeste. Something happened here while I was gone.*

"Thank you, Mrs. Ganaway," he finally said. "You may go now."

The housekeeper nodded and rose to leave, then hesitated in the doorway and looked back at him.

"Yes, Mrs. Ganaway?"

"She was a good nurse, Miss Price was."

Graham sighed. "Yes, she was." *She was a good person, too,* he thought. *A kind, caring woman.*

"Do you still want Mr. Palmer to look for someone to replace her?"

He let out a long breath. "Keep looking, but don't commit to anyone until I give you the word."

When she was gone, Graham took the papers regarding the sale of his Liverpool office from his satchel and put them into a desk drawer. He would sort them out later, after he had spent some time with Celeste. He left his office and went toward the staircase, then took an impulsive detour to the left, into the morning room.

What were you thinking about, Theresa? he wondered as he stood in front of her portrait. He had commissioned the painting fourteen years ago, soon after their wedding, as an everlasting reminder of her beauty. But it was not her beauty that he ached for now . . . it was the *friendship* they had enjoyed, the sharing of each other's thoughts, hopes, and dreams. And, unlike her beauty, those things couldn't be captured on canvas.

Beryl had made several hints about moving the portrait to the nursery or somewhere else more suitable, now that he was engaged to be married. He supposed that he would have to do so, at least before the wedding. Then, no doubt, a portrait of Beryl would occupy the same space, gracing the room again with beauty. But would his life be graced with the same intimacy, the friendship, he had shared with Theresa?

"I didn't even think about her when I was gone," Graham confided under his breath to the face in the portrait. True, the negotiations had taken every waking minute, but even when he had settled down at night, his thoughts had not drifted toward his fiancée.

What *had* occupied his mind? He shifted his weight and let his eyes run along the veined marble in the fireplace. *Celeste, mainly.* He had felt the need to make plans, now that business would no longer be consuming most of his time.

One night in his Liverpool hotel room, Graham had found himself wondering if he should buy one of those bicycles and teach Celeste to ride . . . once he had learned how himself. Surely if she stayed on the grass, and he and that boy Albert ran along on each side, she would be safe.

I'll have to see what Miss Price thinks of the idea, he had told himself, but the very idea made him chuckle. After all, *she* had been the instigator of the croquet matches, and of Celeste's driving lessons in the curricle. No doubt she would love the idea of a bicycle. *Where did such a young woman get such an adventurous spirit?* he had wondered, recalling the scattered moments he had spent in her company.

Standing there alone in the morning room, Graham frowned at the memory. *Why* had he spent more time thinking about Miss Jenny Price than about the woman with whom he planned to spend the rest of his life?

He lifted his eyes to Theresa's portrait again and took in a sharp breath. Above the hint of a smile, the blue eyes staring back at him from the canvas seemed to mock him gently. *You know why.*

~

"Why, hello, Father!" Celeste beamed when Graham walked into the nursery ten minutes later. She gave him a quick embrace. "Miss Barton and Albert and I are going to play croquet. Now you can play, too."

"All right," he replied with a nod to the governess. "But first I'd like to have a word with you privately."

"Why don't you and I go ahead and set up the game?" Miss Barton suggested to the stable boy. When they were gone, Graham turned to his daughter.

"Come sit with me," he said, motioning toward the sofa. "I want to ask you something."

The girl's posture stiffened, and the dimple in her cheek disappeared. "This is about Miss Price, isn't it?"

"Just come and sit." When she had taken a place on the sofa next to him, he cleared his throat. "I want you to tell me truthfully if you played any more pranks on Miss Price."

"I didn't. I promise, Father."

"Then why did she leave?"

Celeste's expression darkened. "She left because Miss Beryl scolded her."

"For what?"

"For telling someone at her garden party that I was a spoiled brat."

"Did you *hear* her say it?"

She lifted her chin, meeting his incredulous gaze straight on. "I was inside. But Miss Beryl told me."

"That doesn't sound like something Miss Price would do," Graham insisted, shaking his head. "Are you absolutely certain?"

The look of defiance on the girl's face softened into a lip-trembling sadness. "I thought she *liked* me," she said, and her voice became piteously younger.

~

The next day, Graham and Beryl sat at a window table in Isola Bella's in Soho and ordered lunches of bouillabaisse and mackerel with fennel sauce. Bits and pieces of conversations drifted from other tables, accompanied by a trio of stringed instruments playing in a back corner.

"Celeste asked to come, too," Graham told his fiancée when the waiter had left. "But I told her we would bring her next time."

Beryl's gloved hand reached for his on the tabletop. "I hope she understood, darling. After all, she gets to spend more time with you than I do."

"I believe she does." In truth, Graham had not wanted to leave the girl, for the forced gaiety he had witnessed since arriving home yesterday was disturbing. He would not have had the liberty to speak frankly with Beryl, though, had his daughter been present. "I don't understand the circumstances that led to Miss Price's resignation," he began after taking a sip of his coffee. "I simply cannot believe that she would refer to Celeste as a *brat.*"

With a shrug of her shoulders, Beryl answered, "You said yourself that Miss Price was outspoken when it came to Celeste. Why should this surprise you?"

"A *brat?* And she said this to whom? Someone at your party she had just met?"

"I heard it with my own ears, darling. I'm just thankful that

Celeste happened to be in the house, or she would have been brokenhearted."

"That's another thing. If you were concerned about Celeste's feelings, why did you tell her about it afterward?"

Beryl's posture went rigid, and her hand slipped away from his and back down to her lap. "Just what are you accusing me of, Graham?"

"I'm not accusing you," he answered. Reaching out to touch her arm, he said, "I just don't understand why she had to know."

The defiance in her expression relaxed. "It wasn't my intention to tell Celeste, darling," she said earnestly. "But the child was blaming *herself* for Miss Price's departure. I simply didn't feel that I had any other choice."

"I suppose you didn't," Graham conceded after a sigh. "And I do appreciate your taking the time to console her. But I still can't imagine Miss Price saying—"

Beryl took his hand again. "Let's talk about something other than Miss Price now, shall we?"

31

"I HAVE been wondering what to do with the house that my grandmother left me," Elaine said to Logan Fogarty Thursday afternoon when his lesson was finished. A pleasant noon rain had washed the air, and the scents of green things and damp earth wafted through the lattice of the gazebo. Elaine had found herself wishing, as the Irishman seated next to her read, that the tutoring sessions could last longer than an hour.

Mr. Fogarty, his elbows resting on his knees, nodded. "Aye. 'Tis a hard decision."

"If I sell the house, I'll have more than enough money put away for my later years."

"Ye want to be considerin' that." The man nodded again.

"But if I open a boarding school for girls, I can keep the house *and* have some income . . . and I would still have the opportunity to teach."

He looked at her with an expression of wonder. "Why, that would be just right for ye."

"It would seem to be," Elaine replied. "But for the past two days . . . I've had another idea."

"Other than the boarding school?"

She nodded. "Have you ever had a thought that wouldn't leave you?"

"Aye." He smiled. "That's how it was with me when I first started thinking about readin'. I couldn't even sleep sometimes."

Elaine smiled back at him. She had known instinctively that Mr. Fogarty would understand. "May I tell you my idea, and see what you think about it?"

The Irishman sat up straight and put a hand to his chest. "You're wantin' *my* opinion?"

"I would value your opinion very highly." Elaine took a deep breath. "I would like to open the house to orphaned children."

"An orphanage, Miss Barton?"

"Yes. But for boys *and* girls, so that children who lose their parents aren't also separated from their sisters or brothers."

Mr. Fogarty's blue eyes filled with warmth. "I think it's an even grander idea, Miss Barton. And think of all the little children ye could give lessons to!"

Elaine laughed. "I would have to hire some other teachers, too. A cook and kitchen staff as well."

An expression of worry replaced the smile on his face. "Aye, but then how would ye pay them? And what about food and clothes for the little ones? Not to mention books . . . and doctorin' when they're ill?"

"That's what has kept me up for two nights. The funds that were left to me would hardly last a year under those circumstances."

"Then what can ye do?"

"I don't know," Elaine said, sighing. "Most, if not all, of the orphanages in England are sponsored by churches. I don't know how to go about appealing for sponsorship, how to set up accountability for the funds that come in, or even how to go about gathering the children."

"Why don't ye ask Mr. Harrington's advice?" the Irishman suggested after a moment's thought.

"Mr. Harrington?"

"You're talkin' about operating a charity, but I would imagine you're goin' to have to treat it like a business, too."

"A business?" Somehow that tainted the whole idea, and Elaine shook her head in puzzlement.

"Not for makin' a profit, Miss Barton, but so's you'll have a plan." He waved a hand out toward the lawn. "We gardeners . . . we don't just throw seeds up in the air and see what happens. It takes proper plannin' from year to year. Like a business."

That made sense, but then the enormity of the whole project threatened to overwhelm her. "But how can I know if this idea is from God, and not just some sympathetic impulse on my part?"

"Perhaps ye should ask him to give ye peace about it, ma'am."

"I've already done that."

"Then wait for it," he suggested. The smile came back, softening his rugged features. "But I have a feelin' that it was the Lord who put this idea in your heart. According to my pastor, Jesus had a good deal to say about widows and orphans."

~

Celeste was just waking from her nap when Elaine got back to the nursery. While the girl was in the lavatory, Alma approached Elaine in the schoolroom. "The child spoke in her sleep today," the maid said in a low voice.

"What did she say?" Elaine asked, although she had a feeling she already knew.

Alma looked back over her shoulder. "It was the name of her nurse, Miss Price."

Thirty minutes later, as Elaine sat on a bench watching the three young people play croquet, her thoughts returned to what Alma had told her. Celeste missed Jenny, that was certain. But for some reason she was working very hard to cover up her heartbreak.

"They're rather lively today, aren't they?" came a voice from behind Elaine.

She turned to see Mr. Harrington standing there in his shirt-sleeves and a pair of fawn-colored trousers. "I believe Celeste is catching up with Albert today," she said, nodding toward the croquet match. "But Gerdie has yet to be beaten."

He stepped to the side of the bench and waved at Celeste, answering her request that he join them with, "Next game." Then he turned back to Elaine. "Do you mind if I sit here? There are some things I would like to discuss with you." She gathered her skirts and moved over to make room for him.

"She's rather taken with this game, isn't she?" Mr. Harrington remarked, staring out at his daughter.

"That was Miss Price's doing," Elaine said with a cautious sidelong glance. "*And* the fact that she seems to enjoy the challenge of a fair contest."

"Do you think Celeste misses her?"

"Very much so, although she won't admit it." She told him what Alma had said about the child talking in her sleep.

Mr. Harrington furrowed his brow with thought. "That settles it."

"Sir?"

He turned to Elaine. "It has been my policy for years to try to hear all sides of a situation, and it has served me in good stead. What is missing here is Miss Price's side."

"You're going to write to her?"

"That's another reason I wanted to speak with you. She left no forwarding address with either Mr. Palmer or Mrs. Ganaway. Would she possibly have left one with you?"

Elaine shook her head, then suddenly remembered Saint Thomas's. "Surely the school would have it. Or you could even post a letter to Bristol in care of Price's Bookstore, and it would reach her."

"I'll do that." He was quiet for several seconds, then cleared his throat. "Miss Barton . . . can you imagine Miss Price referring to Celeste as a spoiled brat?"

Elaine gaped at him. "Absolutely not! That would be completely out of character for her."

Mr. Harrington nodded, his mouth set in a determined line. "I'll post the letter in the morning." He shifted to the edge of the seat, and it seemed that he would get up and leave. When he did not, Elaine sent him a puzzled glance.

"Is there something else, sir?"

The lines of concentration deepened along his brow and under his eyes. "I had a rather strange dream last night, and it has not left me all day."

Not knowing what she was expected to say, Elaine waited silently for him to continue.

"It involved the leys jar in my library," he finally offered. Quirking his eyebrows at her, he continued. "And . . . you, Miss Barton."

"Me?"

"I dreamed I felt compelled to give you the leys jar. You

held an infant in your arms, and I remember saying, 'Sell this and use the money to take care of your child.'"

Elaine's breath caught in her throat, and pain in the palms of her hands made her aware that she was digging her fingernails into them.

"I'm not one to take great stock in dreams," Mr. Harrington went on, apparently not noticing the shock that *had* to be all over her face, "but I can still remember every detail of this one. You don't have any children, though. I can't imagine why I would have such a peculiar thing on my mind. This morning I even asked God to give me clarity concerning it, but I have received no answer."

When she could finally speak, Elaine hugged her arms to her sides against the strange chill that was coursing through her body. "I'm the *least* qualified to speak for God, Mr. Harrington," she replied. "But may I tell you what has happened to me?"

~

Saturday dawned fair and breezy. There was a general chatter of excitement from Graham Harrington's servants as the groups drifted down the carriage drive to the stables for their rides to the Saint Mark's fair. The barouche, coach, curricle, and even the wagon had been pressed into service. Once the entire Harrington household had been delivered to the area near Holland Park, the groomsmen and drivers would find places to tie up the horses and have their own turns at the fun.

"So Mr. Harrington has offered to solicit a board of sponsors," Miss Barton was saying to Logan when the stables were in sight. She shook her head in an incredulous manner. "I asked God for a sign, and when Mr. Harrington offered to donate one of his valuable artifacts, the peace you advised me to wait for finally came."

"Does that mean you'll be leaving here?" Logan asked, though he knew it could mean nothing else. He had shyly offered his elbow, as he had observed gentlemen do, and the governess had, without hesitation, taken it. He wished he had the nerve to tell her how wonderful she looked to him, with the early sunlight glinting off the auburn curls that peeked from under her hat. Right now the light pressure of her hand in the crook of his elbow brought a feeling of companionship and security that he had never experienced. How *lonely* life would be again once she was gone.

"There are still details that will have to be attended to," Miss Barton answered, her jade-green eyes lighting up with the wonder of it all. "And I did promise Mr. Harrington I would stay here until his wedding, for Celeste's—"

"Hey, you dumb mick!"

The sound of George's voice from behind him caused a knot in the pit of Logan's stomach. *Pay him no mind,* he told himself as Elaine's hand tightened on his arm.

"I see they'll be able to commence with the dog and pony show!"

Next came Healy's mocking lisp. "How obligin' of you, Fogarty, to bring along your own dog!"

Logan froze. "They're just trying to provoke you," Miss Barton whispered, but he could see the hurt on her face. Gently, he removed her hand from the crook of his arm and turned. Some ten feet away, George, Healy, and Dudley had also come to a stop. They were clad in their finest clothes, their hair shining with macassar oil. The faces of the first two gardeners were twisted into sneers, but Dudley wore a mask of uncertainty.

"Look, Fogarty," Dudley quavered, holding up both palms and taking a step backwards. "Weren't me what said anything."

"Aw, hold yer ground," George ordered, his eyes meeting Logan's with challenge. "He ain't gonna do nothin'." But Dudley, after a second's hesitation, turned to make tracks back to the gardening cottage.

His hands clenching into fists at his sides, Logan took a step toward the other two gardeners. *"Please,* Mr. Fogarty," came Miss Barton's voice from behind him, and he felt her touch on his shoulder. "It doesn't matter."

Logan turned his head long enough to give her a sad smile. "Aye, but it does, ma'am." Facing the two again, he lowered his shoulders and barreled into George like an angry bull. He picked up the gardener, who was too stunned to offer any resistance, and threw him across his shoulder. Healy, mouth and eyes wide, turned to run away, but Logan had him by the seat of the pants before he could take another step.

"Let me go!" Healy yelped as Logan tucked him under his arm. Logan paid them no mind. The anger that had accumulated for weeks seemed to give him an almost supernatural strength. Accompanied by shouting and hooting servants, he took long strides toward the back of the stable.

"You're gonna be sorry if you don't put us down!" George howled.

"Aye," Logan answered, averting his face sharply to avoid Healy's kicking feet. He glanced to his side to see Mr. Horton limping along with a grin as wide as a shovel blade. "I'm going to put ye down presently."

When he reached the manure pile, at least six feet tall and glistening with the morning dew, he allowed Healy to drop to the grass. Before the shorter gardener could scramble away,

Logan put a boot into the small of his back and pressed him to the ground. He grabbed George's feet with both hands, did a mighty turn with his shoulder, and swung him into the pile, as effortlessly as tossing turnips into a crate. Then he bent down and did the same with Healy.

Logan barely heard the roar of approval that rose from the servants gathered around or felt the claps on his shoulders as he turned and weaved his way through them, back toward where Miss Barton still stood with her hand at her mouth. His heart hammered forcefully against his chest, pumping courage and determination through his whole body.

"Miss Barton," he said when he stood before her. "Ye will be needin' someone to keep up the lawn of your orphanage, as well as to grow fresh vegetables for the children."

Her green eyes widened. "Why, Mr. Fogarty . . . are you applying for the position of gardener?"

"No, ma'am. I'm askin' to be your husband."

Her hand dropped to her heart. "My *husband?"*

"Aye." Her reaction caused a bit of uncertainty to creep in. "That is . . . if ye will have me." By then, the other servants had caught up again, roaring approval from all sides.

"What do you say, Miss Barton?" he pressed.

Slowly her face eased into a smile. Logan's heart resumed its fierce pounding when she held out a hand to take his arm again.

"Please call me Elaine . . . *Logan."*

~

The crowd had finally thinned out enough so that Celeste, her father, and Miss Beryl could make their way to the glassed-in exhibit at the other end of the tent. A shiver ran down Celeste's neck at the sight of the two-headed snake, but she wasn't repulsed enough to tear her eyes away. "How do they know which way to go?" she whispered to her father, who was holding tight to her hand.

"Perhaps they toss a coin," he suggested with a twinkle in his eyes.

Celeste smiled appreciatively. It was good to hear Father make a joke. He had seemed so preoccupied for the past week. *Ever since . . .* She shook the thought from her head. *He's just been tired, that's all.*

"Well, I think it's grotesque," Miss Beryl whispered forcefully as she wiped at her neck with a handkerchief. She turned to glare at a man who bumped her elbow when he leaned closer to the exhibit, then said to Father, "I'm going to wait outside."

Celeste stopped looking at the snake long enough to watch Miss Beryl work her way back to the entrance of the tent. She wished her father's fiancée was having a better time, but from the minute they had stepped from the coach onto the grounds of Saint Mark's, she had found something to complain about. *Perhaps she has a headache.* That had to be it. She recalled how beastly irritable her own headaches made her feel. *And she still wanted to come with us,* Celeste thought, admiring Miss Beryl's unselfishness.

When she and Father walked out of the tent, she was relieved to see that Miss Beryl, standing several feet away, was actually smiling.

"Graham . . . Celeste!" she called, beckoning. With her stood a lady that Celeste recognized from Miss Beryl's garden party. She had worn a hat with ostrich feathers then, but now she wore one that was decorated with ribbons coiled to look like rosebuds.

"This is my good friend Jeanette Worthy," Miss Beryl said to Father as the lady offered her hand. "I don't think you've ever met her. She has been living with her aunt in Florence for the past two years."

"I'm charmed to meet you," he said, brushing her hand to his lips. Then the lady turned to Celeste and smiled.

"And of course I remember this delightful young lady. Are you having a good time?"

Celeste nodded and pointed to the tent they had just left. "Have you seen the snake with two heads?"

The lady's lips seemed to twitch just slightly. "I haven't gotten around to seeing it just yet," she answered with a glance at Miss Beryl.

"The exhibits are frightfully packed anyway," Miss Beryl remarked, turning to Father. "Perhaps we should wait to see the rest when the crowds die down."

"I have a better idea," Father said to her. "Why don't Celeste and I see the rest of the exhibits while you and Miss Worthy keep each other company? We could meet in a couple of hours."

Celeste felt her shoulders relax and found herself hoping that Miss Beryl would agree. After all, fresh air would likely cure whatever was ailing her.

Miss Beryl glanced over at the snake tent again, then nodded. "If you're sure you won't mind . . ."

"I'm positive." Father smiled back. "Let's meet where that chap was selling meat pies. I'll be good and famished by then."

Taking Celeste by the hand, Father led her in the direction of the next tent, where a sign boasted a magician who could supposedly make a live pigeon disappear. He paid a collector at the entrance twopence, then looked down at her with concerned eyes. "You don't mind that Miss Beryl wanted to spend some time with her friend, do you?"

Celeste shook her head and tried to peer inside. "How do you suppose he's going to make that pigeon disappear?"

Almost an hour later, the two of them stood outside still another tent. "Are you sure you don't need some time to rest?" Father asked her.

"I'm not tired yet," Celeste replied, then pointed to the sign in front of them. "May we see that?"

NOAH'S ARK ANIMAL-SHAPED POTATO COLLECTION . . . A MIRACLE STRAIGHT FROM THE GROUND . . . ONLY ONE PENNY!

"Noah's ark in potatoes?" Father dug into his waistcoat pocket for still more change. "We wouldn't want to miss that, now would we?"

The tent was stuffy and packed with people, and the only faint light came from a lantern suspended over a table at the back.

"Why is it so dark in here?" Celeste asked.

In spite of the dimness, she caught the smile that her father gave her. "I imagine that 'Mister Noah' has done a bit of carving on his potatoes." Just then another group of people filed into the tent, pressing into their backs, and Father took her hand and led her over to one of the canvas sides. "Why don't we just wait here until the crowd clears out a bit?"

Celeste nodded. It would be impossible for them to work their way over to the exhibit now, anyway. She spent her time studying the people who were jockeying forward for better positions. They were curiously quiet, speaking in hushed tones that could only be described as reverent. *It's as if we were in church,* Celeste thought. She wondered if the onlookers actually thought there was something holy about the exhibit, then suddenly she heard a female voice speak her name.

"Celeste was actually spying on them from outside a window?"

The voice filtered in through the canvas behind Celeste, and she recognized it as coming from Miss Beryl's friend, Miss Worthy. She opened her mouth to say something to Father, but he put his finger to his lips and inclined his head against the canvas.

"Oh, the wretched little sneak has done worse than that." This time it was unmistakably Miss Beryl's throaty voice. "I caught sight of her spying on Graham and me from the other side of the conservatory door one time."

"Did you tell him?"

"Why? And risk my engagement? His precious little prima donna can do no wrong in his eyes. Besides, it worked to my advantage this time."

The scorn in Miss Beryl's tone cut through Celeste like sleet through a fog. She swallowed, missing whatever Miss Worthy had said, then heard Miss Beryl's voice again.

"I'll never forget the look on that nurse's face. She's likely somewhere washing bedpans now!"

The sound of giggling came next. Blinking back the stinging tears in her eyes, Celeste looked up at the blurred image of her father. "Come here," he whispered. He pulled her to him, gently covering both of her ears with his hands.

They stood like that for at least five more minutes—Celeste hearing nothing as her father listened. When he finally removed his hands from her ears, he bent down and scooped her into his arms. There in the dimness he gave her a smile that eased some of the ache she was feeling inside the pit of her stomach.

"I'm sorry you had to hear that," he said as he wiped her cheeks with his hand.

Celeste bit her trembling lip and sniffed. "Perhaps it was good that I did," she answered, although she couldn't help but wish that she hadn't. "Are you still going to marry her?"

"No. Do you mind terribly?"

A lump welled in her throat at the thought of not having a mother, but she shook her head.

"Have you ever been to Bristol?"

"Bristol?" Celeste cocked her head at him. "You know that I haven't."

"Would you like to go?"

Then she realized what he was saying. *Miss Price is from Bristol.* "You and me?"

"We could leave right now," he said, his eyes smiling. "Unless you'd rather we stay here and look at potatoes and the like."

"Right now? Shouldn't we pack?"

"Not if we want to make sure we arrive in Bristol before dark. We can buy anything we need when we get there."

"I would love to go!" she said, throwing her arms around his neck. A sudden worry caused her to pull her head back. "But what are you going to tell Miss Beryl?"

"I'm going to tell her that she's not invited," her father answered, hoisting her up higher into his arms on his way out of the tent.

~

Outside, Graham saw the two women standing over to the side of the tent, about seven feet away. He locked eyes with Miss Worthy immediately. The woman's mouth gaped open and she motioned to Beryl, who turned to look at them with a startled expression.

"Oh, there you are, darling," Beryl said, reverting to her usual composure as he approached with his daughter in his arms. "I thought Celeste would have tired of the exhibits a long time ago. Is she all right?"

"She's fine." Graham smiled at Celeste and reached into his waistcoat pocket again. Bringing out a sovereign, he held it out to Beryl. "This is for your carriage, when you're ready to leave."

Her cheeks reddening slightly, Beryl glanced at Miss Worthy and then down at the coin in her palm. "You're going home now?"

"Not quite. But the two of you may want to stay and see some of the exhibits. There is a giant pumpkin a couple of tents back that must weigh twenty stone."

"And just where are you going?"

"Paddington Station." Graham started to turn, but Beryl caught his arm. Her thick lashes batted demurely against her cheeks, and her voice suddenly took on a softer, pleading tone. "But I thought your business in Liverpool was concluded."

"We're going to Bristol."

"We? You mean, Celeste and you?"

"Yes." Graham gave his daughter a wink. "My little prima donna and me."

32

SATURDAY afternoon, Jenny was in the office of Price's Bookstore, seated on a stool next to her mother as they looked over an order form at the work desk. "Mr. Berthold would like more German poetry," she said, watching the neat row of printing taking shape under her mother's pen.

"And we're almost out of Mrs. Beeton's cookbook," Mother mused out loud. "This time I'm going to double our order."

The bell tinkled from inside the shop. Jenny glanced over her shoulder from habit but didn't get up. Father, along with the shop assistant, Helen, could take care of the steady stream of customers. If they found themselves overwhelmed, one of them had only to stick a head through the curtain and ask for their help.

As soon as Jenny had turned her attention back to the order, she heard Helen's voice behind her. "Jenny, there are some people here to see you."

"Me?"

"Some of your old friends must have found out you were back," Mother said, the pen still moving in her hand.

"I wonder why Helen didn't mention their names?" Jenny said as she got to her feet. On her way out the curtain, she tucked the loose strands of hair back into her chignon.

"Miss Price?"

Jenny let out a gasp at the sight of Mr. Harrington. He was holding his hat in one hand and Celeste's hand in the other.

"We've come to apologize for what happened to you," Mr. Harrington said without preamble. "And to ask you to come back to London."

Celeste looked up at her, and her bottom lip began to tremble. "I'm sorry, Miss Price. I told Miss Beryl all your secrets, and then she told them to everyone. I didn't know she'd—"

"You?" Jenny shook her head. "But how . . . ?"

"She was listening at the window the day you told me," Mr. Harrington explained, his hand on his daughter's shoulder.

"You mean—?"

"Jenny?" From behind the curtain, Mother appeared with her pen tucked over her ear, her gray eyes questioning. Jenny recovered enough to make introductions and had to make them all over again when her father, sensing something amiss, excused himself from a customer and joined them.

"You'll have to pardon the condition of our clothing," Mr. Harrington said, brushing at a wrinkle in his coat sleeve. "We didn't take time to pack any other clothes."

"You must have been in a hurry."

"Quite so," he replied with a meaningful look at Jenny. "In fact, we left a fascinating potato exhibit to come here." He turned back to Jenny's father and motioned toward the curtain behind the counter. "Mr. Price, I take it that there is an office back there?"

"And a storeroom." A smile crept to her father's lips. "A stove, with hot water for tea as well."

"Tea would be nice." Mr. Harrington turned to Jenny's mother. "And would you happen to carry children's books?"

"We have a wonderful children's section," Mother answered, her expression filled with understanding. Holding out a hand toward Celeste, she said, "Would you like to browse through them together?"

"Yes," the girl answered, but before taking Mother's hand, she stepped forward to put her arms around Jenny's waist. "I love you, Miss Price."

~

A few minutes later, Jenny and Mr. Harrington sat at right angles to each other at a small table near the office stove.

"Are you sure you wouldn't like me to brew some tea?" Jenny asked, weaving her fingers together in her lap. She sat awkwardly, twisted sideways in the chair. A second ago she had accidentally bumped his knee with hers, and she didn't want to do it again.

Mr. Harrington shook his head. "I'd rather you tell me that you're going to come back with us."

Jenny had hoped against hope, during the quiet times that she couldn't fill with activity, that he would show up one day and say those very words. But now they caused a terrible ache, because they stemmed from Mr. Harrington's concern about righting a wrong and nothing more.

"I suppose I shall have to," she answered. "I'm still obligated for the two years, unless Miss Nightingale decides to send me elsewhere. She should have received my letter by now."

"We'll have to pay her a call as soon as we get back to London," he said thoughtfully. "Before she has a chance to consider any other assignment."

Jenny took a deep breath and nodded. "I can be packed and ready by morning."

A puzzling look of disappointment settled across Mr. Harrington's face. "Just like that?"

"Like what, Mr. Harrington?"

"You're agreeing to come back without an argument?"

"Well, I still care about Celeste. And now that I know . . . "

He leaned closer across the table, staring at her with his dark eyes. "Now that you know *what,* Jenny?"

He had never used her given name before, and it took her by surprise. "Now that I . . ." What *had* she meant to say? While she groped for an answer, he spoke for her.

"Now that you realize *I* didn't tell your secret to Beryl? That *was* why you left, wasn't it?"

The memory of how she had felt that day sent a cold chill through her. "Yes."

"You were hurt because you thought I had betrayed you, weren't you?"

Why is he asking me this? Jenny thought. "It doesn't matter now, Mr. Harrington," she said, her voice sounding flat and hollow in her ears.

"It matters to me. If you were hurt . . ." Mr. Harrington cleared his throat and shifted in his chair. "May I see your hand, please?"

"My hand?"

"Please."

Jenny unclasped her hands and put her right one on the table. She watched in stunned silence as he covered it with his own. "Now, look at me." His voice was gentle, a caress that floated across to her.

She raised her chin and looked at him. On his face was the most tender of expressions, and she wondered if he could hear her heart beating loudly against her chest.

"This past week has been miserable for me," he said. "I have never missed anyone so much since . . ."

"Theresa," Jenny whispered.

His dark eyes sparkled. "I have longed for our talks. The intelligence of your gray eyes and the beauty of your face. The sense of balance and adventure that you brought to our household."

He paused, as if collecting his thoughts, and as he went on, a trace of worry clouded his expression. "I said to you once that your sense of humor reminded me of Theresa. But I hope you don't think I will be constantly comparing you with her. I'm not expecting you to be a copy of my first wife."

Jenny shook her head. "I don't know quite what to think, Mr. Harrington."

"Please call me Graham."

"Graham," she complied, marveling at how natural the name sounded from her lips.

"Think about this then, Jenny," he said, leaning still closer. "Think about the fact that I . . . love you . . . and so does Celeste. I would be the happiest man in England if you would consent to be my wife."

"Your *wife?*" Jenny's other hand went to her pounding chest. The recollection came sweeping back to her, of herself peering down from a window while Graham and Celeste sat together in the carriage. She had so longed to be a part of their lives. *Say yes,* her heart urged.

A face flashed across her thoughts. "But what about—"

"Beryl?" Graham sat back and gave a regretful shake of the head. "Unfortunately, she and Mrs. Courtland will have to enjoy truffled dog with someone else."

When she smiled at the memory of their private joke, he

lifted her fingers to his lips. "You haven't answered my question, Jenny. If you'll say yes, you'll save me the trouble of having to ask you every day for two years. Remember your obligation, Nurse Price."

A sense of awe overwhelmed Jenny. In spite of her misgivings, God had pieced together the puzzle of her life, giving her a dream she had not dared to pray for. The next thing she knew, she was on her feet, drawn into Graham Harrington's arms. His lips were warm and sweet, and she returned his kiss with an ardor she did not know she was capable of.

"You know, our coming here was done under such impulse that I neglected to think all of this through," he murmured into her hair. "This changes things dramatically."

"It does?" She knew instinctively that he was not the kind of man to play with her emotions, but still she held her breath and waited for an explanation.

"Propriety and all that. We can't live under the same roof now . . . not without being married."

Jenny wondered why that hadn't even crossed her mind. "I'll just have to stay here until the wedding."

"I suppose so," Graham agreed, and she could feel his chest rise and fall with a sigh.

"What's wrong?"

After a hesitation he said, "Beryl wanted the most impressive wedding in London. It was taking her several months to make arrangements, but I was in no real hurry, so it didn't matter."

She smiled against his shoulder. "Are you worried that I'll take that long as well?"

"That did cross my mind. Isn't there *any* way that wedding plans can be hurried up a bit?"

After a moment's thought, Jenny answered, "My father's family owns a bakery here in Bristol, so the cake is taken care of. The dress is the only problem. Perhaps six or eight weeks?"

He took hold of her shoulders and stepped back to grin at her. "You mean it?"

"She means it!" piped up a child's voice.

They both turned to find Celeste standing just inside the curtain, her eyes wide and a hand clasped over her mouth. "I wasn't spying, honest," she said quickly, and held up a thick book. "I just wanted to show this to Miss Price—there are two hundred stories in here!"

Graham opened his mouth as if to scold her, but Jenny reached up and put a finger to his lips. Smiling, she turned back to the girl. "And I suppose you'll be needing someone to read them to you at bedtime, won't you?"

The dimple appeared in Celeste's cheek. "A mother can't have too many bedtime stories."

Editor's Note

EPILEPSY has been in existence for centuries. The treatments used in this book for epilepsy are accurate and appropriate for the late 1800s; however, there is a far better understanding of epilepsy and seizures today. The Red Cross now advises the following when a person has a seizure:

- DO NOT try to place anything between the victim's teeth.
- Remove any nearby objects that might cause the person having the seizure harm, and protect the victim's head by placing a thin cushion under it.
- If there is fluid in the victim's mouth (vomit, blood, etc.), roll him or her onto one side so that the fluid drains from the mouth.
- If the seizure occurs in a public place, ask bystanders not to crowd around the victim.
- When the seizure is over, check to see if the victim was injured; be reassuring and comforting. Stay with the victim until he or she is fully conscious and aware of surroundings.
- If the victim is known to have seizures, you do not need to call Emergency Medical Services (EMS)

immediately. The victim will usually recover within a few minutes.

- DO call your local EMS if the seizure lasts more than a few minutes; if the victim has repeated seizures, appears injured, is pregnant, or is a diabetic; if you do not know the cause of the seizures; or if you know that the victim has never had a seizure before.

A Note from the Author

Dear Reader,

Looking back over the pattern of your life, can you say, as Jenny Price ultimately did, that you're grateful that you did not get something you really thought you wanted? Before I started writing, I was offered a part-time job at the reception desk of a clinic at a small private college. It would be during my children's school hours, and as I'm fond of young people, I just knew it would be fun and interesting.

But alas! I had committed myself to a project that would not be finished for weeks. I was heartbroken, tried to rationalize quitting the project, but ultimately had to turn down the job. Three months later, I landed a dream job conducting sessions in local schools that gave students tools for saying no to drugs and unhealthy peer pressure. The hours were even better, the pay twice as much, the work was fun. I thanked God every day for it!

And I thank *you* for reading *Jewels for a Crown,* my friend. May we both strive to handle disappointment with an eye toward the future, when it's just possible we will look back and say, "That was the best thing that could have happened."

God bless you!

Lawana Blackwell

About the Author

Lawana Blackwell is an accomplished novelist whose books have found a strong following. Her books include *The Widow of Larkspur Inn, The Courtship of the Vicar's Daughter, The Dowry of Miss Lydia Clark*, and *The Maiden of Mayfair*. She and her husband live in Baton Rouge, Louisiana, and are empty nesters who love every opportunity to get together with their three recently married sons and their wives. Besides writing, Lawana enjoys Home and Garden television, vegetarian cooking, and garage sales.

Lawana welcomes letters written to her in care of Tyndale House Author Relations, P.O. Box 80, Wheaton, IL 60187-0080 or by e-mail at lawanablack@yahoo.com.

Turn the page
for an exciting excerpt
from Lawana Blackwell's
next HeartQuest book,
Song of a Soul

ISBN 0-8423-7229-6

Song of a Soul

Sure enough, Miss Knight was at her usual place at the head of the dining-room table, with her nephew adjacent to her on the opposite side. He stood when Deborah came into the room and took a step around the table to pull out her chair.

"Oh, please sit down," she said, reaching the chair and pulling it out before he could make his way to her. After seating herself, she turned to Miss Knight on her left. "I do apologize for being late. I lost track of the time."

The elderly woman smiled in her direction. "We only arrived ourselves a moment ago, dear. Isn't it wonderful that Gregory could join us?"

Deborah lowered her eyes to the place setting in front of her, then became irritated at her sudden bashfulness. *It's not his fault that Avis and Bethina have fanciful ideas,* she reminded herself, lifting her chin to smile at him. "I'm glad you were able to stay, Mr. Woodruff."

"Thank you, Miss Burke."

At the head of the table, Miss Knight shook her head. "Would you two mind doing an old woman a favor?"

"Of course not," Deborah and Mr. Woodruff replied at the same time.

Miss Knight sighed. "Forgive me for saying so, but I'm beginning to find it tedious to hear you young people address each other so formally. Now that you'll be spending Sunday afternoons together, why not use your given names?"

Deborah eyed her hostess suspiciously. Surely it had to be a coincidence—Avis fussing over her appearance upstairs, and now this request. But there was nothing but innocence on Miss Knight's face as she sat there waiting for an answer.

"If I'm meddling too much . . . ," Miss Knight began, but Deborah reached over to pat her hand.

"Of course. It *is* silly to be so formal week after week." She smiled at the man across from her. "Isn't that so, Gregory?"

"I agree completely," he replied, but he had to swallow before adding, "Deborah."

"Now, see?" the old woman said, beaming. "I just know you two are going to become good friends."

"To friendship," Deborah said, lifting her water goblet. "Who won the dominos match?"

Gregory smiled, his blue eyes filled with quiet humor. "Mrs. Darnell, both times."

"One day I shall insist upon the blindfolds," Miss Knight said.

Bethina brought in a tureen of blue-and-white jasperware and dished out a clear chicken-and-leek soup to start the meal. "Missus?" she said when finished.

"Yes, Bethina?"

"It's the boy, Thomas. He's down in the servants' hall, worryin' over if he should have the trap ready after supper."

"Oh, dear. I didn't even think to send word to him that Gregory was staying."

"Mr. Darnell told him," Bethina reassured her.

"How good of him." Turning to her nephew with a

worried expression, Miss Knight said, "I've never sent Thomas out after dark. Do you think he is too young to . . ."

Gregory touched her arm. "I'll walk up to Bridge Street and flag down a hansom. I don't think he should be out either."

"Are you sure, dear?" Because he could harness up the barouche and Mr. Darnell could accompany him for the ride back."

"That's too much trouble. It's only a short way to Bridge Street." He turned to Bethina, who was waiting just inside the door. "But please tell Thomas . . ."

He hesitated as his eyes met Deborah's. *What was wrong?* he wondered.

There was something familiar in his expression, something that she herself had felt before. Concern for the boy? *I'm not the only one who wonders about him,* she thought. *Does he know something that I don't?*

"Yes, Mr. Gregory?" Bethina asked at the door.

"Just thank him anyway for me, please."

After the three shared pleasant conversation over a main course of turbot with lobster, Miss Knight turned and said, "I wish you could stay for the rest of the evening, dear Gregory, but I shall worry if you're out looking for a hansom too late."

"They don't run all night, sir," added Bethina, who had come in with Gwen to clear the dishes. "One time my sister's boy, Eston, had to walk all the way from Sidgwick to Newmarket because he waited too long to flag a hansom. It took him two hours to get home."

Gregory smiled at her and pushed out his chair. "If you'll excuse me for leaving so soon after the meal . . ."

If you don't ask him what he knows about Thomas now, you'll have to wait another week, Deborah thought. Rising from her own chair, she said, "I'll walk you to the door, if you don't mind." She caught the look that Bethina and Gwen exchanged but ignored it.

"Of-of course not," Gregory stammered. He went around the table to Miss Knight's chair, leaning down for a kiss on the cheek. "Good night, Aunt Helene."

"Good night, you dear boy," she told him, her face wreathed in smiles.

Once Avis was at Miss Knight's side, Gregory walked over to Deborah and offered his arm. She did not look at either maid as they walked out of the room.

The two walked down the hallway without speaking, passing the staircase and winding up in the entrance hall. "I would like to ask you about Thomas . . . the boy who drives you," Deborah said when she was sure they were out of earshot of any of the servants. "You seemed a bit worried about him earlier."

"Shall Mr. Darnell secure you a coach, sir?"

They both turned their heads to see Mrs. Darnell standing there with a derby and umbrella. Gregory thanked the housekeeper for his things and reassured her that he could find the cab on his own, then waited until she was gone to say to Deborah, "Would you mind if we talked about this outside? That is, if it's not too chilly for you."

"Why don't we see?"

He opened the door and ushered her out into the night air. The branches of the sycamores and elms lining the street hid most of the light of the stars and moon, but streetlamps along the walkway shed enough light for propriety's sake. Though the air felt heavy with humidity, it was comfortably cool after the arid heat of the dining-room fireplace.

"Would you like my coat?" Gregory offered.

"Thank you, but I'm fine," she told him. "I didn't feel I should ask you about Thomas in front of your aunt. I wouldn't want to worry her."

"That's a wise idea." He nodded appreciatively, and Deborah wondered if all young men were as concerned about their loved ones as Gregory Woodruff.

"Thomas drives me back and forth to my lessons," Deborah went on. "Sometimes there is such a sadness about him—I assumed it was because he missed his mother. But then he assured me that he still sees his mother. When you seemed concerned about him in there, I wondered why."

"I don't know the boy well at all, Miss Burke . . . Deborah." He gave her a little smile. "It may take me a while to get used to using your first name."

"You don't mind, do you?"

"Oh, not at all," he said quickly. "I rather like it."

"So do I," she told him. "What about Thomas?"

He shrugged uncomfortably. "I don't know if it's my place to mention anything."

"So you've noticed something."

Hesitating for several seconds, he replied, "Something."

"Please tell me," she urged.

Again there was a silence, broken only by the hissing of the streetlamps and the ringing of a set of hooves upon the cobblestones. Gregory motioned toward the steps. "Why don't we sit?"

"But your carriage . . ."

"Please . . . not *you* as well," he groaned, which made her laugh.

"No one wants you to have to walk home," she told him, still smiling. "That's why everyone is rushing you."

"Well, that's exactly what I plan to do," he replied with a smile. "It's good exercise, and I've a good umbrella if it happens to rain."

He has such a nice smile, Deborah thought, then forced her mind to return to the subject at hand. *Ask him what you came to ask,* she told herself as they sat down on the top step. *He probably has to study, and you're wasting his time.*

"Regarding Thomas again," she said, gathering the skirt of her dress behind her knees. "Would you mind telling me what you've noticed?"

He stared ahead at a streetlamp. "All I feel at liberty to tell you is that it appears the boy might be in some kind of trouble."

"Trouble?"

"It seems he doesn't want anyone who lives here to know about it. And it doesn't sound good."

"What can I do to help him?"

After a thoughtful silence he said, "I suppose you should just be kind to him. Show him that you're willing to listen if he's ever willing to confide in you. Trying to force him to confide in you may work the opposite way . . . which is likely why he would barely talk to me this afternoon."

Deborah sighed. "I'll do my best."

"But don't be hurt if you make no progress," he warned. "I believe the only reason he mentioned anything to me is that I'm not connected to the household."

"But you *are* connected. You're Miss Knight's nephew."

"Yes," he said quickly. "I mean . . . I don't live here."

Deborah nodded. "I'm sorry for Mr. Henry—he's the coachman here, whose toe was broken—but it's good that

Thomas has to drive you on Sundays. Perhaps he just needs to get used to you."

"Perhaps so."

Suddenly she realized that she was keeping him from going back to Pembroke. Gentleman that he was, he wouldn't leave her sitting there alone. She reached for the wrought-iron railing beside her, but he was immediately on his feet and extending a hand.

"Please allow me," he said, and helped her to her feet. He did not look her in the eyes as he did so and let go of her hand as soon as she was standing under the portico.

How curious it was that he seemed to be stricken with bashfulness in her presence. Her self-inflicted discipline of practice and schooling had not allowed much time for socializing with young men in the past. Somehow she had naively assumed that men never battled the occasional bouts of timidity that some women suffered.

"I do appreciate your speaking with me about Thomas," she told him.

At last his eyes met hers. "It's good of you to be concerned. Not many people would take the time to worry over a servant boy."

"Well, my family has always had a heart for servants. My mother was a maid-of-all-work before she married my father."

"I didn't know that," Gregory said, his expression surprised. "I would be interested in hearing how that happened."

Deborah smiled and looked out at the dark street. "It's a very long story. I'll have to tell it to you when you're not pressed for time."

He looked strangely reluctant to leave. "I have the time right now. That is, if you have."

"Are you jesting? I'll make time to talk about my family if you like. But we should sit down again." She settled back onto the steps, making sure that the hem of her dress covered her ankles. "My mother was taken in at thirteen by a couple whose occupations were extortion and blackmail. . . ."

"Blackmail?"

"One was a murderer as well." She went on with the story of how her mother, Rachel, had escaped that sordid life and ended up as an artist married to Adam Burke. When Deborah finished some twenty minutes later, Gregory shook his head.

"She must be an incredible person."

"Of course I think so." She smiled. "And what about your parents?"

"My mother is a good woman, just like Aunt Helene," he answered, then held out his hand to help her to her feet again. "I should be on my way now. I hope you have a good week."

"And you as well," she replied, startled at the warmth that came out in her own voice. He seemed just as surprised as she and glanced away.

"Good evening, Deborah."

"Good evening."

He walked down the steps, but at the bottom he turned back around and looked up at her. There was an air of expectancy about his posture, and Deborah wondered if he had thought of something else to say. "Gregory?" she asked.

Lifting the handle of his umbrella to point at the door, he said, "You shouldn't be standing out here alone after dark."

"Of course." She gave him an appreciative smile, but for some reason that she couldn't fathom, she felt strangely disappointed.

Must-Reads!

THE PERFECT MATCH
Her life was under control,
until he set her heart on fire.

HEART QUEST

OVER A MILLION BOOKS SOLD!